Expelled Mossad agent, Ronen, has disappeared following a failed assassination attempt on the life of the Hezbollah operative responsible for suicide bombings in Israel. Feared to be on an unauthorized mission that will bring catastrophe to his country, Ronen must be found and his former commander, Gadi, takes it upon himself to track him down. The resulting physical and intellectual scuffle between the two men becomes one of deeper, moral inquiry.

Mishka Ben-David served in the Mossad for twelve years, becoming a high-ranking officer. He is now a full-time novelist living outside Jerusalem.

"... high stakes, and the brutal complexity and fear of today's fragmented Middle East ... Ben-David delivers spy thrillers with all the authenticity and inside knowledge of an ex-Mossad agent."

Simon Sebag Montefiore, author of
Jerusalem: The Biography

DUET IN BEIRUT

DUET IN BEIRUT

MISHKA BEN-DAVID

Translated by
Evan Fallenberg

HALBAN
LONDON

First published in Great Britain by
Halban Publishers Ltd.
22 Golden Square
London W1F 9JW
2013

www.halbanpublishers.com

A CIP catalogue record for this book is available from the British
Library.

ISBN 978-1-905559-58-9

Originally published in Hebrew under the title *Duet b'Beirut*
by Keter Publishing House Ltd, Jerusalem, 2002

Published by arrangement with The Institute for
The Translation of Hebrew Literature

Typeset by Spectra Titles, Norfolk
Printed in Great Britain by
Berforts Information Press, Stevenage

DUET IN BEIRUT

Prologue

THE ILLUMINATED SIGN above the terminal welcomed Gadi to Beirut International Airport. He had opted not to bring the passport he had used the last time – the one with the valid visa – because he had no way of knowing how seriously the authorities had investigated the events of the previous year, and whether his name appeared on some blacklist. He figured he wouldn't have any real trouble passing through as long as the visa clerk, the border officer or the customs officer didn't have an especially good memory.

He moved forwards with the other passengers from the Alitalia flight from Rome, mostly Lebanese, with some Italians and a smattering of businessmen from other countries. As usual, the businessmen hurried to the front, but Gadi hung back with the tourists. Wearing a jacket with no tie – he had taken it off in the plane after observing the other passengers – and carrying only hand-luggage, he looked like something between a well-to-do tourist and an informal businessman, an image that suited him.

The renovated terminal was sparkling clean and nearly empty; the duty-free shopkeepers stood in the doorways of their shops watching the thin column of travellers pass by. Gadi rode an escalator up to the second floor, to the visa window. Peering over the heads of two Finnish backpackers he could see the very clerk who had checked his visa on his last trip to Beirut.

While it is true that the level of fear decreases with the number of trips an operative makes, it is also true that the fear never entirely disappears. Gadi's subordinates were surprised to learn, when he spoke to them about justifiable fears and how to deal with them, that even he got butterflies in his stomach. It would be inhuman not to feel fear as you disembark on enemy territory, knowing, as you approach say, the border officer, that if something goes wrong you're in huge trouble.

What helped Gadi lower his level of fear was the knowledge that he was lying, smuggling, and using false documents all for the good of his country. It wasn't that he was a liar: he was lying for a cause. He was an emissary. But now he couldn't hide behind that logic; he was lying to his own country, too, entering an enemy state without permission and about to carry out a mission that no one had approved.

Suddenly he felt anxious about what he'd taken on. What if his calculations were wrong? What if he'd been mistaken in thinking the right way to act was to reach Ronen and convince him to come home? How had he dared to take on such responsibility, to play with the destiny of an entire nation? So much was in the balance here. Who did he think he was anyway, Superman? He wasn't even James Bond.

The tourist in front of him had finished. The clerk motioned him forwards.

"Good evening," Gadi said as he handed him his passport and the fee.

The clerk looked him over, flipped through the pages of his passport, then looked up at Gadi again.

"First time in Lebanon?" he asked in a low voice.

Gadi answered that it was, and smiled. The expression on the clerk's face – a mixture of disbelief and an attempt at remembering – disappeared as quickly as it had appeared. His eyebrows arched momentarily into an expression that said, *so be it,* and he took the dollars and stuck the visa into the passport. Gadi thanked him and moved along to passport control.

One of the officers looked completely unfamiliar to him, so Gadi stood in his line. The two Finnish women were ahead of him again, poring over a small map of Beirut.

"Do you need help?" Gadi asked, smiling.

"We're only staying in the city for one night," answered one.

"Need a hotel recommendation?"

"We booked a room over the Internet, at the Intercontinental."

The officer motioned the Finns forward. They were stamped through immediately. Gadi approached the counter.

"I'll meet you downstairs," he called after them,

smiling at them and at the officer all at once as he handed over his passport.

The officer compared the photo on the passport to Gadi, located the visa and stamped it.

"Have a pleasant stay, Mr…" he glanced at the passport, "…Ford."

Gadi moved on, traces of a smile still on his face. He didn't have a clue how he managed the transformation. Not that he found it particularly difficult to smile, but it still surprised him that it was easy for him to do so in the line of duty. He'd been weak at manipulations, acting and pretending in the training course; let him fight, man a stakeout, tail a target any day, just don't make him lie. But time had had its effect on him.

Gadi descended to the bottom floor of the terminal, to the Hertz counter, and rented a Ford Mondeo with only a few hundred miles on the milometer. The car-hire agent walked him to the car.

"Here in Beirut I need to explain to you exactly how to travel, since there are some very dangerous neighbourhoods," he said.

"That's okay, I'll manage," Gadi told him as he slid his suitcase onto the passenger's seat and sat down behind the wheel.

"Are you familiar with Beirut?" the Hertz agent asked.

Gadi started the engine. "A city's a city. I know lots of cities." He smiled and drove off.

The agent mumbled to himself with genuine concern, "But there are…it's dangerous…"

*

Gadi had a strange feeling cruising the main street of Beirut on the way to Abu-Khaled's office. He noticed the new buildings that had sprung up, but still it seemed as though nothing much had changed in the year that had passed since he last patrolled these streets. He recalled his very first time in Beirut, more than ten years earlier, when everything had seemed unfamiliar to him. Operatives loved working out the puzzle that was a city; it was true, a city's a city. Or to be more specific, the cities of each region resemble one another: European cities almost always have a ring road, pedestrian zones in the centre, and a cathedral, court and town hall near an old castle. Arab cities have a central souk, wide boulevards that bisect the city and are dotted with government buildings and hotels, and a refugee camp on the outskirts.

In Beirut, the Corniche served both as the ring road and as the main avenue. It was a wide, circular road that began in the north at the port, ran the length of the bay, became the promenade along the beach to the west and then turned eastwards, becoming the border between the old Christian and Moslem city and the southern, Shi'ite quarters, in the centre of which stood the refugee camps. Each section of the Corniche had a different name and a different character; Gadi's squad members called it Corniche el Mazraa after one of its sections.

Every city has its surprises, too. Khartoum surprised them with its verdure, which spreads through the city along the river as it splits into the Blue Nile and the White Nile. In Damascus it was the number of trees and the grass and huge parks; in Amman, the neighbourhoods filled with enormous villas built of chiselled stone, not just by wealthy Hashemites but also by rich citizens of Saudi Arabia and the Gulf Emirates. In Beirut, it was the liveliness of the beach: the restaurants and cafés, the walkers and joggers. The other surprise in Beirut, less pleasant than the first, was the huge number of policemen and soldiers. At every intersection there were at least two well-armed members of the security forces. Some were Syrian and some were Lebanese, and together they formed a tight ring of security that surrounded the city, making it difficult to gather intelligence or find escape routes for the squad. This was always mentioned in intelligence summaries, but seeing it personally gave new meaning to its operational aspects.

Far worse was the situation south of the Mazraa. Dahiyeh, where the main concentration of Shi'ites lived, comprised two neighbourhoods. Bir-el-Abed, to the north, was reminiscent of other Arab cities, with multi-storeyed private homes and quiet, narrow alleys. But Haret-Hreik, in the south, was an awful, crowded heap of six- and eight-storey apartment buildings with streets far too narrow to contain the masses of pedestrians and cars that created an ongoing and endless traffic jam.

In the heart of Dahiyeh was the autonomous area of the Hezbollah, whose borders and roadblocks were manned by armed Hezbollah guards who stopped and inspected nearly every car. While the drive along the bay was still relatively free, even when passing the refugee camps and the poorest neighbourhoods, entry into the Hezbollah-controlled area required an unshakeable cover story and nerves of steel. Even Christian residents of Beirut didn't dare try to enter.

Just over a year earlier, Gadi, as squad commander, and Udi, one of his most experienced men, had made their way as scouts to find Abu-Khaled's whereabouts. They were sent a few days after a suicide-bomber dispatched by Abu-Khaled, the head of Hezbollah's foreign operations, had blown himself up in a crowded Jerusalem market, killing a dozen people. Gadi and Udi were relieved to discover that his office was in a building on a wide street that separated the two neighbourhoods, a street that connected the coastal road with the Beirut-Damascus road at a spot where traffic was heavy but moved fairly freely. They called the road by the name of the neighbourhood nearby, El-Obeiri. The shops on the street level of the building enabled Udi to gather information nearly without raising suspicions, though they both noticed that, as in every Arab city, they still drew the attention of the occasional local.

It took a little more effort to locate Abu-Khaled's home on a quiet lane of three-storey houses and apartment buildings in Bir-el-Abed. The nature of the neighbourhood made a foot patrol, and even driving around in a rental car, extremely dangerous. One of the buildings fitted the description they had received in an intelligence briefing based on a report made by a local agent and after a few trips through the neighbourhood they were able to pick out, in the parking area of the building, a light green Mercedes that had also been parked at the office. The next morning, as they waited by the entrance to the El-Obeiri road, they spotted Abu-Khaled in the same Mercedes. The pieces of the puzzle were beginning to come together, and when the car was seen in different places with additional Hezbollah activists, new operational possibilities opened up.

Gadi had decided to return to Israel with the early findings in order to plan the next stage of intelligence gathering with officers at headquarters, and to send a second team to gather additional information. Both he and Udi had spent too much time there already; there was no way of knowing which shopkeeper near the office or which security guard at the roadblock nearest Abu-Khaled's home was already suspicious. In a police state the path from suspicion to arrest is short, and in the extraterritorial Hezbollah area the path from suspicion to being kidnapped or murdered is even shorter.

Back in Israel Gadi recommended continuing intelligence-gathering activities, with a focus on placing an explosive device in Abu-Khaled's Mercedes, either at his home at night or even, under certain circumstances, in his office car park during the day. For that kind of operation they would need more information, such as whether his wife and children used the car as well.

And then Abu-Khaled had ordered another car-bomb attack. There were more bodies in Jerusalem, and Gadi's squad was instructed to depart immediately. Without further intelligence, planting a bomb in the car would be problematic. The Prime Minister was reticent, too, since innocent bystanders could be injured and retaliation would follow: yet another car-bomb, or a rain of Katyusha rockets in the Galilee.

Gadi remembered well the day when Doron, the head of the Operations Division, had assembled the staff just after returning from a meeting with the Mossad chief and the Prime Minister. They set up a highly focused operation: since it was Abu-Khaled who had ordered the attacks, and Abu-Khaled who had sent the terrorists, then it was Abu-Khaled who must be assassinated – immediately. All intelligence gathering, even if related to planning escape routes, was suspended.

A mere two days later Gadi, Doron, and the Mossad chief presented their plan to the Prime Minister. Gadi seized an opportunity to state briefly that there would be no time for preparing contingency plans, no time for simulations; that some of his team, including Ronen, the "Number One" – the shooter – were not familiar with Beirut, and that there was no time for them to learn the escape routes – a necessary stage in case of a shoot-out. But he stopped short of saying that this was no way to set out on a mission.

Had he assumed that the chief and Doron had already said all this to the Prime Minister at their previous meeting, when the decision had been made? Did he think it was too late, or that in any event it was Doron's job, as his superior, to say it? Was it so obvious that it was unnecessary even to mention? Or was it that in the heat of activity, with the pressure from terrorist attacks, as part of the division's culture of operational derring-do, such things simply were not said?

Gadi still hadn't come up with answers to all these questions. But a year later the whole process seemed completely insane to him. He was travelling the same streets, everything appeared the same, but back at home an internal earthquake had taken place due to the failed operation.

As he approached Abu-Khaled's office, he was glad it was evening and the shops were closed. There was no need to worry, on this first drive-by, that he would look familiar to one of the shopkeepers in the building.

Still, something inside him reacted when he arrived at the office building. The car park was empty and the pavement nearly bereft of passersby, but two armed soldiers were walking towards him. He couldn't see any signs of security at the entrance to the building itself, but perhaps these two were reinforcements for the two pairs of soldiers stationed at the closest intersections. Putting the building behind him, Gadi felt his breathing returning to normal. He hadn't seen any signs of Ronen yet, but there was no reason for him to be there just now.

At the entrance to Bir-el-Abed he was stopped by a chained roadblock manned by two armed guards.

"Dr Itzmat Abdel-Ganem," Gadi said. The previous year that had been their cover story, which they had worked on extensively, but now there was no substance to it, he would just have to hope these Hezbollah guards were lazy and would not check it.

"Why doesn't he come and get you here?" the guard asked him. It was rare for Westerners to enter the neighbourhood alone.

"I've already been to his house twice," Gadi answered, in American-accented Arabic. "We work together at the Christian hospital."

Gadi was smiling while butterflies tumbled crazily in his stomach. It wasn't the first time that a smile stood between him and jail, but on other occasions there had at least been some opportunity to ground his cover story, like a phone number that someone would answer. But now there was nothing. A couple of idle Kalashnikov rifles were not the end of the world, but still they were pretty close. Two blows and he and his Mondeo would be out of there in a flash. Gadi had already worked out how he would hit them and where he would turn the car around. He had a chance of getting away if they didn't recover quickly and shoot at him, or if their comrades didn't arrive on the run. Just as had happened with Ronen, during the failed operation. Only this time nobody was there to sneak a car into the throng, as Gadi did that day.

The guards lowered the chain.

As soon as his car had turned into Abu-Khaled's quiet street Gadi could see, from far off, the small new guard booth positioned on the pavement at the entrance to the parking area of Abu-Khaled's building: the manifestation of a lesson learned from our operation, Gadi thought. He scanned the buildings on both sides of the street, saw some movement inside the guard booth and turned his gaze in another direction; he did not want the guard to take notice of him on his first drive through the neighbourhood. He still had no way of knowing how alert the guard was, or whether he was the only one stationed there.

That's enough for today, Gadi thought, and turned his car in the direction of a small hotel on the Corniche. Staying at one of the nearby hotels would enable him to justify his presence in the neighbourhood but he had frequented them the year before, and in the other hotels on the south side of the city he would certainly be most unwelcome as a foreigner.

It was Ronen's second night of intelligence gathering in the neighbourhood. He had already learned everything he could from one night-time reconnaissance patrol and two day-trips around the area. He also knew that there was round-the-clock armed surveillance at Abu-Khaled's house. Now he wanted to see whether the guard would check the car, the garden, the neighbour's garden, or whether, like most security guards, he would hunker down in a chair in his booth, reduce his contact with the outside world to a minimum and even nod off for a while.

Ronen drove past the guard in his rented BMW, verified that he was inside his booth, turned right at the first intersection, stopped, got out of the car and entered the grounds of a neighbouring building. He'd staked out this spot earlier in the day, a house built on pillars, with ample space underneath, surrounded by a tall hedge. It was the perfect spot for watching Abu-Khaled's house: located across the street, it was two buildings down from the guard, close enough to observe his movements but far enough away not to draw his attention. He could be fairly certain that the guard would not even look in his direction.

The more palpable adversary was the close surroundings, every neighbour who might come down to his car, every child playing ball, every gang of roving youth. A foreigner did not stand a chance of surviving a minute here; all it would take were a few shouts and dozens of armed men would descend from every building. He knew the feeling well, and the fresh memory of it made his skin crawl.

Ronen walked around the building, passed between the parked cars, and stopped next to the furthest pillar. He had a good view of the guard booth and had chosen a spot in the hedge through which he could run to his car if one of the neighbours spotted him.

He decided he needed to be there for more than an hour; if the guard had instructions to patrol once an hour, then he would find that out. But if the guard stayed inside for more than an hour then it was safe to assume he did not patrol at regular intervals.

A stakeout like this was not normally difficult for Ronen, who had spent hundreds of hours in similar circumstances. But this time he felt completely different; a sense of urgency was coursing through him and he found himself checking his watch every few minutes. Sounds that in the past had not bothered him now frightened him: water running through a sewage pipe, a tomcat, the slam of a window. He would duck when a car drove past, especially if it turned right and its lights shone directly on him. There was no one to inform him from another observation point that the light in the stairwell had lit up and he had better get out of there.

And that wasn't all. Something about him was not working as it usually did. That was the only way he could explain the in-depth interrogation he had undergone at the airport. He had noticed when the visa clerk motioned to the border officer, and how the border officer had signalled the customs officer. He was the only westerner whom the customs officers called aside and investigated, emptying everything from his suitcase and asking him the same questions as the visa clerk and the border officer. He answered them testily. It was no wonder they had zeroed in on him: he was unshaven, wearing jeans, a polo shirt and a jacket. He felt they could read his intentions, the evil in him, even the craziness on his face. That was what Naamah had said was happening to him. They could see his crazed tenacity. So there, Gadi, Ronen thought: there's a stage even beyond "criminal tenacity".

Ronen knew that the sense of urgency or compulsion he felt did not stem from the real tactical difficulties facing him. He was breaking every rule but would not allow these feelings and thoughts to penetrate his consciousness. He knew that the decision to assassinate a target was made carefully and after ample deliberation somewhere high above him, at the level of the Prime Minister, the Defence Minister, the Mossad chief, the Research Division and probably included a host of other factors. Now he was making the decision on his own. True, the decision to assassinate this particular man, Abu-Khaled, had already been taken, so if it was justified then, then morally speaking and in terms of the effect it would have on Hezbollah, it was still justified now, particularly after a further attack in the Israeli city of Afula. But since when did a Number One decide on his own not only the appropriate moment to carry out an assassination, but to assassinate at all? And what thought had he given with regard to the potential complications he could cause, whether he succeeded or failed?

He hadn't, nor did he wish to; he only wanted to set right what he had screwed up. Then again, who was he kidding? He wanted to succeed at what he had failed at. He wanted to prove he was capable, that he was just like Gadi, his commander, and, especially, just like Naamah, his wife; even more than that, that he could do it all on his own. The previous year it had simply been his first time, and there was that little surprise no one had prepared him for, that possibility no one had ever mentioned in contingency planning. Now it was his second time, and he had graduated: he could do it alone now, something nobody had ever done before except in films.

Now too, just like the last time, he was under time constraints. But this time he would manage. It wasn't the pressure to carry out the assassination before Abu-Khaled could order another attack, and it was a fact that Abu-Khaled had planned many attacks and would most undoubtedly continue planning others. It also wasn't the pressure of the surroundings: it wasn't easy working alone, when no one was covering your back and someone could surprise you at any moment and decide to shout, but he could handle that, too. It was the Mossad he was worried about. How long would it take them to figure out where he was and try to stop him? How long would it take

Naamah to understand and run to Gadi, thereby setting the entire system in motion against him?

He wanted to finish the job and get out of there as quickly as possible, certainly before the fog inside him dissipated, the fog that was preventing him from seeing clearly what he was doing and was permitting only the most mechanical, automatic actions to penetrate.

The guard stepped out of his booth, stretched, made a short tour around the house and returned to his post. Ronen wanted to see his next patrol up close, to see whether he checked the car. Ronen crossed the street and made for the building two doors down from Abu-Khaled's house. He then pushed through the hedge to the building adjacent to Abu-Khaled's and watched from there. That was where he was standing when Gadi drove by, looking the other way.

I.

IT DIDN'T SEEM like a place where fates are determined. That was what Gadi thought the first time he'd come to the offices of the commission of inquiry: two prefabs on a small military base, one used for the proceedings and the other as offices for members of the commission. A tarpaulin stretched between the two had provided a bit of shade at the outset of the investigation, but was no shelter against the rains that began to fall as the proceedings stretched out into the winter months.

The two buildings had been hastily fenced off, a guard stationed at the entrance. Plenty of secrets had been amassed on the tapes of the proceedings, so it seemed quite right to Gadi that the place was guarded round the clock, though all the essential details were leaked by interested parties nevertheless. The Israeli media updated the public daily, albeit with such distortions that only the people directly involved could discern between the quite narrow factual basis and the commentators' fantastical reconstructions.

In any event, Gadi thought, it's almost all behind me now. Apart from three consecutive days of testimony at the beginning, they had called him in three more times to provide additional details or to cross-check his version of events against that of the other operatives and headquarters staff. And finally today, a summation, which had been postponed several times because he had been on the road during the past month. The squad had been tracking a shipment of weapons from two former Soviet republics to Iran via a long and circuitous route, and losing sight of one of the trucks they were tailing as it left its base in the Ukraine – even for a moment – would have shut down the entire operation. Gadi would have been indispensable even if he had not been in charge: his Russian skills enabled him to clear up problems or read a sign or speak with a suspicious policeman or register at a hotel, so that the presence of a few Europeans travelling the length of the Caucasus from Georgia to Azerbaijan would not draw attention.

Gadi arrived precisely at the appointed hour. It was not a place he enjoyed spending even a single spare moment but Rikki, the commission secretary, spotted him and motioned him to join her in the office.

"They haven't finished with the person ahead of you yet," she said with a complicitous grin. "At least," she added, "I can offer you a cup of coffee."

"So today's the day they finish with us, right?" he said as he entered the office.

She smiled as she leaned over to pour the coffee, turning her enticing, pear-shaped bottom towards him.

Freeze, he wanted to tell her: that's the position I like, don't move. He knew, however, that this was no time for flirting, and he would never say something like that. He wondered if any of those being interrogated had exploited her rather obvious admiration to find out what was happening on the commission. Gadi restrained himself from even asking who was being questioned at that moment, but just then the door opened and Ronen walked towards the office looking pensive, his shoulders a bit stooped, but his tall frame and black clothes still made for an impressive sight. He was carrying a biker's jacket over his shoulder, holding the collar with one finger. Gadi admired the fact that Ronen had not dressed to impress the commission. As he reached the office doorway, Ronen noticed Gadi and recoiled for an instant, then smiled, seemingly embarrassed by his reaction.

"Interesting place to meet," said Gadi.

Ronen had taken temporary leave from the squad two months earlier, when he'd figured which way the wind was blowing with the commission of inquiry, and had been teaching surveillance and counter-surveillance in the Mossad's training school.

"Interesting? I don't know, we've been in more interesting places than this," he said, adding, "but not necessarily more dangerous."

His face serious, he levelled his gaze at Gadi. Gadi could guess that Ronen was not in good standing with the commission; he hoped Ronen did not blame *him* for that. The blame could be evenly divided between the two of them, he thought, but the members of the commission had favoured him throughout the proceedings, excepting, perhaps, Shalgi, who kept setting traps for him.

"Gadi, they're waiting for you," Rikki said.

Gadi ignored her and approached Ronen, proffering his hand. Ronen, half a head taller than Gadi, shook his hand firmly, his long, bony fingers clasping Gadi's in a strong, intense handshake that expressed all that he could not voice. Gadi, broader and burlier than Ronen, recovered from his initial surprise and strengthened his grip so that the two men grasped hands in matching intensity.

"Good luck," Ronen said, relaxing his grip and turning to go. "We don't want them to accuse us of collusion," he said by way of apology for departing, a faint, bewildered smile returning to his face.

That's not the man I know, Gadi thought disconcertedly as he watched Ronen's figure grow distant. Ten years had passed since Ronen had first reported to the squad's training facility and only recently had he completed the Mossad's long classifying process and had been sent on a training course for operatives. At the time, Gadi was in charge of training, and at the end of the course, eight months later, was scheduled to become the squad's deputy commander, bringing with him a new batch of operatives.

The group consisted of three recruits who were former seals in the Navy Commando Flotilla, a new immigrant who had served as a commando in the French army, and two fighter pilots; Gadi was relieved that at least he would be spared the traditional competition between the seals and the paratroopers, in which he, a former paratrooper, would never manage to remain neutral. The three seals managed to rile him quickly enough even without paratroopers around, thanks to their natural cockiness. Only later did Gadi learn to differentiate between the light, youthful, even charming arrogance of the seals and the snobbish, slightly pompous arrogance of the pilots, preferring the former.

In order to deflate the airmen's egos a bit, Gadi began to put an emphasis on activities requiring physical strength – like hand-to-hand combat, which he himself taught – because the pilots were weaker. But it was tall, lanky, muscle-bound Ronen who provoked him most of all, becoming his chief training adversary, not to mention his punching bag. Ronen's fighting sense began to grow on Gadi, the way he would absorb a blow, fall, and sputter something like, "Okay, but wait 'til you see what I can do in another year." Then he would absorb another blow, fall again and say, by this time only semi-conscious, "Make that two years."

Two years later Gadi was on his way to becoming commander of the squad and Ronen was a young, overly abrasive operative. Ronen had not learned to adapt himself to the flexibility and glibness necessary for someone required to move about in foreign, enemy territory, where the only weapons available to him were his quiet demeanour, his ability to blend in with his surroundings and his smile or eloquence when dealing with aroused suspicions. Gadi had wondered whether he should renew Ronen's contract at the end of his third year, but a wise and experienced division head had told him that the more valuable a gemstone was, the harder – and more worthwhile – it was to polish.

As the person who had certified Ronen at the end of his training, Gadi felt responsible for him and continued to give him chances to prove himself. Still, after dozens of additional missions, Ronen had not lost his rigidity, had not learned to blend in. Gadi, who had in the meantime been appointed squad commander, had, for all practical purposes, given up on him, assigning him to simpler missions, chiefly in Europe, and had refrained over the years from naming him team leader or Number One, the guy who pulls the trigger. That is, up until that miserable operation in Beirut, when he had finally given Ronen a chance.

Gadi walked the few feet to the building in which the proceedings were being held, and turned to take a last glance at Ronen. Ronen was bent over his motorcycle, which was parked in the bushes next to the gate, and did not look back. Gadi took a deep breath and entered the room.

One wall of the old prefab had been removed to enlarge the conference room and, perhaps, to give the impression of a courtroom atmosphere of respect and civility. That it never acquired. The commission members sat at the back of the room behind three small tables covered with a grey-green army blanket; each had a microphone and notepad. Gadi made his way across the room to a small witness table with microphone that stood facing the panel members. The two junior commission members, Shalgi and Tal, were busy writing while the chairman, Nov, peered amicably at Gadi from behind thick-rimmed glasses.

Before being appointed to the commission, Nov was the chairman of the board of a large company, Tal a brigadier general in the reserves who had only recently retired, and Shalgi a senior army officer in the reserves, too, and head of a public company. To the Mossad agents it was clear that without someone on the panel with an understanding of the considerations and nuances in the field, someone who was familiar with other operations and could put things in perpective, the Beirut mission would seem like the act of madmen. Who would believe it was feasible to shoot Abu-Khaled, chief of Hezbollah's overseas terror operations, at their heavily-guarded headquarters in the heart of the Shi'ite quarter of Beirut, and slip quietly away? In the humiliation that followed the mission's failure, the request for such a panel member was made too quietly and went unheeded.

The panel had been dubbed the Commission of Inquiry into the Mossad's Failure in Beirut, which clearly defined the parameters of the investigation: it would not be dealing with the process for selecting and confirming the target, nor would it be investigating the decision-making process; instead the focus would be on the operational aspects. The Prime Minister and his advisers in the government and the army who had approved the target would be left out of the investigation. In the beginning that decision had drawn criticism, but as the investigation dragged on the critics had desisted, all that is exept the agents in the Mossad's Operations Division, who grumbled bitterly amongst themselves.

The relationship between a person under investigation and his interrogators is a strange one. Here before him, Gadi thought, were three people with whom he had little in common, yet they were the ones who, in just a few days' time, would determine his future. During the months of investigation a considerable amount of mutual respect had developed between the panel members and Gadi. It had started as it did with most outsiders, with the ambivalence reserved for people who take part in such operations – and fail at them. But the more the details of this operation and others like it became clear to the panel members, the more Gadi felt their admiration for him grow, especially in light of his decision to abandon an academic career in favour of sticking his head again and again into the lion's mouth. Which is exactly what he had done at the climax of this operation, after Ronen's screw-up, thus preventing far worse consequences.

Gadi had a good feeling about the results of the inquiry, even though he felt he was in no small degree responsible for the failure. Still, even if the commission were to absolve him of all responsibility, he nonetheless felt his days with the Mossad were drawing to a close.

The circle of people who had enveloped them on their return from Beirut were first and foremost glad to see them alive and well. But soon thereafter it became clear to Gadi that nobody was about to forgive them. There are acceptable mishaps, but an operative who draws a gun and then decides not to shoot, causing an angry mob to chase after him, is not one of them. True, Gadi himself had intervened at the last moment, saving Ronen and John, both wounded, from certain lynching. And it was also true that the whole escape plan had worked as it should, and no wounded were left behind. But these were hardly mitigating circumstances. There was no way of erasing the smiling face of Abu-Khaled from all those television screens, telling of how Mossad agents had bolted.

It was inexcusable to fail in such a manner, especially when such an incident hits the media and makes them all look like fools. The Operations Division was hurt and angry, but only later, when Gadi learned that people in the less glorified divisions of the Mossad were privately rejoicing, did he understand that the exposure of their failure in the media was only the lesser of the evils.

After that he continued to run a number of operations around the globe, some even more complex than the failed operation in Beirut, but it was clear to him that everyone involved in the failure would be forced to leave the Mossad sooner or later. It didn't matter whether the commission of inquiry found him guilty or innocent: the corridors of power had already sent down their verdict. Nor did it matter how much of the division's glory had been earned by Ronen, himself and others over the past decade; that glory was based on the bits and pieces of information cobbled together by other Mossad employees and the even scantier information that drifted down to the public, like the assassination of Khalili, head of the Islamic Front, as revenge following a massive terrorist attack at Beit Lid. But who remembered that now? And who even knew about the hundreds of successful covert operations that brought invaluable intelligence vital to Israel's security? Gadi and Ronen had now turned the Mossad into a laughing stock, and they were the ones who would have to pay the price. So the commission of inquiry could change precious little.

"Gadi, if you were asked to sum up in two sentences the reasons for the failure, and to point to the guilty parties, what would you say?" asked Nov.

The long months of investigation had not prepared Gadi for that question. The panel members had dug deep into the procedures, into the drills, into the command responsibility, into what had really happened there, in Beirut, but this sudden switch in roles – from being interrogated to pointing the finger – caught him by surprise. Until now he had answered their questions easily and willingly, at least from the time he had decided not to worry about the outcome and begun to harbour the hope that finally someone from the outside would shake the dust off old procedures and off the unwillingness to say about an operation that it was "too dangerous", or "not really necessary"; but that ease had suddenly disappeared, replaced by a heavy burden on his shoulders: did they really expect him to tell them who he thought was guilty? He, Gadi, one of the parties most certain to share in the guilt? Did they really think he would point the finger at his subordinates? Or his commanders? Or himself?

He heard himself talking, uncertain when exactly he had formulated an answer. He could see himself as if from the side, stoop-shouldered, a bit downcast, levelling his gaze at Nov while all three panel members watched him with interest. It felt more like an anthropological study than a legal trial. Or rather, a test of integrity. Or perhaps the panel members were testing themselves to see how close their findings were to what the people under investigation thought.

"I commanded the operation. Authority in the field can't be divided, and neither can responsibility. So if you need to figure out who was responsible, then hierarchically speaking it's got to be me. And one more thing," he said, moving his gaze from one panel member to another. "You dealt with the planning aspects of the operation in great depth. As the squad commander I too was responsible for the planning. So once again, I can only point the finger at myself."

"You don't sound totally convinced of that," Nov said.

"That's what taking command is all about," Gadi answered. He paused, thinking about what he had just said. "I know you've heard our work described in general terms and you understand that an operation like this one is really an exception. Our division is assigned the task of gathering intelligence through special operations. We're asked to carry out assassinations only when the need arises, simply because we're the best trained to pull them off."

Shalgi, tall and fair-haired, interrupted in a tone that sounded to Gadi like impatience. "Yes, we understand that. Just like the IDF Special Forces Commando Unit is assigned the task of bringing intelligence from behind enemy lines. But when there is something else that needs to be done they do it, because the most experienced fighters are there. And yet, a mission is a mission."

Gadi continued, ignoring Shalgi's interjection. "You understand that gathering intelligence in an Arab country is sometimes as complicated and dangerous as carrying out an assassination. And, due to the conditions and circumstances, there have been assassinations that were no less complicated than the one in Beirut, as in the case where the target was on an island from which it was difficult to make a getaway. We plan each operation according to its complexity. But this time, due to a spate of terrorist attacks and pressure from above, we were put on an especially tight schedule and," Gadi searched for the right words, "we blew it."

He lowered his gaze. Nov waited a moment to let his words make their impression, then said, gently, "Gadi, please note that we did not ask you about responsibility. The chain of command and the responsibility and authority are quite clear to us. I asked you about guilt."

"Ronen also took responsibility upon himself in his role as final decision-maker in the field, but he understood that the guilt lay with his superiors as well, and with the planners," Shalgi added. "Let me put it like this: it's clear to you that you are not the only guilty party. So, in terms of percentages, how would you divide up the guilt among the others involved?"

Gadi paused again, gazing in Shalgi's direction, then answering slowly. "First of all, I'm sorry you told me what Ronen said. That's not right, and I hope I can ignore it. If you're asking which particular action could have been performed differently to prevent the mishap, I'd say it was Ronen's. But if you're asking about everything that wasn't taken into account in the preparations, contingency plans that weren't discussed carefully enough, simulations that weren't practised enough, then I'm guilty, me and my superiors right up the chain of command. I didn't set the crazy schedule, but I also didn't demand more time. That was because of the recent terrorist attacks, and also because we never say, 'I can't' or 'I'm not ready yet'."

The three panel members exchanged glances.

"Would you say that the guilt should be split fifty-fifty between Ronen and his superiors?" Tal asked.

"I wouldn't know how to make a calculation like that," Gadi said, a note of anger in his voice. What's happening here? After months of inquiry the commission members needed him, Gadi, to tell them how to apportion the blame? What meaning could that possibly have coming from one who himself was undergoing interrogation? Were they looking to see how far off their own conclusions were? Suddenly he understood that even after all these months they hadn't caught on, they hadn't understood the nuances of this kind of work, or the true dangers. Or, for that matter, the abilities.

Only now, as they reached the end of the inquiry, could they perceive this. And really, what chance was there that Tal, a brigadier general, whose life had been spent moving forwards under the protection of tanks and aeroplanes, would understand the complete loneliness a Mossad agent feels in a foreign city – surrounded by people who, at any second, can become his enemies – as he risks responding in a language that he is not supposed to know, meets someone who recognises him from some other situation and under some other identity. How could the brigadier understand that he must work in this antagonistic environment in opposition to its rules of reasonable behaviour, that he must observe, follow, and gather intelligence without standing out, that he must dress like everyone around him, that any mistake he makes driving on unfamiliar roads might bring him into conflict with the police? That each time he enters or departs from his hotel – nearly always at odd hours because that's what his line of work demands – he may be arousing suspicion? And to counterbalance all these dangers he has only a forged passport, a fake identity, a cover story and a smile that is meant to project reliability and self-confidence.

What chance was there of making these members of the commission understand how many years of experience on the street, how much familiarity with the chaotic rules ruling it, were necessary to enable you to go with its flow or spot a lurking whirlpool that you needed to avoid? How could you explain to someone who does not live by these rules that even with days and hours of manoeuvres and simulations, and long nights of analyzing contingency plans, and plotting escape routes, that in real time, on the street, different rules applied. Only the almost extrasensory ability to notice the signs – that the couple in the fifth car from the right are private eyes, that the dog of the old man approaching is growling and may attack, that the two youngsters about to cross your path are going to speak to you – determined, ultimately, the success of the mission. Sometimes that ability was there, and sometimes it wasn't.

So maybe only now were they figuring out that what had happened on that street, in that particular second, was as connected to all the training manoeuvres and planning of this particular operation as it was detached from them, separate, connected to the personality and abilities of one lone man on whose shoulders rested the mission.

Their appeal to Gadi now, just as they had appealed to Ronen before him, was a cry for help.

Gadi continued. "Every level carries its own responsibility. The hand that pulled out the gun and failed to fire belonged to Ronen, but on that hand the entire chain of command – from me up to the Prime Minister – was hanging. That hand did not act alone or in a vacuum. It acted as a result of something of which we were all a part."

"One more question," Shalgi interjected, curtly. "You mentioned the Prime Minister. You know the expression, 'The buck stops here?' That's the place where decisions are made and responsibility is taken."

Gadi nodded. He knew there was no way that Shalgi's personal history would permit him to accept wishy-washy conclusions. There had been slip-ups in his military career that had caused him major setbacks and now, acting as a judge, he wasn't going to let anyone off lightly.

"Don't you think that expression should be placed on a desk somewhere in the Mossad? On the chief's desk? Does it seem fair to you that responsibility should be rolled so easily out of the doors of the Mossad?"

"I don't think I need to respond to that," Gadi said quietly. "I'll just remind you that in this instance, unlike any other I've experienced, the time constraints were imposed by the Prime Minister."

The smell of the sea was for some reason stronger in winter, Ronen thought as he turned off the main road towards the street leading into the village where he lived. He picked up, too, the scent of citrus blossoms and wet earth; as he raised the visor on his helmet to breathe them all deeply into his lungs, he dropped into a low gear, coasting in near silence on a path between the fruit groves.

He had never quite got over the excitement of returning home, first from the army, then, after joining the squad, from frequent overseas trips, to this place that was like no other, an oasis of calm. Then to Naamah, who had herself already seen and experienced everything he had but awaited his return nonetheless, full of curiosity and love; he had never stopped fearing that one day he would return and she would be gone. After that, to the scaffolding of their new house, which they had built in his parents' garden facing the sea, nearly everything he was meant to finish with his own hands as yet left undone. And, most recently, to his tiny daughter's scent and her wonderful laughter, which now roused such mixed emotions in him.

He navigated the streets of the village passing the old, weather-beaten houses, passing his parents' home then turning down the narrow lane that led to his own. Drinking in the heavy sea air he could hear, even before turning off the ignition, the waves breaking on the rocky beach below. He paused for a moment, perched on his motorbike; his nightmarish day was over, or then again maybe this had only just been its preamble. Everything around him was perfectly suited to his mood: the encroaching darkness, the wind, the rough sea; inside, Naamah and Lital each waiting to pamper him, a pleasure he felt incapable of enjoying; his parents, in their house, whose worry weighed heavily on him and made him angry; and beyond that not a soul, not a single one of the friends who once gathered every Friday on the verandah of his parents' house to swap army stories. When it became impossible to provide details of his escapades, their numbers dwindled, and they disappeared altogether when he brought Naamah here, preferring to spend his rare days off with her alone.

Ronen pushed on the door handle with his elbow and entered the house carrying two bags of groceries. Soft music and the aromas of food swirled together with the roar and scent of the sea that billowed in with him. He closed the door with his foot and in an instant cut himself off from the outside world.

"Ronen?"

The sound of the slamming door had alerted Naamah, who had been reading a book in the dining room, from where she could keep an eye on a pot simmering in the kitchen. Ronen placed the bags of groceries on the work-top and Naamah, who had left her book upside down on the table, came to the kitchen and hugged him from behind.

"Was it rough?"

Ronen turned around slowly. It was so easy for him to be tough outside, on his motorcycle, in the wind, against his interrogators, but Naamah's words, her touch, the warmth of the house, the aromas, the music, all conspired to cause his whole body to tremble. Were the tremor to reach his protective shell it would crack it irrevocably, like a chick emerging from an egg.

Even without looking at his face she knew he was terribly worried.

"Why did you have to go back there today?"

"The summing up," he said, moving the groceries to the refrigerator. "They wanted me to give the bottom line on who I thought was to blame."

"And...?" Naamah asked.

Ronen closed the door of the refrigerator and moved away, escaping the need to look at his wife.

"I said that as Number One it was my decision whether to carry through or not. I was the one who read the situation incorrectly and made a wrong decision. What about that isn't clear?"

Naamah, who had followed him, stopped, surprised.

"You simply told them you were to blame? Only you?" Something between disappointment and a rebuke had crept into her voice.

Ronen turned on her sharply. "Yes, the bottom line – it was me," he said angrily. "But there were other lines," he added quietly. After a moment, he said, angry again, "In any event they're going to dump it all on me."

He glanced at his watch, a diver's watch.

"The news is on. I want to see what lies and leaks they're reporting today." On his way to the living room, he stopped to pick up a toy that Lital had left on the floor and lobbed it straight into the toy chest in the corner of the room. Every evening he sat in front of the screen, lapping up every word and cursing; he swore he would catch the person leaking information and rip off both his balls – one for leaking and the other for distorting everything so that each and every person in the Mossad came out tarnished.

Naamah paused for a second before following him. He surely would not want her to patronize him now. When they had first met, at a party for new recruits, he was brand new, while she was not only a former operative, Number Two on a number of missions, but also Gadi's ex. In the eyes of Ronen and the other new recruits, Gadi's trainees, this made her practically the commander herself. But really there was no need for additional reasons to admire Naamah: tall and dark-skinned with a chiselled Sephardic face, straight nose, pointed chin, dark, bright eyes and long black hair, she could pass for a flamenco dancer.

Rumour had it that Naamah had left Gadi when he was appointed deputy commander of the squad, with all signs pointing to his eventual rise to commander, a job that would demand every waking hour of his life. The squad commander not only accompanied every overseas operation – unlike the operatives themselves, who shared the burden – but at home was also responsible for taking part in and observing training exercises, participating in discussions at headquarters, and planning operations. As the commander of one of the "long arms of the State of Israel" there was no time for anything else. Ronen was taken by surprise when Naamah, who only had to click her castanets for all the dancers surrounding her to bow, had actually selected him; he, too, would be travelling a lot, participating in drills, might rise one day to a command position. And still, she chose him.

At first, he would tell her in great detail everything that happened to him. How he had stood on a street corner surveying the target's shop, until someone had asked him if he'd lost his way; Naamah would laugh and produce, in a flash, three or four methods for doing it better (was there perhaps a bus stop opposite the shop, or a café from which he could sit and observe?). Or how one night he had been waiting for the target in a car, along with another operative, when a policeman rapped on the window, demanding to see their papers, since a suspicious neighbour had phoned to complain; Naamah would burst out laughing, wanting to know where the female operatives had disappeared to and advising that if it had to be two men stationed together then at least they should kiss from time to time. Ronen would find himself jealous of Gadi and the other operatives who had been Naamah's partners through an infinity of nights like those, then he would swing her up and throw her onto the bed, coming to her with the strength and childish emotion she loved so much.

With time he became less open to her advice, and

eventually she began to feel a certain reserve on his part. But that's okay, she thought, figuring he'd gained enough experience not to remain her trainee, and so she stopped offering advice, simply listening, interested and alert, to descriptions of his operations. In her head she listed his mistakes, so easy for her to see, and stored them away for some more appropriate occasion.

But now it was no longer a matter of his experience as an operative: now, his entire character was on the line, and suddenly it was perfectly clear to her that all those old wolves, his superiors, had effortlessly torn him to shreds. He had not even sensed the danger, thanks to his innocence, his goodheartedness, his integrity, all the qualities that made him a wonderful husband and father and a great friend but were not suited to the street life of the squad, and certainly not to an interrogation room. How had she never thought of that before? she wondered, angry with herself. How had she not spoken to him of this, not advised him to defend himself? And what was the point of saying something to him now, when it was all over?

She watched him sitting on the sofa, pressing the remote-control, and a wave of love for him washed over her. Where do you find a man like this these days, she said to herself, repeating verbatim the words of her friend Dalia, whose advice she had petitioned about Ronen years earlier. So what if he's younger than you, and innocent, Dalia told her then, failing to mention his tall, handsome physique. Nor could Dalia know anything about the great tenderness that coursed through his large, sinewy hands as they passed over Naamah's body. He's such a dish, Dalia had said, a real catch.

Tears brimming from her eyes, Naamah sat next to Ronen, pulling her feet onto the sofa and leaning her head on his shoulder. He recoiled, and Naamah removed her head immediately. Oh, I'm sorry, I forgot, she mumbled, and the pain of his bullet-ridden shoulder, which forced him to remember the shame of Beirut on a daily basis, penetrated her as if it were her own. Ronen continued to watch the screen, which was now filled with scenes from the West Bank.

"Lital wanted to stay awake until you arrived, but she fell asleep here, on the couch. I moved her just a little while ago. Do you want to go in and see her?"

Ronen did not react. Something bad was happening to his relationship with their daughter but she could not tell precisely what. Too many troubles all at once. She passed her fingers lightly through the hair on his neck.

"I don't think they'll blame you for it all. What about the others? I know what the bottom of the chain of command is, it's still part of the chain. After all, they could have blamed you right from the beginning. Why would they need to sit for so many months? I'm sure they'll have criticism for the entire system."

"In your time there were no commissions of inquiry," Ronen said after a short silence, without moving his eyes from the screen. "It was all taken care of internally. So the lessons learned were for real, and each person actually accepted responsibility for his own mistakes. Now it's a whole different story."

Milken, the television commentator who covered, among other things, intelligence issues, appeared on the screen. Ronen leaned forward, avoiding Naamah's touch.

"The Commission of Inquiry into the Mossad's Failure in Beirut heard today the summary statements of the affair's heroes," Milken said. "As predicted, the operatives blamed the senior staff for faulty planning and administration of this operation, while the senior staff blamed the squad for the faulty implementation of a good plan."

Naamah tried to say something but Ronen silenced her.

"Or," continued Milken, "as one of the key witnesses expressed so colourfully, and I quote, 'Hanging from the hand that drew the gun were all those that deserve to be hanged.' In short," he said as he turned to face the anchorwoman, "there are no big, righteous heroes in this affair. Tomorrow we'll hear if the members of the commission agree with that, or whether at least some of them are still blinded by the rhinestone halo of the Mossad: the Agency for Intelligence Gathering and Security Screw-Ups." He turned a suppressed smile to the camera, nodding as if to affirm his own words, while the anchorwoman thanked him. Then his face disappeared as the next item came on the screen.

"Is it true what Milken said?" Naamah asked Ronen, a worried look on her face.

"I only know what I said, which was just the opposite," he answered as he turned off the television with the remote-control button. "That piece of trash has been tossing around lies for the past six months but it doesn't seem to be bothering anybody."

"Maybe he quoted the others accurately. Maybe only you blamed yourself. I mean, he can't just be making it all up."

Ronen stood up and looked at her.

"He can't just be making it all up? You yourself told me that the day we got rid of Khalili you heard Milken explaining who this Ibrahim El-Sheikh who'd been assassinated was, and that every single detail was so wide of the mark that you began to think we'd killed the wrong guy."

"That's true," Naamah admitted. The squad had zeroed in on Khalili at a stopover on a small island in spite of his disguise and false identity, and the journalists had understood, thanks to the style of the hit, that he'd apparently been a terrorist. They didn't yet know that Ibrahim El-Sheikh was the false name of the head of the Islamic Front, so they spoke in general terms – in fact, complete fabrications – to avoid getting the story wrong.

"So that's it," Ronen said, ending the conversation as he turned to go out, "when they don't have information they make it up."

"But it can't all fall on you. We have to prevent that from happening," she said, though it was unclear whether she was talking to Ronen or herself. "I want to talk to Gadi," she said, reaching for the phone.

"Don't you fix things up for me with Gadi," he grumbled in a low voice. It didn't matter to Ronen at that moment that it was Naamah who had ended the relationship with Gadi, that Gadi had a wife and two children, that they had Lital; he couldn't accept an appeal from Naamah to Gadi to help him. Not when deep inside he blamed Gadi for his failure.

He removed the receiver from Naamah's hand.

"Ronen!" The sound died in her throat.

"What do you mean, *Ronen*? How do you expect me to keep my cool when the first thing you do is run to Gadi?"

"The first thing? We haven't spoken once in the six months since the operation and the inquiry. And anyway, in the ten years you've been with the squad we've barely been in touch. He's your commander, he's *supposed* to be in touch!"

"So that's what's bothering you?" he asked, a bitter smile settling on his lips. "That he hasn't called? Don't worry, he hasn't forgotten you. Don't you think I notice how he's been testing me all these years, if I'm good enough for *his Naamah*? And don't you think he's the one who's stood in the way of my promotion to Number One, even when I was just about the most experienced member of the squad, so you'd see that I don't measure up to him?"

"Ronen, it was over between us before you even joined the squad," she sputtered dispiritedly, rising from the couch. But Ronen continued without listening to her at all.

"He barely let me be Number Two. And you, of course, were his permanent Number Two. He even let you shoot. So don't you think he wanted to prove that I wasn't as good as you?"

"I don't believe that's really what you think. After all these years…"

All at once all the fears, suspicions and anger between them had a single focus: Gadi. What was it her friend Dalia had said when she'd told her she was going out with one of the new operatives to annoy Gadi? Don't play around, it's too dangerous. One day it will blow up in your face.

And when she first started going out with Ronen it really was in defiance of Gadi, who had not wasted time in finding a beautiful college student from Denmark after Naamah informed him she wasn't willing to lead the life of a wife of the squad commander. The invitation to Gadi's wedding had arrived soon after that. At first Ronen couldn't ignore Naamah's lingering interest in Gadi: what does Gadi think about us dating? Nothing? It really doesn't bother him? What about the men? I don't talk about you to the others, or to Gadi, Ronen answered, a bit hurt.

When she discovered that what was between her and Ronen was love, it was already too late to uproot the seed of jealousy, or suspicion, that she herself had planted in his heart. She hoped their marriage would do that, hoped that Lital would do that, hoped that never mentioning Gadi's name would do that. But here it was, proof that nothing had worked.

A human barricade of television crews and reporters brought the official Toyota to a halt several feet in front of the barred entrance to the car park of the Prime Minister's office. Nov smiled ineffectually as he alighted from the

42

front seat of the vehicle, an attaché case in his hand. In an instant he was surrounded by reporters thrusting microphones into his face. Shalgi and Tal reluctantly climbed out of the back seat, and reporters who had failed to push far enough into the throng surrounding Nov rushed to shove microphones in front of them.

"Is it true you recommend firing the head of the Mossad?" asked one reporter, while a second interjected, "Will this be another case like the Night of the Hanggliders, where the private guarding the gate takes the rap while the senior commanders walk away unscathed?"

Nov smiled patiently without answering, attempting to ply his way through the throng to the guard booth at the entrance. Shalgi and Tal were trying to follow close in his wake. As they passed by the journalist who had asked about the Night of the Hang-gliders, Shalgi smiled and said, as though sharing a secret, "I didn't allow that to happen."

A reporter for Channel One news held Nov's arm for a moment. "Doesn't the public deserve to know the results of your findings?"

Nov turned towards him, and the crowd of reporters pushed in closer to listen, shushing one another.

"The commission of inquiry was appointed by the Prime Minister, hence the findings will be delivered to the Prime Minister. Most of the report is indeed top secret, though some of the conclusions are not, and those will be made public by the Prime Minister if and when he so chooses. Thank you, gentlemen."

As Nov and his entourage disappeared into the

building, the rash of questions hurled at him was caught by the plate-glass door that slid shut behind them. The radio reporters blathered their impressions into microphones, the print journalists into voice recorders and the television reporters faced the cameras.

"Six months after the failure in Beirut," reported the Channel One journalist to the camera, "the commission of inquiry today handed in a thick report of findings and testimonies, and a thinner volume of conclusions. While the panel members have naturally maintained a discreet silence, the main conclusions have come to our attention: according to the panel members, a systemic failure is what brought about the aborted operation in Beirut, which was doomed to failure from the outset. By a majority decision the commission places the blame at the operational level, while the dissenting opinion of commission member Shalgi states that the head of the Mossad should also accept responsibility and should step down from his post."

A couple of dozen young men and women – nearly the entire squad – were gathered in the briefing room waiting for Gadi and Ronen to arrive from their meeting in the office of the Mossad chief. They had heard the news broadcasts of their failed mission in Beirut, had learned that every single person involved was held responsible for the mishap. Whole sections of the commission's report were already available on the Internet, but the operatives had no way of knowing whether this was a leak of real information or a fabrication. There was nothing to do but wait for the official version. The fact that only Ronen had been summoned to the office of the Mossad chief, alongside Gadi, seemed to indicate that the findings focused on the two of them.

This was in keeping with what most of the operatives thought anyway: while nearly all of them had played a part in the operation, it was clear that the central roles had been occupied by the commander and his Number One. Further, it was hard to pinpoint any special shortcomings in the work of anyone else. The surveillance team had performed effectively, as had the evacuation team and the car positioned as an obstruction. Ronen's back-up team, too, at his side in the event of a jammed weapon, had not acted but was cleared of any blame. Ronen had not notified them of any problems, he had simply decided not to shoot, and the back-up team had been given no instructions to fire in his place.

Gadi entered the room in a rush, blank-faced, Ronen just behind him, downcast. Immediately there were questions, but Gadi asked the squad members to be seated. They shoved together on the sofa and armchairs facing the television in the corner of the briefing room. Others dragged chairs over, forming concentric circles that filled the room. Ronen took a seat, too, while Gadi remained standing.

"The head of the Mossad read us a summary of the commission's conclusions," Gadi started right in, skipping the formalities. "I'll get right to the bottom line. The commission established that there was a series of bad decisions, each at a different level of responsibility. The head of the Mossad bore administrative responsibility for sending out the team. There was a minority opinion that thought he should step down but the commission recommended keeping him in his job. I am responsible for parts of the plan that were incomplete, including failing to establish a code word for carrying out the shooting, so Ronen was stuck with the decision. However, according to the commission my actions did not contribute directly to the failure of the operation, so there are no recommendations with regard to me personally. As for the rest of you," he said as he scanned the faces of his squad, all but Ronen's, who sat close by, "there are no comments. Ronen was at the end of the chain of command, but the commission established that his actions alone could cause or prevent the mission's failure. They note that even after their investigation it is unclear to them why Ronen drew his weapon but failed to shoot, that perhaps he was too quick to draw and too hesitant to shoot. Therefore, they recommend excluding him from operational activities in the future. The summary of the report is right here, whoever wants to read it later."

Gadi produced a sheaf of photocopied papers from his jacket pocket and tossed it onto a small table outside the circle of chairs. Nonetheless, a few people grabbed for them immediately.

"But first of all, I want it to be perfectly clear," Gadi said, before the whispers and murmurs could grow too loud, "that I am no less responsible than Ronen, even more so. I knew we didn't have time to gather intelligence as we should have, I knew we didn't do simulations as we usually do, and yet I didn't pound on any desks, I didn't threaten to resign. I would feel more comfortable if the panel's conclusions were not what they are, but unfortunately that's what they had to say.

"I informed the chief that I would like to hand in my resignation, but his answer was that he doesn't care to engage in mass breast-beating and that what the commission recommended is what will be."

Gadi didn't know whether and to what extent his people would believe him. No one could know how guilty he felt, how much better he would have felt if the commission had placed the guilt on his shoulders and not, as it transpired, completely on Ronen's. After all the tests and trials he'd put Ronen through, year after year, a combined mishap in which he'd been found innocent and Ronen guilty had created not only a very problematic situation with regard to their relationship but also with Ronen's status among the operatives, and in his relationship with Naamah, too.

"What does it mean, 'from operational activities'?" asked David, one of the younger operatives. "Does that mean he can't be Number One or that he can't take any part in operations at all?"

"Ronen is forbidden from participating in operational activities. The commission did not differentiate between the various roles in an operation," Gadi answered.

"But they *did* differentiate," Sharon said, glancing at Ronen's downcast face. Sharon had been Ronen's partner on a number of overseas missions. "How is it that the head of the Mossad can continue to confirm operational activities and you can command them, but Ronen can't participate in them?"

Another voice cried out, "And what about Doron? Can he continue to head the Operations Division?"

"And how about the Prime Minister? Is he allowed to continue pushing us into such ridiculous time frames?" someone called out from the back.

"Settle down, guys," Gadi said. "I understand how you feel and I feel pretty much the same way. But we don't appoint Prime Ministers and we don't decide who gets to give us orders. We need to do some soul-searching, and work out how we should act when we're given such orders."

"There's nobody here who could have performed any better than Ronen under those circumstances," said Danny, a young operative who had been Ronen's charge when he'd first joined. "The conclusions about Ronen are really about all of us."

"Don't get carried away, okay?" Izzy, one of the older operatives, said angrily. Just before the Beirut operation he had been named Gadi's deputy. "And, please forgive me," he said to Ronen, then turned back to Danny, "but suddenly you've forgotten our own criticism of Ronen? You've forgotten how angry we were that before drawing his gun he didn't take a few steps backwards, didn't open his eyes wide to take in everything, didn't open his ears to hear everything. What's going on here? We're not rookies and this isn't Hollywood here, where you draw your gun and whatever happens, happens. Have you forgotten that we've discussed all this? So don't put us all in the same boat, okay?"

"Izzy, we're all wise after the fact," Udi, the oldest operative, said in his English accent. "Analyzing our actions in the field later, under a microscope, is a no-brainer. Just as planning in controlled weather conditions and then carrying out a mission in the street are two totally different things. We all know this. You and I have seen each other make enough mistakes which were not predicted in the planning stages and which, in the post-operation analysis, shouldn't have happened at all. But they happen, and we all know it, because the street has its own rules."

Ronen remained seated, as if the discussion were not about him, while his peers continued arguing. Not one of them voiced opposition to the guilty verdict; even his close friends in the squad were angry with him, clear that a mishap like this should not have happened. Their criticism was essentially that only Ronen would pay the price even though the list of those responsible was considerably longer. They were angry, too, about his complete dismissal from operational activities in spite of the hundreds of missions he'd participated in without incident in the past. True, he shouldn't be Number One, but not even a regular operative?

Gadi continued to stand, listening pensively. The question he'd not been asked by the commission was always there, in the background: why had he chosen Ronen to be Number One? Gadi was the one who'd once said, after a mission, that before shooting he felt as though his eyes became one giant eye that sees everything, as if from above, and that his body reacts to every movement on the street. When he carries out an operation he becomes an enormous receiver, sensitive to the slightest rustle, his thoughts as clear and sharp as a computerized chess program. Everything is taken into account, weighed, and he sees clearly what he is about to do and what the reactions will be of each person in the vicinity, always three steps ahead of real time. Simultaneously he can see himself from the outside, as if in a film. He knows exactly where he is and how he appears to others. And then he makes his move, lightly, unnoticed. The step, the drawing of the weapon, the shooting. Suddenly there is a very faint noise and someone collapses as though a string holding his various body parts together has snapped and his body hits the ground like a marionette torn from the puppeteer's hands, all so different from the way it happens in films. And he sees the reactions of passersby, the ones who glance and continue walking, the ones who steal a look over their shoulders, the ones who move away in shock, the ones who stop as though thunderstruck, and the ones who bend down to help. And he – a shadow, a breeze – he blends in with the passersby, knowing precisely what is happening behind him and how many steps he will need to take before turning down the alley where the escape car is waiting for him, and only after turning does he feel a blow to his ribs, as if his soul were suddenly returning to his body, as if someone had restored the sound to the film. All at once he is assaulted by the noise and scents and sights on the street and the crackling from his transmitter. He is grounded again, has come back to all his senses and to the earthly mechanism he is responsible for, leading his people out of danger and reporting on his transmitter, in his deep, peaceful voice, that the operation went off without a hitch.

Again and again he asked himself which of them were capable of performing as a Number One. This work is comparable to nothing else: not the navy commando, swimming stealthily underwater towards his target, not the fighter pilot sitting right on the tail of an enemy plane and not the paratrooper storming a fortified target in a hail of fire. Perhaps the war dance between two seventh-degree *dan* masters is the closest approximation. It was similar to how he himself had sat in the lotus position while the old master stood behind and over him, a wooden sword poised in his hand for attack, for one very long minute as Gadi – without seeing him or even hearing his breath – had to sense the split second that the sword would land on him and move his body aside at lightning speed. This sense was what elevated him to the rarefied status of the Ninjitsu masters. There was nothing mystical about it, just a supreme moment of concentration, the ability to sense vibration in the air, complete control of his mind and body, and near-control of the space around him. Who of his people could reach this level of control?

One in a thousand applicants is suited for recruitment to the Mossad and one in a hundred Mossad recruits finds himself in this squad, whose job it is to gather intelligence behind enemy lines and execute special covert operations. At any given time on the squad, he mused, there are maybe one or two people who can handle carrying out the shooting itself, who can do the job and then fade into a passing shadow. It's easy to raise Mafia tough guys, who work their own territory. Iranian hit men leave the embassy in cars with diplomatic plates and weapons in diplomatic pouches; they shoot and then, under the protection of diplomatic immunity, return to the embassy building. But to steal into an enemy capital without the protection of a special diplomatic passport, to pass innocently between alert guards, to wait, like a street cat that nobody notices, until just the right moment, to strike and slip away without leaving a single fingerprint, to have set it up so that at no airport do they have a clue who they're looking for as you pass right under the inspectors' snooping noses, your heart pounding but your face serene on your way to the plane and to freedom – that's an art of an altogether different calibre.

He'd trained two, both of whom had left. When Izzy announced he was planning to leave, Gadi appointed him his deputy and now he was only hanging on because Doron, the head of their division, was talking about making him the next squad commander. Udi had never been suited to that kind of job, and the next in line, according to seniority, was Ronen. On the eve of their departure for Beirut, with Ronen as Number One for the first time, he wondered whether he had refused to select Ronen all those years because of Naamah. Could it be that he had read him incorrectly, blocked his advancement for no good reason, blamed him unfairly for being too rigid, inflexible? He should already have started training the next generation but couldn't find anyone better among the younger operatives. It wasn't right to keep splitting up the execution of their operations between himself and Izzy, especially since Izzy had been handling all the logistics in his capacity as deputy. And that's how Ronen's turn came and together they had brought everyone down.

Together with the feelings of guilt plaguing him from the time of the mishap and the unpleasantness of walking away blameless while his subordinate had not, Gadi felt deep sympathy for Ronen. True, he wasn't flexible or capable of manipulation, and his acting abilities were limited, but couldn't the same be said about Gadi himself? Hadn't he already learned, and not just with Ronen, that the stronger and more forthright a person was, honest and innocent and goodhearted, the less capable he was of impersonation? And Ronen really was a good guy, in the best sense of the word; he made up for his inability to be manipulative by being willing and tenacious. Gadi gazed at Ronen, his shoulders hunched and his eyes downcast, and a terrible sadness gripped him in the pit of his stomach.

Gadi wanted to set the discussion on a different track. He raised his hand and, after a few more murmurs, silence fell.

"I want to reiterate that we have no business criticizing our superiors or chewing the fat over what's come out of the investigation. Our consideration is first and foremost Ronen. We all know what stuff Ronen is made of, we've all seen him carrying out operations that any of those who judged him would have shit their pants over. I hope that we'll be free to interpret the recommendation of the commission in a way that will let us keep Ronen with us, and I'll put pressure on whoever I need to. In any event, one thing's for sure: Ronen is not leaving us and we're not leaving Ronen. He'll be part of our family in the future just as he is today, part of all our social activities. We're not giving up on him."

Gadi himself wasn't happy with the tone of his words, it was simply what came out of his mouth when he looked at Ronen. He picked up on some murmuring when he finished talking that did not please him: Naamah's name was being tossed about. When the room settled down again Gadi turned to Ronen.

"Would you like to say something, Ronen?" he asked quietly.

Ronen shook his head. He, too, had heard Naamah's name and had understood the connection; he knew exactly how the squad was split between his supporters and his critics. The younger ones, whom he had trained during their first year in the squad – David, Danny, Sharon and others – were fans of his. After eight months of training, when they already thought they knew everything there was to know, they began jetting about with him and discovered that the training course was one thing and the streets of Athens were something entirely different. "You know these streets better than a taxi driver," David said once with admiration, when Ronen was showing them the escape routes from the centre of the city. And Sharon sought him out, with a certain coyness, for extra tips after their normal working hours, in his hotel room.

The group that had been in the squad a bit longer, three to five years, had watched, more than once, as Ronen stayed a tad too long at the lookout, until someone had come along and asked if he were looking for something; and he, who was incapable of smiling or asking for help, answered brusquely and walked away, leaving behind him a trail of suspicion. They understood why they, and not Ronen, got the more sensitive jobs and the more dangerous assignments. Ronen, who was always willing to take on any assignment, never complaining about a full night of surveillance in the snow or driving twenty-four hours straight in order to reach a certain place, was the king of Europe, Africa, Asia and South America, but they had already clocked more time in Tehran, Damascus and Beirut than he ever would. They still gave him the credit he deserved as their senior, but did not refrain from criticizing him in debriefings.

The most experienced operatives, like Izzy and Udi, had not spared the rod when it came to criticizing him, which they did after nearly every operation. Udi, who now only engaged in "clean" jobs, like renting hotel rooms and cars or making inquiries in offices and companies, rebuked Ronen gently, while Izzy delivered his criticism harshly. After a surveillance operation in Vienna during which Ronen had acted particulary brazenly, Izzy had shouted: "Go back to the navy. You've never stopped behaving like you're in combat and you'll never learn to be a spy."

And then there was Gadi, who saw everything in a more severe light because of Naamah. Of course because of Naamah. It was a fact that nobody else was as critical of him as Gadi. But hadn't he proved that Gadi was right? Maybe another member of the group wouldn't have pulled out his gun under those circumstances, or at least would have finished the job instead of freezing with a gun in his hand. But would it have happened if he'd had proper preparation beforehand, if he hadn't been suddenly thrust into a battle for survival in the heart of the Shi'ite quarter of Beirut after ten years of biding his time, taking part in the easier assignments? It was a final examination of sorts, performed in seconds flat, in which everything you know and everything you are is tested. But what did it matter now? The results were known, and everybody had an opinion about them. He'd had his say in front of the commission of inquiry, and even before, through long days of internal debriefings in the squad and comprehensive debriefings in the Operations Division. He'd heard himself and everyone present so many times; he had made practically no slip-up over the years that hadn't been discussed and analyzed, even though for every mishap there were complex situations he'd handled well, respectably, even elegantly at times. What was the point of mentioning that now?

Gadi waited for a moment, watching Ronen's blank expression change to bewilderment, bitterness and resignation. He continued.

"I want to share with you my own personal conclusions," he said, pausing to allow the operatives to disconnect themselves from the issue of Ronen. "First of all, I think we need to introduce a new concept into our lexicon, criminal tenacity. Its cousin is criminal negligence." Again he paused for a moment, to ascertain whether they'd absorbed what he was saying.

No one present could know that Gadi had already used this term in a discussion with the previous head of the division and had angered all the department heads at that meeting. The head of the Planning Department had presented plans for a highly complex operation deep in Lebanon, one that required the operatives to hide in the hills with a view of the road until the right moment for carrying out the mission. Gadi had asked for the floor.

"I'm not saying this because I'll necessarily be the person who has to carry out the mission with his people; you could just as well send Rami, with his Mistaravim squad of operatives posing as Arabs, or whoever you want for that matter. I'm simply looking at our operations over the past year and I see a very clear path: we are constantly raising the level of risk. It's like a pair of scales, one of which is labelled 'lack of tenacity' and the other 'criminal tenacity', and they're tipping further and further towards the latter. In my opinion the only operations that justify taking such risks are those of strategic importance, like foiling delivery of a shipment of non-conventional weapons, or those of national importance, like freeing our missing soldier Ron Arad. And that's not what we're talking about here."

The room fell silent when Gadi finished speaking, and for a moment he didn't know whether to read the looks he was getting as agreement or astonishment. Those present were the senior command staff of the division: three commanders of operations squads, including Gadi, who held a rank comparable to colonel in the army, and the heads of the Planning, Intelligence and Weaponry Departments of the division, who were taking part in the discussion. Kobi was there too, formerly head of planning and now the senior representative of the division overseas, as well as Doron, who was in the process of taking over from the outgoing director of the Operations Division.

The division head cleared his throat and said, "We do not get involved with the merit of a mission, only with whether we can or cannot carry it off. This is not a case of 'cannot', we clearly can carry off this mission – with risks, which we'll present to the boss. He'll decide."

It wasn't really an answer to the issue Gadi had raised, even though it fit the way the division head perceived his role. Two staff officers questioned the expression criminal tenacity but Kobi went on the attack. "If you think there are criminals here then get up and leave," he said. The others, including Doron, remained silent. Only the director of the Intelligence Department dared to admit that the scales had shifted from where they had been two years earlier, but no one supported Gadi publicly. Afterwards, in the corridor, Rami slapped Gadi on the shoulder with a smile, and Yankol, another head of squad said, "Tell me, have you decided to leave? That's not the way someone who's planning on staying in the system talks."

Gadi had realized then just how entrenched was this defective institutional culture in which no one dared come out publicly against an operation, and certainly not against an operation that was supported by the head of the division. Even the squad commanders, who must have felt as he did, had not dared speak out. Shortly afterwards a string of mishaps took place, in Amman, Beirut, and in Austria where Yankol was head of the squad. If headquarters won't internalize this, Gadi thought, at least I'll drill it into my own people, if it's not too late.

"I can't think of a better expression than criminal tenacity for summing up what happened in this operation," Gadi continued, "there's no point in blaming the Prime Minister – no one pointed a gun at our heads to get us to perform this mission, and we knew we were heading out without sufficient practice. None of us felt good about the fact that we were to locate the target and finalize a lot of the details in the field, but we did it anyway. And that's criminal tenacity."

"Have you forgotten why we acted so quickly?" Izzy called out. "Don't you remember the attack in the souk?"

"I haven't forgotten anything," Gadi said brusquely. Suddenly we're all just fine in Izzy's eyes. Izzy, the one the commission of inquiry had nothing to say about because Gadi had cleared him of all responsibility. My deputy had no specific role in the operation itself, Gadi had claimed, and there were no problems with the logistics that Izzy took care of. The fact that Izzy had been involved at every level of the process did not disqualify him – either in his own eyes or in Doron's – from taking over from Gadi as squad commander. And now Izzy was starting to build up his status among the other operatives.

"I still think," Gadi said, returning to his original point, "that it was our responsibility to say that we were not prepared and we need to look to ourselves to see how we deal with the instructions passed down to us. We have no right to please our superiors, we have no right to consent to their demands, if we aren't absolutely certain we are willing and able to carry them out. The State of Israel is unwilling and unable to pay the price of our failure, which was proved in this case at every level, from the Prime Minister down to the lowliest journalist, right through to our own friends and neighbours who don't even know we were there and joked with us about the 'losers' in the Mossad."

Gadi's last words caused a few of them to squirm in their seats; most had had the unpleasant experience of listening to criticism of the Mossad from people who didn't know they were talking to Mossad agents.

"So my conclusion from all this is that we're done with being yes-men. The fact that each of us knew we shouldn't take on this assignment but kept quiet about it stems not only from criminal tenacity, but from excessive good manners and obedience. It's not nice for us to say to our bosses, 'What? Are you crazy?' But if we don't, they have no way of knowing the real demands they're making on us. They're not aware of the little details."

Gadi tried to gauge the effect he was having on his audience but couldn't get a clear picture. It's not easy for people who see themselves as spearheads – like the seals from the Navy Commando Flotilla and members of the IDF Special Forces Commando Unit – to grasp that they are really just a pack of good little boys. But Gadi knew them, and that's exactly what they were. You couldn't say that about your average criminal from Jaffa or Ramle, but the Mossad doesn't take natural-born killers or thieves. They take nice boys and teach them to lie, break in, kill. And there's a price to pay for that.

"In my opinion keeping silent is a way of expressing that we, the long arm of the State of Israel, are in the end just a bunch of nice, polite yes-men. So as far as I'm concerned, at least, that's finished, and I hope that's true for all of you, too."

Gadi understood that both Ronen's failure and that of the whole operation stemmed from the same source. Only nice boys allow a brazen operation like this one to take place, and only nice boys hesitate at the last moment. Ronen had already paid the price, and now Gadi wanted to treat the malady of the entire organization. It's true that the system could deal with each element separately, and it's a fact that almost every operation had worked. But the organization couldn't possibly succeed in the untenable combination of a nice boy serving as Number One in an overly bold operation.

The operatives glanced around the room uncomfortably, their mouths shut tight only out of respect for Gadi; he understood they were not with him. He wasn't sure he had succeeded in making his claims clear. It had taken him, too, a while to understand the hidden connections between cause and effect, which he had tried to point out. Whatever they understood, they understood, he thought, looking at Ronen again.

"Ronen, perhaps you've changed your mind?"

*

Ronen raised his eyes, a bitter smile on his lips. He had, in fact, been listening, recalling the many times Gadi had spoken to him of his excessive tenacity, saying that it was better to bail out and try again later under more advantageous conditions than to charge ahead at any cost. But now what stood out in his mind was the connection between Gadi's reproach about their being yes-men and this meeting, in which his friends were as quiet as if they'd been reprimanded, like children who say nothing when the teacher removes a trouble-maker from the class, simply relieved they weren't the one to be thrown out. How quickly they'd dispensed with their watered-down criticism of the commission's findings.

"Yes-men," Ronen said into the tension-filled silence, "are the ones who think that the conclusions of others are what counts, who do what others decide for them." Suddenly he felt that he couldn't stay there any longer, that his continued presence would be an admission that the commission's conclusions were correct, that he was willing to accept the non-operational jobs he was bound for. "A yes-man doesn't consult his own conscience, he just does what he's told. God help all the good little yes-men."

The transparent wall separating him from the rest of them seemed to fog up until he could barely see anyone on the other side. They hadn't merely betrayed him, these friends he'd spent days, nights, months and years with in surveillance, chases, infiltrations and escapes on five continents; they were completely different from him.

Ronen felt almost physically that something had

broken inside him. And to think that Naamah had told him he was too naive, too good. So who are these people? Gadi was right, they really are just a pack of good little boys, a bunch of yes-men, but he's wrong if he thinks something will change in them. Nobody who hasn't been affected personally will change. He, Ronen, had taken the brunt of the blame. Should he have fought back? Lied? Cut corners? Had he been too straightforward and honest? No, the opposite: his integrity up until today was nothing compared to the way he'd behave from now on. Gadi says they should say what they really think, that they shouldn't just do what people tell them to? Well that's exactly what he was going to do.

The room was silent, people were waiting for him to continue. Gadi, perplexed, was speechless too. He thought, Go on, Ronen, get it off your chest. It'll be good for everyone if you do. But Ronen didn't want to get anything else off his chest, no new words formulated themselves in his head, and the only feeling he could discern in the darkness that was spreading through him was slight nausea. He stood up and left.

Ronen plodded heavily to his room which was primarily a place for studying, writing reports and resting between manoeuvres, but ten years on the job had turned it into a repository for things that told his entire history with the squad.

A large cork board hanging over his desk was covered haphazardly with photos of Ronen: wearing a suit, drinking coffee with Arab sheikhs; eating with local businessmen in a restaurant decorated in an Oriental style; standing by a small private jet at a snowy airport sporting a Russian fur hat; riding in a speedboat among opulent yachts at an unnamed marina; during squad manoeuvres, in a wet suit on a rubber boat, in a group hug with squad members in various world capitals.

He opened a spacious flight bag and began stuffing it with the photos. After that he carefully cleared the shelves of dozens of mementos he'd collected: boxes decorated with coloured stones that formed the names of various exotic and not-so-exotic countries, knives sheathed in ivory, gold, silver and copper. With great care he added to the bag horses made of wood and leather, camels, elephants and, last of all, a wool and leather llama given to him by a young woman who had fallen in love with him on a short trip to the area where Brazil, Argentina and Paraguay meet. In several towns at that particular spot Hezbollah had decided to build an infrastructure, and it was from there that the men who bombed the Israeli Embassy in Buenos Aires had set out. He, Danny and David posed as three among thousands of tourists coming to see and sail the magnificent Iguaçu Falls nearby, roaming back and forth until they had mapped out where the Hezbollah men lived, prayed and gathered, then returned with Gadi, Izzy and a bunch of tiny monitoring devices. From now on we'll know in advance when they're going to blow up one of our embassies.

Ronen placed two suitcases, one large and one small, on the bed in the room, and began filling them with clothes he was removing from the narrow metal locker:

two suits and several summer and winter jackets, more white shirts than he would ever have use for, a wide variety of ties he would no longer need. From drawers in the locker he withdrew jeans and corduroys, jogging trousers, sweatshirts and checked flannel shirts – clothes for every occasion on five continents. He briefly wondered whether clothes purchased from his annual wardrobe budget, which covered about a quarter of his actual costs, were his to keep, but he continued tossing them from the locker into the suitcases. Are these suitcases even mine? he asked himself as he pulled a soft-sided travel bag from under the bed and began stuffing it with black shoes and brown shoes, elegant shoes and plain shoes, winter boots, hiking boots and trainers.

And suddenly he stopped. He wondered why he was packing all these clothes when he didn't want or need any of them: neither the suits nor the elegant shoes nor the suitcases. That period of his life was over.

Sharon walked into the room and Ronen turned to her. With tears in her eyes she hugged him, her hands grasping his shirt and the skin of his back. Ronen returned the hug lightly.

During their first trip together, as during their training exercises in Tel Aviv, he wasn't sure whether it was merely the admiration of a new operative for her trainer, who was showing her every day how little she'd actually learned on the course. By their second trip it was becoming clear that her desire to *consult* and *analyze* events did not stem solely from professional concerns, certainly not in his hotel room or hers as she desired. She was a tall woman, and fairly attractive, too thin for his tastes but there was a certain magic in small, hard breasts topped by a long, thin neck, or in a firm ass atop long, beautiful legs up to Vogue standards. He ignored her and she made do with hints. Until Paris.

It was a simple mission, exposing an Iranian terrorist infrastructure in the French capital: where the Iranian intelligence people were going, who they were meeting, where their secret apartments were.

"I don't know if there's anything about falling in love with your trainer in squad regulations, but I can't trust you to figure it out on your own," Sharon said as she knocked on his hotel room door.

Ronen smiled, playfully ruffling her short, boyish blonde hair. "The regulations aren't what counts. And thank you. But let's leave it at that," he said. She blushed, and he added, "You're very cute."

"Cute?" She gave him a look of surprise, resentment and defiance all rolled into one.

Ronen, a few years older than she, was still a boy when it came to women. Naamah was everything he could – and did – dream about.

"I mean, the way you say that. And you're beautiful, very beautiful. Attractive, too. But let's leave it at that," he said again.

Sharon drew close, pulled herself up on her toes and kissed the tip of his nose. She turned around and walked out, but not before Ronen caught a glimpse of the small, secret smile of victory on her lips. She knew it was only a matter of time.

Another year passed. Sharon was now a full participant in operational activities. She and Ronen had stolen into a factory supplying Iran with components of non-conventional weapons. While they were still working they were notified by the agents on guard outside that unexpected guests had arrived. The team spread out as planned. Ronen and Sharon retreated to a nearby thicket on the other side of which waited a car for their getaway. After an hour on the road they found a hiding place in the one available room at a small hotel in the mountains.

They didn't waste any words after showering and devouring the sandwiches they found in an automatic dispenser, washing them down with machine-dispensed coffee, too. Ronen didn't try to make excuses to her, or to himself for that matter. He had forgotten how exciting the touch, the scent, of a different, unaccustomed body could be, the wonder of a small, slippery tongue exploring his mouth, the magic of a pair of long, thin legs wrapped around his waist, a languishing voice pleading for more. Pleading, not demanding, like Naamah.

Ronen managed to justify himself the first time, but when it happened again he felt bad about Naamah. He also knew how hard it was to keep a secret in the squad, and thinking about the next party, at which Naamah would be mixing with people who would know what had happened between him and Sharon, was unbearable.

Ronen didn't talk about it with Sharon, he merely arranged that situations in which they would find themselves together in a hotel would not arise again, and she had apparently given up.

Now she was enfolded in his arms, sobbing, and he did not know whether it was for him or because their affair had no future. His hands, which held her back, remained lax. He felt her relax her own hands, finally releasing him and leaving the room in a rush.

There were only three framed pictures remaining on the walls. Ronen removed them slowly, one after the other, gazing at each in turn. The first was of him in the desert, surrounded by Ethiopian children. An inscription written by the Prime Minister read, "To the few who turn Zionism from a fairy tale into reality." That had happened during his first year in the Mossad, one of his first missions. The second was a certificate of appreciation from the Mossad chief for "determination in achieving the goal in very difficult conditions behind enemy lines, in an operation that brought invaluable intelligence and security to Israel". Ronen removed the third from the wall.

It was a poem by the poet and songwriter Haim Hefer, entitled *The Address*. The last stanza read:

> The people of this nation wish to toast the health
> Of our friends behind the scenes working in secrecy
>   and stealth.
> We'd send a hearty thank you if only we could guess
> Where to send the letter, and to what address.

It was inscribed by another Prime Minister: "To Ronen, who participated in Operation Explosive Lightning: I, who do know the address, wish to thank you."

Ronen gazed at the framed poem and the inscription, slowly dropped all three frames into the small rubbish bin, and left the room.

2.

ALL THE TIME in the world to surf the waves behind his house. Ronen took his surfboard out of the tool shed, peeled off the plastic flaps and, after he had applied a bit of oil and paint, it was as good as new. He surfed alone; no one else was crazy enough to ride the waves before the surfing season. Now and again he caught sight of Naamah watching him from the garden of their house up on the cliff. His body reproduced the moves fairly quickly, slaloming adroitly from wave to wave, and he hoped to reproduce, too, the feelings; but the contact with the cold water, day after day and week after week, hovering over the waves and taking control of the sea, failed to invoke even the memory of immense joy, the victorious feeling that had pealed inside him as he surfed.

All the time in the world to plant roses, even in the salty ground that was so ill-suited to them. There was time to dig large holes, fill them with soil, plant the roses, water them and remove from the petals the salt borne by the wind. And between the roses to plant small flowering annuals, and in the pale, salty earth to arrange patches of dark brown flower beds set apart by borders made by Ronen from pocked beach rocks, the beds dotted with reds and pinks and purples and whites and watered with a small watering can. When Naamah asked whether it would be a good idea to lay a pierced irrigation pipe as spring approached, he told her it wasn't necessary, he had all the time he needed for watering.

And all the time in the world for completing the clean-up of the basement, where he planned to set up a small gym. He brought in sand and cement, poured a thin layer of concrete on the ground and smoothed it down, painted the concrete walls white, fixed up the bench press and ordered a Multi-Trainer and a treadmill. At the start of the rainy season Ronen stopped running on the beach, shifting to the treadmill instead and later adding an extra hour with the weights. While Lital slept, Naamah would come down and work out beside him, their paced breathing and panting replacing the need for talk, obscuring the lack of words.

All the time in the world for putting the final coat on the walls of the tiny attic, which might serve as an office for him, when he worked again. When these self-imposed months of inaction were behind him. From the dormer window he could see nothing but the sea, and he found himself staring for hours on end at the view, bewitched, the thin planks of wood he'd carried upstairs lying idly beside him. Almost every time he passed in front of that window the view trapped him there, and each time the sea had something different to say. Sometimes it was the deep, deep blue of infinite possibility, sometimes it was the dull azure blue of an uncertain future, sometimes it was a shimmering green and sometimes a grey filled with danger. In the afternoons it was a blinding gold that blocked all vision or thought. And at twilight – well, twilight he preferred to spend on the verandah facing the sea, since the view from the attic window was too small in scope.

Each patch of sky and each patch of sea had a different shape and colour at twilight, which Ronen devoured whole with his eyes. With a hot cup of coffee in hand – the temperatures dropped with the sun and the wind from the sea grew in intensity – he sat absorbing the pink that turned to orange, then crimson and then an ever-deepening purple, each patch of sky different from the next, shifting by the moment. Even after the sun disappeared, its rays continued to paint in gold the edges of the clouds directly above the spot where it had set, while the clouds in the north and south had already turned from purple to the deep blue of night. The clouds in the west, however, continued to enjoy the light hidden inside them, relinquishing it only gradually, and not without a fight, losing the colours of the prism one at a time; first the gold, then the pink, then the orange, and finally the inevitable darkness.

Clouds, in fact, have rules of their own. Each has its own shape and colour, which changes with the moment. Some soak up the sun's golden rays and refract them back in pink. Some shatter them into hues impossible to name even using the paint catalogue he had consulted to select the shades for painting the attic. Only the direction was clear: everything moved towards darkness. It was only a matter of time, time he tried to catch and preserve each evening. Only recently had he noticed that two or three minutes passed between the moment that the orange sun touched the horizon – which sat not on the waterline, but slightly above it – then began to flatten, becoming the shape of an onion-dome on a Russian Orthodox church, then the dome of a mosque and finally an old batik lampshade, sometimes crowned with the halo of a bomb-burst – and suddenly all that was left was one shining strip over the sea, and then it was gone.

Season after season it was possible to find consolation in the beauty of the time after the sun had set, which lasts much longer. Fifteen minutes pass until minus six degrees, when the sun is six degrees below the horizon and you are still visible to the enemy and have to stay underwater, since the sun's rays are continuing to fight for their lives, colouring the tops of the hills and reflecting as a prism from the clouds; another fifteen minutes until minus twelve degrees, when you can lift your head from the water and swim your way quietly into shallow water, since the sun has acquiesced, its battle lost and the deep purple and blue that it trails behind are already paving the way for the kingdom of the night; and another fifteen minutes until minus eighteen degrees, complete darkness, when you can move forwards, crouching, past the fences, taking up positions, waiting for the order to attack. All this was from some other film, far off, one in which he was no longer certain he had once participated.

The beauty of the encroaching night offered consolation, too, as it crept in a wide arc, capturing first the flanks and then encircling the centre in silence, without fanfare, only in the knowledge that this could end no other way. And even before the battle on the central front had been completed, the night allowed remnants of light to raise a white flag directly in front of him on the horizon. Here a star, there a star. The moment the battle ended, flag-bearers raised the white flag from the trenches again and again, though perhaps these were really gravestones, masses of casualties of a battle whose outcome is predetermined, "who shine like the glow of the heavens". Doomed to failure from the outset, the commission of inquiry had called it.

But maybe it wasn't like that at all, but rather, When the Lord closes a door He opens a window, and instead of one malevolent, blinding, arid sun, the one that had accompanied him on endless marches in the army, there were multitudes of tiny stars also useful for seeing things at night, as in solo navigation training. When they were plentiful he could see their haloes conjoining, and suddenly the Milky Way was clear, and from charts in books he had studied he knew where he was in relation to the shining band above him, which was only a single spoke in the wheel of one hundred billion stars circling him and the earth and the entire solar system.

Did he really know where he was? It was funny just thinking that thought. In fact he didn't even know what the *he* of *where he is* meant. Was it the childhood Ronen of the beach, of his mother and father and the friends on the verandah, or the Ronen of the Navy Commando Flotilla carrying out raids in Lebanon, or the Ronen of surveillance and infiltration on the streets of Europe; or Naamah's Ronen, enjoying nights of such happiness and such immense passion that he could not contain them, and they would touch some inner pain so that tears suddenly rolled down his cheeks and Naamah would lick them off and hug his head with all her might and say, tearful too, I didn't know it was possible to love so much, and these were the only times Ronen believed her; or Lital's Ronen, who preferred not to leave home since each packing and departure tore his heart in two; or Ronen the liar – the Ronen who succumbed to Sharon – returning home angry with himself and transferring his anger to his parents or Naamah; or Ronen the bungler, who, in one critical moment, a moment for which he'd lived and trained for ten years on the squad, and five years before that in the Naval Commando Flotilla, in that moment when every bit of him should have been Number One, he went back, suddenly, to being Lital's father, and a boy playing on the shoreline, and his world turned upside down and an entire nation had landed on his shoulders and crushed them.

But even if he didn't know who *he* was, or even how long he would continue to exist, he could still take consolation from the darkness, from the wind that blew in from the sea, from the foam on the crashing waves he could see through the moving and breathing darkness below him. Sometimes he would fall asleep like that, and Naamah would approach on tiptoe and cover him with the knitted woollen blanket that had been with him since he was that boy.

*

"Mrs Dolev, to you," Naamah said into the receiver in a voice that contained more rebuke than mirth. Gadi, on the other end of the line, was confounded. "I'm sorry I haven't phoned, Naamonet," he said, and his former nickname for her, which belonged to a different time and situation, made her flinch. How could he think to call her that?

After all this time to call her Naamonet no less. As if she hadn't told Ronen – and herself – countless times that what there had once been between them was over. But life has its own rules, its own course, and Gadi was always in the background.

"I know I should have called sooner, and I wanted to, also, it's my job, after all, but ever since Ronen told me not to call, it's been a problem," he said, hesitantly, "and this has been a crazy month. I've barely had two days at home between trips."

"At home." A home that could have been hers, if it weren't for her aggressiveness, which had caused her to give him an ultimatum, if it weren't for his obstinacy and pride, which had caused him to refuse even to negotiate with her. As if that love hadn't existed, as if they hadn't shared such unique and amazing experiences as a couple, as if they hadn't engaged in all that wild screwing. Who else had sat behind her lover on a motorcycle, pulling up with him alongside the car of the representative of the Popular Front for the Liberation of Palestine in Cyprus, who was hosting three PFLP agents from Syria just a few days after their attack in Nahariya; had pulled out a mini-Uzi in unison with her lover and fired a long round of ammunition – he at the passengers in the front seat, she at the men in the back – leaving them full of bullet holes, then tightened her grasp as Gadi zoomed forwards and, three quick turns later, reached a hilly road near which was parked a windowless van. The driver quickly lowered the ramp and in a flash they and the motorcycle were inside, quickly throwing off their helmets, changing out of their leather clothes, handing over their weapons and receiving the keys to the little Fiat parked nearby in which they made their way back to the city, straight to the hideaway apartment. And the sex the moment Gadi closed the door behind him. He hadn't even managed to turn around when she was already hanging from him, so wet that he asked if there was a washing machine in the apartment: I don't want to walk around with your smell on my trousers all day. He'd barely managed to get his trousers off and she was pushing him inside her, and he said, The neighbours are going to show up any minute now, settle down a bit, and she bit his shoulder and dragged him to the bed and pushed him down on his back, swaying back and forth, front to back instead of up and down so that he wouldn't slip out of her, and he said, Too bad it took a few Arabs to die for you to come like this. As they sailed home that same night they celebrated the "lowest fuck on the Mediterranean" and she said, I've had sex with lots of other men, but I only *fuck* with you. She was in love, and was certain this love was the one meant to be.

"…I'm sorry for being out of touch," he said, completing his thought and tearing her away from her memories.

"Don't be sorry," she said coldly, "'Love means never having to say you're sorry.'"

Gadi smiled on the other end of the line. There goes Naamah again with her double entendres. He wasn't even sure she was aware she did it, years of playing games that lead nowhere. He couldn't let that happen as long as Ronen was his subordinate, and definitely not now. Which is why he had severed contact with her: it would be awful if he discovered she had actually wanted him and that a stupid game had sent each one in a different direction. It wasn't as though it wasn't good with Helena, but there were paths created by nature and paths created by humans. The path he shared with Naamah was the former.

"Okay, so I'm not sorry. But not a day goes by when I don't think about what you're going through. Both of you." He hastened to soften his tone of voice. "Do you think Ronen is ready to talk to me? I'm on my way to the airport, I thought…"

"Hang on a minute." Her voice was again distant, and cold.

Naamah crossed the kitchen to the door that lead to the garden. Ronen, wearing an old pair of army trousers and a blue shirt, was kneeling in the flower beds removing tiny weeds with his hands, his back to her.

"It's Gadi," Naamah said, covering the mouthpiece of the telephone. "He's on his way to the airport and wants to say hi."

Ronen turned his head sideways and remained kneeling. "Tell him I'm busy."

He went back to his tiny weeds with renewed vigour.

"Come on, Ronen," Naamah said in a tone that was both a reproach and a plea, but Ronen did not answer. His back stiffened and his fingers pulled angrily at the weeds. Naamah sighed, went back inside and put the receiver back to her mouth.

"I'm not making any progress with you two, you with your 'job' and him with his weeds. It appears that the weeds are more important. He doesn't want to talk."

"Well, at least the garden is blooming."

"Yes, it is well-tended, too well-tended," Naamah said, refusing to play his game, "but Ronen is wilting. And I really don't like the fact that the garden has become an obsession."

"I thought he wasn't doing anything, at least that's what you told me last time we talked." When was that last time, two months ago when Ronen told him not to phone again?

"Yeah, but he's obsessive about doing nothing. It was a mistake to leave the Mossad completely." After a moment of reflection she added, "His principles got in the way."

"I did everything I could to get them to find a job he'd be prepared to do," Gadi said.

Once again he was apologizing to Naamah, who had turned into Ronen's spokeswoman, completely on his side as though she hadn't seen what really happened and didn't really understand the need for the organization to react.

"I really wanted him to stay with the Mossad, and I wish I could have done more," he added.

"But you didn't," Naamah summed up simply and succinctly, putting an end to the conversation.

Gadi was left to his thoughts. It wasn't Naamah's distance that was gnawing at him now, it was Ronen's unwillingness to speak to him. An unwillingness that was already there when he asked Gadi not to make him any more job offers, that he didn't want to talk to anyone any more, that that part of his life was over. But still Gadi tried; Ronen had become his personal failure. He was the one who had taught him, trained him; he was the one who now should be shaking up the Mossad on Ronen's behalf. To hell with the commission's recommendations, we're talking about a man who has served the country from the age of eighteen, and wants neither a free lunch sitting at a desk at headquarters until the age of sixty-five nor a fun time training new operatives on the streets of Tel Aviv. How many men like that are there?

In the beginning Gadi wanted to keep him on the squad itself as chief trainer for weapons and self-defence, responsible for training exercises in Israel, but all the options were dismissed both by Ronen and by headquarters. "That's not in the spirit of the commission's recommendations," the division head told him. Ronen said, "You can't fuck halfway. It's either or." When it became clear that Ronen was unwilling to remain even at the periphery of the squad, Gadi felt freer to fight for him. Now nobody could whisper about his wanting to keep Naamah close at hand.

This state of pretending nothing had happened while Ronen was rotting at home had become unbearable to him. He himself knew it had nothing to do with Naamah, and that was enough for him. It was between a commander and his subordinate. Between two operatives. Between two friends.

Yes, friends in spite of it all. On trips abroad, when they'd sat for long hours on stakeouts, or while they tailed a target by motorcycle, or just sat in a hotel room in a foreign city, Gadi felt very close to him, as if with a younger brother, a partner, just as he felt towards most of his squad. Gadi simply loved his people. Each one had his own manner of dealing with fear, with being far from home, with being in a hostile environment; each had his own unique blend of courage, cleverness, agility, judgement, faith. Some, too, were manipulators, and they weren't easy to deal with, but at least with Ronen he'd been spared that. And they all had their idiosyncrasies; after all, someone completely normal would never make it there. It took a certain sparkle, a hint of madness, to do this thankless work which nobody outside could ever know about.

And now this younger brother of his was wounded and he'd had a hand in it; Ronen was in need of help, and Gadi could offer it. Naamah was fading into a dull, intangible background. He wasn't doing it for her; this was between him and Ronen. He knew he'd already made a name for himself as a pest with his incessant phone calls to the heads of other squads, and to various department heads, but even when his peers responded favourably and found interesting jobs for him, Ronen remained steadfast: he wasn't going to become a member of headquarters staff, wasn't willing to be "Trainer of New Recruits".

On the eve of his latest departure Gadi requested, once

again, that Ronen be given a job on one of the less front-line squads, trailing terrorist activities in Europe, working in security. Doron promised, without sounding over-excited, to raise it with the Mossad chief.

An El Al flight from Helsinki came to a halt some distance from the terminal. The passengers, who were on their feet and in the aisles before the plane had come to a complete stop, pushed towards the doors just as soon as the hydraulic stairways had been put in place. Gadi, David and Ina, a Russian-speaker who had recently joined the squad, remained seated until the line at the front of the aircraft had thinned out. Dressed in business attire and carrying heavy coats and small suitcases, they joined the end of the line but left space between themselves and the last of the other passengers now making their way to the bus waiting to ferry them to the terminal.

It had just turned dark, enabling the three of them to split off unnoticed at the bottom of the stairs and walk towards two Mazda Lantises and a van parked not far from the nose of the plane. Doron, head of the Operations Division, was waiting for them as was Eli, head of the division's Intelligence Department. The three drivers got out of their cars, too, to shake hands with Gadi, David and Ina.

"The chief sends his warmest praise for the operation you just carried out," Doron said, clasping Gadi's hand. Gadi had been on a lot of missions with Doron and had great respect for his professionalism, his courage and his cool composure, which had saved him from quite a number of unpleasant situations. But he had taken several steps back from Doron, with his good looks and his unconventionally long, curly hair, when Doron had disassociated himself from the failure in Beirut and had given Gadi and his people the cold shoulder. As if Doron himself hadn't come up with the method they'd used while he was still a squad commander; as if he couldn't have prevented the operation from taking place if he hadn't been fully sure it would work!

However, Gadi appreciated the fact that Doron had come to the airport to bring the chief's greetings, a gesture customarily reserved for particularly important successes. From the moment that all political efforts to derail the Russian-Iranian arms deal had failed, the only thing left to do was to break into the Siberian military base at which the shipment was being prepared in order to disrupt it in a different fashion. Breaking into the base was not the most difficult part of this operation, nor was it the fear of being apprehended by an approaching patrol; rather, it was the cold. They had entered the base night after night and worked in the dark, in incredibly cold weather, their hands shaking and their teeth chattering, all the while aware that one small technical error could render their entire effort useless.

After a few more words of praise Doron said, "The chief wants to take part in the debriefing, which we've scheduled for tomorrow morning."

"Tomorrow morning!" David was incapable of hiding his disappointment. "But I haven't seen my wife in two weeks!"

"It's better this way," Ina said. "When it's done then we can take some time off."

"You can take some time off," said Eli, "after you've finished writing your reports."

"You're killing us," David concluded sadly.

"Okay, it's a shame to waste any more time. The driver will drop you two off," Doron said to David and Ina.

Gadi put his arms around their shoulders and said to Doron, "We've got a new generation of operatives here who will teach us all a thing or two. Goodbye," he said to David and Ina, "see you tomorrow," as they climbed into the van and it took off.

Another driver gave Gadi the keys to his car and climbed into the second Mazda with Eli. They would be returning to headquarters with Doron.

"I was thinking about Ronen the whole time," Gadi said to Doron as they were parting company. "You know, he's the one who started gathering intelligence for this operation."

"No, I don't recall that," Doron said.

"Yep. Ronen's the one who brought us information about the base, which enabled us to decide how to carry out the mission. Never mind, that's not the issue now. Has the chief answered my request about him yet? I'm planning to drop by on him now and I was hoping to tell him."

"I haven't spoken to him about it yet, but there's no chance. According to the commission's decisions, even working in Europe is considered operational activity."

"How can you compare surveillance in Frankfurt to

an operation in an Arab country, or even Siberia? It's practically on the level of a training manoeuvre."

"And Ronen didn't want to be a trainer," Doron answered sharply.

"Instead of interpreting the decisions of the commission as it suits you why don't you consult the panel members, and, if necessary, confront them? This isn't a question of black or white."

"This is most definitely a question of black or white," Doron answered. "They said to keep him away from operational activities."

"Those were recommendations, not instructions. You know as well as I do that if Ronen is given the chance to finish his term carrying out surveillance in Europe or Asia or South America he'll do a great job."

"We're not going to open this up again," Doron said, ending the discussion.

Doron was just a little older than Gadi, and their training had been similar, but during the years Gadi had spent at university Doron had served as an operative and then a team commander in the squad. By the time Gadi was summoned to the Mossad for just one mission, because of his Russian language skills, Doron had already been singled out as squad commander material. They had mutual professional respect for one another, but now, a decade and a half later, in a position equivalent to that of an army general, Doron knew how to pull rank and put Gadi in his place.

"I see," Gadi said angrily. He got into his car, threw his coat and suitcase on the seat next to him, started the engine and drove off.

*

Naamah laid Lital gently in her bed. Lately the toddler had been restless, cranky. It was no longer a matter of teething. An ear test yielded nothing, but Naamah knew it wasn't that anyway. It was Ronen.

"I'll call Daddy to come and sit next to you," she whispered to Lital as she left the bedroom and went into the living room.

Ronen had fallen asleep in front of the television. Naamah could feel the waves of anger rising from inside her: ten minutes earlier she had asked him to spend a little time with Lital before she fell asleep. In a few minutes, he'd said, watching yet another programme on the Nature Channel, which he had become addicted to. And now he was sleeping. Naamah hesitated, then gently shook his right shoulder, the good one.

"Ronen, Lital is waiting for your goodnight kiss."

Ronen opened his eyes but said nothing.

"Go on in, she's going to fall asleep any minute."

He closed his eyes again. Naamah shook his shoulder angrily.

"You can't go on like this. She hasn't had a kiss from you, you haven't held her, for maybe two months. What's up with you? When you were abroad most of the time you were with her more than you are now."

Ronen lifted himself from the couch and dragged himself to their bedroom.

"Her room is that way," Naamah said, pointing in the opposite direction, "in case you've forgotten. And why are you always so tired," she hurled at his back as he returned into their bedroom, "when all day long you do nothing? You don't even work in the garden any more!"

Lital called to her father "Abba, Abba" from her room, and Naamah dropped to the couch where Ronen had been sitting. What's happening to him, and why is Lital bearing the brunt of his detachment and self-imposed seclusion? Where had his great love for her disappeared to? There had been times when Naamah worried that the way he squeezed her with hugs and showered her with head-to-toe kisses and tossed her around and around would hurt Lital, but now he was scarcely capable of smiling at her.

The sound of the doorbell cut off her thoughts. She opened the door and was surprised to find Gadi standing there, a bottle of Russian vodka in his hand. In the split second that Naamah wavered before inviting him in, she wondered how much time had passed since their unsuccessful phone conversation, what the reason was for this unscheduled visit, and what Ronen would think, do or say.

"I've just landed. I wanted to tell Ronen about the operation. It was something he worked on, in the initial stages."

Tell Ronen? Tell your grandmother about it, she wanted to say, and Gadi, who knew the jist of what she was thinking by her expression, asked himself if he had really come here to tell Ronen.

"Yeah, well, he's already sleeping," Naamah said dryly.

"Oops," Gadi said, flicking his wrist instinctively to

look at his watch, which refused to extricate itself from his sleeve.

"These suits," he said. "I'll never get used to them."

"It's only nine-something," Naamah said. "He goes to sleep with the birds."

"Does he wake up with them, too?"

"I wish. If I manage to wake him up when I get back from school, that's good."

"I thought you'd taken the year off."

"That was the plan, so I could be with Lital, but we thought that since Ronen is at home I could go back to work. Next year, when his contract has ended, I'll take my sabbatical and get a job somewhere to earn some extra money."

"So he spends the day with her?"

"'Every plan is a springboard for change.' I take her to a childminder."

Naamah was a physical education teacher at Ruppin High School near their home. Her studies at the Wingate Institute had been interrupted when she joined the squad, and she had planned to complete them that year. The fact that she had suddenly postponed her sabbatical and Ronen couldn't take care of Lital sounded worrying to Gadi. But he decided to veer away from that topic, which would only bring up more bad news.

"Come on, wake him up, he'll be glad."

"No, I don't think so."

"He won't be sorry you didn't wake him?"

"I don't know. He's finally starting to forget you people," she said after a pause. "It won't do him any good to see you like this, on your way back from an operation. In fact, it's pretty stupid on your part."

"Well, it's up to you. But it's a bit of a shame. Can I at least leave this bottle of vodka for him?"

"That's just what I need. I think he finished the last bottle yesterday."

"That doesn't sound good."

"No, It's not. Look, do you want to come in? It's silly to stand here talking."

Gadi followed Naamah into the kitchen. Small bulbs embedded in the kitchen cabinets bathed the kitchen in a faint light.

"Now I feel really bad about this bottle. Do you mind taking it anyway?"

Naamah chuckled and accepted it from his outstretched hand, their fingers touching momentarily. Gadi sat at the kitchen table and scanned Naamah's body, which he could see in profile, as she reached to place the bottle in a cupboard, her long, wild, black ponytail swinging in the air, her tight-fitting jogging suit outlining her breasts and firm, shapely buttocks.

"It's running out," Naamah said.

"What is?" Gadi asked, hastening to avert his glance from her body.

"The drink supply. You don't mind if I stick your bottle in here, do you? That way Ronen won't feel obliged to drain it in your honour."

Naamah returned to the table and sat down.

"You know, we returned from the mission in a strange mood. Well, I did, anyway. Even the reception at the airport wasn't what it used to be. Nobody talks about 'strengthening the nation's security' any more and all that other bullshit you remember? Nothing is like it was."

After a short silence, in a soft, quiet tone, he added, "Even you're not what you were once, Naamonet. Sorry, Mrs Dolev."

"Tell me about it," she said.

Ronen staggered out of the bedroom; the voices from the kitchen had dragged him from his bed. As he drew near he was surprised to hear Gadi's voice, and stopped in his tracks. From where he was standing he could see only their shadows on the opposite wall. There was no mistaking the romantic atmosphere created by the soft lights and low voices, but he had no strength left to fight on yet another front. And now even his relationship with Naamah was falling apart before his eyes, just as it had with Lital; the friends that had deserted him, his plans for the future, all were conspiring against him and it was all interconnected, beginning with that one moment of error, of hesitation. That was the root of the matter, that was where he needed to get back to. Like a tent that collapses, it wouldn't help to lift one flap or another; you had to get right in the middle and lift the central pole and then everything else would rise up and settle peacefully back in its place.

But for now he would not stand here eavesdropping like a spy; he would either join them or return to his dreamless sleep, the only place he found true repose. No, he would not enter the kitchen.

*

"What would you like to drink?" Naamah asked Gadi as she rose from the table and turned on the overhead light.

"Better not. I'll come another time."

"Well you're here now despite of that; I've already told you Ronen doesn't want to see you. For every two steps forwards, a visit like this sends us back one and a half."

Gadi couldn't help but notice her use of "us." "You don't want me to visit any more either? Are you still mad at me, too?" he asked quietly.

"It's not important what I want or feel. It's not good for Ronen. Right now I've only got his interests in mind, okay?" She levelled a defiant look at him.

"Sorry. I didn't mean to sound like a bastard."

"Apparently you have a problem with that. You keep sounding like one without meaning to."

Gadi scratched his head, confused. Naamah smiled, slapped the back of his hand, which was resting on the table, and left her palm on his for one longish moment.

"You're a big boy, you'll get over it. And there are so many men, and women, who would like to console you."

"Not anymore," Gadi said quietly. "It's amazing how an air of failure, when it sticks to you, drives people away. It's like a litmus test that separates the true friends from the sycophants. But that always bothered you, didn't it, all the people around me all the time?"

"You belonged to everyone and I wanted someone who would be mine alone."

"And is that what Ronen is?"

"He belonged to you, to the Mossad. But now that he's at home, I really understand him, his solitude. So now, yes, he's mine alone."

Gadi sighed, stood slowly and left the kitchen, with Naamah close behind. He opened the front door, turned around and kissed her cheek. She accepted his kiss coldly.

He smelled her scent, a pleasant mix of shampoo and lotion and under that the smell of her body, so close and yet so far away, and suddenly he thought that of all the differences between Naamah and Helena, with her blonde hair and blue eyes, her clear skin, her soft, round limbs, her pleasant voice, the light and goodness in her eyes, the gentleness of her love – it was the difference in their smells that defined them better than anything else. Naamah smelled like the sea, like fire, like a storm, while Helena smelled of flowers and grass and springtime unperturbed by encroaching summer, or by the autumn and winter to follow.

"But, is there anything I should know about? Is there anything I can help with?" He brushed the back of his hand against Naamah's cheek. She removed it gently.

"I don't think so."

Gadi turned away and receded into the darkness. Naamah closed the door noiselessly and leaned against it, her heart contracting as it always did when she saw him walking away.

"Who was that?"

She was still leaning against the door when Ronen's voice, coming from the bedroom, caught her by surprise.

"Gadi. He had just come back from an operation in Russia and wanted to tell you about it."

"But didn't have time to wait around. Typical of the bastard."

"I told him you were sleeping."

"Don't protect him, okay? That asshole could have woken me up. He's probably happy, he can cross 'visit the operative I got rid of' off his list."

"*He* got rid of you? Oh really, Ronen. It wouldn't hurt you to remember that he got you out of there a minute before they slaughtered you."

"I'm sick of how you're always on his side," he said, cutting her off. "Maybe he came by to see you, so it suited him that I was sleeping."

Ronen came into the kitchen, noticed that the overhead lights were back on now that Mister Romantic had gone home. He went to the drinks cupboard, ignored the new bottle of vodka and instead pulled out a near-empty bottle of whisky.

The long minutes that had felt like an eternity to Ronen, during which he had willed himself to stay in bed, not to leave his room, not to listen to their conversation, not even to imagine what they were saying, had practically caused the veins in his temples to burst. How many awful thoughts can pass through one's mind at such times, and how difficult it is to return to logic and balance. It was true that Gadi had saved his life and that they almost never mentioned that fact; it made sense, too, that he would come by to tell him about the operation on his return from Russia; logical, too, that they would whisper in the dull light of the kitchen so as not to awaken him. But the voice inside him saying these things was too weak, and only served to increase his anger. He didn't want any favours from Gadi, wasn't willing for Gadi to pull him out of the swamp he'd sent him to, didn't want to hear about the operation that he, Ronen, had begun but for which Gadi would get the credit, didn't want Gadi to be nice to him, while sitting with his wife in the darkness. He wanted Gadi to get the hell out of his life.

Naamah stood in the doorway watching him, and the bottle.

"You don't need that. Why are you doing this to us?" she pleaded.

"*To us*?" Ronen thundered, taking a glass to the table. "I'm doing this *to us*?"

He sat down heavily, poured himself a glass and drank down several mouthfuls too quickly, his face contorted as a result. He held out his hand to Naamah. "Come, show me that we're still *us*."

Naamah conceded unwillingly. His twisted expression had not disappeared, and was so unlike the Ronen she knew, her Ronen. And Lital might wake up.

"It's not because of you," he said, with a laugh that made her shiver. "I was sleeping, so I have an erection like in the morning." He pulled her towards him.

"You're drunk," she said as she sat on his lap, and his penis, which had poked through his old pyjama bottoms, stood between them like a gear stick. Ronen wrapped his arms tightly around her, pressing her buttocks with his hands and moving her so close that his penis was trapped

94

between her thighs and rubbed against the top of her vulva. Naamah lowered her face to his and kissed his hair, his forehead, his closed eyes, his mouth drenched with alcohol. His lips and tongue began to respond slowly to her. Now the little boy she loved so well and the drunk man were beginning to merge. The confusion of love and disgust caused her stomach and temples to heat up. With a few dexterous twists she managed to pull her knickers off and sat back down on his lap, squeezing his penis with her labia and moving gently up and down. For one short moment she was the Naamah who knew how to soften him, how to win back his heart, convince him of her love; but in an instant she reverted to being a wife whose husband had estranged himself from her for months – had performed like a machine the few times they had had sex – and now he was awakening to her, wanted her, causing her whole body to fill with renewed hope.

Ronen pulled at her top and pushed his head inside, sucking on one breast and fondling the other with the palm of one hand, the fingers of the other prodding the sensitive spots on her back, making her buck and groan with pleasure, her face tilted up, enslaved, her hands clinging to the hair on the back of his neck. Her big, grown baby.

She lowered her hand to his penis, lifted herself up a bit and slid him into her, barely needing to move before she felt that wonderful explosion, which burned her with a fire more pleasurable than should have been allowed and returned her, for a short moment, to her once-upon-a-time love.

Lital and Naamah, basement and attic, sea and garden – three bands closing in on him. He wasn't choked by memories and thoughts as he had been during the first few months, but now they were swirling together and creating something new, something as yet unclear but threatening nonetheless. Occasionally he managed to break through all three bands on his motorcycle, tearing along the relatively empty roads during the late morning hours. The thought of encountering a policeman, or a sharp curve in the road, or a truck that had wandered from its lane didn't bother him; he wouldn't even see them since the shield on his helmet was raised to let the wind whip his face and his eyes were narrowed to a slit. And if the road should lead to the promenade along the Tel Aviv shoreline, as it did lately with increasing frequency, well, that wouldn't bother him either. It was the same sea, the same scent, but the narrowed eyes widened, there was more to take in there: the sounds of people, colours and sights and unfamiliar smells of food cooking. Still, somewhere deep within, the unwanted pregnancy, the illegitimate child of unpleasant thoughts and angry memories, betrayal and desertion, continued to grow and thrive.

When had he chosen this particular café two blocks from the sea where Bograshov Street slopes downwards, a gathering place for yuppies and brokers and journalists? Seated at a small round table on the pavement next to other small round tables on whose cushioned metal chairs perched the who's who of Tel Aviv – whom Ronen tried hard not to identify – peroxide blonds in suits, ties and earrings next to him in his leather biker's jacket and boots. And when had he ordered a large espresso brought by a waitress in a miniskirt, who forced him to widen his eyes even more when she stood between him and the sun? A line of cars at the corner of Ben Yehuda Street was moving at a snail's pace, creating a slow-motion kaleidoscope, and the bitter coffee felt good inside him, all the way from his tongue to his bowels.

That's how he found himself, entranced for a long moment, when a voice brought him to disagreeable places far from that pleasant sunshine. He tried to push it away but Milken's voice was insistent: "Go in and tell her that I want my usual. She'll know."

Ronen's head turned as mechanically as a robot's, only the zoom worked noiselessly while his eyes tried to remain immobile. Yes, it was Milken in the flesh, only without makeup he looked significantly older and uglier. Milken's cell phone rang: "Yes, exactly, I just finished talking to him now," he said in a loud voice, as if he were on air. "You wouldn't believe what a pain in the ass this guy is, I told him I could give him major help running for mayor of Hadera, I have a whole page in a local there. So what does he answer me, that jerk? Hadera doesn't interest him! Like *I* owe *him*! After he got himself into so much trouble and they nearly made him take a polygraph test, all that bullshit. I told him, Sorry buddy, that's what I've got to offer…"

Someone pushed in between Ronen and Milken and sat down. His face was young and familiar, though Ronen

97

could not place him. Milken continued: "Of course he'll calm down, now he's the one who needs me, not vice versa."

He folded his cell phone shut, made a gesture of victory and smiled at his young colleague. "Have you ordered?" he asked.

"Yeah, the food's on the way. I ordered the same as you." Milken flashed him a look of surprise. "The same? Aren't you in a bit of a rush?" he chuckled. "You're going to have to sweat a lot more until you get to the point where you can sit in a café waiting for the news to come to you instead of chasing after it."

"I'm not lazy," the young man said. "Anyway, the news doesn't come to you. You *make* the news."

"Well put," Milken said with a satisfied smile. "That's the way you run a country. But first of all you have to work. Let's get back to what happened a few days ago in Austria."

Ronen actually felt his ear muscles straining as he involuntarily swung his head again towards the table next to him.

Yankol and his squad had been engaged in a routine operation in Austria: once again it was a Lebanese national connected to Hezbollah, who had set himself up in a European country that does not cooperate with the Mossad, and had begun to build an infrastructure that would enable terrorist attacks in Europe or the safe-passage of terrorists to Israel. Once again a squad was on his tail, the kind of work they'd engaged in hundreds of times, following up on his connections and exposing the entire network. But this time something went wrong and the police were notified. After getting his people out safely, Yankol had stayed behind to finish the job. But he didn't manage to get out before the police arrived.

Ronen knew Yankol by name only and he didn't know the people who were with him, some other Ronen or Sharon or David, young people who, instead of studying at university during the day and spending their evenings in pubs, gather intelligence by day and take part in infiltrations and bugging by night.

When he'd heard about the mishap in Austria his heart had constricted. Another failure, another humiliation, another mediafest, as if it were an Egyptian squad, and not an Israeli one, that had been caught. He dismissed the spark of acknowledgement that told him a failure in a relatively safe environment would reduce the severity of his own failure in Beirut. But they probably had a reduced schedule, too, and didn't want to wait for ideal conditions either. Ronen didn't even want to think about Yankol's dilemma, whether to take the emergency escape route with his people and leave behind a trail, or the chance that the police would be held up for a few minutes and allow him to finish the job and clean up the evidence. Maybe it was once again a case of criminal tenacity, but he himself would have done exactly the same thing, and Gadi certainly would have too. What a huge difference there was between finishing the job and escaping by the skin of your teeth, and leaving the wires exposed, only to tear your hair out when you learnt that the police had been held up and you would have to explain back at headquarters why you "ran away".

Certainly Yankol hadn't thought to organize his people, stun the policeman and make an escape. That wasn't in the regulations, just as Ronen had not even considered shooting the Lebanese policemen who had lined up in front of his escape car. The bullet wounds in his shoulder testified to just how many holes there were in those regulations.

"I've already got the address of the guy they put in jail," Milken said. "Don't ask me how, it's a fact. Go there, sniff around. Find out who he is, what his record is, something colourful – maybe he was thrown out of school – what this big hero did in the army, stuff I can use in my report."

So the bastard is going to expose Yankol. He'll probably just call him Y but he'll give enough poisonous details to entertain his viewers and turn Yankol into a laughing stock. What Milken won't say is that throngs of Israelis can ski in the Alps in peace, or that there hasn't been a terrorist attack in Europe for ten years, thanks to all the Yankols who are constantly on the tail of every Hezbollah member in Europe, or that only months and years of hard, constant, dirty work has prevented the rise of terrorist cells in heavily populated Islamic areas of Europe who would be capable of crashing planes into Tel Aviv's Azrieli Towers.

"Doesn't it seem way over the top to you that they'd send people to break into some basement in Austria in the middle of the night just to know if some 'Abu' living there is with the Hezbollah?" the young man said. "Don't those suckers have anything better to do?" Suddenly Ronen remembered who he was: his last name was Haramati. He sometimes reported on intelligence issues for the radio and shot off his mouth in a column in one of the newspapers.

"The truth is," Milken said carefully, "they're not suckers, but if we say they're heroes then what are we? And if they don't screw up occasionally, what would we have to talk about? Hey, have they forgotten about our order? So what if I'm not a food critic?"

"I'll get it," Haramati said as he rose from his chair and walked into the café. A moment later he re-emerged with a large tray loaded with food. The path back to his seat took him close to Ronen's table.

Ronen casually extended his leg. Haramati tripped, falling, tray and all, right onto Milken.

Haramati and Milken both stood up, astonished; both turned to glare at Ronen, who did not even bother to return his extended leg to its place under the table. He just stared back at them with growing interest, peacefully, a small smile at the corners of his mouth. They looked so ridiculous, dripping with pasta, salad and juice, so hopeless and confused and angry.

The waitress came running out, apologizing for not bringing the tray out herself. "Shut up, you fool," Milken sputtered furiously as he and Haramati pushed their way into the café.

Ronen finished his coffee, which now tasted especially good. It had been a long time since his ride home was so relaxed, attuned to the sights and smells of the fields. Still, he didn't feel that the fire burning inside him had disappeared, only that the flame had diminished a bit.

*

More bodies, this time at the central bus station in Afula. Ronen stationed himself in front of the television earlier than usual, his stomach in knots. Paramedics attending to the wounded, police holding curious onlookers at bay, ambulances, people crying. He was thrown back to the terrorist attacks that had tossed him into the vortex of events culminating in his escape from Lebanon. Waiting anxiously for more reports he prayed that there would be no connection between the two. But the newscaster announced that once again Hezbollah had claimed responsibility for the attack.

And as if to add to the horror he felt, Milken's face appeared on the screen. Ronen could taste the bitterness of the coffee on his tongue just as he had the last time they'd met.

"This is the first attack by Hezbollah within Israel itself in more than a year," Milken said, "since the string of suicide attacks in Jerusalem. It is a slap in the face to those who dared claim that the Hezbollah leadership was so stunned by the impressive ability displayed by Mossad operatives in their failed assassination attempt on Abu-Khaled in Beirut that they'd instructed their international terror network to desist from attacking Israel."

Abu-Khaled, smiling and bearded under a Shi'ite turban, appeared briefly on the screen. His appearance was just like the photograph the intelligence officers had provided before the operation, along with a file containing the few facts known about his home, his car, his daily routine, his wife and five children, and his "charge sheet", the quasi-legal document describing all the terrorist activities in which he'd had a hand. He was the one who had come up with the idea to move Hezbollah's struggle to parts of the world where Israel was more vulnerable: to Latin America, Asia, Africa and eventually Israel itself. He was the one who had flown to Tehran personally to receive the blessings of the Revolutionary Guards and their logistical assistance in blowing up the Israeli embassies in Buenos Aires and London. He was the one who authorized every suicide bomber sent to Israel. He was the one to whom the agents and controllers in Europe reported, like the one in whose basement Yankol was arrested. All roads led to him and all instructions came from him; he was personally responsible for the deaths of more than two hundred people. The document had cautiously suggested that putting Abu-Khaled out of commission was likely to curtail Hezbollah's ability to carry out operations for a certain period, in Israel or around the world.

The year of peace and quiet that had passed since their disastrous assassination attempt caused some people in the Mossad to hypothesize that it really had served to deter someone in the Hezbollah leadership. But here they were, on the screen, the shredded bodies and Abu-Khaled's grinning face which, like Milken's razor-thin smile, proved the contrary.

For nearly a year Ronen had harboured in his heart of hearts the illusion that perhaps the damage he'd incurred wasn't so terrible after all. Moreover, some commentators had suggested that if he had pulled the trigger, Hezbollah's retaliation might have ended in scores of deaths, as when al-Musawi, the previous secretary-general, was assassinated and Hezbollah took action in Argentina. There were times when that theory alone gave meaning to Ronen's life just as everything else seemed to be crumbling around him. And now here he was again, whether he liked it or not, in a commotion of bodies of which his actions and failures were an integral part.

Milken was right. In spite of the in-your-face sarcasm that characterized him, he was right. Ronen felt the truth of this hardening in his entire body. He pulled himself heavily from the couch and made for the bedroom. From under a pile of clothing in a cupboard he carefully removed a metal box, opened it and took out his gun, a heavy silver and black Jericho pistol he'd been presented with when he had completed his training to become an operative. He weighed the heavy weapon in his hand and couldn't help but feel the heat radiating from deep inside himself. Weapons had become appendages to his body these past fifteen years: after handing in his army-issued M16 it was an elegant Beretta that he was loath to part with, but he quickly grew accustomed to the efficient, almost ugly conventionality, of a Glock 17. However, this Jericho, which symbolized all his hopes when he joined "the close-knit Mossad family", as the enlistment notices called it, was dearest to his heart, even now, when his estrangement from that family seemed so cold and final. From the dresser drawer Ronen withdrew a steel-grey magazine filled with 9mm bullets. In the background he could still hear Milken.

"Furthermore, I would claim, without making any wild guesses, that if it weren't for the Mossad's failed missions in Amman, Beirut and most recently again in Austria, today's attack might not have happened."

Screw him. Ronen lumbered back into the living room, returned to his seat on the sofa and stroked his pistol. It was too dry, he thought; he hadn't touched it since the last time he'd gone to the shooting range, when he'd had to renew his permit, and the light oiling he'd given it then was barely perceptible. He pushed the magazine into place.

Milken turned a half smile to the anchorwoman on his right. "Perhaps it would be more efficient," he said, "if the Mossad were to ask their Jordanian, British, French or Austrian counterparts to do the job for them –"

This was the third time Ronen was obliged to curse Milken to hell, since – in spite of his unbridled nastiness, which brought good ratings and no apparent reprimands from his superiors, his *schadenfreude* (the deranged sources of which Ronen failed to comprehend), his unwillingness to give credit where credit was due, and even his latest haughty, cynical statement – everything he said contained a grain of truth.

A grain of truth, that was all a commentator needed. Armed with that grain of truth, no matter how partial or shady it was, made it possible, with a complete lack of professionalism, to create a distorted picture and live quite well with that. But in my case, he thought sadly, only one hundred per cent success was tolerated, nothing less.

Ronen aimed the barrel of the gun at the floor and

cocked it. The heavy breech-block moved backwards on the drop of oil on the track. He relaxed the grip of his fingers and the firing mechanism sprang back into place, collecting the top bullet in the magazine on its way and entering it into the barrel. The hammer, which remained cocked, rubbed the base of Ronen's thumb.

Milken smiled into the camera to complete his sentence: "I feel quite certain that the results would have been far better."

Unlike that last, cursed time in Beirut, the pistol in Ronen's hand now felt comfortable, right, stable. He raised the barrel slowly.

Naamah was in the kitchen with Lital, who sat next to her in her highchair, eating. She had given up on encouraging Ronen to participate in the daily rituals of family life, even on those occasions when he had returned home from his inconclusive wanderings and was actually in the house. When he wasn't doing his renovations in the attic or gardening or working out in the basement – he had no energy for those lately – he sat like a lumpy sack in front of the television. She knew if she reprimanded him or called him to help with Lital that he would end up downing yet another bottle of whisky. The only bottle he didn't touch was the vodka Gadi had brought, as if he didn't see it there.

The news of the attack in Afula set off warning bells in Naamah's mind. It was a brutal picking at the scab that had begun to form on Ronen's open wounds. She could hear Milken's voice, and knew what effect that had on

Ronen. She would join him in the living room as soon as she finished feeding Lital and had put her to bed.

The roar of a single gun shot followed by a terrible explosion sounded as though it were inside her head. Lital's face contorted and she burst into bitter tears. Naamah ran to the living room, terrified by what she might find there.

Ronen sat motionless on the couch. The pistol was lying limply in his hand against his thigh. Smoke was still rising from the barrel. On the other side of the room the television lay shattered.

3.

EIGHT O'CLOCK IN the morning was the regular meeting time for squad members and their headquarters staff at the training facility, but two or three of the younger ones would arrive an hour or even two hours earlier than that to start the day with a workout and self-defence training. These were the squad members that Ronen had trained, bequeathing them a tradition he'd learned from Gadi. From the time of Ronen's departure from the Mossad, they continued their early morning sessions without him.

Gadi entered the facility a few minutes before eight, as usual. As a squad commander he had the use of a car, but would leave it overnight at the training facility, driving it to job-related appointments or when he needed to take others with him. Otherwise he rode a motorcycle; that way he was able to exert full control over his schedule, avoiding the daily traffic jams both to and from work. Many of the squad members were motorcycle freaks, and they divided into three categories: the Suzuki enthusiasts, the Honda fans and the aristocrats, the BMW boys.

When Ronen bought himself a wedding gift – a Suzuki 600, which had only recently come on the market – Gadi felt it was right to phone Naamah, after a period without contact, to warn her that it was a suicide machine. Naamah, who herself ran around on a speedy little Vespa, did not manage to foil Ronen's purchase but quickly traded in her Vespa for a small sports car, which proved serious competition to the Suzuki for Ronen's love. Gadi had begun his career with a small, solid Honda 250, whose classic look he'd never stopped loving even years later, when he'd switched to a BMW 850. True, the size of the BMW didn't always pay off in traffic jams, but it provided the safety necessary when Helena rode pillion.

Gadi was greeted by the familiar smells of cooking. After an early morning workout the squad members indulged themselves with a post-shower protein-rich breakfast, and Gadi would usually join them for coffee. In the kitchenette the smell of omelettes cooking mingled with coffee, shampoo and after-shave, producing a particular, unique aroma that Gadi loved.

"You won't believe it, but I found Sharon and Lesley here at six this morning, writing their report on Warsaw," David said, his blond hair still wet.

"When I left last night they were writing. I hope they didn't spend the night here," Gadi said.

"Nope, they came in with me a little before six," Danny answered.

"I'll pop in on them," Gadi said as he poured himself a cup of coffee from the percolator and left the room.

"I managed a backwards flying hook kick this morning," Danny called after him.

"I'll be right back," Gadi said, continuing down the corridor, missing David's comment, that "that sort of thing" no longer interested Gadi as it once had. Danny added that in general, since the Beirut mission, and especially since the commission's findings were made public, Gadi had changed, doing only what was necessary, "without putting his heart into it".

Sharon and Lesley were sitting with their backs to the door. Dozens of photographs were spread out on the desks in front of them and on their beds, which stood across from one another occupying the two longer walls of the room.

"Oh, it's a good thing you're here, you can help us make some decisions," Sharon said. "The single shots came out better than the panoramas, but the intelligence officer likes panorama shots better."

"Think which you would have preferred to get before your first time out in the field and decide according to that," Gadi said. "And what's this over-the-top diligence all about anyway?"

"He wants our report by this afternoon in order to brief another squad," Lesley answered. "Tell me, did they make James Bond write reports after every trip, too?"

On the way back to his office Gadi passed the small weights room. The sound of metal on metal made him peek inside; two squad members were lifting weights, and Gadi pointed to his watch. It was exactly eight o'clock, and they needed to be at a briefing in preparation for manoeuvres they'd be doing later that day. Moshe, the intelligence officer assigned to the squad, was already waiting with maps and briefing folders in his hand. One by one the participants began to assemble.

Tamar, the squad's secretary, wound her way around the computers – a cup of coffee in her hand – turning each one on, entering the password and switching on the printer. When she saw Gadi she sent him a cheerful "hi". Gadi responded with a smile as he entered his office which also served as the squad headquarters meeting room and the meeting place for division officials who had business with the squad. The walls were covered with certificates of appreciation from the Israel Defence Forces chief of staff for operations in which the squad had enabled IDF troops to land quietly on some distant shore or reach their targets deep in some Arab country. On the walls, too, was a mosaic of photos of squad members around the world, and the shelves were crowded with special mementos from a variety of operations. The contents from containers the squad had dismantled and costumes they'd used featured prominently alongside Turkish coffee pots, narghiles and jewelled swords.

A long T-shaped table surrounded by narrow chairs extended into the middle of the room. Gadi sat at his usual place at the head of the T, which set him at a distance from the others and waited for the printouts Tamar would bring him. Even though the Mossad had become a paperless office some years earlier, he preferred to read his material as hard copy and not on a screen, highlighting with a marker the information he wanted to reread and delve into more carefully. Facing him on his desk were two medium-sized photographs, one of Helena alone and the other of the four of them, he and Helena with their children, Ami and Ruth, on a trek in the Dan River Nature Reserve.

Tamar buzzed the intercom.

"Ronen's Naamah is on the outside line."

Naamah's phone calls to him at the facility were so rare that he picked up the receiver immediately.

"Ronen has disappeared," Naamah said, without preamble.

Gadi's heart skipped a beat.

"When?"

"Yesterday."

"And you have no idea where he is?"

"That's just it. I do. And it's bad."

"What, what are you talking about?" he stuttered. "What did he tell you?"

"He didn't tell me anything. Yesterday morning he left and didn't come back. By last night I was worried, and after phoning all the hospitals and the police I noticed that his carry-on suitcase and his flight bag were missing. His toiletries too, and all sorts of clothes. I hoped he would come back or at least phone, but he hasn't."

Gadi knew what Naamah was thinking, and even before she said anything he felt she was right.

"And you think...?"

"Yes, I think he's gone back there," Naamah said, finishing Gadi's sentence.

"There?" Gadi hoped to be proven wrong.

"You know exactly where I'm talking about, I can't say any more over the phone. Yes, he went back to finish off what he didn't manage to complete a year ago."

Gadi couldn't find the appropriate words. He pulled his shirt away from his skin; he'd begun to sweat.

"But did he say anything, drop any hints?"

"Gadi, I live in this house with him, not you," she said, cutting him off. "I simply know it."

"Hang on, I'm on my way over," he said.

Gadi hung up the phone and pressed the intercom. He needed confirmation even though this was one of those instances where gut feelings were more important and accurate than any logical analysis. During discussions at headquarters after the attack in Afula, Gadi, too, felt that something must be done about Abu-Khaled. He had requested the reinstatement of Abu-Khaled as a priority target. He was informed, however, that it wouldn't work: immediately after the Afula bombing Abu-Khaled was promoted to a senior political position at Hezbollah headquarters and his name had been removed from the hit list altogether.

Gadi switched from investigative mode to active mode. Doron was abroad, and not a moment could be wasted.

"Tamar, please arrange a meeting for me with the chief, as quickly as possible. I mean within the hour."

"That'll be tough with Doron overseas. The new chief insists on division heads being present at all meetings with headquarters staff."

"Tell him it's an emergency," Gadi said. "I'm driving to Naamah's, and then I'll go to his office. Ask Hillel to step in now."

Hillel, one of Gadi's administrative assistants, appeared in the doorway with Tamar peering in curiously over his shoulder. Gadi had no desire to disseminate unnecessary information at this point but knew his instructions to Hillel would clarify matters.

"Hillel, please check if any of Ronen's documents are missing, and verify with the Shin Bet if anyone has left Ben Gurion Airport using Ronen's name." This was the kind of assistance the Shin Bet, Israel's internal security service, regularly provided to the Mossad, its overseas counterpart.

"His real name, Ronen Dolev, and all his aliases, on all departing flights from Ben Gurion starting from yesterday morning."

He stood up, grabbed his jacket and, as he passed Tamar and Hillel, said, "Call me on my cell phone with the results. And don't talk to anyone about this."

Riding a motorbike enabled Gadi to weave his way north to Ronen's house on the coastal highway with great speed, but an unexpected traffic jam forced him onto the dirt roads that wound through the small agricultural settlements of the Sharon Valley and out to the old Tel Aviv–Haifa road, where he could pick up speed again. His self-imposed distance from Ronen in the past few weeks had boomeranged back at him: if Ronen had in fact continued to deteriorate, Gadi hadn't seen it. Why hadn't Naamah called, why hadn't she said a word? He only hoped she was wrong, and that he himself was wrong, too.

His helmet in his hand, Gadi knocked on the door. When Naamah opened it he entered without formalities. She was dressed in jeans and a snug-fitting tricot shirt and was just finishing a telephone conversation with her mother.

"I can't find him anywhere. I've tried everything."

"Since yesterday morning, you said?"

"Yes. But I only started worrying last night. He's been disappearing for hours lately, but he always comes back at night."

"So why do you think he's gone to Beirut?"

"Because he's stuck there. For a whole year he's been thinking about nothing but that."

"Did he say anything about it to you?"

"He didn't need to. It was clear. And in any case we've barely been on speaking terms lately," she said, lowering her gaze.

Gadi hesitated, then placed his palms on her shoulders and looked into her eyes.

"Naamonet, listen carefully. I'm going to recommend sending a team to Lebanon to detain him."

"Detain him?" she freed herself from his hands.

"To prevent him from taking action and to bring him home. Otherwise it will be a disaster."

Naamah turned her back on him. It was probably the right thing to do but this idea of Gadi and his people setting out to catch Ronen agitated her.

"It's not against Ronen, it's to help him. Do you know

what kind of trouble he'll bring down on himself if he's really set out to kill Abu-Khaled? Not only on himself but the whole country. If he succeeds they'll start firing Katyusha rockets all over the Galilee. And if, God forbid, he gets caught there…"

She did not react. She knew that everything he was saying was true, but which option had the best chances? That Ronen would return home alone, unharmed? That Gadi and his squad would bring him back against his will? Or that Ronen, Gadi and his people would get into trouble there? From what she knew of Beirut and the players involved, she gave even chances to all three. She couldn't oppose sending a team out, but she couldn't support it either.

"Naamah, I want you to think again, because if you're wrong, if there's some other explanation, then we're taking a tremendous risk for no reason."

She turned back towards him. "The attack in Afula a few days ago completely deranged him. He thinks he's responsible for the people who were killed there."

"I feel shitty about it too," Gadi said quietly. "But that's not proof he decided to assassinate Abu-Khaled. I'm on my way to meet the Mossad chief and I have no real evidence to give him."

Naamah was completely certain she was right. True, Gadi couldn't know that Ronen had destroyed the television set or be aware of any of the other signs of his recent decline, but his insistence on having proof angered her.

"Don't worry," she said mockingly, "I'll take the blame. I'll even tell the inevitable commission of inquiry that I knew without doubt that he was in Lebanon, okay? So once again you'll come out clean; don't let *that* bother you. The question is whether you can handle him there, under Abu-Khaled's nose. After all, he's not exactly going to help you out and come back home with you willingly. He blames you for much that happened to him and that's what you're going to have to deal with now."

"Naamah! I…"

"Oh come off it, Gadi," she said, cutting him off even before he'd decided what he was going to say. "Can't you see for yourself? Everything's connected to everything else, and nobody can disentangle it all now. Ronen is not capable of forgiving anyone, but most especially you."

Gadi remained silent. The "most especially you" needed no further clarification. It was all so perfectly clear that there was no reason to contradict her. Gadi was even glad, somehow, that Naamah had placed herself so squarely on Ronen's side. At least *she* had. And it suited her, too, and aroused in him the desire to pull her and Ronen out of the mess they were in. They didn't deserve this: not Ronen, who had done everything he was capable of doing even when the situation he'd found himself in – which Gadi had got him into – had been more than he could handle; and certainly not Naamah, who had devoted the past year to rehabilitating her wounded, traumatised patient and hadn't allowed either her hates or her loves to keep her from her mission.

"True," he answered, contemplative. "There's no disentangling now. And if I go to Lebanon it will be for you, too."

Gadi turned and walked towards the door; Naamah remained where she was. She knew it was true, it would be for her, too, just as it would be for Ronen and for the state and for Gadi himself. She saw how tortured he was, how he felt not only an obligation but the *desire* to solve this new problem. But her compassion for him did not measure up to other feelings she had, mostly fear for Ronen who could at that moment be in grave danger.

She couldn't imagine how Ronen might be brought home safe and sound without endangering people she loved, and she found herself trapped in a web, a mess of the more-guilty and the less-guilty, a mess in which there could be no winners, only bigger losers and smaller losers. And what should she feel at this moment? Gratitude that they were going to bring her husband back?

"Just don't expect me to say thank you," she said.

Sarah, the Mossad chief's longtime secretary, greeted Gadi brightly. She had known him since he'd been promoted to squad commander and had begun to take part in meetings in the chief's office, but she had seen him even before that, when she'd accompanied her bosses to squad meetings, a privilege reserved only for the chief's closest and most trustworthy associates.

Daphna, the other secretary, sat next to Sarah. She was very young, and her eyes still sparkled with excitement and admiration at meeting squad operatives. A relatively small number of Mossad agents actually skipped around the globe carrying out surveillance, staging break-ins or planting bugging devices, and only a small percentage of those comprised the squad assigned to intelligence-gathering behind enemy lines. Even within Mossad headquarters only a handful of staff members ever saw their faces.

Gadi had little occasion to visit the chief's office. Discussions involving squad operations only took place there when there was a need to involve headquarters staff from other divisions, and even then the head of the Operations Division would represent the position of the squad in most cases. Only rarely was it necessary to hear what the squad commander had to say in this forum, particularly when operational nuances could affect the activities of other divisions.

Gadi stood by the secretaries' reception desk. Tamar had been told that the head of the Mossad would be occupied until the afternoon, and Gadi was angling to move things with the help of his bureau chief, Avigur, who had now appeared through one of the inner doors.

"Gadi, I tried, believe me, from the moment Sarah told me you had an urgent matter. The earliest he can meet with you is in at least another – " Avigur shook his watch free from the sleeve of his suit jacket – "two hours."

"Tell me, am I speaking Chinese?" Gadi asked. "Don't you understand that urgent means urgent? Have I ever made a request like this before?"

"I understand, but there's a problem. He's in a meeting with his Italian counterpart and his senior staff and it's clear that he can't talk to you now."

Gadi realised that without making a small scene he would never get what he wanted, so, taking advantage of the anger that was mounting inside him, he leaned over the counter towards Avigur and said quietly, "I'll tell you what's clear. It's clear that if you don't pull him out of there I'm going in like this, just as I am, and I'll tell him what I need to."

Avigur shrugged in the manner of a person with no choice. Even though he was about Gadi's age it was unbearable for him to imagine Gadi walking into what was actually a cocktail party in his leather jacket and motorcycle helmet. "I'll try again," he sighed, and turned towards the reception room. When he opened the door Gadi could see a long table loaded with sandwiches and cakes surrounded by men in suits holding cocktail glasses. The door closed and the trail of happy voices behind it faded.

Sarah leaned towards Gadi. "In the past you wouldn't have been made to wait like this," she whispered.

"Is it only me, or everyone from Operations?"

"I really believe he's afraid of the people in Operations," she said with a smile.

"Times change," Gadi said, imitating the voice of the new Mossad chief.

Avigur emerged from the reception room and motioned to Gadi to follow him to the chief's office.

"I guess this proves that might still makes right," Gadi said to Sarah with a smile. He asked Daphna to call his office. He wanted Hillel and Tamar to hurry up with their investigations.

The Mossad chief's modest office was located on the third

floor of a new building north of Tel Aviv, a building that resembled a Hyatt Hotel. Hanging planters on each floor created a curtain of green foliage which cascaded downwards into a central atrium. The hundreds of headquarters staff who had been selected for employment and who spent twelve-hour days there, had turned the building into a highly effective factory for absorbing, processing and assessing intelligence. This was where orders were issued to gather intelligence and to carry out operations, all of which were controlled by the centralized office in which Gadi and Avigur were now waiting.

Gadi's cell phone rang. Hillel was on the line.

"Your feeling was right," he told Gadi. "One of the 'little notebooks' is missing."

"Which one?" Gadi wanted to know.

Hillel hesitated, searching for the right way to pass on this information.

"The one we took out of commission, the one we decided not to use any more."

Gadi tried to remember Ronen's various passports. It was true, there was one passport they'd frozen. Jesse Smith was Ronen's name on that passport.

"Jerry Seinfeld?" Gadi asked.

It took Hillel a moment to realize Gadi was using initials. He laughed and confirmed Gadi's guess. "And a man by that name left Israel for Paris yesterday afternoon," he added.

So their fear was becoming reality.

This was Gadi's first personal meeting with the new Mossad chief. He wasn't even sure how to address him.

Chief? By his first name, as he had called his predecessor? Perhaps by his code name, Beaufort, given to him in the days when he was responsible for contacts with the Phalangists in Lebanon?

During the time he had spent as a field agent, as a team commander, deputy squad commander and squad commander, Gadi had served under four Mossad chiefs. Each of them had taken upon himself, as a first priority, to meet the field agents, the ones who, after all, did the work – and there weren't so many of them to meet. The new chief hadn't seen fit to do this yet.

Beaufort had been called to the job when it seemed his long career had reached its end. He had held a number of positions in the Foreign Relations Division, the Intelligence Division and as head of Personnel. He had been perceived as a highly suitable deputy to the Mossad chief, but never as his successor. His close personal connection to the Prime Minister, which dated back to the Lebanon War of 1982, when Beaufort's agents led IDF forces straight into Beirut, surprisingly paved his way to the top. Still, at nearly sixty, Beaufort felt the exigencies of the job were beyond the capabilities of a man his age.

He read the intelligence briefings with great interest as soon as he arrived in his office each morning at six-thirty. He was in full control of the details, and capable of constructing a complete picture from the details with great speed. At seven-thirty he began his meetings with the various divisions. He had no trouble making decisions with regard to topics in his fields of specialization: giving the right emphasis and directions to intelligence-gathering missions, or deciding on matters of administration or personnel. He was especially fond of dealing with relations between the Mossad and its counterparts in other countries, and with states with whom Israel did not have diplomatic relations. Here he would even take part in junkets and secret meetings. Still, he couldn't avoid having to meet with the people from the Operations Division; their invariably urgent meetings, which could never be postponed, the quick decisions that needed to be taken because they had 'people in the field'. And so they would lay decisions on his doorstep with regard to operations whose success or failure depended on slight nuances of behaviour in the field, on one single code word that was given or not, on the decision whether the command room would approve an action or whether that authority would be delegated to the commander in the field. How did they expect him to decide these things? Again and again he was forced to set up additional meetings late in the evening; again and again he finished his workday late at night, exhausted and bleary-eyed.

Why couldn't they make do with gathering intelligence in the traditional manner to which he was accustomed, by making use of local agents and foreign intelligence agencies? These Tarzans he worked with, however, wanted to handle everything themselves: their work had to be one hundred per cent Made in Israel as they called it.

As a gesture of appreciation for fruitful cooperation, Beaufort had invited the people from the Italian secret service, whom he knew from the period he'd served as head of the Mossad's European office, for cocktails. But even before he could begin to enjoy their company, Avigur had called him out for an urgent meeting with Gadi.

The Mossad chief entered his office with an air of impatience. Leaning back in his chair, he listened to Gadi with narrowed eyes. Gadi took in the man's face – that of a professor and not a military man – the flaccid body, the small belly bulge that even his expensive suit could not hide, and felt sorry for what he was about to drop on the man's desk.

Gadi had often thought about what it must be like to run the Mossad, one of the most complex and sensitive organizations around. Research and organizational skills or the ability to maintain good relations with other organizations were no less important than the ability to lead complex missions, but he couldn't help feeling that someone without extensive experience as an operative would understand neither the situation he was describing nor the options for getting out of it. He doesn't know me, Gadi thought, he knows little about me, and he can't possibly attach the proper importance to what I'm about to say.

After Gadi had said his piece, Beaufort paused, refusing to believe what he had just heard. It sounded to him like hogwash. If Doron were here, he thought, he would already have separated the wheat from the chaff. "So tell me," he said, "what do you think I'm supposed to do with your gut feelings? Call up the Prime Minister and tell him that one of my people has departed without authorization in order to assassinate Abu-Khaled, but that

I'm not quite sure about that? All because of your gut feelings?" What had started as a complaint had turned into an attack.

"It's not just a gut feeling," Gadi said quietly. "I've known Ronen for nearly ten years, and his wife Naamah, too. She was one of my operatives, even before he was. She's sure he's there, and I know I can rely on her."

The chief surprised Gadi. "Yes, I've heard all about that, and I can't say it seems like a healthy set-up to me. In any event," he continued, "it's still just in the realm of guesswork. Correct me if I'm wrong, but we don't have any real *information* that Ronen has set out to kill Abu-Khaled."

"Ronen is the kind of man who's liable to take the law into his own hands. He lives by his own set of rules. And now he's very angry at the entire system because of his dismissal…"

"His *resignation!*" the chief said, cutting him off. "He resigned, he was not dismissed. I'll ask you to keep in mind that he rejected offers for a non-operational job."

"As far as Ronen is concerned, it's all the same. He was led to understand that people would be happy if he left. Just like I have been led to understand that my own days here are numbered," he added after a brief pause, "since I can't help noticing that people avoid talking to me about promotion and that my replacement has been lined up behind my back. But that's not what we're here to discuss."

"It's *really* not what we're here to discuss," the chief said quickly, stretching in his chair as if he were about to stand up. "So don't bother me now about your career."

"No, but what I *do* need to bother you about is the huge mess that the Mossad and the State of Israel are going to find themselves in if we don't do something to stop Ronen." Gadi could feel the anger creeping into his voice.

"Do what exactly, when any operation we carry out in Lebanon just means a bigger mess?"

Gadi detected true helplessness in Beaufort's response. At that instant he understood that his chances of getting him to send a team to apprehend Ronen were nil, as were his chances of exploiting the secret service of some other country with a permanent presence in Lebanon.

"I can stop him," he said. "I know where he'll go to find Abu-Khaled. If you'll let me take one or two other men with me, we still have time to leave today and reach him before he manages to get to Abu-Khaled. In a worst case scenario we could overpower him."

"Sounds just lovely. Mossad operatives brawling at the entrance to Abu-Khaled's house in the heart of the Shi'ite quarter of Beirut. I know Beirut a bit, so allow me to continue the scenario: you catch the attention of the guards, you down a few of them and are downed yourselves by a few dozen others who show up in seconds. Sound familiar to you?"

Gadi lowered his gaze. The Mossad chief's anger was palpable, and in large part justified, Gadi had to admit. He remained silent, and Beaufort continued. "Or, no less awful, Hezbollah takes you captive. In your opinion can the State of Israel afford another three kidnapped citizens?"

Gadi did not say a word.

"You still have no positive confirmation that he's reached that destination, right?"

"Right. Only that he left for Paris yesterday."

The chief stood up. The different possibilities passed quickly through his mind, each worse than the last. And still there was a chance, a good chance, that Gadi was wrong. He needed to hear Doron's opinion, needed to have the various possibilities presented to him in an organized manner. There was no way he would make a hasty decision based on one man's conjectures.

"From Paris a person can fly anywhere," Beaufort said. "As soon as you confirm he's on the list of passengers entering Beirut, let me know. In the meantime I want you to inform Doron and bring your planning and intelligence people into the picture. Have Doron phone and give me his assessment. Start working on suitable plans."

The Mossad chief turned to go.

"There's one other option that would at least shorten response time," Gadi said, causing Beaufort to turn back to him. "I can get things started in the division and then set out for Europe so that if you decide to take action in Lebanon, I can be there within hours, even this evening."

Beaufort returned to his chair and considered Gadi's words.

"There's some logic to what you're saying, but how will you take part in the planning?"

"Doron and I communicate well, we think alike. In the worst case the squad members who come after me will supply me with the details."

"Okay, I'm approving your departure for a stopover in

127

Europe, but mobilize the planning process here first. Let Doron know. If you're not going to be here then Doron has to come back for the planning."

He stood up and left the room in a hurry. Gadi remained seated, perplexed. A lot depended on being able to reach Doron, give him as many details as possible by code, share gut feelings with him. At the same time, every moment that passed made the danger in Beirut graver. He felt it was already grave enough for the top echelons of the Mossad to do everything in their power to find a solution, but instead he was being sent to "mobilize the planning process".

Everything had fallen on his shoulders. Gadi rose from his chair, angry, and left the room. "Tell me, does it ever happen that decisions are made around here *not* based on a policy of cover-your-back? Real decisions based on the seriousness of the situation? Or is it just another opportunity to leave us in the field with the real decisions?" he said as he passed Avigur on his way out. He gathered his jacket and helmet from the reception counter and hurried down to the Operations Division, leaving three surprised people in his wake.

In the office of the head of the Operations Division Gadi learned that they had been trying to reach Doron for an hour. He asked them to send another urgent message and to book him a ticket to Rome and a hotel room there, before setting off to mobilize the planning process with the heads of the Intelligence and Planning Departments.

It was important to Gadi that the staff of the

Intelligence Department pass on requests for information from relevant intelligence-gathering sources and to receive updated information: it was highly possible, for example, that Abu-Khaled's promotion had entailed moving to a new office or even a new apartment, or that he was now driving a different car.

While Gadi sat planning with his friends, Eli, the Intelligence Department head, listened attentively and agreed with what he was saying, whereas Arye, head of the Planning Department, who was responsible for carrying out the work schedule for the entire division, rejected Gadi's theory and went along with the planning process only because he was instructed to do so from above. "If you ask me," he told Gadi angrily, "I can't see the justification for the division to enter into such a risky situation just because Ronen's taken off. I have more than a dozen requests for operations from different departments in the Mossad and Military Intelligence that I'm busting a gut trying to fit into our work schedule and can't, because the squads have an insane workload and don't even have time to breathe. So we have to waste time now for *this*?"

Eli immediately pointed out that they couldn't leave one of their men in the field, but Gadi did not think the head of planning's outburst was worthy of a response. Arye's *this* was a person, a trainee of his, a subordinate, a comrade in arms. As far as Gadi was concerned, the question of whether to rescue Ronen was not up for discussion. He calculated that there would still be a need for a first planning meeting and the preparation of an updated intelligence profile, even though he had already learned that Abu-Khaled had not changed offices or homes. In the best-case scenario hours would pass before Doron returned, then they would have to get the Mossad chief to approve the general plan, fill in all the details, test it out, obtain the Prime Minister's authorization – all a matter of two or three days at the very least. Yet tomorrow, or the day after at the latest, Ronen was liable to take out Abu-Khaled, or get caught trying to do so.

Gadi checked the list of flights and connections. The plane to Rome, which would be leaving in less than four hours, was the last one that would enable him to make a connecting flight to Beirut that same night. Any hold-up would delay his arrival by one full day. Only one solution remained; he alone could find Ronen – and only if he left immediately. The personal danger was tremendous, but he felt he owed it first and foremost to Ronen, and then to everyone else – Gadi did not even stop to name them – affected by this turn of events.

Eli allocated one of the intelligence officers from his department and Arye one of his deputies in order to start initial planning. Gadi used the office to pass along a more detailed message to Doron: Leaving for Rome as stopover. Planning process in motion. Waiting urgently for you, call Beaufort immediately. No one at headquarters knew that Gadi had already made up his mind to continue on to Beirut. If he were to be granted approval, fine, but if not, he'd deal with the repercussions when he returned.

On her return home from the regional school where she taught English, Helena was surprised to find her husband in their bedroom in the middle of packing. He told her all that had happened that morning as they sat together on the bed, a suitcase open between them.

Mossad regulations allowed Gadi to tell Helena about the operations in which he took part, though he declined to tell her about the most dangerous or violent ones. Even without knowing he was in an Arab country she had spent enough sleepless nights, and days in which concentration was impossible. This time he knew that the likely complications were such that he would have to tell her everything, even his decision to continue on to Beirut with or without permission. He did not want her to discover that this had been a personal mission to save Ronen after the fact.

Helena did not need to say a word for Gadi to discern how upset she was. The sparkle in her beautiful blue eyes was snuffed out the moment he mentioned his visit to Naamah, and a tremor of anger, so out of character, quivered at the corner of her mouth when he told her about his meeting with the Mossad chief. Gadi's heart sank and he leaned over the suitcase to kiss her lips, which remained sealed.

Her entire married life had prepared her for this moment, because that was precisely who Gadi was. The very first time she met him, at the university swimming pool shortly after she'd arrived in Israel to study for a year, she recognized the contradictions in his personality that would become so familiar to her through the years. A brawny man tanning himself in a lounge chair, he sat reading *The Idiot* in Russian, which she had learned as a second foreign language in Denmark. They talked briefly and he told her, with a winning smile, that after reading only three pages he already knew it was the most wonderful book he'd ever laid his hands on. A man who loves Prince Myshkin so much must be a good person, she told herself. Gadi was older and more introverted than the other students, but that in fact suited her. She fell in love with his gaze, which was in those days as soft and loving as it could be tenacious now. She fell in love with his ways of thinking, speaking and behaving, which were straightforward and honest and somehow different from all the other Israelis she'd met – softer and gentler.

Some time before they were married they were sitting with Gadi's close army friends as they told tall tales about each other in turn. One of the tales was about a navigation exercise on a rainy night when they encountered a prickly cactus hedge at least a hundred feet long. To their amazement, Gadi began cutting through it with the butt of his rifle, and passed through the hedge while all the others went around it. Gadi said they should follow a straight navigational line as planned, and that if they went around the hedge they might not stay on the same line. He was the only one who managed to reach the exact reference point, a certain olive tree in a thin grove at the entrance to an Arab village in the Galilee. Everyone laughed appreciatively, and Helena knew this small story was the perfect example of one side of Gadi's character: his straightforwardness, his seriousness, his refusal to cut corners. But this was after he'd been wooing her for a while, and revealed more of himself to her, aspects of his personality she was loath to share with others: his devoted, doting love, his softness, the silliness and laughter he saved only for her.

Helena knew that the kiss he wanted to give her now was a soft kiss of love, but his eyes spoke of penetrating that prickly cactus hedge. A jumble of thoughts was running through her head: how could she stop him? What would keep him from leaving? The words burst forth randomly. You can't go without permission and without assistance. Why you, why do you always feel that everything is on your shoulders? You've told the Mossad chief, now it's in his hands, he knows what the risks are. If the decision is not to do anything, that's legitimate.

Gadi smiled. Here she was talking like a native-born Israeli: you've told him, now it's in his hands. Certainly that would suffice for many of his friends if they were in the same position. And that was precisely the nearly unbridgeable gap between him and them. What was it that Shalgi had said? The buck stops here. He wasn't going to pass on the responsibility, nor would he blame his superiors, either.

"Ronen is my personal responsibility," Gadi answered quietly inside the small cloud of her delicate perfume as he moved his unrequited lips away from hers. "Just as he was tossed aside, I could have been tossed aside, too. So now that he's got himself, and all of us, into terrible trouble, I have to get him – and us – out of it."

He could imagine the muddle in her brain just then.

Helena had been trying for years, without success, to build a home in which he would leave his work outside, on the doorstep. Even though many of their neighbours in the small communal settlement were employees of the Mossad and security institutions, Helena had not developed relationships with their wives. She was far removed from the squad's culture, knew what she needed to about her husband's past, including Naamah, but the information never added up to a full picture; the puzzle in her mind was never complete and there were missing pieces that bothered her.

Helena knew Gadi would leave on this insane journey even without permission, and also that this was probably his most dangerous trip – alone, perhaps without assistance, against a double opponent: Ronen and the surroundings. It was clear to her that Naamah was involved in his decision; after all, he'd visited her at home, she must have asked him to rescue her husband, and Gadi was just the knight who'd be prepared to risk his life doing so. Helena might have been able to refrain from saying anything so as not to darken the moment of their parting. But she understood that if she were to put matters on the table, instead of keeping them inside as she usually did, Gadi might come to his senses.

"Are you looking after him, or after Naamah?"

He flinched, then gathered all the tenderness he could muster, and said, "Where did that come from, Iloush?"

"Can't you see for yourself? If you heard that story from some other woman would you be so quick to move?"

Gadi knew he needed to give a clear answer. Helena's

present distress came from deep within, and there was no way for him to search it out and squelch it in the short time remaining. Again he felt his love and compassion for her swirling around inside him.

"Naamah wouldn't make such things up. I know her well enough to be sure of that."

"Too well," Helena spluttered with a bitterness that had accrued over the years, and which she'd thought she had managed to tuck away in her deepest recesses, perhaps even obliterated by her husband's love.

Gadi stood up and went to the wardrobe. He removed a tie and began to put it on. There was no point in reiterating that the affair with Naamah had ended long ago, he'd said all that in the past. To his surprise Helena stood up too, opened the other wardrobe door and removed the right jacket for the trousers he was wearing.

"I have no other explanation for this madness," she said into the continuing silence. "Do you want to tell me that it wasn't Naamah who came to you, that she didn't appeal to you to go?" All mixed up inside her were the desire to use Naamah to keep Gadi from going and the need to express her worry and the insult she felt.

Gadi embraced her. "She called and told me what had happened. She never thought of the possibility that I'd go there."

This, in fact, sounded right to Helena. Such a crazy idea could only take shape in Gadi's all-or-nothing brain. She let him hold her, did not move. Then she pulled away from him and went downstairs, his jacket in her hand.

Gadi came into the kitchen a minute later, the suitcase locked and his tie pulled tight into place. The coffee machine, which he had turned on before he went up to pack, had brewed a pot, so he poured himself a cup. Helena refused his offer to join him.

"Give yourself a few more hours to think about it. Maybe something else about Ronen will come to mind. Maybe they'll send someone else with you." Once again, scrambled thoughts were tumbling from her mouth, each one another rope she hoped Gadi would grab onto in order to swing away from his crazy intentions.

"Unless they get their asses in gear it'll be too late. And if I don't catch the plane to Rome and make the connecting flight to Beirut this evening, I could be too late."

"You two are both going to wind up in some Hezbollah dungeon. He'll naturally want to take you to hell with him. He must hate you."

"I believe that when he sees me he'll understand the game's up. He's not out to commit suicide," Gadi said as much to convince himself as Helena, realising that he really had no idea how far Ronen had deteriorated recently, and which Ronen exactly he would find himself up against there.

"If anything happens to you, nobody will know. Even just a traffic accident. And nobody here will be able to help you."

Gadi knew that day-to-day Helena, like the wives of other Mossad operatives, lived with the feeling that the omnipotent Mossad would ride in to save them from any mishap. And so she couldn't even begin to imagine the feeling of complete loneliness that was his lot in every mission he'd carried out on his own, in which his fake passport was good for first impressions only, and if he were to slip up and someone decided to check on him, he'd be powerless. A fourth-degree *dan* in Ninjitsu would do him no good in the middle of Beirut or Tehran; no one could rescue him from the cellars of the Hezbollah or the Revolutionary Guards.

"If I had an accident in Kazakhstan nobody would know it either, even if I'd been on duty," he said. He glanced at his watch and began to make his way to the door.

"Can't you at least wait for the kids to come home? It's almost never happened that you've left the country without saying goodbye to them."

Helena and Gadi both knew that she was now using a weapon she'd never before used. Gadi was crazy about his two small children. Even Helena did not know about the times he had arrived in Europe from an Arab country and had called home, the tears flowing when Ami or Ruth answered. But she did know about the many nights he'd arrived home late and had rushed to their beds in the hope that they hadn't yet fallen asleep. He would rest his head on their small, sleeping bodies, and when he left their room it would seem to her that his eyes were moist, which would bring a tear to her eye, too. Still, both of them knew that nothing would keep him from going.

Gadi glanced at his watch again and shook his head no, with sadness.

"If God forbid something should happen to you, they'd never forgive you," she said. "I wouldn't either."

Gadi put his empty cup down, walked over and hugged her. "Hate my job, not me, Iloush."

That was her Gadi: expressions of love, winning words and uncompromising tenacity. It was a package deal with him.

"At least promise me you'll talk to headquarters and think more about it in Rome."

"I promise."

"You're creasing your jacket," she said with a laugh amid the tears.

"It's the last time, I promise."

"Yeah, just like the kids," she said into his shoulder. "After the last time, there's the very last time, and then the very, very last time, and then…how many years have you been telling me that's it, soon you'll be mine alone?"

Gadi tightened his embrace, melting under her accent, which he loved so well, and Helena made a sound that was half laughter and half sob.

4.

GADI MADE THE promised telephone call to headquarters – a call he would have made anyway – from a public phone on Piazza Barberini, in front of his hotel. He even reconsidered his plans. But as he anticipated, things were sluggish back at the office: Doron was in the air on his way back to Israel, a late-evening meeting planned for his arrival. Eli told Gadi that Doron was pretty angry about being called back by "hysterical situation assessments" and that he, Eli, had trouble believing the division would shift into true battle protocol. "If the director-general doesn't shake things up here," he told Gadi, "no one's going to do more than the bare minimum."

There was no way anyone was going to give him permission to continue to Beirut that evening, and little chance it would happen the next day, either. Gadi knew that flying to Beirut now would be a flagrant violation of Mossad conduct and discipline. Even though there was an operational edge to making another step forwards, this was certainly not an operation carried out by the book that could lead either to an official commendation – if the operation succeeded – or demotion, dismissal or imprisonment if it failed; this was a no-win situation whichever way you looked at it. Still, he had to give it a chance. This was the first time in his life that Gadi was departing for a mission with no rules, no preparations, no back-up – a mission whose success could reek of failure.

His check-in at the hotel went smoothly. Just like the car rental and his renewed visit to Dahiyeh, a little earlier. When the receptionist requested that he leave his passport, Gadi acted surprised and asked why and for how long. "Until tomorrow morning," he was told, "but if it's really important to you, you can have it back in two hours." A short while later, as he sat sipping coffee in the lobby, Gadi watched agents from the Mukhabarat – the secret police – approach the reception desk, take the passport and depart.

A gamble: the photo in this passport was similar to the one he had used the previous year. Would they compare them? How in-depth had that investigation been, anyway?

If asked he would act surprised, would smile even at the similarity between himself and some man named Martinson who had visited Lebanon a year ago. And in the meantime he would have to be patient, tighten his stomach muscles, and wait. After all, there were far more difficult aspects to the job than that. If you couldn't handle it, then you needed another line of work.

Gadi finished his coffee. He needed to locate Ronen's hotel. It was late, and making too many inquisitive calls would arouse suspicion. He couldn't phone from his room, and using the public telephone in the hotel lobby would draw unwanted attention.

Gadi crossed the street and went into another large hotel. From a public phone in the lobby he began calling Beirut hotels asking for Mr Jesse Smith. The lobby was a little too empty and the hotel security guard gave him a thorough once over. Gadi had decided on a ten-call limit, after which he would move to another hotel, but fortunately for him on the seventh call, to the Mar-Elias, he struck lucky. The operator was about to put him through to Mr Jesse Smith but Gadi told her he would call back and hung up. He quickly left the lobby, in case Ronen's phone was being tapped. At least he is operating correctly, Gadi thought: the Mar-Elias, a small hotel on the Beirut–Damascus road, made it legitimate for him to use the El-Obeiri road, where the Hezbollah office for overseas operations was located, at almost any hour of the day.

Gadi looked at his watch; it was nearly midnight. Should he go to the Mar–Elias now and settle matters with Ronen? A visit to a small hotel outside the city could arouse suspicion, and who knew what kind of tail Ronen was dragging around after a day and two evenings of reconnaissance in the city. If he showed up at the hotel he could find himself falling straight into the arms of the security forces, who might already have staked out Ronen's room. It would be better to catch him in some neutral location, so he decided to start early, perhaps to ambush him outside his hotel, or near Abu-Khaled's house. He hoped that in the meantime Ronen wouldn't cause too much damage.

First, however, Gadi wanted to get his passport back.

*

A city that never stops, Gadi thought to himself with a smile as he drove away from his hotel very early the next morning. A surprising number of passersby were out and about. Joggers were running along the promenade and a platoon of Syrian soldiers from a nearby base was running in formation across the street. He drove along the wide boulevard that encircled the downtown area, eyeing pairs of armed policemen stationed at intersections, weaving between early-rising pedlars and their carts, taxis, and the clapped out vehicles of workers making their way into central Beirut from the suburbs.

He turned south. After only a few minutes he had left behind the congestion of the main street; Abu-Khaled's neighbourhood was not yet awake, and at the sleepy roadblock the guards barely paid him any attention. There was very little traffic on the narrow street that led to Abu-Khaled's home in this familiar neighbourhood of three-storey houses and apartment blocks built on pillars, beneath which residents parked their cars.

Gadi had planned his moves carefully. Abu-Khaled's was the fifth house on the left. He would, therefore, turn right out of his house on his way to the office. If Ronen were lying in wait for him he would almost certainly be hiding at one of the first four houses on the left, out of the guard's line of vision.

Gadi slowed to a leisurely pace. His eyes scanned left and right, his head barely moving. Parked cars and more parked cars, along the street, on drives alongside gardens, under the houses, building after building. As he was approaching the guard booth at Abu-Khaled's house, he noticed what appeared to be a rental car in the inner parking area of the third house on the left. In a split-second decision he pulled over and parked, still out of the guard's line of vision as long as he stayed within his booth.

Before stepping out of his car, Gadi glanced up at the building. All the shutters on the verandah windows were closed. He strode into the parking area and made for the rented BMW, which was parked between several other cars. At first it seemed empty, then Ronen sat up, averting his glance in anticipation of their meeting.

Gadi sighed deeply, walked round to the passenger door of the BMW, and climbed in. "Start the engine and drive off," he said.

Ronen stared straight ahead, not a muscle moving in his face. And then, slowly, without turning his head, said, "Get out of the car and away from here. I don't want you mixed up in this."

"First, we both need to get away from here. After that we'll talk."

Ronen continued to stare ahead, his hands gripping the steering wheel. "I have no intention of discussing anything with you. Get out of the car and away from here before it's too late."

Gadi was about to disagree, but then he noticed the tension in Ronen's jaw and in a flash his private hope – that his being here would bring Ronen back to his senses – was dashed. Ronen was not his subordinate here, he was full of resentment against him and the whole system and would never accept his authority. Right now it was Gadi's job to calm him, to ensure he didn't act in haste. And he had a Plan B: that was to tell Ronen that an operational squad was on its way to Beirut. Gadi could also say that a warning had been passed on to Abu-Khaled, but then Ronen was liable to perceive himself to be at war with the entire system and Gadi would lose the opportunity to persuade him of anything. He changed tack, softening his voice.

"If we leave here quietly nobody will ever know we were here. Nobody knows I'm here yet, you have my word on that."

Although Ronen had suspected that the Mossad would become involved and try to stop him, he was astonished at the speed at which they had acted.

He turned his head slowly towards Gadi.

"It's been a long time since your word meant anything to me. Still, it's too bad you're mixed up in this," he said, surprising Gadi. "Get out. How did you get here anyway? How did you know I was here?"

It was then that Gadi realized just how disconnected Ronen was from everything happening around him. True, he couldn't have known for sure that Naamah would guess he had left for Beirut and would engage the Mossad so quickly, nor could he know how efficient they would be in gaining access to passenger lists from foreign airlines, but to be amazed that they had located him? Ronen was one of those operatives who trusted the intelligence reports, believing they would be reliable and accurate without ever asking how they were obtained. There were other operatives, less innocent, more suspicious, who grilled the intelligence officer about every piece of information. The intelligence officer would try to wriggle his way out of answering, since the operatives were meant to set out for missions with only as much information as they absolutely needed. It was none of their business if hacking into a school computer had provided details on a target's children; if a local agent had been sent to the target's home disguised as a salesman; if an aerial photograph had provided details on the target's car or if another operative had passed by his office on a previous intelligence-gathering mission.

The contradiction between Ronen's outward severity and his naivety had never been more obvious. Gadi understood it would be as much a mistake to answer his question, to mention Naamah, as it would be to lie to him now. He decided to ignore the question. Tense and decisive he continued to speak softly.

"Ronen, think about it. This isn't just about you. You're dragging an entire country into this mess, as well as the Mossad. And me."

"I've thought this through," Ronen answered, his expression veiled, "and I have no intention of taking anyone else into consideration, just like nobody gave a shit about me."

Persuasion and sympathy are not going to work either, Gadi thought. "Ronen, get a grip on yourself. You're not talking like a sane person."

For an instant a spark shone in Ronen's glazed expression as he turned his head to face forwards again.

"Maybe I'm really not sane any more," he said

145

pensively. "Do you think a crazy person knows he's crazy?" he asked, turning to Gadi.

He knew Gadi would think he was pulling his leg, but that had not been his intention at all. For several months Naamah had been telling him that if he didn't get help he would end up in bad shape. Benny, the division psychologist, had come to the house twice, but Ronen had refused to meet him. I'm allowed to be depressed, he had thought to himself: other operatives couldn't say they had caused the Mossad a major mishap, the worst ever, something to talk about for years; other operatives hadn't been implicated by a commission of inquiry and booted off the squad.

"Maybe if I know I'm crazy that proves I'm normal?" he asked Gadi without seeking an answer. "Let's just agree that I had pretty good reason to go nuts," he said, falling silent.

How unbelievably stupid of me. Gadi cursed himself for making a direct though unintentional hit on Ronen's open wounds. How could he have suggested that Ronen was crazy? He needed to neutralize the situation as quickly as possible.

"One crazy guy says to another, 'Let's go crazy,' so the other one says, 'Are you crazy?'" Gadi put his hand on Ronen's shoulder and Ronen gave a short laugh.

Suddenly they froze. A figure appeared on the other side of the parking area. He got into his car and turned on the engine: the path to the exit would pass by the BMW. Ronen and Gadi exchanged glances, the uneasiness between them dissipated; now they were simply two experienced operatives at a decisive moment. Gadi leaned forwards and Ronen lay his head on Gadi's back. They heard the car pass by but Ronen waited another moment before lifting his head a little, looking about and straightening up. Gadi did the same.

"Ronen, we can't stay here. Other neighbours will be on the move soon, and you know as well as I do that every other person around here is a member of Hezbollah."

"So go!" Ronen answered furiously. "What do you want from me? That asshole is still blowing people up, I'm going to wipe him out!"

"First of all, let me bring you up to date. He's been promoted to some administrative job. And second, do you really think you're helping Israel this way?"

Ronen clamped his mouth shut and refrained from looking at Gadi. He had no intention of leaving. Gadi could sense his own fury rising; he was angrier with himself for being so sure he could bring Ronen home than with Ronen himself.

"You're such a blockhead. Just so tenacious, right? You've decided, so that's that. No talking you out of it, eh? Okay, so listen Lone Ranger, the game's up. Listen closely to what I'm going to do."

Think hard, Gadi heard from a small voice in his head. Think hard. This is not some argument between two angry drivers on some road in Israel and this is not some leadership exercise on the squad. This is an operation, the real thing. You were here once before and you failed because of inadequate planning. And here you are making the same mistakes again. This is not the time for improvisations and spontaneity. What's more, as he expected, people and cars were starting to pass up and down this small street and the slightest spark could set the whole area on fire.

But that small voice was weak. Gadi decided to take a gamble. He could only see the immediate danger, that something would happen and they would find themselves surrounded once again by an angry mob, a danger that Ronen, in his blinkered pursuit, could not envisage. He had to get him out of there.

"I'm going over to the guard in the booth at Abu-Khaled's building," he said without taking into consideration what chance there was that Ronen would believe him. "I'm going to tell him that I've seen someone suspicious in this parking area. It'll only take a few seconds for him to show up here and for their security forces to seal off the area. Is that what you want? Don't you understand," he said in a tone that was nearly pleading, "that I can't let you muck things up for everyone?"

He knew he had created a situation which was almost entirely in Ronen's control. Of course he could stay in the car, but then *all* the cards would be in Ronen's hands.

After a short silence Ronen gave him a scornful look: "So go on. Go. Now who's talking about being a blockhead. Go on."

Their eyes locked in anger. Ronen was prepared to go all the way with his crazy plan, and if his nerves held he would steal the entire act. But then Gadi recognised a glint of disbelief in his eyes. It was not that he was prepared to take a chance on getting the guard involved, it was that he did not believe that Gadi would involve him, that he would break the golden rule of the squad: standing by one another. Even if you could make a clean break you would stick your head back in the lion's mouth to save your friend.

Gadi had proven this rule a year earlier, not far from where they were at that very moment, when a round of ammunition fired at the car in which John and Ronen were trying to escape hit them both, causing John to veer to the side; the vehicle hit the kerb and came to a stop. Gadi, overseeing the operation, was standing next to his car on the opposite side of the street, facing Abu-Khaled's office. He jumped into the car, nosed it across the street against oncoming traffic, dispersing the dozens of onlookers who had already gathered around the bullet-ridden car, the scent of a lynching hanging in the air. He fired into the air, Ronen and John leapt into his car, and he sped away.

And now he had announced he was about to break that rule, and Ronen didn't believe him. He knew Gadi would not turn him in, knew he still believed in the codes and rules. I have a thirty-second walk to make to put his trust to the test, Gadi thought. If trust wins out then my gamble has failed. Gadi looked right and left. Nobody was around. He had a window of opportunity. He got out of the car and walked towards the street.

A picture of what was happening took shape in Ronen's head. This was not some riddle, some brain teaser, nor was it a cockfight between two of Naamah's suitors. Gadi was here to stop him at all costs, including Ronen's own head. Fuck you, Gadi, he mouthed. That much? You hate me that much? Enough to hurt me? I mean that little to the organization? You're that submissive a servant of the Mossad? His frozen limbs seemed to be thawing as a roiling wave of anger and distress washed through him. To hell with everything.

He jumped out of the car. Gadi was nearing the street when he heard the car door open, heard Ronen's approaching footsteps. He slowed down, thinking, Good, it's working.

Ronen caught up with him, threw his right arm around Gadi's neck and bent him sideways with tremendous pressure.

"You're not going to stop me," he hissed in a choked voice. "Certainly not like that."

Ronen's grasp was so tight that Gadi practically passed out. It took him a second to recover enough to understand that once again he had erred in his assessment: his actions had not caused Ronen's logic to trip in. He rammed his left elbow into Ronen's solar plexus and, using the same hand, followed up with a fist to his balls. Ronen moaned in pain. Gadi lifted his heel, stomped on Ronen's foot, and swung his right hand around blindly, hoping to catch Ronen in the face. He hit something. Both his hands now gripped Ronen's forearm – which was still firmly around Gadi's neck – and were pulling hard. The noose around his neck relaxed and he jerked his head free. Without wasting a second he bent Ronen's arm behind his back and pushed him in the direction of the car.

"Are you nuts?" Gadi whispered. "Do you want to attract attention? Haven't you learned anything from last time?"

The moment they were under the building Gadi released his grip on Ronen and pushed him onto the bonnet of the BMW. Ronen broke his fall with both hands and turned around quickly.

"Don't you dare speak to that guard."

"So get out of here."

Ronen slowly stood up straight and eyed Gadi, looking him over. His arm was sore from where Gadi had bent it backwards, and the other limbs that had absorbed Gadi's short, powerful blows hurt, too. He could not understand how Gadi had got the better of him so quickly. His entire consciousness filled up with the image of Gadi standing in front of him, solid, quiet, tenacious, blocking the path to his goal. Gadi would once again return home the victor; the commission of inquiry would once again find that Ronen had screwed up and that Gadi had put things right. And Naamah would look at him once again and acknowledge, without words, which of the two was better, what luck it was that Gadi had once again intervened in the nick of time. The squad would say that Ronen had once again failed, in spite of the secrecy of the mission and the element of surprise. This time, though, he was not the last in the chain of command; he was the entire chain. And here was Gadi facing him, his shoulders slightly stooped, his arms hanging at his sides, having made his short pronouncement, and waiting silently for Ronen to obey his command. Not this time. Not this time, damn it. This mission was complex enough, his life was complicated enough, the decisions he had to make were difficult enough. Just let him disappear!

Gadi saw it coming, in Ronen's eyes, and for a second hoped that Ronen would succeed in damming this fresh outburst of anger, but prepared himself against attack nonetheless. He saw Ronen push off from the car in his direction, enraged, and his body pulled taut. So many years of karate, he thought in an instant, and Ronen still hasn't learned that you fight with your head, not your heart, with your eyes, not your body. He reached his arms first right and then left, deflecting Ronen's wildly flailing fists. Gadi stepped backwards, bringing his hands down in an X in order to block Ronen's foot, which was about to connect with his balls. How has it come to this, he thought, brawling with Ronen two doors down from Abu-Khaled's house, just like the Mossad chief had predicted? Insane.

Ronen renewed his angry charge. Gadi moved backwards in small steps, blocking another series of blows, and was pushed out of the parking area to a place where anyone could look down on him from one of the verandahs. He shook Ronen off, dodging forwards and right, returning two short blows to Ronen's rib cage and stomach. Ronen was momentarily winded and Gadi turned around, slipping his right arm under Ronen's left armpit and placing his hip against Ronen's stomach to enable him to lift Ronen off his feet and hurl him to the ground. Ronen's legs made a full circle in the air and he landed with a thud. Before he could even begin to comprehend what had happened to him, Gadi threw his heavy body on top of him, his arm encircling Ronen's neck like a vice, his shoulder pushing Ronen's head into the ground. Ronen had no air in his lungs, he couldn't make a sound and felt his consciousness slipping into a fog.

"Mufik, come quickly!" came the frightened voice of a woman right above them.

"Shit," Gadi muttered, releasing his grip. They were only a few feet from the shelter of the building, they would have to get out of there immediately. A mix of voices drifted down: the woman, her husband, neighbours who had been alerted by the shouting. They appeared on their verandahs in various stages of wakefulness and dress. The woman was excitedly describing to her neighbours the scene they had missed.

Gadi picked Ronen up, dumped him in the passenger's seat, lept across the bonnet and slipped behind the wheel. Armed Hezbollah men would be there any minute now. He turned on the engine and sped onto the street with a screech. In the rearview mirror he could see the guard from Abu-Khaled's building running after them. He made a right turn and then a quick left, the fastest route towards the centre of town.

Scarcely a minute had passed when a Land-Rover with a siren blaring passed them going the other way, with two guards from the roadblock hanging off the back. By the time the neighbours had given them a description of the car, Gadi and Ronen had disappeared.

*

As he merged with busy traffic on the Corniche in the direction of Ras-Beirut, the westernmost point of the city, Gadi slowed down but still drove tensely, surveying the policemen and soldiers at intersections and checking the rearview mirror to see whether some unexpected patrol might pop up behind them. He occasionally glanced at Ronen, who sat hunched and lifeless. As a result of the scene in front of Abu-Khaled's neighbours, he hoped Ronen would restrain himself when in a public place, so that was exactly where Gadi was heading.

A complex of restaurants at the northern edge of the city, next to the marina, seemed at first to be the best place to spend the next hour, but looking at Ronen – his clothes creased and dirty – convinced Gadi they could not go there. He recalled a large restaurant in the heart of the western quarter, not far from the promenade they were on at the moment, that was popular with labourers. There they would attract less attention, so Gadi turned the car onto a side street that wound its way up a hill filled with garages, warehouses and building supply stores. Ronen was starting to return to his old self: he sat up straighter, took notice of where they were. Gadi drove about a hundred feet past the restaurant and parked in front of a large shop.

Ronen was still confused by the events of the morning so it suited him to keep quiet and do whatever Gadi decided. He, too, understood that in operational terms it was preferable that they leave the car and find temporary refuge. Ronen patted himself in an attempt at removing some of the dust and dirt on his clothes, and when he turned to get out of the car Gadi used his hands to brush, very gently, the dust that had stuck to his jacket. Ronen stayed put, allowing Gadi to finish. For a brief moment he was once again the disciplined, trusting subordinate.

Gadi chose a table near the window, overlooking the street, and sat so that he could see the BMW. If a patrol car were to stop, the police would assume they were inside the shop and he and Ronen would have a few moments to make a getaway. The only other customers were further inside the restaurant, by the counter, and the waiter did not try to hide his displeasure at having to make the trip over to their table.

"Full breakfast," Gadi said, pointing at the menu.

"Coffee," Ronen muttered as though he were being forced to order.

When the waiter walked away Gadi said, in a tone that was somewhere between admonishing and reminiscing, "You know, don't you, that it wasn't using our wits that saved us back there – it was luck?"

"Luck?" Ronen said disdainfully. "The moment I saw you I really felt like I'd hit the jackpot."

Gadi laughed, then tried to change the topic. He knew he had to soften Ronen before he could talk about their current situation again. "Luck is the name of the game in our screwed-up profession, even after all the preparations."

"No, that's not the case," Ronen said gravely. "But because of the rules we're forced to rely on luck."

"What's it got to do with rules?"

"Everything, that's what. When I got stuck with you that time for an entire day in the ceiling of that chemical company in Karachi, it was only because of the stupid rule that says we can't harm innocent people. Otherwise John and Danny, who were outside, could have made sure that the watchman wouldn't find us and we could have walked out like VIPs."

The arrival of a boy who came to arrange the cutlery on their table gave Gadi the chance to replay the scene in his mind.

"The night watchman just arrived, he's approaching John's car," Danny's voice had come over the transmitter in the dead of night.

John was parked in a dark spot just outside the entrance to the building. In case of a disturbance he could run down anyone who turned up at the door and Gadi and Ronen could escape from the building and jump into the car. But Gadi had decided otherwise.

"Don't show yourselves," he said quietly. "We'll spend the day here and you can pick us up tomorrow night, half an hour after the watchman on the day-shift leaves."

He could have arranged a hasty departure with the intention of returning the next day in the window of time between the end of one guard's shift and the start of the next, but headquarters would never give him permission to return. Why had the night watchman shown up so early? How could they be sure he wouldn't arrive early the next evening, too? Had they not left evidence behind them in the office?

Gadi could recall the smell of Ronen's outstretched body as they lay head to head on beams that supported the acoustic ceiling of the company archives. Beneath them, a hair's-breadth away, they could see employees coming and going.

Next evening Danny reported that the day-time watchman had gone and the building was empty. This time they finished photographing the materials and copying files from the computer before the night watchman arrived, slipping away through a toilet window, a sewage pit and the basement to John's car.

Back home, in the debriefing, his decision had been analyzed from every angle, but there's no arguing with success. It used to be said that, "Nonsense that works is still nonsense," but lately it seemed that everything was measured by results.

The waiter brought Gadi his breakfast.

"You've got to be kidding. What did you expect, that John would run him over?" he said after the waiter had gone.

"That's exactly what I wanted then," Ronen answered. After a short pause he added, "What do you think I did in Buenos Aires, when you and Lesley escaped through the tunnel?"

"I don't recall anything unusual coming up in the debriefing," Gadi said.

"Of course not. Would I be crazy enough to report it? You wouldn't be here today if I'd played by the rules."

"You don't say," Gadi said, smiling.

Ronen understood: Gadi would not be there, in Beirut,

if he, Ronen, had played by the rules. "That's not what I mean. I mean *here*, among the living. Two policemen started chasing you two, and it was clear to me that they were about to draw their guns and start shooting. So I backed the car up onto the pavement. The space between them and the tunnel was about the width of a car, and I decided there was no choice – I would cut them off and even run them down if necessary."

"And…?" Gadi glanced up from his plate when Ronen fell silent.

"What do you mean, 'and'? They jumped backwards, pounded on my windows with the butts of their guns, I made a little scene and by the time I'd pulled away you had disappeared out the other side. They shouted after me to wait and ran after you. Naturally, I took off."

"Well, first of all, a belated thanks," Gadi said. "Secondly, that's exactly the problem. You think the rules were not made for you." He motioned to Ronen not to answer, since the waiter was again approaching, this time with a jug of coffee for refills.

"Rules are for the people who made them, so they can cover their asses while they screw us," Ronen said finally.

"What's the matter with you?" Gadi said angrily. "Don't you understand the difference between harming a Hezbollah activist and harming an Argentinian or a Pakistani policeman? What have they ever done to us?"

"I have a problem with anyone who wants to harm us, even if it's because the guy happens to be a policeman and it was his bad luck to be at the wrong place at the wrong time. You know as well as I do that one fart back on that ceiling and we would have cried for the rest of our lives about the fact that John hadn't run down that watchman."

"How would the Mossad have looked if Yankol's squad had hit the Austrian policeman who came to detain them? They could have easily, you know."

"Exactly. That shows just how stupid the rule is. In the morning someone would have found the guy passed out in the basement and nobody would have known who did it." Ronen's voice was growing louder.

"Listen, it didn't come up in the debriefing about Beirut," he continued. "After John picked me up from Abu-Khaled's office and I didn't shoot those two policemen who came out of nowhere and opened fire on the car, we crashed into the kerb and all those people started gathering around us. There were a hundred people in less than half a minute, they knew something was going on when they heard Abu-Khaled shouting. They had murder in their eyes, I could see it. The gun was still in my hand, and when one of them opened the door I rammed the barrel in his face. I knew I was going to have to ruin a few faces if we wanted to get out of there alive, but then suddenly there were gunshots and everyone stopped and backed off. I didn't know what was going on, and then you showed up and pulled me into your car. If you hadn't, I would surely have had to shoot at them, even though they were, really, just your average citizens. Citizens who wanted to lynch me," he added. "Now every time I sleep on my left side I curse the fact that I didn't fire on those two fucking policemen."

Fire you should have, Gadi thought, but on Abu-Khaled, with a silencer, and not those policemen.

Everything would have gone according to plan. But this was not the time to talk about that. Gadi weighed his words. "I really hope you don't mean what you're saying," he said quietly. "A few shots in the air were quite enough. There was no need to shoot ordinary people to get away safely. You've been watching too many KGB movies."

"That's just it, you and your bosses haven't learned a thing," Ronen answered. "You think you can do dirty work and stay clean. Use your brain, man, it doesn't work like that. Shit sticks to you and reeks. But we're sanitation workers in white shirts. It's high time to show that whole stupid and self-righteous organization that in this profession there's no room for bleeding-hearts. No room for nice little yes-men."

"Calm down," Gadi said when he noticed the waiter watching them.

"Immediately you take the side of management," Ronen continued. "And what about us? How am I supposed to get away safely from all these tight spots when your 'clean' rules tie me down?"

"You think I'm on the management's side right now?" Gadi asked. "Can't you see that I'm here to make sure you get out of this safely?"

Ronen lowered his gaze, abashed. He gulped down his coffee, stood up suddenly, grabbed the car keys from the table and left the restaurant in a hurry.

Gadi called the waiter over urgently. The waiter, however, was in no great hurry. Gadi pulled out his wallet, removed a twenty-dollar note, waved it at the man and asked, "Is this enough?"

The bill for his breakfast and Ronen's coffee was barely more than half that amount, but Gadi couldn't afford to wait for the change. Let the waiter think whatever he wanted to. He smiled, pleased. Gadi left the note on the table and hurried after Ronen. As he reached the door he saw the back of the BMW disappearing up the hill.

5.

GADI HAD TO admit that Ronen had succeeded in pulling a fast one on him, and that once again he would have to start looking for him in places where Abu-Khaled might be found: and for that he needed the Mondeo, which he had left next to Abu-Khaled's house. Abu-Khaled would be amazed to learn who it was that was keeping him safe these days...

Gadi checked his watch. Only two hours had passed since he had met up with Ronen that morning. The neighbours had seen them drive off in a rental car, had seen there were two of them and that they had been fighting. It would not be hard for them to guess that the second rental car, parked by the kerb of the same building, was theirs also. The Mondeo might well be under surveillance. He could hire another car, but leaving the Mondeo in Bir-el-Abed would certainly arouse suspicions, and an investigation would lead to him. The faster he could get it out of there, the better. He decided to take a taxi, and once again, using the old cover story, he gave the driver the address of Dr Itzmat Abdel-Ganem. The drive necessitated driving down Abu-Khaled's street and stopping at the corner of the next one, where he paid off the driver and climbed out of the taxi.

The area was quiet. He could see no signs that the Mondeo was being watched. The guard in his booth radiated apathy as Gadi drove away. At the roadblock the guards were not suspicious, and were primarily concerned with incoming vehicles. So he was clean, he was not being followed, but still that didn't mean no one had checked to see who had rented the car left on that street. Although he still had the option to switch hotels, that would only serve to delay the Mukhabarat officers searching for him, and such a move would in itself raise suspicion.

Ronen must be having these same thoughts, Gadi realized, so it made sense to find out whether he had left his hotel. Gadi continued driving slowly, paying close attention to the area around Abu-Khaled's office and the other places he had frequented during their previous intelligence-gathering mission. Ronen wasn't at any of them. Nor was Abu-Khaled's car.

After checking a number of addresses, Gadi drew up by a row of public telephones at a shopping centre in West Beirut. Helena was undoubtedly worried, he needed to phone and tell her he was fine. He also needed her to pass on messages to headquarters and to Naamah. Some of the phones had been ripped out and all the booths were covered with graffiti, which was none too inviting, but the hotels, which were more hospitable, were far away. He simply had to reach Helena, he owed her that.

Helena's voice, partially obscured by static from the satellite connection that turned the inconspicuous international number he was dialling on to Israel, answered after several rings.

"Oh, thank God, I've been so anxious to hear from you!"

In English, which she was accustomed to using for their overseas phone conversations, her Danish accent was more pronounced than in Hebrew, and a pleasant feeling washed over Gadi just hearing her voice. What had she done to deserve this, his beautiful Dane? All she'd wanted was to study in Israel for a year – the very same year that Gadi was to spend in the very same univerisity finishing his master's thesis. And so she had wound up married to a Mossad operations squad leader and had become the mother of his two small children. She had been forced to understand what went through the head of a man who had personally put a number of people to death, to believe that his tenderness really was tenderness, that his sweet words really were sweet, that his love really was love, and that there did not exist, somewhere deep down, a stockpile of violent mysteries that would break out one day and bring everything to ruin. Still, even an Israeli woman would have found it hard to understand this complete split, the brain that could access its killer compartment on command or by decision, and afterwards seal off that compartment, accessing once again the tenderness.

"I'm really sorry it's taken me so long to call," Gadi answered. "I continued my journey last night. I've met Ronen and we've spoken, but I still haven't convinced him."

Gadi knew he was presenting matters in a more positive light than they really were, but it was important for him to allay Helena's fears and to pass on a soothing message to the others. Now that he had made initial contact with Ronen, and was at the beginning of rapprochement with him, he didn't want anyone to come up with any strange ideas.

"God, I've never been so tense before. I cancelled my first class this morning, I simply couldn't leave the house without hearing from you. Then I realized it might take a while, so I went to school. But I left my head at home."

Gadi laughed. "I was with him from early this morning, so I couldn't call earlier. In fact, calling at all is not strictly according to the rules."

"I'm not complaining, it's just that I was so anxious to hear from you. I didn't know how things would develop. I knew my students would kill me, too, because in the second lesson they had a test on Chaucer. I think that's the only reason I went in."

"Is that how you spend your nights when I'm away from home? With *The Canterbury Tales*?"

"I wish I had a head for that right now," Helena said with a sigh that contained, Gadi could hear clearly, her innocent love for him. Only with him was everything complicated, half of him obscured in darkness. In that sense, he and Naamah were soul mates, capable, without uttering a word, of being so much closer to one another than he and Helena could ever be. With Helena he needed to nourish his love.

"How are the kids?"

"They were a bit angry that you didn't say goodbye, but I explained it was an emergency. And one more thing," she added after a short silence, "I told them that this was the last time you'd be travelling for work. I don't know if I should have said that, but I had to make them feel a bit better."

"That's okay," Gadi said, attempting to maintain a level voice. "That's what I promised." If it hadn't been Helena, whose thoughts and intentions were as light and lucid as the colour of her hair, he would have suspected that she was trying to tie him down. But now was not the time to open it up for discussion. He needed to muster all his tact to pass his message on.

"Can I ask you to do something that's a bit… sensitive?"

Helena murmured her consent.

"I want you to call Doron and Naamah. Tell them I'm here, that I've met Ronen, and that I'm working on it."

"Hasn't he called her?" Helena hoped to avoid having to talk to Naamah.

"I don't think so. Please do that for me, okay?"

She did not ask him why he could not call Doron himself. Did she understand the problem in phoning a number linked to the Mossad? Or did she realize he was in a delicate position vis-à-vis the Operations Division? He had no way of knowing whether he had become a public enemy or a hero back there but what he did know was that the distance between the one and the other was, in the tense, zealous atmosphere of headquarters, next to nothing. Without being able to gauge where he stood in their eyes he could not risk a telephone conversation with Doron, who might well explicitly order him to return to Israel. Not to have understood that continuing to Beirut from Rome was subject to approval was one thing, but disobeying an order was something else entirely.

Their phone conversation was already longer than Gadi felt was acceptable under his present circumstances. Helena wanted to know if she should say anything to his parents; after thinking for a moment he asked her to send his regards but not to let them know that this trip was different from any other.

He looked around him, did not notice anything suspicious, and got into his car. Why had he not thought about his parents until now? He knew how they suffered when he was gone; nothing made them happier than hearing from him after a journey, safe at home. He never called them from overseas, even when he could. He thought it would set a bad precedent, and they were willing to be sent regards through Helena. This was another way of bringing her closer to them. They had been suspicious at first that this Nordic fairy would carry their son off to her icy homeland. Only later, when the nature of the time he spent overseas became clearer to them, did his mother say that maybe it would have been better for him to sit quietly in Denmark, that the years of worry when he and his older brother had served in the paratroops had been quite enough for her. He knew that on top of the worry there was no small amount of pride, especially where his father was concerned. He knew, too, that he was doing this for them, or, more accurately, *because* of them. Because of their own personal histories under Soviet rule and German occupation. Because of the grand dream that had carried them to Palestine, and so that this grand dream could become reality with time.

This, too, was the reason he had stopped working on his master's thesis on Russian literature when the Mossad had approached him, promising it would be just one mission – because of his Russian language skills – which "nobody in the whole State of Israel could do" but him. He developed a taste for it and was soon hooked; suddenly his studies seemed like a luxury at a time when renewed waves of terrorism and the development of non-conventional weapons by Moslem countries meant that Israel had not yet actually completed its War of Independence.

After a few more minutes behind the wheel, Gadi was convinced he was not being tailed, and so he stopped at another public telephone. He was not surprised to learn that Mr Jesse Smith had checked out. Now Gadi would have to wait an hour or two before beginning his phone calls to hotels all over again.

Doron had never looked more miserable than he did on his way to the office of the Mossad chief. His request for an urgent meeting had been granted immediately, so he raced up the stairs. He had returned to Israel the night before, as soon as it became clear that Ronen had indeed landed in Lebanon on a Middle Eastern Airlines flight from Paris. The chief had apprised the Prime Minister of the situation and had instructed Doron to prepare several operational alternatives in his division and to bring them to him for approval the following morning.

Doron's report, earlier that morning, had relayed the information that there was no contact with Gadi and that he had not checked into the hotel room reserved for him in Rome. The Mossad chief instructed Doron to make use of the intelligence-gathering apparatus to locate Gadi and to prepare operational plans that would suit this new situation. He postponed the meeting in his office until he had done so, preferring in the meantime a summary by Doron of the various options for action that had been raised in the division. And now he had to relay news that was doubly, triply worse.

Doron entered the office and closed the door behind him without being told to do so.

"I have two matters to report," he said as he took a seat facing the chief, who was busy with a pile of papers.

"Bad news and good news, I hope." Beaufort's well-developed sense of sarcasm was in place as usual.

"Fairly bad news and terrible news," Doron said, preparing the chief for what was coming.

"Start with the bad news."

"Gadi arrived in Beirut last night."

The chief's eyes narrowed. "I had a feeling we'd find him there, that Rambo of yours. The terrible news is that he's in cahoots with Ronen?"

"No, no," Doron said, shocked at the very idea. "That's why I said 'fairly bad'. I spoke to Gadi's wife just now. It's clear he set out to detain Ronen, and there's apparently some sort of hope he'll succeed. She recounted that Gadi has met him and that he's 'working on it.'"

"What does that mean, he's 'working on it?' And where did he meet him?"

"Nothing's clear yet. That's exactly what he asked her to pass on to us, and I can't even know if it's correct."

"I agree that we can't rely on this information," Beaufort said, and then paused to think a moment. "Something's rotten in your realm, Doron, some sort of lawlessness that we're going to have to shake up from top to bottom when this is all over. Tell me," he continued, "is there any good reason why it's taken you a full day to come up with this information?"

"With Ronen there was a problem checking passenger lists from all the flights leaving Paris. With Gadi, well, we only began looking a few hours ago…"

"I wasn't expecting an answer," the chief said, cutting him off. "But I'm not satisfied with receiving passive reports from Gadi's wife. Why, in your opinion, didn't he call you directly?"

"I can only guess. He figures we'll tell him to come home immediately."

"All right. Move on to the other matter."

Doron tried to swallow but his mouth was too dry. "It appears that Ronen paid a visit to the squad's old weapons warehouse. According to an investigation we've made, a charge is missing."

"An explosive charge?" Beaufort asked, astonished. "How did Ronen get in there?"

Doron nodded in response to the first question and

answered the second. "He knew the combinations on the locks. And we have positive identification thanks to his magnetic card, which he used to get in."

"He still has his card?"

"Yes, it appears it was never taken away from him. The charge was a prototype," he said, racing ahead with his desperate, hopeless explanation. "When the Weaponry Department passed it on to us for testing, we decided not to use it, so it was put into storage in the old warehouse."

"Is there something special about this charge, or some problem with it that I should know about?"

"It's comprised of two components, the charge itself and a small receiver with an antenna for long-distance operation. But there was some sort of electrical circuit that connected the cable that ran between the charge and the antenna to a timer. So whoever disconnects the cable actually activates the timer."

"In other words, it's a sort of booby trap."

"Exactly. The timer could blow whenever it was set in advance or in twenty-four hours. We came to the conclusion that that wasn't a good idea for a charge with remote-control, so we put a stop to its development."

"What are the chances that Ronen managed to get it in to Beirut?"

"Since we didn't finish developing the charge, the metal cover was never attached to it, only a temporary cover made of plastic. So the charge won't be picked up by a metal detector, only by sniffer dogs. In the airports he's passed through dogs aren't used."

"This brings us to a completely new phase," the chief

said after pondering this information for a moment. "Are you people ready with the options that take Gadi into consideration?"

Doron confirmed they were.

"From what you told me earlier this morning, the fastest option is to use your squad that operates undercover as Arabs, the Mistaravim?"

"Yes, if we want to avoid entering Lebanon via a stopover in Europe, all that sort of thing. We'll have to bring them into Lebanon by one of the established methods, by helicopter or from the sea."

"Do they have Lebanese documents?"

"Yes."

"And they're as skilled as other squads? They're prepared to handle an abduction?"

"They're an operational squad like any other. Most of them worked in similar units in the IDF and the Shin Bet."

"Prepare a detailed plan and report back here as soon as you're ready with all the relevant people. I'll contact the Foreign Relations Division and you bring the psychologist from your division with you. I want to hear from someone who understands the relationship between those two. And do something about our failure to communicate with Gadi except through his wife. I find that completely unacceptable."

The chief turned towards the row of telephones on his desk and Doron left the room. Even with all the complications and risks inherent in the operation the chief had just saddled him with – without fully understanding how dangerous it really was – Doron felt relieved. At least they were doing something, and doing something was his expertise. Who exactly was their target, who exactly was their enemy? That much still needed to be defined.

"Get me the Prime Minister," he heard Beaufort instructing his secretary over the intercom on his way out. "It's urgent."

As he pulled away from the restaurant where he had ditched Gadi, Ronen felt satisfied by the astonished expression on his commander's face. True, Gadi presented another obstacle in his path, but Ronen had no intention of giving up.

He could not allow himself to drive his car to Bir-el-Abed, even though Abu-Khaled was likely still to be at home. He guessed that Gadi would be running around the neighbourhood searching for him, the neighbours might identify him, and it was even possible that police or Hezbollah patrols had been provided with a description of the BMW. He needed to let things cool down. Ronen continued in the direction of his hotel. He would shower, change out of his dirty clothes and plan his next moves.

In his room at the Mar-Elias, Ronen turned on the television and the radio to local stations, as he always did. After showering he heard an announcement about a lecture that was to be given by Sheikh Fadlallah, the spiritual leader of Hezbollah, that evening at the Sheraton Hotel. Ronen's Arabic was good enough for him to understand, and the implications were quite clear: the entire Hezbollah elite would be on hand, Abu-Khaled included. He broke out in a sweat. He couldn't have hoped for a better set-up. But he would have to alter his plans – again – and fast. First he had to move to the Sheraton; that way he would ensure himself free passage among all the security agents who would undoubtedly inundate the hotel.

Before approaching the reception desk at the Sheraton, Ronen scanned both the outdoor and below-ground parking areas. For the second time in a hotel lobby his rather odd appearance drew the attention of security personnel, but no one dared search his belongings: his American Express card, along with his foreign passport, did the trick as they almost always had. It didn't matter if you were wearing jeans and a t-shirt and were unshaven. It didn't even matter if the components of an explosive charge were hidden in your belongings.

In the room, Ronen glanced briefly at the elegant furnishings – carved armchairs covered in green velvet and a huge canopied bed – then quickly arranged his few articles of clothing in the wardrobe. The chambermaids would undoubtedly pay a visit to his room shortly after he went out, and he did not want them making a suspicious report to wary hotel security officers.

He hung the Do Not Disturb sign on the doorknob, locked the door, bolted it with the chain, then removed, one by one, the components of the charge, which had been hidden separately from one another in his suitcase and flight bag. He then shut himself in the luxurious marble bathroom and began to fill the bath, so that even a cheeky hotel employee – the kind you find everywhere – would close the door on hearing the running water, even before encountering the chain.

It did not take him long to assemble the main components of the charge, wrap them up and put them into the flight bag along with a set of tools. He stuck the remote-control to a piece of adhesive tape which he then affixed behind one of the drawers of the bedside table, so that the remote-control would not be on him while he was carrying out such a delicate undertaking. After dressing in dark clothing and his overcoat he was ready to go. There remained only one small thing left to do: plant the charge on Abu-Khaled's car.

Shortly afterwards, Ronen parked his car in the centre of town, took the flight bag with him and hailed a taxi. This is something they had never done in the Mossad, he thought to himself: riding in a taxi with a set of tools and a nearly-ready explosive charge.

It was almost dark when the taxi passed by Abu-Khaled's house, but Ronen could still make out the guard sitting in his booth and a Mercedes in the parking area. He hoped it was indeed Abu-Khaled's Mercedes; in the dark it was hard to tell whether the car was a light green colour.

Ronen asked the taxi-driver to drop him off on the street behind Abu-Khaled's. He needed to enter the garden of the building that backed onto Abu-Khaled's home, then slip through to the Mercedes.

It would have been far better to start working later at night, when the residents had turned in for the night and the guard was sleepy, but Ronen knew he could not wait any longer. Within two hours Abu-Khaled was likely to leave for the Sheraton, and by then Ronen would need to be back at the hotel, ready to activate the remote-control.

He could only hope that no one was sitting on a verandah in the dark, watching him. He circled the building, made for the bushy hedge separating the garden from Abu-Khaled's, and verified that the Mercedes was indeed his. Now he had to assemble the charge almost under the guard's nose – or, more precisely, behind his back.

Ronen searched for a suitable place. Nowhere in the garden was suitable; any car entering the parking area would reveal him immediately. Never, ever, would the Mossad have allowed me to take such a risk, he thought as he knelt down close to the ledge. He shed his overcoat, removed the various components from their wrappings and began to assemble them.

He needed only two or three minutes since the screws were already in place and the wires were marked with adhesive tape so that they could be identified in the dark. Ronen worked quickly, surprised he could not hear his heart beating.

Then came an interruption from straight ahead: a car had entered the parking area surrounding Abu-Khaled's building, had wound its way back to the hedge behind which Ronen was kneeling and was flooding the hedge with light. He froze; there was no point in lying down or backing away. His only chance was that the driver would not notice him through the hedge. One blinding headlight shone directly into his eyes, so he was forced to lower them. The time it took for this invisible driver to finish whatever he was doing in the car was endless. What was taking him so long? Had he noticed him? Ronen was afraid to move a muscle. And if the man had noticed him, what should he do? Attack him? A small dagger he had bought as a souvenir was in the flight bag. And what if the guard had left his booth? Or if there was more than one person in the car? Should he run away? To where? He didn't even have a car in the vicinity. And what about the charge, which was lying there exposed? Should he leave it as it was? These were the problems of new recruits; you could get kicked off the course for such idiotic planning. What had he been thinking? That just because he really wanted it to happen it would? That standard operational conduct – which would have required an entire team for such an operation – had come about haphazardly, and illogically?

The engine died and the light faded. Ronen was surrounded by silence. He lifted his eyes and his muscles grew tense. He had to be ready for anything. The door of the car swung open and the inside light went on, reaching Ronen as well. Don't move, don't breathe. Only his eyes moved, in the direction of the place where the driver would step out. He could see the man in shadow as he bent to remove something from the car.

The voice of the security guard, asking something like, "Worked late today, huh?" made Ronen's blood freeze. The guard was outside his booth. The man stood up straight and answered, "As usual." They chatted for a few minutes

– Ronen could not understand the conversation – while the car door remained open and the light continued to shine on him.

Ronen moved involuntarily when the door slammed shut. The double beep of the car alarm caused the car lights to shine on him once again, but the voices of the driver and the guard were fading, and now Ronen could hear the beating of his heart, as if for the previous few minutes the volume had been lowered to nothing. They were saying goodbye to one another. The man entered the building and the stairwell lights went on. And the guard?

Ronen peered through the hedge. The guard had returned to his booth. Time to get back to work.

He quickly finished assembling the charge and picked it up carefully, even though there was no real danger of an explosion without the remote-control. Still, nobody enjoyed handling several pounds of explosives. He lifted first one leg then the other over the hedge and, stooped, crept towards Abu-Khaled's car, removing the tools from his pocket and slid under the car.

The attachment went quickly and uneventfully. Occasionally metal would hit metal and he would freeze, but what sounded to him like a gong did not even reach the guard in his booth. He affixed both parts of the charge into place with duct tape and reinforced them with metal bands, checked to make sure that the antenna cable connecting the two parts was fastened tightly and then slipped back out from under the car. He listened for a moment; the guard was apparently still inside his booth so he crouched once again and made his way back to the hedge, stepped over it stealthily, gathered the empty wrappings into his bag, took his overcoat, and walked towards the street. In the street light he could see just how dirty he was. He put his coat on and continued walking towards the centre of town. In two hours Abu-Khaled and his friends would be flying sky-high.

Ronen parked in the farthest corner of the underground car park at the Sheraton. This would allow him – if necessary – to traverse the length of the garage on foot in search of Abu-Khaled's car. There was as yet not a sign of enhanced security. He took the lift from the car park straight to his floor thus avoiding passing through the lobby, where he risked others noticing the dirt on the bottoms of his trousers, on his shoes and on his face.

The magnetic card opened the door with a light click. Ronen closed the door behind him and turned on the hall light. He removed his overcoat, hung it on a hook by the door and made for the elegant bathroom. His shirt was indeed dirty, and there were oil stains on his hands and face. He took off his shirt and washed his hands and face. With a towel draped round his neck he left the bathroom and went to turn on the television.

There, sitting comfortably on a cushioned armchair at the other side of the room, he found Gadi. Ronen recoiled for an instant then burst out laughing. He finished drying his hands on the towel and turned on the lights.

"Why should I be surprised? You've found dozens of 'Abus' and broken in to their rooms, so of course it wouldn't be a big deal for you to catch up with me. Still, congratulations on a job well done. I haven't been here long."

Ronen could not tell whether Gadi was enjoying the situation or whether he was still being the professional when he said, quietly, "You're no 'Abu' to me, Ronen, but yes, the technique is the same."

"The goal, too," Ronen said, finishing his thought.

"It's really too bad you feel that way. I'm here for you. If I haven't made that clear to you yet, then I've failed miserably. But we'll both pay the price."

"The door is that way," Ronen said, motioning grandly with his arm.

Ronen had no desire to reignite their debate. It wouldn't get them anywhere, since Gadi's arguments were predictable and his own mind was set on carrying out his mission at any cost. How could Gadi be such a pawn, such a puppet? A year ago he had wanted not only to pick off Abu-Khaled but to wait until they could get him together with a bunch of his cronies. His request had been turned down, and he had accepted that. Now it seemed that the Mossad wanted him, Ronen – the one who was about to achieve exactly what they had originally set out to achieve – apprehended, so naturally Gadi would comply.

Ronen went to the mini-bar, took out a small bottle of whisky and poured two glasses. He handed one to Gadi and sat facing him.

Gadi, however, was not about to abandon his efforts at persuasion.

"Let's say you don't care about anyone. Let's say

everyone screwed you. So what? What right do you have to decide that you're going to kill a man, complicating matters for an entire nation. Who do you think you are, God?"

Ronen finished his whisky and clamped his mouth tightly shut for a second, then said, "I really don't feel like I'm God, but you know who does? The Prime Minister, who selects who he wants to kill from the hit list you people give him. And you too, all of you who dare to put such lists together. It doesn't matter to me if that's the Research Division or the Intelligence Department or the Mossad chief – and you, Gadi, you're a part of that. You act like God's adjutants: yesterday you decided to put someone to death and today you're going to pardon him because he has a new job. Or perhaps you're all omniscient, like God, and you know whether tomorrow he's going to kill someone or not."

Ronen stood up and paced the room clenching his empty glass. Gadi studied him with interest. This was a different Ronen; he was talking about things that all the squad members lived with for years without daring to discuss. Each did his own private soul-searching, which they usually managed to repress, shielding their hearts behind protective armour since just about anyone looking for decisive answers to such questions would need to put his gun aside and admit it was not for him. Even the very few who could manage to continue this work would have to confirm for themselves each and every target, would need to be convinced that warning the target or merely injuring him was not an option. But no organization could withstand such behaviour.

Gadi himself could not help but interfere with the considerations of the Classification Department, whose job it was to recommend whether to spy on a target, or recruit him as an agent, or even, rarely, kill him. He asked questions, clarified matters and posed obstacles with regard to the need for assassinating every single target. Could they be certain he had "blood on his hands" and that he was continuing to carry out attacks? Had they considered and eliminated every other possibility? He was very suspicious of "bureaucratic" assassinations: the researchers felt obliged to give warnings, the Classification Department felt pressure to point the finger, the managers wanted to provide work for their employees and the Operations Division needed to justify its existence. As a squad commander and the spokesman for his subordinates, the difficult questions he posed were somehow bearable, even though there were complaints against him that he was poking into other people's business: there were those who did the research, those who suggested targets, those who made the decisions, and those who carried out the operation.

Gadi had always had the feeling that Ronen was unable to shield himself in that protective armour, but now he was saying much more than that.

"I was a foot or two away from his daughter. I waited for you to tell me to abort the mission because she was there. But God doesn't have mercy on the children of terrorists. Nor does the Mossad, or you for that matter. And I was only the messenger. So don't you dare accuse me of thinking I'm God."

The implication was clear, even though Ronen did not volunteer to finish his line of thought. But nevertheless he had revealed something that he had not dared to even when his colleagues had incriminated him.

Gadi replayed the whole scene in his mind. He had been standing across the street. John, in the escape car, was parked by the building next door. Ronen was at the entrance to the building, at the top of the stairs. Abu-Khaled got out of his car, which had stopped at the bottom of the staircase, waved goodbye and began mounting the stairs. Ronen had approached him and pulled out his gun. Just then a little girl jumped out of the car and ran up the stairs after her father, calling, 'Yabba, Yabba'. No one knew she was in the car. Abu-Khaled turned back towards her; the driver, startled, got out of the car and was coming after her. And there was Ronen, standing with his long silencer gun drawn, not shooting.

Shoot, Gadi said into the mouthpiece of the transmitter clipped to his shirt collar, Shoot now. But Ronen stood, frozen. The driver saw him and shouted. Abu-Khaled turned in the direction his driver was staring and froze in horror, face to face with the barrel of the gun. His daughter was clinging to his trousers, calling him. Fire, Gadi said. Instead, Ronen lowered the gun, and moved to the side of the staircase, never taking his eyes off Abu-Khaled.

Gadi knew that in a moment there would be rioting. "John, now, get him fast!" he ordered. John took off with a screech, passed Abu-Khaled's car and threw open the door. Ronen raced down the stairs and jumped in.

The picture became clear in Gadi's mind. So that was what had prevented Ronen from shooting! They had seen the girl, she'd even been mentioned in the inquiry. But Ronen had never even hinted that that had been the reason he had failed to shoot, and no one from the squad had ever raised that possibility.

It had happened that the squad had called off hits when a car they were about to bomb was found to be ferrying family members, but no one had ever failed to pull the trigger in the presence of a family member. And like everyone who had studied the history of their division, Ronen had heard about such operations, about men killed next to their wives, about fathers killed in the presence of their children. He had heard and had kept silent. Was he ashamed? Was that why he hadn't revealed the reason? Did it seem unprofessional to him? Naive? Childish? An abuse of the trust put in him at long last? Perhaps even stupid and irresponsible, in light of the consequences?

Gadi placed a hand on Ronen's shoulder. "No one can blame you for failing to shoot under such circumstances," he said quietly. But at the same time he heard deep inside him another voice which said, Either shoot or don't draw your gun; assassinations are not a game for boy scouts. And a third voice asking, Is it true that professionalism is more important than the look in the eyes of a small child? And what would he himself have done had he pulled out his gun and only then noticed the child? In the past he had seen, while gathering intelligence, the children of his victims. But he had never stood facing them as he fired his gun.

Gadi did not have a chance to answer his own questions. Ronen shook off his hand and walked to the other side of the room, bristling. "First of all, you're only beginning to understand what went on there. And second, it's a little late now."

"So think about his little girl now, Ronen," Gadi said.

Ronen turned on him sharply. "Right now all I can think about is those people killed in Afula because of him, and about *their* children. And about how that may be because of my failure. I hate all of you for the fact that now I have to choose between the children of some Abu and the children of some Cohen."

"Choose your own daughter, Ronen, who's going to be fatherless soon."

Ronen went to the mini-bar and took out another small bottle. "Enough. Leave me alone. I don't have the strength for your bullshit *and* mine at the same time. You're not my commander here."

Ronen filled his glass again and moved towards Gadi, whose own glass was untouched, and it was then that Gadi noticed the dirt on his shoes and trousers. His face darkened.

"You've been messing with his car."

Ronen froze in his tracks, astonished, then followed Gadi's gaze to his trousers and his shoes. Gadi put his glass down and rose from his chair, pushing brusquely past Ronen on his way to the bathroom. All the sympathy and compassion he had felt for Ronen in those past few minutes evaporated the moment he laid eyes on the dirty shirt on the marble counter and the residue of dirt and oil in the sink. He emerged from the bathroom with the shirt in his hand.

"You've wired his car."

"Good job, Sherlock," Ronen said with a cynical grin on his face.

Gadi's face was grave. Where had Ronen got hold of an explosive charge? Had he improvised something, had he managed to smuggle in the materials, or perhaps bought them in Beirut? In any case, why wasn't he already on his way out of the country? Or had he caught him just as he had been about to leave?

Gadi went to the wardrobe and saw Ronen's clothes hanging there. No, he hadn't been planning a quick getaway.

"So it's a delayed-reaction charge," Gadi said, thinking aloud. Ronen watched as Gadi continued searching, his attitude one of interest mixed with scorn.

"You're getting warmer, but you're still a long way off I'm afraid, my dear Watson. I see I was wrong calling you Sherlock."

Gadi was figuring it out, the pieces were fitting together. Ronen was too relaxed, he had time, so it couldn't be a delayed-reaction charge. It must be one he could detonate from a distance! But why had he switched hotels, and to the Sheraton of all places? Ronen was not the type of person to want to commit suicide in luxurious surroundings…it must be taking place right there!

"Abu-Khaled is due here, and you're going to get rid of him using a remote-control." The smile vanished from Ronen's face.

Gadi walked to the window, which overlooked the entrance to the hotel, and parted the curtains. A number of Mercedes were on their way down to the underground car park.

"They're starting to arrive," he said as he turned around, letting the curtain fall back into place. He held out his hand, his face grave. "Give me the remote-control."

Ronen tried to smile. "Of course, sir. That's exactly what I came here to do."

"Ronen, this is no time for games," Gadi said in a tough voice.

"Are you uptight, commander? Maybe we should play hot-and-cold. Start with the acoustic ceiling, maybe I hid it up there?"

"Ronen!" Gadi cried with impatience.

"No? Okay. So what will you give me instead?" he said with a childish smile.

"Ronen," Gadi said, a warning in his voice.

"You've completely lost your sense of humour. Maybe you'd like to torture me? After all, that's the only way you're going to get out of me where the remote-control is hidden."

Gadi went to the window again. The tail of another Mercedes was just disappearing into the underground car park. He turned, slowly, picked up his glass of whisky and drank it down in one gulp. Without a word he handed the glass to Ronen, who took it with a smile.

Gadi had made his decision before handing the glass to Ronen: Ronen refused to give the remote-control to him of his own volition, and a struggle could end in one of them accidentally blowing up the car, either empty or full of people. He would have to put Ronen out of commission if he wanted to locate the remote-control, which was undoubtedly hidden here in the room, and he would have to do it without making any unnecessary noise.

As Ronen was about to open the mini-bar door, Gadi took two quick steps forward closing the gap between them. He raised his right hand over Ronen's left shoulder and planted a shoto chop squarely on his neck. He'd even managed to plan the intensity of the blow which could, if employed to its fullest, kill, by breaking a neck or the vertebrae; it could also cause intense pain if performed with slight hesitation. As he needed Ronen down for only half an hour or so and then alive and well, the blow had to be absolutely precise in its intensity and placement.

Ronen's head bobbed, his knees folded and he collapsed onto the thick carpeting. Gadi's glass fell from his hand.

Gadi leaned down to him immediately, lifting his eyelids and checking his pulse. Ronen was in a deep faint. Gadi lifted the drooping body and placed him on the bed. He removed the laces from Ronen's trainers, which were next to the suitcase, using one to tie Ronen's hands together and then to the headboard, and the other to tie his feet together and to the foot of the bed. He stuck his finger in the space between the shoelace and Ronen's wrists, and then his ankles, to make sure the knot was not too tight, wouldn't cut off his circulation. The space would enable Ronen to break free when he awakened, but it was preferable to cutting off his blood supply.

Now Gadi began searching for the remote-control. If he found it he would prevent Ronen from carrying out his plan and it would give him time to decide – perhaps even with the permission of headquarters – whether and when to disengage and remove the bomb from Abu-Khaled's car. As long as the remote-control was not in his hands, Gadi knew, Ronen could not plunge them all into deep trouble in a split second.

He turned the pockets of Ronen's coat and trousers inside out. He then dumped the contents of his suitcase on the bed – nothing. He looked for a secret compartment in the suitcase but found none. He shook out the pile of clothing in the wardrobe, and the socks and underwear in the wardrobe drawer. Then he overturned the flight bag, and a collection of empty containers tumbled out. Gadi stopped to breathe deeply. This was where Ronen had been keeping the components. So there really was a charge, it was not just a wild guess. The guy was courageous, and not stupid. Crazy, but professional. Gadi felt enormous pressure building inside him. He lifted the mattress, shifting Ronen a bit. Nothing. He climbed onto a chair, lifted the acoustic ceiling and peered in. There was almost no chance of finding it there. The drawers of the desk were empty, and there was nothing behind the seat cushions nor behind the pictures on the wall.

Where, damn it, could it be? Gadi checked Ronen. He was still out cold, but would not be so for much longer. And how long could he keep Ronen tied up, anyway? Under the present circumstances the best option seemed to be to keep him restrained until the gathering was over and the participants had dispersed. The immediate danger would have passed and then he would figure out what to do. But it was impossible to predict how Ronen would react when he came to, he was liable to go wild. Gadi could not stun him again, the damage would be too great.

The need to disassemble the charge while Ronen was neutralized was becoming more and more acute. A feeling of desperation seized Gadi; he sat down in an armchair. This really was not in his plans: it was one thing to catch up with Ronen, to speak frankly with him, to argue with him, even fight with him. But now, under terrible time constraints, to locate Abu-Khaled's car, sneak under it, and remove an explosive charge – that was complete madness. The place was undoubtedly swarming with security guards and drivers. And Ronen could, in the meantime, wake up, and simply activate the bomb while he, Gadi, was under the car. It was all too depressing, but what choice did he have if he really wished to avert this huge mess?

Gadi stood up heavily. He recalled seeing a screwdriver in Ronen's flight bag; he picked it out and put it in his pocket, but among the rest of the tools he found neither a torch nor cutters. How could he succeed in removing the charge in the dark? He glanced at Ronen, still out cold. He had no choice. He would simply have to get the job done in the five or ten minutes he still had at his disposal. If he could not manage to defuse the bomb or remove it from the car then at least he would disconnect its antenna cable.

Gadi went to the door, hung the Do Not Disturb sign outside, pressed the lock button and closed it behind him.

Aloni, head of the Foreign Relations Division, which was responsible for contacts with overseas intelligence agencies, entered the small meeting room next to the chief's office with three of his department heads. Doron and Benny, the division psychologist, were already seated across from Beaufort while Avigur, the office chief, sat at his side. Beaufort was reading a draft proposal of the operational order prepared by Doron and did not look up. Aloni was oblivious to the sombre atmosphere. He proffered his hand warmly to Doron and Benny and took a seat, his aides at his side.

The previous evening Beaufort had briefed Aloni on the situation and asked him to look into whether there was some foreign intelligence service – preferably West European, and particularly strong in Beirut – that could be approached and asked to check out Abu-Khaled's home and office in order to find Ronen and detain him, or at least give him a message. He had spoken again to Aloni, giving him the news of Gadi's presence and now wanted to hear the opinions of Aloni's relevant department heads.

The man in charge of contacts with the CIA spoke first and stated right away that no US embassy vehicle would go near the Shi'ite neighbourhoods and that American intelligence capabilities in Beirut began and ended with electronic surveillance. His counterpart in the Western Europe department estimated that there were several intelligence services that could patrol the Shi'ite areas but that they would do no more than that. "We've observed them during joint operations in other Arab countries; they know how to speak eloquently, and of course they can move around in diplomatic vehicles and engage in wiretapping from their embassies, but they have no operational squads, certainly not the kind that could abduct Ronen." He also expressed the worry that information about two Israeli operatives on the loose in Beirut could leak from the embassies; who knew what kind of connections these services were cultivating, under the table, with Hezbollah and with Syria.

The Mossad representative in Germany, who happened to be in Israel and was asked to join the meeting, said that the German secret services were not equipped for a hostile operation like an abduction in Beirut. "Worse still," he added, "they would certainly exploit such a request to lend legitimacy to their overtures of friendship towards Hezbollah, just like they did towards the Iranians when we asked for help tracking down our missing soldiers and Ron Arad in particular. There's no point in giving legitimacy to that."

No one present felt it was possible to trust any of the East European services in such a sensitive matter, even if it were portrayed as a measure to save the Middle East from renewed conflagration.

They discussed the possibility of requesting that their Western colleagues open the gates of their embassies to Gadi or Ronen in the event that they needed asylum, or if Gadi were to overpower Ronen. Indeed, the conversation that Doron had had with Helena made it clear that there was contact between the two, but not the nature of that contact. After briefly analyzing the various options, Aloni rejected that one: "If Gadi or Ronen reach an embassy with the Lebanese in pursuit, no delegation will open its gates, even if they've promised to do so. And if a foreign embassy does admit them to their premises, and the Lebanese find out about it in the course of an investigation, the result will be a political crisis in which Israel will be stuck in the middle. I can even envisage a scene in which Hezbollah lays siege on the embassy, demanding that the 'Zionist agents' be turned over. God help us – and the foreign delegation – figure out what to do if we find ourselves in *that* situation."

Doron added that in any case there would be no opportunity to notify Ronen and Gadi that they could seek asylum in a certain embassy even if there was a delegation that would agree to it. Finally, the danger of a leak quashed that option.

The bottom line that Aloni presented was that no foreign intelligence service operating in Beirut was capable of providing assistance. In other words, his division had nothing to offer. There was no safety net in Lebanon, no possibility of a soft landing; any failure would be total.

Beaufort thanked Aloni's team and dismissed them, but requested that Aloni himself stay. Before the three department heads had even departed, he had picked up the draft of the operational order again and continued to peruse it.

*

Doron's face was inscrutable. The meeting had given him a melancholic feeling of déja vu: the plan to stage an operation in the Shi'ite quarter of Beirut using a sloppy battle procedure, a banner of failure already floating above it all.

He knew only too well the consequences of the operational order that Beaufort had instructed him to submit and which he had had the head of the Planning Department prepare according to his own guidelines. There had been Israeli operations in Beirut before – Doron himself had participated in and commanded some of them – so it was clear to him that the common denominator between all those that had succeeded was meticulous planning, highly detailed intelligence gathering and uncompromising preparations. Success was built on small details, each and every one given proper attention.

Similarly, failure there was built on haste. The common denominator of all failed operations – there had been very few, but failures tended to reverberate – was a foreshortened schedule from which they were forced to cut whole sections of the battle procedure. True, this too was part of Mossad heritage: in the seventies and eighties, when he was a young member of the squad, they would land in Cyprus, Athens or Rome on the heels of a terrorist just arrived from an Arab country; it had happened that they had received intelligence briefings at the airport, had done their basic planning while searching for the target in cafés frequented by Palestinians. The strength of the squad back then was in its advance reconnaissance work, which led to close familiarity with contacts, nightclubs, mosques, brothels and meeting places frequented by terrorists during their short visits.

The worst mistakes were made when this rolling method of operations – in which the squad was given the freedom to locate the target and make its hit according to the judgement of the commander in the field – was employed in places with stringent security, places less familiar to the squad. You could not perform a rolling operation in Beirut, nor could you in Amman. In those cities the operation had to be planned down to the last detail and carried out only after intensive intelligence gathering and meticulous preparations.

Doron had been called to army headquarters when someone discovered he had a foreign passport. After a short training course he found himself chasing terrorists all over Europe. The list of his operations and successes was in the hundreds. Ironically, it was Doron – who had started during the days of improvised operations – who would present proper planning methods to the squad, and later to the entire division. Ironic, too, that he had now presented the Mossad chief with the draft of an operational order for a mission that shouted of appalling improvisation, violent, coarse activity in territory that was not familiar enough: an operation that would be nearly impossible to carry out without drawing undue attention and that stood little chance of succeeding without casualties.

In the end he had submitted his plan because he felt Beaufort's distress at having to present the Prime Minister with some solution – any solution – to this entanglement, and because of his own feelings of guilt that it was two of his own subordinates who had brought it about. Doron was well aware he had alienated both of them, that each had a bellyful of complaints and anger against him, at least enough to hide their true intentions from him. Not only Ronen, whose fall he did little to break, failing to find him proper employment; but also Gadi, who was not blind to Doron's attempts at removing him from his position. It wasn't that he didn't trust him any more – Doron knew that Gadi would perform any mission better than anyone else – but because Gadi had been walking around since being acquitted by the commission with his guilt written across his face. Around Gadi, Doron's own guilt at being exonerated stood out, guilt that he refused to acknowledge. He would feel much better if the head of his main operational squad was a person who owed him his appointment, not someone who felt himself Doron's equal and flaunted his independence too much.

In the document he'd submitted to Beaufort, Doron emphasized the risks: an exchange of fire with guards at the target's office or home, pursuit under fire, the possible need for rescue by sea or air. That was how the Mossad chief would have to present it to the Prime Minister.

He knew, however, that with these kinds of risks one did not embark on an operation. So how was it that he, with his brilliant, prudent record, had fallen into the same trap once again? Why couldn't he say to the chief, Sorry, I have no adequate plan to present to you? And weren't they trying to return to "zero mishaps", a slogan that had been empty of meaning for quite some time. Was it simply because it was not the tradition of the division to say I have no plan, or I can't do it? For a moment Doron felt strange in his own skin. This was not him – the moderate, cool-tempered guy whose considerations were always to the point.

He would sit, later, face to face with the Mossad chief and tell him this. After all, what was written in the operational order was entirely theoretical to Beaufort. The nuances escaped him; he couldn't know whether the squad would really manage to pass themselves off as Lebanese, or how awful an escape under fire would be. He had to explain it all to him. Later.

Beaufort finished perusing the five pages in his hands, placed them on the desk without a word, removed his glasses, leaned back and glanced at the men assembled.

"This plan of yours needs a lot of discussion," he said, looking at Doron with a poker face, "as does the impotence of *your* people," he added, turning his gaze to Aloni. "But first, to have a better idea of what's in store for us if we don't send anyone in, I want to talk about Gadi and Ronen, so I've asked the division psychologist to join us."

Benny cleared his throat. The chief looked at him and continued speaking. "Assuming we know what each of them set out to do, I want to hear your assessments with regard to the anticipated consequences. I have to present our recommendations to the Prime Minister this evening."

He had no intention of letting them float all kinds of

plans that were in his eyes unacceptable and then having to present those, too, to the Prime Minister. "Allow me to define the main options," he said. "The first is to let Gadi do the job. The second is to send him assistance, which would probably be the Mistaravim squad, more or less along the lines of the plan you gave me, Doron. The third is to try and bring Gadi back home and leave Ronen to his own devices. Whatever happens with him, happens; we won't take any responsibility. Perhaps you are not aware of this, but Ronen is an independent citizen of the State of Israel who travelled to Lebanon of his own free will, without authorization. He is not on any mission for the State of Israel or for the Mossad. The fact that we are gathered here to discuss the possibility of rescuing him is beyond what justice calls for. Legally we have no obligation towards him. Morally, well, that's up for debate. We can only guess at his motivation, and we have reason to believe his mental health is shaky. I say all this in relation to the third option, which we cannot completely disregard. But let's start with the first one. Doron."

"Both Gadi and Ronen are familiar with Beirut," he began, to the point as usual, "which means that Ronen should have no trouble locating Abu-Khaled. And Gadi has apparently managed to find Ronen. But it's not clear to me what exactly that means. I imagine that the arena for their meeting will most probably be around Abu-Khaled's office, which is on a major road, and not around his house, which is a very dangerous area."

"That's not what I meant when I said consequences," the chief said, cutting him off. "And as I've already told you, you need to solve this problem of lack of communication. It is unacceptable that we have only indirect contact with Gadi and we are forced to feel our way in the dark."

Doron blushed and ignored the reprimand, for which he had no good answer. He continued straight to the bottom line of Beaufort's brief. "If Ronen places the charge, Gadi's chances of preventing him from setting it off are very slim."

"I'd like to say something," Benny said, breaking into the embarrassing silence that followed.

"Please," Beaufort said, gesturing with his hand.

"The question of how the meeting between them will end is not just an operational question. Complex interpersonal relations are involved."

Doron, who was not pleased with what Benny was saying, interrupted. "I don't think the chief is interested in a psychological profile. He wants the bottom line."

Benny, taken aback by Doron's sudden aggressiveness, restrained himself from addressing the insult and simply answered the question: "The bottom line is that Ronen is apparently sufficiently deranged to pull this off, and Gadi may not be the person to prevent him from doing so. The issue is not Gadi's operational capabilities versus Ronen's, but rather Gadi as a representative of the organization versus Ronen, whom the organization abandoned and deserted – in his eyes," Benny hastened to add when he saw the sharp expression on the chief's face. "Gadi as the successful one versus Ronen, who was blamed for the failure and needs to prove otherwise. And ultimately, the competition over Naamah will always be in the background. Even if Ronen perceives his mistake, the moment he sees Gadi he is liable to carry out the assassination simply to score a point."

"That's one fat bottom line," Doron said with a smile that contained no small measure of mistrust. But Benny continued, unflustered.

"As for Gadi, I can't ignore the possibility that subconsciously he might *want* Ronen to go all the way with this madness, just as I can't ignore the possibility – again subconscious – that Gadi will let Ronen beat him in order to settle the score. The complexity is such that I would not attach too much importance to the simple fact that contact has been made between them."

Deep inside, Benny couldn't help feeling admiration for Gadi's tenacious madness, whose goal was to take a sword to the Gordian knot that the entire division – operatives, Mistaravim, intelligence officers, technocrats – and certainly all the rest of the Mossad were unable to untie. Still, he felt that these two men who believed the organization owed them something might team up in secret.

"I've been talking with their wives since this business began," he said, as if to give credence to his words. "They've each got a lot to get off their chests, and if you'd hear them out," he said directly to the chief, "you'd get a feel for the complexity of the matter. Incidentally, Gadi also has complaints against the Mossad, feels he's being undermined, and I can't pretend there won't be a situation in which there could be some sort of collusion between the two of them."

Now Benny could see the dissatisfaction in the chief's eyes, too. Beaufort could already sense the impending commission of inquiry that might pit him against two widows.

"Set up a Ladies' Day for me tomorrow, let's hear what they're feeling, let's figure out how we can help them and how they can help us," the chief said to Avigur. "I asked a simple question," Beaufort returned to the men facing him, "and I didn't ask you all here to lecture me. What I understand from you," he said to the psychologist, "is that the Gadi-option is not good enough. Psychologically speaking, we can't be certain of the outcome. Which is the very same thing I understood from you, Doron, operationally." The two men nodded.

"So, practically speaking, we're down to two real options: the Mistaravim squad or leaving Ronen to his own devices." Beaufort thanked Benny, who stood to leave with a heavy heart. He had had a lot more to say.

Sarah took advantage of Benny's departure to slip in with a small tea trolley. There was soda water and black coffee for the chief, cappuccino from the machine for Doron, Aloni and Avigur. The chief sipped his coffee and felt a certain sluggishness seep through his body. He knew what the two division heads had to offer: war on the one hand, surrender on the other.

In the draft Doron had given him he had found expressions like "fighting on the streets of Beirut"... "wounded"... "military intervention needed for rescue": in short, a real calamity. Slippery old Aloni had brought his team of department heads so that he would not have to say himself that he had surrendered in advance, that he could not offer any assistance, and that in fact he did not want to ask for any help from other agencies, as though his main concern was gaining points with them. When Beaufort himself had been active in Lebanon he had, in addition to pulling strings with the Phalangists, made sure to forge bold connections with the local heads of several foreign intelligence services operating in Beirut in the event that the Phalangists changed their tune. Aloni had neglected that area.

Thirty-five years in the Mossad had taught Beaufort to mistrust the rising stars, the up-and-coming youngsters. Not that Aloni was young anymore, but when he himself had left the Foreign Relations Division he was a decade older than Aloni. A decade meant lots more contacts, personal connections, joint operations, secrets that offered him a link to the heads of other agencies. When he and the head of foreign relations for the Italian secret service cooked together during reciprocal visits, it wasn't only pasta they were preparing: a relationship was formed enabling classified activities that would never have received official approval. Now was precisely the time to make good use of those relationships. But since today's stars barely lasted one two-year term in office on their climb to the top, there was no opportunity to forge such connections.

As far as Doron and his people were concerned, the chief had even graver misgivings. They had not yet comprehended that the James Bond era was over, that no

European nation was prepared to have Mossad operatives roaming its streets and wiping out Palestinian terrorists. Nearly every country in the world had come to an understanding with the Palestinians and were unwilling to serve as a battleground for Middle Eastern "tribal warfare". He was well acquainted with the heads of various secret service agencies around the world: polished, well-educated analysts they were, highly skilled at intelligence gathering and analysis but far removed from any sense of adventure. All they wanted was peace and quiet, and they were all of a generation for whom Israel was a strong nation occupied with oppressing another. It was only in theory that they knew of the circumstances that had brought about the present situation: the Holocaust or Israel's struggle for independence against ongoing aggression by its Arab neighbours or Palestinian unwillingness to accept Israel's right to exist. Their considerations were global; Israel was a mere drop in the ocean vis-à-vis Arab countries and the Islamic world. Even when Islamic terror hit them and they decided to fight back, they did not want Israel's assistance, and certainly had no tolerance for Israeli machismo on their territory. But this was what Doron and his predecessors, and their men, too, were far from comprehending.

The reactions of the man in the street, the media, and the country's leaders to the few failures over the previous years had taught him something else, which this, too, the operations people had not internalized: the Israeli public had no tolerance for failure. The media would tear to pieces anyone who had failed or was in any way responsible for a failure. They would dissect the circumstances, the plan, the deviations in carrying it out; no stone would be left unturned in the witch hunt. Each correspondent would outdo the next in exposing damaging data, each commentator would compete with the next in sarcastic remarks, each politician would claim greater innocence than his colleagues, each army officer would make denials of his knowledge or involvement faster than his comrades. Whereas it had been possible to present the Israeli public with justification for the mission that had failed one year earlier in Beirut, what was there to offer the public *this* time?

Beaufort watched the two silent division heads seated in front of him, the one with downcast blue eyes and the other with a dark, intelligent expression that was scanning with interest his own impervious face with what seemed like a hint of provocation. Would salvation come from these two?

The frustration that Beaufort was feeling because the two generals facing him had brought no good news was compounded by an additional realization: that he had brought this situation upon himself. Gadi's requests for various positions for Ronen had reached his desk, and he had rejected them out of hand. Further, he had backed up Doron in his attempts at bringing Gadi's tenure with the Mossad to an end. He had allowed him to make a deal with Izzy, Gadi's deputy, about taking command of the squad in the near future, had instructed the head of personnel not to offer Gadi any suitable position.

He knew about Gadi's long list of successes, knew that the organization owed him a lot and that there were few appropriate jobs for him at headquarters. But he had adopted, too easily he saw now, the stance that it was preferable to distance anyone touched by failure from the Mossad. Further, he had convinced himself too quickly that such a stance would pass along a positive message: that failure was not tolerated. For some time the word around the Mossad had been that his hiring and firing policies were bereft of all humane consideration. But was that not the efficient way to run such an organization, in which every mistake was critical?

Beaufort could not deny that he had imagined himself telling the Prime Minister that he had, quietly, dismissed all of those involved in the Beirut fiasco; there would follow a small laudatory announcement in the papers under the title, "Spring Cleaning Among Mossad Personnel". Now, instead, there would be an article entitled "Mossad Spinning Out of Control" and he would have to explain to the Prime Minister how it was that, under his nose, a dismissed operative had become deranged without the organization knowing a thing about it and a high-ranking commander had gone after him without authorization. On top of all this he would have to present two miserable options, which, in his opinion, weren't options at all. He'd known that even before they'd sat to discuss them.

205

At the bottom of the emergency stairwell to the underground car park, Gadi realized that he had no logical explanation for what he was doing there. Because he had known about the parking problems at the Sheraton and that the concierge would insist on parking his car for him – especially since he looked European – he had left it at his hotel and taken a taxi. Now he would need to spend time in the underground car park, and possibly emerge from there filthy dirty. He bit his lip at this realization; if he had thought about it just minutes earlier he would have taken Ronen's overcoat and wrapped himself in it. But stupidly, he hadn't. Damn it! How had he got himself into another unplanned operation, and on the same target? But really, what choice did he have?

A small and opportunely unlit hallway led Gadi from the stairwell to the car park entrance. Pressing himself up against the wall, he peered into the darkened space. Someone walking around at the far side of the car park drew his attention to a row of Mercedes. On closer inspection he could see two guards, one who was patrolling around the cars and the other who was stationary. It was possible, too, that a driver or two was sleeping in the cars. Gadi bent down low and crept forwards. The Mercedes were all alike in the darkness, he would have to get right up close to them and identify Abu-Khaled's car by its number plates.

He crouched behind a car that was only a few feet away from the row of Mercedes. To reach them he would have only a few seconds, from the moment the patrol guard passed until he reached the end of the row and turned around. Taking into consideration the fact that several minutes had already passed since he had left Ronen and the sound of a huge explosion could strike at any time, he hadn't a moment for hesitation. He darted from car to car in the row parallel to the Mercedes, trying to identify Abu-Khaled's number plate. It was difficult in the dark, but he managed to scan all but two. He waited for the guard to pass and then crawled quickly to the two cars in question. Up close he was able to identify Abu-Khaled's Mercedes and he squeezed underneath it.

A feverish search in the usual locations for a charge turned up nothing. Had Ronen broken into the car and planted the bomb inside? Under the driver's seat, for example? That would be logical, if he were using a small quantity of explosives. The thought filled Gadi with fear. If that were the case he would have no choice but to take the guards out – and there were two of them, armed of course. It wasn't impossible, but he had no need of any further entanglements. He would continue to feel his way across the bottom of the car.

Just above the main axle, Gadi's fingers located the charge.

Ronen opened his eyes and tried to get up from the bed, but a sharp pain in his neck kept him glued to the mattress. Slowly comprehension dawned on him: that bastard screwed me once again. A wave of hatred washed through him. He lifted his head off the mattress as far as he could manage and looked around, but could not see Gadi.

"Open these, you son of a bitch," he called in a restrained voice into the room, but no answer came. Where was he? Had he gone to get help? Perhaps some of the squad members had arrived in the meantime? Ronen pulled his arms and legs with all his strength and the canopy bed shook violently; the bed was more beautiful than well-made, so that when he pulled again the headboard came loose. Fortunately for Ronen, the canopy did not fall on him. He sat up, moved his hands – which were still bound together and attached to the headboard – to his lap, and began working at the knot with his teeth. The lightly tied shoelace made his task easy and in no time he was working at releasing his feet. Free, he jumped from the bed, but felt a sharp pain in his neck again. The room was spinning around him and he sank back onto the bed.

When he could focus once more he noticed his belongings strewn around the room, the open wardrobe and drawers. Had Gadi managed to find the remote-control? He lifted himself up, moved to the bedside table and stopped: it was too easy. The bed had come apart too easily, his hands had been tied too loosely, the blow he'd sustained hadn't been that strong, even the obvious way the room was messed up, as if to leave no doubt that Gadi had searched for the remote-control was all too easy. Perhaps Gadi was watching him right now from some corner, to see where he would fish it out from? That old fox was completely capable of it. Afterwards he would smile and slap his back amicably. Ronen looked up; in two spots the acoustic ceiling had not been returned to its proper place. Is that where he was? The round wooden chair that had been in front of the dressing table was directly under one of them, so Ronen climbed on it and poked his head through the gap in the ceiling. Gadi wasn't there. He checked the second spot and scanned the room once again. No sign.

For an instant Ronen felt faintly satisfied, it appeared that Gadi the Great hadn't even thought of this manoeuvre; instead he had gone to get help, or was underneath the car trying to defuse the charge…

Defuse the charge! That would certainly be like Gadi. At this very moment he could be under the car putting an end to my operation, that jerk!

Ronen shot over to the bedside table, yanked out the lowest drawer and stuck his hand inside. The remote-control was still there, stuck to the back with tape. A rush of contradictory thoughts hit his brain: so Gadi hadn't found it, that was lucky. What an idiot I am, I could have activated it by thrusting my hand in so carelessly. I'll have to take it out with caution. What if he's already managed to defuse the charge? And if not, what should I do now, run and stop him? Bring the guards down on him? Set off the bomb? Maybe I can even set it off from here, right now. But what if Gadi's there now? Or what if nobody's there at all, not Abu-Khaled or any other Abu? Each thought brought its own wave of heat or cold, its shivers, which surged together with the dizziness Ronen felt each time he bent over or stood up.

First he would check out the situation, then he would decide. He went to the bed, where his clothes and belongings were scattered, put on a shirt and hurried to unlock the door. He peered into the hall. He couldn't help but smile at the Do Not Disturb sign hanging from the knob. Even in these circumstances, Gadi had remained Gadi. Ronen moved quickly to the lift.

The lift kept moving up and down between the second floor and the underground garage. When at last it reached Ronen, he pressed the garage button but the elevator stopped on the second floor. The doors opened to a hotel security guard with an armed Hezbollah man in camouflage. Ronen's heart stopped for a moment as the two stood where they were looking him over. His appearance appeased them apparently, and they turned around to face the Moslem clerics making their way down the hallway to the lifts. Beyond them, at the end of the hall, Ronen could make out a sea of turbans, head scarves and army berets. Everyone was in motion, the lecture was obviously over. So what now? Would he descend to the basement with them?

The security guard and the Hezbollah man still had their backs to him. Ronen stuck out his hand quickly and pushed the close button. As the doors shut Ronen caught the angry gaze of the two men as they turned around. The lift continued its descent.

The telephone next to Haramati's bed rang.

"It's Milken." The familiar voice shook him awake. "Get a pen and paper."

He lit a lamp to find the pen and notebook he kept on

his bedside table. His girlfriend grumbled a complaint and fell back to sleep.

"You remember that bastard from the café on Bograshov Street?" Milken didn't wait for an answer. "Well, I've got something on him."

That's what he's waking me up in the middle of the night to tell me? A few weeks had passed since then, Haramati thought bitterly. "How do you know who he is?"

"That day I got the waitress in the café to write down the number on his motorbike. I checked out his name and address and put them into my database. Now suddenly I've got something big. Have I told you about my friend the chef?"

Haramati couldn't recall.

"He invites me over for a meal every time he needs to screw someone over in his organization. Pretty high up. I've known him since the time I spent overseas working for the paper."

"Deep Throat?" Haramati joked.

"Something like that. Listen. I just got back from a midnight supper at his place, and there's something happening, something very, very sensitive. I need you to fill in a few details for me. He didn't give me everything. Are you ready to write?"

Haramati murmured that he was.

"So, I got two addresses from him, and the first one sounded familiar. I checked it out and bingo! It's the guy from the Bograshov café. Just goes to show you, crime never pays."

"I have no idea what you're talking about," Haramati dared to admit.

"Patience, boy. The second address is somebody important in the Mossad. The story isn't all that clear, but there seems to be some sort of mutiny in the Operations Division and both of them are involved. Some people went out on an operation without authorization – he hasn't told me what or where, but it's going on right now. I need you to work urgently on those two addresses. Who, what, when. The wives are sure to know what's happening, they'll be hypersensitive. So tread carefully. This may be the big opportunity I've been promising you."

Haramati wrote down the addresses.

"I don't hear the killer instinct in your voice," Milken said. "It's not just the scoop: you should start making the world understand that they shouldn't mess with you, that every dog has its day."

"I'll make the rounds tomorrow, and I'll call you for more background," Haramati said, ignoring the end of Milken's sentence.

It's all over for *that* poor slob, Haramati thought with something close to pity, imagining what was in store for the man who had apparently tripped him up that day. He pretty much had it coming, but Milken wouldn't ease up until he'd presented him as a walking joke; within the boundaries of censorship he would distort his name in a way that would allow all his acquaintances to identify him, and he wouldn't stop until he turned him into the village idiot.

✧✧✧

The charge was not affixed in the standard regulation way, but it was attached firmly with metal wires and thick duct tape. Gadi's hands probed the different sections of the charge – the body, the cable, the receiver – in the darkness. He tried with the screwdriver to locate the four screws in the body of the charge but was unsuccessful. He searched with his fingers; there were no holes for screws. The cover of the charge was made from something other than what he was accustomed to. What had Ronen done here?

The lift bell rang. There were footsteps and voices. How could he dismantle the charge and defuse it if there was no way of opening the box? It was all one big improvisation, apparently something Ronen had pulled together. He would have to detach the entire charge from the car, and get it away somewhere to be dealt with later. An engine was turned on in the adjacent row of cars, its lights right on Gadi. He froze. The car pulled away and he continued. Once again his hands, which were sweating, located the metal wires and the duct tape; he began untwisting the knotted wires. The tips cut into his fingers.

The lift bell rang again and again. More voices, more turning on of car engines. Gadi continued undoing the wires. Blood was trickling from his fingertips. There were at least three more metal rings wrapped around the charge and the small receiver. He heard talking and laughing, the door of a nearby car open and shut, and he understood that the conference had ended and that people were beginning to leave. When the pain in his fingers was too great, he began ripping off the wide bands of duct tape that filled the gaps where there were no wires. At best he had only a few more minutes. The cars to his left and right were still in place; at least one had to remain so that he would have somewhere to take cover if he were taken by surprise by Abu-Khaled or his driver.

What he was doing was sheer madness; he would never have authorized a plan like this or carried it out. Suddenly he understood how far he could be drawn in in the heat of the operation itself, how needy he was of boundaries that would keep him from finding himself so dependent on luck. What would happen if all three of the owners of these cars were to arrive together? He should have got out of there before now, he should get out now, he thought: he had tried and failed, now he should get back to Ronen and deal with the remote-control. But what if Ronen was already awake and lying in wait for the Mercedes by his window, the remote-control in his hand? All he needed was perhaps two more minutes to finish dismantling the charge. Perhaps he had the time. At least he could detach the cable that connected the charge to the receiver which would take only a few seconds, and Ronen wouldn't be able to cause any more damage. It was the lesser of the evils. There would be hell to pay when they found the bomb, but at least it wouldn't explode.

The beep of the automatic door lock sounded right in Gadi's ears. A pair of shoes suddenly appeared very close to him and stopped, their tips pointed straight at him. He held his breath. Shit, he was down to the last band of metal around the charge and one around the receiver, and a few rings of adhesive tape. He took a deep breath and continued. The door opened. Another pair of shoes appeared, on the other side of the car, and the passenger door opened, too. He heard voices above him, then more voices coming closer, more feet, and then the back doors opened. One leg disappeared, then the other leg, and the bottom of the car dipped towards his chest. Now he wouldn't be able to roll out as there wasn't enough room for his shoulders in the narrow space left. He would have to slide out on his back, like an upside-down snake. If there was time, that is. Should he go to the right or the left? There were voices on his right, there was no time to unwind even one more wire. The only thing left to do was to detach the antenna cable. His hand felt for the cable, located it and pulled. The whole charge shook, shifted position, but the cable would not come free. The engine started, its shuddering pounded his chest. Gadi began pulling himself out from under the car, the hand holding the cable pulling with all his strength. His head was already exposed, the reverse lights were on, and he continued pushing himself out. Now his legs and torso were exposed, too, but his hand still grasped the cable. The car began to move.

Knowing that the stream of Hezbollah people moving towards the underground car park would hamper him from taking almost any kind of action, Ronen tore off a small sprinkler attached to the ceiling of the elevator and rammed it into the space between the lift door and the garage floor. The lift shook when it received a call from upstairs, but stuck firm.

He scanned the garage, taking note of people milling about the row of Mercedes. He moved quickly towards the adjacent row. One Mercedes, its reverse lights shining, had begun backing up, then it straightened out in the direction of the exit. Ronen tried to make out the passengers. The man next to the window was familiar, and when the passenger in the front seat turned his face towards Ronen, he recognised Abu-Khaled.

Ronen looked away instinctively and thrust his hand into his pocket for the remote-control, but he could not have been seen in the darkness. He aimed the remote-control at the car, which had begun moving slowly forwards. Suddenly, from the corner of his eye, he noticed movement under the car that had been parked alongside Abu-Khaled's Mercedes. He turned his gaze to the dark spot under the car, where he saw a leg disappear. He knew in an instant it was Gadi.

Abu-Khaled's car was moving further away from him, and Ronen was still aiming the remote-control at it, his finger hovering above the button. But the car was still too close to Gadi and the charge underneath it was just level with his body. Fuck you, Gadi, Ronen whispered, a disappointed look spreading across his face. He couldn't press the button, he would have to let the car move at least fifty feet ahead and only then activate it. That would still be in range of the remote-control…

People were walking quickly from the lift, calling

216

angrily. Responses came from the area where the Mercedes were parked. Ronen crouched down and peered through the window of the vehicle nearest him. Another car had edged its way in between him and Abu-Khaled's Mercedes. Every second put distance between Ronen and his prey. Now, at last, Gadi was out of danger. Now at last, whatever would be, would be. Abu-Khaled was almost out of range.

Ronen pressed the button, crouched down and plugged his ears against the roar that never came.

6.

THE TRAINING FACILITY of the Mistaravim squad of Arab impersonators was once, during the British Mandate, a British military base, and several of the buildings, with their long, arched roofs, were still standing. The dunes of coarse sand descending to the sea and an obstacle course left over from the days when the base was used by the cadet corps were now used by Mossad operatives for physical training, while the private strip of beach enabled them to practise marine landings, swimming and deep-sea diving. A large hangar, built between the old buildings and the service road, served as a garage for preparing vehicles for use by the Mistaravim as well as a sports facility and briefing room. The early morning chill hung heavily inside the hangar, so Doron suggested finding a patch of sun outside.

Next to a tree bent away from the angry sea winds was a bench. Two operatives brought another bench from the hangar and placed it behind the first. Four Mistaravim and the squad commander sat wrapped up in their parkas on the first bench, cups of strong black coffee in their hands.

Behind them sat the department heads from Intelligence and Planning and officers from Weaponry and Communications. A few other officials were standing nearby. Doron, head of the division, stood before them.

In spite of the fact that just the day before Doron had instructed headquarters staff to continue with their preparations, he had, nonetheless, had trouble believing his ears when Beaufort called him at midnight from the Prime Minister's office to inform him that the second option had been selected.

"You mean the option involving Rami?" he wished to verify, naming the head of the Mistaravim squad. The Mossad chief answered in the affirmative; that was, indeed, the Prime Minister's decision.

Doron did not know who had been with the Prime Minister, apart from Beaufort, when he had made this decision. Probably his military advisor, perhaps even the IDF chief of staff, but not Doron himself because at a meeting the night before he had recommend the first option: doing nothing. "Better one more abduction than a blood bath in Beirut," Beaufort had replied at the end of their meeting. But the Prime Minister had chosen the second option. Doron could not know how or even whether the risks and potential complications had been explained to him, whether Beaufort had tried to persuade him, oppose his decision, stand up to him, or if Beaufort had made do with the fact that he "recommends otherwise". And now the Mossad had taken upon itself another frenzied operation that it did not want.

It stood to reason that a Prime Minister with a military

background would understand the potential entanglement and prevent it from happening, but Doron had already seen in the past that the considerations of a Prime Minister were vastly different from tactical considerations, and they were difficult to predict or even understand after the fact. Just as farsighted strategic deliberations could lead to the approval of a dangerous mission against a strategic target, so could upcoming elections; similarly, a visit by the Prime Minister to the US could lead to the cancellation of an elegant operation they had been working on for months, in order to avoid potential embarrassment. The Prime Minister's control of the Mossad – any Prime Minister – was absolute: he appointed the Mossad chief and he alone decided on the most sensitive operations, a situation with which Doron had often felt uncomfortable. Not every Mossad chief could stand up to the Prime Minister, and not every Prime Minister would refrain from using the Mossad not only to serve the interests of the country but his own political interests as well. There had been two or three operations in Doron's long career that he suspected had been undertaken for this hidden motive; in the current situation as well, he could not disregard that possibility entirely. But what could he do about it? He would talk to Beaufort, but where would that lead? And in the meantime, there was no time to lose.

After receiving confirmation of the decision, Doron had spurred the division staff to action, called in reinforcements and worked with them right up to the time he had left for this briefing at the Mistaravim facility. The team now assembled in front of him, hunkered and drowsy, already knew what was happening, but he, Doron, was about to inform them officially that the State of Israel had decided to gamble with their lives. What was the right way to go about this? Or how could it be prevented? Doron decided to cut straight to practical matters. That was his strong suit, and anyway he would have to solve the other issues with his superiors.

"I understand that you've already been briefed on the background and the urgency for bringing you here so early in the morning," he said. "We have teams that have worked all night on plans, weapons, transmitters and vehicles so that you could start your preparations immediately.

"We want to reach Beirut in the shortest time possible, and the fastest way is to drop you this evening into the Mount Lebanon area, which is a little over an hour from Beirut. We've made the necessary arrangements with the Air Force. I know you have more experience in that sector with sea landings, but that would cause us to lose another day. It's likely that if, as we believe, Ronen is planning to attach an explosive device to Abu-Khaled's car he would do it at night – if he hasn't done it already – and then activate it in the morning, during Abu-Khaled's drive from home to the office. It could happen over the course of the next hour, but if he's taking his time then we may still have a chance to stop him. That's why we need you to get started right away. It should be clear to you that you've been selected for this mission because you're the most experienced at working in Lebanon."

Yoav, the commander of the team selected, raised his

hand. He was around thirty, had commanded a similar unit in the West Bank and after his discharge worked for the Shin Bet in Lebanon. When the IDF cleared out of Lebanon he was recruited by the Mossad.

"If Ronen resists, are we supposed to abduct him?"

"If he resists then we have no choice. Some of the training you'll be doing today involves carrying out an abduction," Doron answered. He wanted to get on with the briefing, but Yoav spoke up again.

"An abduction can be pretty violent, and pretty ugly if someone well-trained like Ronen puts up a fight. To what extent are we permitted to use force? What is he to us, an enemy?"

Doron did not like the use of this word. "He's not your enemy, he's your opponent. He's one of us, but he's against us. I expect you to use your good judgement."

Yoav shifted uncomfortably. Some two years earlier he had taken part in a large-scale operation with Ronen, a combined mission carried out by their two squads. Now he was his opponent. He wanted clear guidelines but instead had been given permission to use his own judgement. What exactly was permissible? Threatening Ronen with a weapon? Giving him a blow to the head? Abandoning him and getting out of there if he continued to put up a fight? Why should he have to decide? He resolved that later he would clarify the point further, but in the meantime he still had a few queries.

"If there's a struggle with him near the house, my assumption is that their forces will become involved and we'll have to engage in combat," he said.

"There's no way of knowing where Ronen will decide to stage an ambush," Doron answered. "It's more likely that he's planning on Abu-Khaled's office, on the main road, which would enable him to disappear in traffic. You'll have to scan the entire route from the house to the office, it's not that long. But in any event, you're about to see the arsenal that's been prepared for you. You'll be able to subdue whatever you're confronted with and get yourselves out safely. You'll be practising that today, too."

Yoav wouldn't be put off. "After we get ourselves out safely they'll chase after us. Where do you want us to escape to?"

"If you can't shake off your pursuers then we'll stage a daytime rescue. If you can hang on until nightfall then you'll leave like you came in, on a Yasur helicopter, or else by sea. The Navy has been alerted," Doron said. "This means you'll also have to learn the routes to the hideaways, the landing fields and the beach, so I need you to allocate someone for that who will sit with the intelligence officers."

There was a moment of malaise when Doron finished speaking.

"The schedule is a little crazy for an operation like this, don't you think?" Yoav said. "Seems to me that planning the escape routes alone should take about two days." He knew nobody would accuse him of cowardice; he had taken part in quite a few operations in which – posed as an Arab – he'd plucked out wanted terrorists from the heart of the kasbah in Nablus or Hebron, escaped from an angry mob under fire, and, in the employ of the Mossad, had already penetrated deep into the inner sanctuaries of the Hezbollah, Hamas and Islamic Jihad to gather essential intelligence. He had the credentials to put matters on the table. But he had not been there long enough to understand that it was Mossad practice to discuss such matters with the division head alone, not in front of the operatives. Even though Doron was receptive to such remarks, he decided to put an end to their dialogue.

"First of all, you're already at the stage of contingency planning while I'm still talking about the general plan. There are, in fact, contingency plans for a struggle with Ronen, for a rescue under fire and for escape, but we envisage that your presence will cause Ronen to abandon his plan, and that you'll all get out of there peacefully. And even if you don't, there's no guarantee that the abduction of a foreigner in Beirut will necessarily bring about an immediate reaction. You're not abducting one of their men. Apart from all that, I'm hoping that after today's training session, together with the experience you already have, you'll pull it off, as we say, quickly, powerfully and elegantly." After a short pause to let his words sink in Doron continued. "Furthermore, we don't have much choice. If we don't make our move this evening it could be too late. Don't forget that our basic premise is that this whole thing can and should end quietly."

Moussa, one of the Mistaravim operatives on the front bench, leaned towards Daoud, his neighbour, and whispered, "They haven't learned anything from their last cock-up."

The plan seemed too hasty and hazardous to the two

of them, but they had returned safely from other apparently dangerous operations and had learned to believe in the system: somewhere up there matters were surely taken into careful consideration before decisions were made.

Doron looked at the two dark-skinned young men in front of him, surprised at the speed at which once again he had turned into a representative of "the system".

"I hear muttering. Are there any objections?"

No one spoke. Moussa and Daoud glanced down; it was Yoav and Rami who were supposed to express objections, not them, and Yoav wasn't making a bad job of it.

"If not," Doron concluded, "then we have a lot of work to do. Rami will fill you in on today's schedule."

Rami stood up. "If you don't interrupt then we'll get to the dining room before the omelettes get cold," he said by way of an opening, to the laughter of his men, some of whom understood that this was veiled criticism of the dialogue that had taken place between Doron and Yoav. Rami had not liked Doron's answers, much as he hadn't liked the fact that Doron had refused to let Rami's own squad members take part in the all-night planning session, forcing him to make the initial plans with the Intelligence and Planning departments only.

In Rami's squad, as in all the other squads of the Operations Division, there was on the one hand discipline even stricter than in the army, and on the other, the camaraderie of people without ranks who had matured together through a very large number of operations. He was aware that some of his subordinates – and certainly the team commanders selected ad hoc for certain operations – had as much experience as he himself had, experience garnered, as was his, during years of commanding IDF Mistaravim in the West Bank before joining the Mossad. Some of them, who were in the West Bank during the Intifada, had managed to gain more combat experience than he had; Rami had spent those years gathering intelligence in the refugee camps in the heart of Beirut, Tyre and Sidon, bringing back much valuable intelligence.

What motivated the few dozen operatives in his squad was both the mutual esteem in which they held one another and the fact that they were all involved in planning and carrying out missions: they were partners. He did not like the decision to present them with a plan from headquarters. A plan prepared by the operatives themselves, in which each imagines himself on the street, is always wiser but Doron had not wanted to waste time on ideas and arguments, nor had he wanted – so he said – to waste their precious sleep time. Rami's people did not like what was happening, that much was clear. Yoav spoke with the authority of a person only recently appointed to command an operation whose outcome was shrouded in fog, but he was not alone in his displeasure with the fact that a plan like this had been imposed on them.

Rami announced that the team would first of all have a full intelligence briefing, then Yossi the driver would stay with the intelligence officers for navigational instructions. Moussa was to join him any time he was otherwise free.

Yoav would sit with Rami, Doron and the head of the Planning Department to work on the details, including contingency plans; Eli was to allocate one more intelligence officer for this purpose. After that, the team would practise abductions in several situations followed by a series of shooting drills. After learning the navigation of various routes, Yossi would practise operational driving.

"We'll sum things up this evening at seven," Rami concluded. "That leaves less than twelve hours, which is very little time. At eight tonight we'll have a briefing with the division head and at nine with the Mossad chief. After that there'll be time for personal preparations before a night departure, the exact hour of which will be announced. So now if there are no questions – and I am certain there are none, because otherwise we'll have to stick the omelettes back in the oven – then let's get to the food. I'm told there's a table prepared for the guests, too, in the hangar."

Ronen made his way back to the underground car park very early the next morning, well-dressed, shaved, his hair combed. He told himself he was starting a new round – climbing back into the ring as it were – and needed to make some adjustments; at least his outward appearance ought to have a calming effect on his surroundings. He did not know what the situation was vis-à-vis the explosive charge, what Gadi had managed to do and what he had not. Had it not exploded because of Gadi or because of the distance and interference between him and

Abu-Khaled's car? Gadi had lain there and done something, or tried to do something. Afterwards he had not returned to Ronen's hotel room; perhaps he had gone to Abu-Khaled's house to complete the job of dismantling the charge. If I have any chance left at all, Ronen thought, I'd better take advantage now, the moment Abu-Khaled leaves his house. He knew that Gadi might be there, but then again he could be anywhere.

Ronen crossed the car park. Nothing in the morning silence even hinted at the events that had taken place there just a few hours earlier. At first he had felt like a person who, at the critical moment when his entire personality, his past, and everything he stood for all needed to come together for one small action – the pressing of the red button on the remote-control – had failed to act, just as he had failed back then, his finger on the trigger, when faced with a child, Abu-Khaled's "Lital".

When Gadi was out of the range of danger and he had pressed the button, it was already too late. The hours following were filled with rage and frustration as he sat fruitlessly waiting in his hotel room for Gadi to return so that he could settle the score with the man who had stood between him and success.

Now, after a light sleep and a shower, things suddenly looked different to him. No, it hadn't been a failure; in fact, it had been another kind of success. He couldn't have risked harming Gadi. *Not* pushing the button – in spite of the fact that Abu-Khaled and his cronies were in that car just feet away from him, was the supreme test of that moment. It went against his initial, crude desire, against all the preparation and hopes and his will to succeed. His values had not become so confused as to make him believe that Gadi's life was a fair price to pay for successfully completing the mission. So there, he hadn't failed the test of crazed tenacity after all. Even the previous operation in Beirut should be seen in a new light.

Still, it was Gadi who stood between him and his real aim.

Ronen opened the door of his BMW. The passenger seat was in the reclining position and in it lay Gadi.

Ronen climbed in and sighed. He did not know whether to laugh or cry.

"You're a real bastard, you know?" he said as Gadi began returning his seat to the upright position, his eyes crusty with sleep. "Did you wait for me because you knew I would go out and blow him up this morning?"

"I apologize," Gadi said as he finished raising his seat.

"You know, I only noticed you at the last moment. I was on the verge of pressing the button. You would have gone up to heaven with those four martyrs in the car, three hundred and fifty virgins would have been summoned for the lot of you. But by the time they pulled away from you there were cars in between and the whole business didn't work."

If that's the case, Gadi figured, Ronen was not crazy and did not hate him; still, he couldn't allow his gratitude to deflect him from his plan. "My sincerest thanks, it was very considerate of you. But anyway, I think the calculation is three hundred and sixty virgins, seventy-two virgins each if I'm not mistaken."

229

"I'm getting pretty sick of you, you know?"

"I can imagine. But maybe you'd better tell me about it outside. There's a guard patrolling this area. Can you take me to my hotel?"

Ronen sighed again, nodded despairingly, turned on the engine and drove out of the underground car park.

The BMW coasted down the city's main thoroughfare, still quiet at this hour, without disruption. Gadi's eyes scoured the area but turned up nothing in the vicinity of the hotel. A patrol van was parked at the corner, as usual, the policemen drowsy. The traffic was light this morning, appropriate to the time of day. Gadi opened his window and breathed in the cool air; a pleasant scent of the sea wafted into the car. He could scarcely stifle the deep sigh of relief that was trapped in his chest.

"You have no idea what an operation you ruined for me," Ronen said. "Apart from Abu-Khaled I identified their chief of staff – we saw him arriving at Abu-Khaled's office several times – and a couple of others as well. You know what it would have been to blow them all up together? Do you know what that would have done for your country? For the prestige of your Mossad?"

"Turn left," Gadi said.

Like Ronen, Gadi had not stopped thinking about the events of the previous evening. After crawling out from under the car, the front wheel had grazed his arm. The Mercedes had stopped and then with a terrible slowness, began to turn towards the exit. For one very long moment he had no way of knowing whether anyone had noticed him. He pressed himself under the adjacent car like a giant python while Abu-Khaled's car took its time pulling away. A fourth-degree *dan* in Ninjitsu and a screwdriver in his hand, that was all Gadi had to defend himself with. No cover story, no explanation. Would they even give him a chance to get out from under the car before opening fire on him? This was Hezbollah, after all; the rules for opening fire were none too strict.

Finally, the Mercedes moved out of sight and there, directly facing him, Gadi could see Ronen crouched between two parked cars, his arm extended. It was clear what he was holding in his hand, clear why he was standing in that position, clear what would have happened had he not disconnected the antenna: the flimsy body of the charge would have exploded in every direction and a spray of shrapnel would have struck the four passengers in the car as well as Gadi himself. What if he hadn't completely severed the cable, what if some small part had remained attached? After all, the whole charge was dangling, had almost detached from the car. What a heroic ending, consigned to Hezbollah's Tomb of the Unknown Soldier.

In the midst of that strange situation something illogical inside him wanted the car to blow up at that very second, along with its passengers. What an impressive closing of the circle, what poetic justice: the plan he had conceived one year earlier carried out by Ronen. What a pity that he, Gadi himself, would be its victim too.

Ronen turned the corner without looking at him, and without staunching the flow of his monologue. "You've sort of made it your mission to ruin my life. You've been doing it for ten years, butting in when you shouldn't and staying away when you should be showing interest."

"Turn right."

Ronen turned right and glanced at Gadi, noticing his dirty clothes.

"You're filthy. What exactly were you doing under the car? Did you manage to disassemble the charge?"

"No," Gadi answered. He was fairly certain that he had disconnected the cable and that the remote-control could no longer activate the charge but under the conditions in which Ronen had pressed the button, there was no way of verifying it. In any event this was not the time to tell him, he didn't want Ronen to go crazy again or to find some new way to finish off Abu-Khaled. Gadi's mind was occupied with devising ways to keep Ronen out of as much trouble as possible back at home.

"I apologize if I've made your car dirty," he said, changing the subject. "Because I was so dirty I couldn't go back to you or return to my own hotel. I came to the Sheraton by taxi. Turn right, right here."

Ronen turned at the last moment into an alleyway and stopped next to a small hotel. "You're staying in this dump?"

"My expenses aren't paid on this trip," Gadi said with a laugh.

"Oh, and of course mine are. You know how much this Sheraton Coral Beach Hotel is costing me?"

"Listen, Ronen, let's put an end to this now," Gadi said gently, taking advantage of their mutual good-humoured complaint. "You don't really want to do harm to yourself or to Israel. The operation's over, you know it as well as I do. Let it go."

Ronen looked straight ahead, as if weighing his words. "These past few months I've had a chance to sit in cafés, talk to people, watch television, so I can tell you that Israel isn't the country I joined the Mossad to defend, nor are the people the people I want to defend. I'm finished with looking out for them, now I'm only looking out for me."

"Why? Because everything is based on money and ratings?"

"Not just because of that. I felt like a creature from outer space when I sat in cafés surrounded by brokers and journalists and shaven-headed gays with an earring who don't give a shit about anything but money and fucking. But they're the ones running the country."

"Wait a minute," Gadi interrupted, at first laughing at Ronen's description then growing serious. "First of all, since when did you become this primitive redneck? It doesn't suit you. And second, when we were walking around in temperatures of minus forty in Moscow we knew that people were on the Frishman Street beach, and when we were walking around Tehran in a hundred degrees we knew people were sitting in air-conditioned cafés on Sheinkin Street, and it was okay that we were doing it, basically, for them."

"My attitude has changed during the past year," Ronen said. "They act as if sitting in cafés is a given, just like it's a given that there are suckers who work like dogs to make sure they can."

"What do you expect? That the whole country should

join the standing army, plough the fields and sing folk songs? I would have expected a slightly more balanced world view from you. Anyway, it was always like that; even in the War of Independence there were more draft dodgers than volunteers. That's the way it is in nature, too."

"In nature at least the victors in war get to impregnate the females. Here it's just the opposite. Even the girls have gone through some kind of mutation, they prefer the draft dodgers and the boys who serve their time at desk jobs to the combat soldiers who get home once every three weeks and whose lives are constantly on the line."

"So now you're an expert on what women want, too? Listen, I've logged hundreds of hours of conversation with you and I've never before heard such bullshit. If you want to hate someone, hate me, hate the system, not the whole big world out there. And I have two more things to tell you," Gadi added, glancing around uncomfortably, wishing he were in his room, avoiding the suspicious stares of the receptionist. Still, he felt they were digging up new land mines here that he had to dismantle carefully, since each and every one could set off the explosive charge all over again.

"In nature it's only the species that put willing fighters at the head of the pack that survive, the ones that make sure those fighters are well compensated. If what you're describing is really the case – that our society prefers brokers and journalists and soldiers at desk-jobs – then we're on our way to extinction. Nature's truths are pretty simple: the surviving herds are the ones with enough individuals prepared to fight, and in our herd it's you and me, it's David and John and all the others. If we're not willing then your Lital and my Ami and Ruth are heading for extinction."

Gadi hoped that mentioning Lital would prod Ronen in the right direction. He did not dare mention Naamah since he couldn't predict how Ronen might react.

"The second thing is," he could not resist adding, "we weren't exactly victors. We screwed up, and the reasons are nobody's concern."

"I don't agree," Ronen said, cutting him off with a sharp look. "For every screw-up we have a thousand successful operations, but no one gives us credit for them."

Gadi pondered this, then tried another tactic to end the conversation. "It's amazing how much you still care about the Mossad. Get over it. Instead of being a frustrated homophobe, go with the trend. Let's be suit-wearing brokers or gays with earrings. We'll make everyone else eat shit while we eat the icing on the cake."

"Aha! I knew all those years you were attracted to me, and this is your weird way of expressing it." They both broke out laughing. "You're just lucky you didn't suggest I be a journalist, I wouldn't have been able to stand such humiliation," Ronen said, growing serious. "The problem is, I do still think there are people who want to kill us, all of us, even Lital and Ami and Ruth, and if we don't do anything about it they'll succeed."

The bait has been swallowed, Gadi thought, but he felt no joy. Could it be that society had changed that much, had adopted new value systems, and that only he and his friends had failed to notice it and were still trying to rescue something that almost no one believed in any more, like some tarnished piece of gold jewellery thrown away by people who had no idea of its worth? Still, he had to make one last attempt to gain the upper hand.

"So, it's because you're so concerned for the country that you want to drag it into another mess?"

Ronen fell silent and turned his head towards the window. Gadi switched off the engine and took the keys.

"Do you mind waiting for me for a minute? I just want to change clothes, I don't feel right like this," he said with a smile as he climbed out of the car. Ronen was stunned. Gadi knew it had been a gamble; Ronen could have lost his cool again or simply run out on him, though he thought his message might just have got through, and now he had to show he trusted Ronen. Trust him yes. But not with the keys.

After downing their omelettes, cheese and cake, and with mugs of coffee in their hands, most of the men present drifted to the vehicles in the hangar. There were jeeps and military-style vans, a beaten-up old Mercedes and a newer one from the early nineties that several technicians were still working on, fitting it with a GPS receiver and hidden compartments for weapons. Others gathered around a large table on which weapons for the operation were placed. There were shortened M16s and mini-Uzis, a few anti-tank grenade launchers with grenades, RPGs, rockets, pistols, silencers, knives and hand grenades. "Someone really thinks this could turn into a war," Doron's bureau chief mumbled as he surveyed the table.

"Let's just hope they don't need it," Peter, the chief weapons officer, responded, "because if they do, then I feel sorry for them, sorry for whoever detains them and sorry for all of us. In any event, they'll only be taking a small part of this along with them. They have to choose their weapons."

Tiny transmitters that fit in the ear were lying on another table, along with larger transmitters used for longer distances and for maintaining contact with Israel. Avi, the communications officer who had brought the apparatus, added GPS personal navigation equipment to the table. Only a small portion of this equipment, too, would travel with the team, in keeping with a "minimum equipment" policy.

Eli called them together from another part of the hangar. He was standing by two free-standing partitions of thick cardboard, each about seven-by-seven feet and folded into a V-shape. The first contained a map of central Lebanon on a scale of one to fifty thousand with a spread of aerial photographs of that same area. On the other was a map of Greater Beirut with the appropriate aerial photos. Arrows from the map and the photographs led to a series of enlargements and colour shots placed around the edges of the partition, with identifying labels: the target's house, headquarters of Hezbollah's overseas terror operations, police stations, various numbered roadblocks.

It took some time and prodding, but eventually the squad members seated themselves in chairs facing the partitions. Some of the headquarters staff joined them, while others drifted off.

Eli presented a general survey of the first partition. "Preferred routes from the landing area into Beirut are in green. Permanent roadblocks – the ones we know about – are in red, and diversions to avoid the roadblocks are in blue."

He moved on to the second partition. "These are the various routes from the entrance of the city to Dahiyeh. The route Abu-Khaled takes from home to the office and back each day is outlined in blue, and here," he said, gesturing to a row of enlargements of aerial and ground photos, "are the buildings between his house and his office. These Xs show the best of surveillance spots for Ronen's purposes – the whole length of the route. Ronen could be at any of them, so it's important for you to search thoroughly. Over there," he said, pointing to two folded partitions lying on the floor, "you'll find everything you need on escape routes. There's a lot to take in," he said, turning to Yossi and Moussa. "I hope you had a good night's sleep and your heads are clear."

"Even with a clear head and a good sleep I'd need a week for all this," Yossi chuckled.

"I thought you knew the area and this was just a refresher course," Eli joked.

"Ah, what do I care? You're the one who has to sign off at the end of the day that I know the routes," Yossi said.

"But you're the one who has to get us around there, bird-brain," Daoud said, cuffing him on the neck.

"Don't worry, Eli," Moussa said. "Yossi knows those roads pretty well, and we'll learn them now. But tell me something, just between us," he said, casting a glance

238

around him and lowering his voice. "Is this insanity really justified?"

Eli did not answer. He had kept four intelligence officers working all night updating intelligence and preparing materials, had told Yitzhaki, the intelligence officer usually assigned to the Mistaravim squad, to focus on planning the escape routes, and they had barely finished their work by morning. There was no way Yossi and Moussa would manage to learn the material satisfactorily. In those terms, there was no justification for this madness. And what about in other terms? Cost versus benefits, for example, or risk versus chances for success?

Again, Eli did not have an answer. He had grown up here, too, among field operatives, and like so many others had embarked on a path that vacillated between work in the field and headquarters. After the operations course, when he had come to the division and it was "discovered" that he had had intelligence training in the army, he was assigned, as an intelligence officer, to the squad commanded by Doron, and took part in its actions. After holding a number of positions, among them several years stationed overseas, Eli was appointed to head the Intelligence Department of the division. Even there, where he was responsible for the work of a dozen or so intelligence officers, some of whom were assigned to various operational squads, he sought out ways to position himself in the field during operations, as close as possible to the operatives themselves. He felt close to them now, and could feel their unexpressed frustration rising from Moussa's question.

No, Eli did not have an answer, only a suppressed hope, unknown even to him, that at the last moment there would be no need for "this insanity". There were so many operations like this that fizzled out when someone at the top came to his senses, or when the moment for the final decision arrived. Perhaps it would happen this time, too.

Gadi returned to the car after a brief shower – he felt leaving Ronen alone too long was asking for trouble – in new clothes, and clean-shaven. He suggested that they switch to the Mondeo to let the BMW cool off, and to go somewhere they would draw less attention. About half an hour later they stopped at an observation point above the Jounieh marina. A local family was looking out at the view from a car parked nearby and alongside them was a car whose passengers were clearly tourists. Gadi and Ronen got out of the Mondeo and leaned on the guard rail, taking in the view of the marina, each lost in his own thoughts.

"Ronen," Gadi said after a while, turning tenderly to his friend, "for your own sake and your family's, give me the remote-control." Again he refrained from mentioning Naamah's name.

Ronen did not react.

"It's clear you'll be put on trial back in Israel, so it'll be better for you if I can testify that you changed your mind and gave it to me of your own free will."

"If you hadn't stuck your nose into my business then

no one would have known, so don't make it sound like you're helping me out in the trial I'm going to have because of you," Ronen said angrily.

"If Abu-Khaled had been blown up, you don't think they would've known it was you?" Gadi added, pensively, "Ronen, whatever I do, whatever I say, you don't believe that I'm here for you."

"Not until you prove it," Ronen said, returning his gaze to the sea.

"The only proof I can think of will damage your appeal for a lighter sentence."

"What?" Ronen scoffed, surprised.

"All right," Gadi said in the tone of voice of someone who has reached a decision. "Listen to me, and I'll deny that I ever said this: your remote-control is useless."

"Why is that?" Ronen asked suspiciously.

"Because when I was under the car I disconnected the cable. It won't do you any good."

An expression of utter astonishment spread across Ronen's face and he broke out in a sweat.

"You did what?" he shouted in a voice full of panic and dismay. Everything was lost now that Gadi, with his own overly zealous hands, had brought about another fuck-up which, once again, Ronen would be responsible for.

Gadi, for his part, remained apathetic to Ronen's emotional outburst. He figured Ronen had simply realized, at last, that his personal mission had ended and that he was mourning this new development. "I disconnected the antenna cable from the charge," he repeated dryly.

Ronen hoped he was mistaken: he had'nt had enough time, there was no light; perhaps he disconnected something else. Maybe Gadi was just saying that to trick him into handing over the remote-control.

"Are you sure that's what you disconnected?" Ronen asked, tense.

"Yeah, I'm sure," Gadi answered. Back in Israel, under investigation, he could say without lying that he had not been sure he had disconnected the cable, or in other words, that Ronen had handed him the remote-control without knowing his operation was over.

Ronen returned to the car and collapsed onto his seat like a deflated balloon. Perfect timing as far as Gadi was concerned. Now that the promenade was coming to life with joggers, and yet more tourists, it was preferable for them to draw less attention to themselves. Gadi sat behind the wheel; Ronen was hunched in the passenger's seat, wiping sweat from his brow.

"You didn't notice what kind of charge it was," he said quietly, as if to himself.

"Regular, no? But with some cover you improvised," Gadi said, as he exchanged glances with a dark, lanky, long-haired young woman jogging past them. "I felt the two components, with the cable in the middle."

"No," Ronen said in a near whisper. "I didn't have access to the regular charges. From the old warehouse I found a charge that had been taken out of service…"

Gadi, pale, cut him off. "Wait a minute, the one with a timer?"

"Yes, you idiot," Ronen said quietly. "The one that

automatically activates the timer when you disconnect the antenna cable," he said, presenting the full picture.

There was not a hint of criticism in Ronen's voice, nor was there a trace of provocation in what he was saying. He barely felt angry; Gadi should never have assumed that the charge was a regular one, especially if he had taken into consideration the fact that Ronen had prepared it himself. At the same time he could not have been expected to recall – under those pressured circumstances, beneath the car, with people approaching – that somewhere in the squad's old warehouse someone had placed an unusual explosive charge years earlier or to know that Ronen had made off with it. Nor was it surprising that he did not consider every possibility when he had not managed to disassemble the charge in time; it was only on the spur of the moment that he had decided to disconnect the antenna cable and render the remote-control useless. Still, this reasoning was good for nothing, the damage had been done. If this time Gadi was the hand that had been the last to inflict damage, then Ronen was the body from which the hand extended. There was no escaping that fact.

The cogs in Gadi's brain were working at a pace that threatened to make him implode. He cursed himself for excessive over-confidence, for making decisions too quickly, for failing to plan his actions and for failing to take into account all possibilities. For having remained, in a manner of speaking, too combat-oriented, like Ronen, and for having failed, after all these years, to internalize the safety precautions necessary in a job like this, especially when it dawned on him that he could have blown himself up the second he detached the cable.

"How long did you set the timer for?"

"That's just it, I didn't," Ronen answered. "I had planned to detonate the charge with the remote-control."

"Wait a minute. That means it must have some default setting," Gadi said, pressing his palms to his temples, where his pulse was beating at breakneck speed. "It would be logical that if you don't set it, it would either blow up immediately or most likely after twenty-four hours." And it hadn't blown up immediately, Gadi thought, not wasting a minute to acknowledge his good luck.

It's not a matter of logic, it's a matter of electronics," Ronen said in such a practical tone that he sounded positively hostile. "Approximately when did you disconnect it?"

Gadi glanced instinctively at his watch. "I don't know exactly. Twelve-thirty or one at night? It was just when you came down. Do you remember when that was?"

Now it was Ronen's turn to look at his watch. "No. But that means we may have time if we move quickly." Ronen had already made his peace with the failure. Whatever would happen with the explosives would happen, now it was time to get out of there.

"Move quickly?" Gadi wondered. "To where?"

"Out of Lebanon, before it blows up and they close the borders."

Leaving behind a ticking bomb was the very last option Gadi was willing to consider. He started the engine and

244

said, "We're not going anywhere until we have disassembled that charge."

"Are you nuts?" Ronen exploded. "If our luck runs out – and as long as you're with me, it's bound to – it'll blow up in our faces." He smiled, "But with a bit of luck it will explode when Abu-Khaled is in the car."

"And maybe his wife and daughter, too, and maybe just then a neighbour will be passing by. We're not leaving that bomb in place. Don't you see that's just another giant cock-up? And It's not only a matter of disconnecting the charge from the car, we'll also have to defuse it. We can't leave it behind in the middle of Dahiyeh."

"Forget it," Ronen said. "Anyway, I have no idea how to defuse it from inside and I have no intention of trying."

"I've defused these kinds of charges in the past," Gadi said. "I hope I'll remember how."

"So we're simply going to take our chances?" Ronen said mockingly.

"Not 'we'," Gadi said earnestly, "I. This time it was me who was the idiot."

"We'll see about that."

Gadi did not know if that was a criticism of the entire plan or whether Ronen had decided to join him and was arguing over the right to defuse the charger. He was about to ask which it was, when a Syrian military vehicle parked just a few feet away from them. There was no time for some cover story. And he did not know whether Ronen was with him or against him. It was hard for him to believe that Ronen had made such a sudden switch in his attitude, but at least for the time being he was not fighting him, and

245

that alone was good. Gadi put the car into reverse and turned it round in the car park, passing the Syrian military vehicle; two officers and two pretty young women were just getting out. He waited for a break in the increasingly heavy traffic and sped off in the direction of the luxurious Maronite villas.

Cruising among the villas, the window open, Gadi continued weighing his options. He recalled the operations in which they had used a time-controlled charge, when they needed to balance the chances of catching the target in his car with the opportunity for the operatives to make their escape. At some point, inundated with facts he was trying to dredge up from his memory, Gadi told Ronen that if the charge had failed to explode immediately then it was safe to believe it would after twelve hours.

"Or twenty-four. It depends on the default settings," Ronen responded.

"Why? It takes the dial twelve hours to complete a full revolution and close the electric circuit," Gadi said.

Ronen burst out laughing. "What dial? It may be an old charge, but it isn't *that* old. It's digital."

Gadi nodded his head as if to say, What an idiot I am.

"Maybe we should call Peter? He'd know," Ronen suggested.

The fact that he said "we" suggested that Ronen was with him, but Gadi decided not to ask him outright. Even though he wanted to involve Ronen, he couldn't take him up on his suggestion. As a member of headquarter's staff,

Peter would have to obtain permission before giving them an answer, and most likely they would be told to get out of Lebanon immediately. Even if Helena's message had got through and they had calmed down a bit, forgiven him a bit, nobody would be willing to take a chance on an operation right in the car park alongside Abu-Khaled's home. They would prefer that the charge explode and then deal with the abysmal fallout rather than see bodies of dead Israelis strewn about. Still, the idea of calling Israel took hold of him.

Gadi parked outside a small coffee shop.

"Let's have something to drink, I need to think," he said. "And there's a public telephone here. Let's call home, tell the wives they can calm down. I'll bet Naamah is climbing the walls."

"You're worried about *Naamah*?" Ronen exploded.

"Calm down! It's simply that I've already spoken to Helena, that's all."

Gadi caught Helena in the staff room while she was having a break. In the moment it took to breathe a soft, elongated "hi" into her cell phone and turn her back to the other teachers – her golden hair spreading into a wide arc in the air, then landing again on her back as she hurried to the corner – she managed to take in the room, how it became suddenly alert, how conversations stopped, how eyes turned towards her and ears pricked. It was all from the best of intentions; her colleagues worried about the pretty teacher whose husband was never around but who never mentioned that fact, and probably did not even know where he was.

They themselves had a shrewd idea, and some had even heard rumours from friends who were in the know. One of them, whose husband was a career officer in the army and came home only at weekends, treated her like a fellow sufferer, asked her how she managed, whether she had arrangements for the kids when they had parent-teacher conferences or other activities at night, offering assistance. They never asked, just dropped small hints here and there. The principal had called her to his office once, after the assassination of Shekaki, the head of Islamic Jihad, in Malta. "Your husband was undoubtedly there, right?" he had asked. "Please send him kudos from me." She hadn't known what kudos was, nor the appropriate reaction, so she uttered an embarrassed thank you and fled the office.

Gadi told her that things were working out with Ronen. He asked her to phone Doron again; they had to know that Ronen was with him, that they should not pull any stunts at this point.

This system of passing along messages was probably no longer necessary, and there was even an element of risk involved as in any case of indirect communication, but Gadi still feared what he might hear from Doron if they spoke directly. He would not be able to explain the situation in detail and they would only mess it up. Now, as the operation was drawing to a close, he wasn't going to share the responsibility for it.

"Tell him there's still a complication I need to deal with, but it's not connected to Ronen. It has to do with what he brought with him." Gadi instructed Helena to

248

emphasize this point, and to add that they would be departing for Europe the next day.

The bell to signal the end of the break cut their conversation short. Behind her, Helena could hear the familiar sound of teachers rising from their seats, rushing to place their mugs in the sink, and in the halls, the sound of students running to their classrooms.

He sent her kisses and said goodbye, leaving her with a dilemma: the staff room was already empty, the halls were deserted. She opened her small address book and rang Tamar. "It's an urgent message from Gadi, can you put me through to Doron, please?"

Doron was not answering his office phone or his cell phone. One of Helena's students poked his head into the staff room to ask if they had a lesson.

"I'm on my way," she answered. "Please ask everyone to wait quietly for me in the classroom." Sometimes these things happened; the kids, too, could sense when it was something important.

"Okay, as soon as you get hold of him tell him they're together," she told Tamar. "Gadi says that's really important. Also that he must sort out something that has to do with what Ronen brought with him, and that they'll be back tomorrow. You know what?" she said, reconsidering. "I'll leave my cell phone open so that Doron can call me back. It will ruin a full year of educating my students about the use of cell phones, but this is important enough. So please get him to call me the minute he can."

✧✧✧

A man sat in a parked car on one of the streets inside the training facility. Moussa approached him from the front, on the pavement, while Yoav and Daoud came from the rear. When he was close to the car, Moussa stopped and gave a loud sneeze, drawing the attention of the driver. On cue, Yoav and Daoud opened the car doors. Daoud slid onto the back seat and pulled a thin wire around the driver's throat while Yoav, who had climbed in via the passenger's side, grabbed his hands.

Yossi drove up, stopping parallel to the parked car, and opened his car doors. Yoav grabbed the driver's head, keeping the pressure on his throat, while Daoud jumped out to help Moussa who was dragging the man by his legs, into the back seat of Yossi's car. Daoud and Yoav, holding his torso and head, followed suit. Yossi sped off.

Rami and Doron were watching from the pavement, along with Micky, the squad's hand-to-hand combat instructor. Eli had been observing from in front and Yitzhaki from behind, and now both joined the others. Arye, head of the Planning Department, and a few other people who had been standing on the opposite pavement, crossed the street. Yossi reversed the car and Yoav's team joined the commanders.

"Seventeen seconds from the sneeze until Yossi took off," Eli said, glancing at his stopwatch.

"They can shave at least five or six seconds off that," Micky said.

"Yes, but what worries me more," Doron said, "is that they left the doors of the abducted car open, and Yossi drove off before Yoav got round to closing his door. That's dangerous and it attracts a lot of attention. We need to work on closing the doors into the manoeuvre."

After all the observers had given their impressions, Yoav said, "Okay, we'll work on it."

"I want you to set aside at least two hours for shooting drills, both individual practice and group combat," Doron said. "It's twelve o'clock now. I'll be back at four and I want to see getting through a roadblock under fire, shooting backwards at pursuers and shaking off a car in pursuit."

Yoav and his team, along with Micky, went off to work on improving their manoeuvres while Doron, Rami, the intelligence officers and the Planning Department chief entered the hangar to finalize the timetable and contingency plans. They sat facing the partition with the maps and aerial photographs.

"Has Yossi got the navigation sorted?" Doron asked.

"I went over it for three hours straight," Yitzhaki answered "the first hour was spent with the whole squad and then with him alone when the others went off to their manoeuvres. I need at least another two hours to bring him up to basics on the escape routes."

"Which you may not have," Rami said.

"If the worst comes to the worst you can continue with him after the chief's briefing, and right up to the time they take off," Eli said. "If you combine all the optional plans here, there are hundreds of miles of roads to learn, some of them dirt roads in the mountains or across fields. There's no way of memorising it all, they're going to have to have some maps with them. Yitzhaki is concentrating on options one and two only with Yossi."

Doron picked up the contingency plans, some of which had been prepared overnight by the Intelligence and Planning departments with Rami's help, while the others were being worked on right up to that very minute.

"I don't like the fact that Yoav isn't a part of the planning," Doron said, looking over the papers in his hands. "There are dozens of cases here, and there's no guarantee that he'll be able to remember any of them or that he'll understand the logic of each suggested reaction from having read through them just once."

"Yoav hasn't got a minute to breathe," Rami groused. "I want him to learn the navigation as thoroughly as possible so that he can choose between the various options. He's got to practise the abduction, before shooting, and then he takes off with the crew."

Doron kept silent. What Rami had permitted himself to say to him, he, Doron, had not permitted himself to say to the Mossad chief. Everyone knew, without daring to say so, that they were setting out on a mission doomed to failure from the outset. Maybe he should take Rami with him to Beaufort to tell him so. Why wait for the chief's briefing when the results were a foregone conclusion?

But after the surprise Beaufort had delivered the night before, Doron knew that asking Rami to join him in presenting his case to the chief would not help. The risks had been well documented in the operational order, and that had done no good.

And of course it was also possible that they would

succeed, that everything would run smoothly; maybe Ronen would give himself up quietly, or perhaps the worst that would happen would be having to give some inquisitive guard a chop to the neck or slit hiss throat. They might just pull it off in style. How could he think about throwing in the towel before they had even begun, when the distress of the Mossad and its chief was so evident and the potential entanglement so great?

Doron glanced at the paper in his hands. "Let's work on the escape route contingency plans first," he said. "We'll deal with details of their touchdown in Lebanon after that, if there's time. Case: you've been spotted during the abduction, a ruckus has broken out, guards have been alerted, you're making your escape from the area and you come to Roadblock 18, which is manned all night. What should the reaction be?"

Yitzhaki pointed to the roadblock on the aerial photograph of the area around the house. As Rami began to answer, Doron's cell phone rang. He turned his back to the others; Tamar was on the line, apologetic, explaining that Helena had phoned with an urgent message from Gadi. He noticed on the screen that there had been several unanswered calls: he would speak to her.

7.

THE LATE-AFTERNOON sun dangled above the sea, its rays muted by the dark-glass windows of the small coffee shop in the upper lobby of the Dan Panorama Hotel. Some boys were playing with a ball on a patch of grass between the beach and the road, which was humming with traffic bound for Jaffa. Only a very few hotel guests were seated in the lobby – which was why Benny, the psychologist, had set up this meeting there – but Beaufort and Naamah nevertheless were talking in low voices as they leaned over the small table set with cups of coffee and cakes.

Naamah was wearing a jogging suit. When she'd left school she had only had enough time to pick up Lital from the nursery and drop her off with Ronen's parents before she dashed to this meeting in Tel Aviv.

"How are they handling it?" Benny asked.

"Terribly," Naamah answered. The dismissal of their son – a source of pride since his days as a naval commando, and later in the Mossad – had been humiliating for them. When the results of the commission of inquiry were made public, no one in their small village by the sea had any doubt that Ronen was deemed responsible, especially when it became clear, a short while later, that he was sitting idly at home. Even in an old, established village, pride in a homegrown hero can quickly become *schadenfreude*.

After months of hanging around the house, there was no way of hiding Ronen's disappearance from his parents, even for a single day. At first, Naamah had considered lying to them, but the truth – which was bound to hit them in the face sooner rather than later – would turn her into the enemy. She did not want to share her suspicions with them, but when another day passed she was forced to tell them he had gone off without telling her where, and that the Mossad was searching for him. In the space of the next two days she watched them wither, as though it were several years that had passed and not days.

"And how are you holding up, Mrs Dolev?" Beaufort asked, as though her one word answer had sufficiently covered the issue of Ronen's parents.

As a young operative, Naamah had held the chief of the Mossad in high esteem. But the more her time with the Mossad became part of her distant past, and her age now grew closer to that of senior commanders, the more it all took on a different perspective. She still remembered Doron as a young, over-confident squad commander, which made her wonder whether he had the proper judgement and moderation she expected to find in a division head. The Mossad chief, on the other hand, seemed worn out; it was easy to see that he was having trouble keeping his eyes open and she felt uncertain whether his drooping shoulders were suited to the task placed upon them. He was certainly intelligent, and she had heard he was very analytical. Eloquent, too. He was also probably good at handling the country's leaders and undoubtedly successful with the heads of foreign intelligence services. But just how capable was he of bringing home her Ronen? And speaking of capable, why wasn't Doron with them at this meeting? Did he have nothing at all to say? Was he avoiding meeting her? Or was he in the middle of an operation to bring her husband home, the operation Gadi had been talking about? And what was Gadi's role in all this? She understood that he had left the country, but no one was volunteering any information, not even Benny, who was in daily contact with her.

"Excuse me for being blunt, but this isn't the time to ask how I am or how I'm managing, or question Ronen's feelings about the Mossad, which is what Benny is interested in and says you too want to hear about. You should have asked *that* a long time ago."

"Please, Naamah, I've been in touch with you every day—"

Benny tried to appease her but the chief cut in: "We've come to ask for your co-operation so we can help him."

Benny sat back comfortably in his chair, amazed at the chief's ability to twist matters around. But Naamah would not be deceived.

"Help him? *Now* you want to help him? Instead of tossing him to the dogs you could have helped him out if you'd given him a commendation for the intelligence he gathered in Russia right before that trip to Lebanon."

"My dear lady, it's entirely possible that at the end of the year he would have been a candidate for…"

"Oh please," Naamah said. "Over a period of ten years he did a dozen things of that magnitude, and he never received a citation. Oh sorry, he got three letters of appreciation, but two were from the Prime Minister, not you. A commission of inquiry, of course, he *did* get. If only the two had at least come together, they could have balanced one another out somehow."

"A citation would have been improper at that time, Mrs Dolev. Think of how it would have looked."

"How it would have looked?" Naamah threw back at him. "To whom? The media? I'm sure you got rid of him in order to make the media happy."

Naamah bit her lip and stopped talking. This conversation was not going the way she had hoped. She hadn't planned to let rip her fury on the Mossad chief, who was looking particularly distressed. As much as she hadn't expected him to be the bearer of good tidings, she had still harboured hidden hopes. Maybe he would pull a rabbit from his hat; perhaps, even, she would be that rabbit. The idea had flitted through her mind, after that last conversation with Gadi, that she would have more success bringing Ronen back than he would, but this was a non-starter: co-operating with Gadi could really cause Ronen to blow his top. Now it was a different matter. Gadi was already there.

"I agreed to come today exactly for that reason, to help him," Naamah said quietly. "I don't know Abu-Khaled's neighbourhood, but I still remember Beirut fairly well.

One of the passports I used, a South American one, was valid for life, and I could use that. I could fly to Beirut, and I think I have the best chance of convincing Ronen to let this whole thing go if you'll just help me get to him."

The Mossad chief and the psychologist exchanged glances.

"Look, this isn't some crazy idea I've come up with on the spur of the moment, I was thinking about it all night. You people sent Gadi out there, but that could lead to a major confrontation: each has so much against the other that at any given moment either one could start fighting or try to outwit – or even harm – the other. With me it would be a completely different story."

Benny glanced at Beaufort, wondering whether he remembered the psychological analysis he had prepared, in which he had said exactly what Naamah was saying now. Her idea was brilliant; her appearance in Beirut could really work magic on Ronen. But she did not know that Gadi had gone there on his own initiative: what she would find in Beirut would alter the way she saw the situation. As a psychologist, could he be certain that Ronen would come home with her like a good little boy? If he really had lost control and was prepared to desert her and their child, to take a risk that could leave Naamah a widow and their daughter fatherless, who could predict how he might react? And who could guess how Naamah might ignite the war between Gadi and Ronen when Gadi himself hadn't exactly been following instructions from headquarters?

Beaufort was thinking along similar lines and, like Benny, kept silent.

This isn't the place and these aren't the people to make such a decision, Naamah thought. Doron should be here. He was the only one who could truly understand what her arrival in Beirut would mean, a South American woman in her mid-thirties wandering around the Shi'ite neighbourhoods. He was the only one who could recommend such an action to his superiors, and to decide, for example, to assign someone to escort her and drive her around. From the favourable expression on Benny's face when she voiced the idea, Naamah understood that he liked it; Beaufort, on the other hand, was poker-faced, and now Benny's eyes seemed to have lost their sparkle, too. It seemed they had reached the cover-your-back stage.

"Look," Naamah said, breaking the silence. "I'd like to suggest bringing up the idea with Doron, to get his opinion on it. You can storm a hill with an entire brigade – and rack up lots of casualties – or you can drop a small team onto the top of the hill using a helicopter. I don't know what you have planned, but I'm offering you a quick and practically risk-free solution."

Naamah's example penetrated Beaufort's consciousness. To drop Naamah in and pull the three of them out together could be a most elegant solution. But he still entertained hopes Gadi would succeed, since a day and a half had passed from the time he had established contact with Ronen. Besides, the Prime Minister had already approved a plan and he did not care to stir things up on that front. How had they not thought of Naamah right from the beginning? Then again, how would it look if things went wrong and Naamah fell into the hands of Hezbollah, too? How would he be able to explain that he had sent both parents of a baby into the lion's den, and that this had been the best solution the Mossad had to offer?

"I'll waive all rights, in advance, to any claims or lawsuits," she added when the two men failed to speak up. "I'm not interested in a contract or an operational order or life insurance, okay? I just want to bring Ronen back. And that's what you want, too. If you prefer, then take it as a request: I made the offer and the risks are all mine."

The drill included a fast approach and a slow approach to an open roadblock and a closed one. They practised opening fire when there were two, three and four soldiers at the roadblock, and when there was a platoon of soldiers on alert in a nearby building. The "guards" were instructed to blockade the car from in front, to approach it from the driver's side, from the passenger's side and from three sides all at once. Sometimes "Ronen" sat quietly, co-operating, so that the objective was to put the guards at ease, make a quick excuse and continue driving; sometimes "Ronen" went wild, so the operatives opened fire on the guards even before the car came to a halt.

It took a matter of seconds. Yoav would say the code word and the mini-Uzis with silencers would be out in a flash, paint balls marking the foreheads and chests of the guards. When a whole platoon was involved, the troops barely made it out of the building before being levelled by several long rounds of ammunition.

Doron felt the drill against pursuers was a success as well. Moussa and Daoud pulled out short-barrel M16s with sights from under the seat, rammed their barrels through the two small holes in the reinforced rear window and covered the windscreen of the car in pursuit with paint. And when those in an armoured vehicle were particularly obstinate and kept up the chase, Yoav opened the sunroof, stood up and tossed a dummy RPG rocket at them.

"Okay, Yossi, let's see what you can do," Doron said, and they moved to the area for vehicle drills. Using the hand brake, the steering wheel and the accelerator, Yossi manoeuvred a skid that turned the car around to face the direction from which it had come; and when he had released the hand brake a little earlier, he pulled off a ninety degree turn when it seemed that there was no chance – or intention – of doing so. He drove off into a gully at the side of the road, climbed a steep incline and, for dessert, performed a vehicle-fitness course on sandy roads and mud that only a four-wheel drive would dare attempt.

The next phase was entering and disembarking from a helicopter.

Towards the end of the day, a Yasur helicopter appeared, as if emerging from inside the orange sun that was barely above the waves. The CH-53 Sea Stallion heavy chopper made its way towards the landing pad at the edge of the training facility, circling before landing. Soldiers spilled out in four directions and took up positions around the Yasur. The back of the craft opened, forming a ramp down which came a Mercedes, slowly at first, and then picking up speed. The soldiers sprinted back inside, the ramp rose back into place and the chopper lifted off, changed course and disappeared. Yossi turned the Mercedes around and drove back to the group of commanders who had watched the landing from nearby.

"You made decent time," Doron said. "Give the soldiers just a little longer to make sure the area is clean, and only then pull out. Slow it down, Yossi." To the junior officer who was serving as liaison between the Mossad and the Air Force, he said, "Tell the soldiers and the chopper crew to stay in place until the car has put some distance between them."

"I want you to do the whole thing again in complete darkness," Doron told Rami and Yoav, glancing at his watch, "in about another hour. After that we'll start the briefings. As soon as the Mossad chief arrives and we've had the final briefing, you'll be on your way."

Helena wound her way through the South Tel Aviv congestion, cursing herself for failing to take the inevitable Jaffa- and Bat Yam-bound traffic into consideration. What a lack of respect, to show up late for a meeting with the head of the Mossad! She was familiar with a few of the Mossad chiefs through Gadi's stories, but she had never before met one. She had only met Benny, the psychologist, quite recently, since Gadi had kept his family far out of the reach of headquarters, and was pleased to find him quite supportive and understanding.

Helena hadn't a clue what to expect of this meeting. She had a few wishes and hopes, and mainly wanted to know what the Mossad was doing to bring Gadi home safely. The longer the trip took and the more angry she grew with herself for being late, the more her fury focused on the Mossad and its chief. What did he want from *her*, after he'd refused to listen to Gadi and Gadi had left of his own accord? Had he summoned her in order to apologize? To explain what he was about to do?

Suddenly she felt that no good would come of this meeting. If they had had an easy solution they would not be talking to her. If they were about to embark on some dangerous adventure, well, what did they want? Her permission? Like the family of an incapacitated patient having to agree before surgery could be performed? Or perhaps they were looking to frame Gadi, to hear from her that he had knowingly continued to Beirut without authorization, fully aware of all the risks. She had heard enough from Gadi during the commission of inquiry to know that that was certainly a possibility. But perhaps there was still some way she could help.

Confused by her emotions and feelings, she spotted the hotel on her left just after she had missed the turnoff. A lengthy Danish curse issued from her mouth as she turned into the car park on her right among the grassy areas that led down to the sea.

*

Helena could not have recognized the driver that had been following her for quite a while and had turned into the car park behind her. It was Haramati.

Early that morning he had telephoned Naamah posing as the rep for a water filter system, and told her he was sorry to hear that her husband was not at home. "Can you tell me where I can reach him, or when he'll be back? This is pretty technical stuff that usually only men understand."

"I have a pretty good technical sense and I'm willing to hear all about it," Naamah said patiently, but Haramati insisted he did not make deals without the husbands, "since the wife listens, then says when her husband returns he'll decide and I have to do the whole song and dance all over again." He asked again when her husband would be returning and Naamah, whose patience with this little chauvinist had just ended, hung up on him.

Haramati had waited for her at the entrance to her village, then followed her to the school at Ruppin Junction. After that he had hurried to the newspaper office where he worked, completed a few assignments awaiting his attention, and returned to Ruppin in the afternoon. He was pleased to find Naamah's car still in the car park, and chose a point from where he could watch out for her. He was enjoying playing the private investigator, or perhaps the spy, but what he had not taken into account was having to fight off sleep for several hours. He dozed off and on until he woke to catch a glimpse of her car racing off. He tried to catch up with her but lost her in traffic.

Naamah's car was not to be found next to her house, so Haramati decided to try his luck at the second address, in a small community settlement. No one disturbed him as he kept an eye on the well-tended house surrounded by low shrubs. About an hour later Helena left the house. Haramati followed her with relative ease. One thing was certain, he told himself, those lucky bastards at the Mossad sure knew how to pick beautiful women.

Helena glanced at her watch; she was only a few minutes late. The sign at the entrance to the car park informed her that in another fifteen minutes parking would be free, so she didn't bother to waste time scratching out the date and time on a ticket. She walked quickly along the promenade towards the hotel. Facing her, not far away, she saw Naamah leaning against a boulder, watching the darkening sea. Helena stopped, her heart beating quickly. Her first thought was how beautiful Naamah was, her face slightly lifted towards the spot where the sun had disappeared into the sea. In the fading light the silhouette of her chiselled features stood out starkly: her straight, narrow nose, her chin. Sea breezes rippled the long, black hair that cascaded down her back. And how cool she is, Helena thought, when she noticed what Naamah was wearing: a jogging suit. She herself had rifled through her wardrobe, had at first selected elegant clothes, then tailored suits, then something sporty but elegant, finally opting for a pretty dress, nothing too festive but appropriate for a business meeting, with which she wore an elegant pair of shoes. She had brought along a thin silk jacket which served no other purpose than to add an air of respectability. How different she was from Naamah, though Naamah, too, was undoubtedly here for a meeting with the Mossad chief; she too was a woman in distress and was doing everything she could to save her husband. All at once the thought that it was because of Naamah that Gadi was there now in that threatening trap, faded away, leaving in its place the realization that they were sisters in distress. A feeling of warmth rushed through her, and with it the hidden hope that Naamah would know what to do. Certainly she would know more than Helena, since she had been there. With Gadi.

"Naamah?" Helena said with hesitation. The roar of the sea swallowed her voice. "Naamah?" she repeated, taking two steps closer.

Naamah turned slowly towards her, opening her eyes. Even in the little light left Helena noticed the slight alarm in them, mixed with grief. A moment later, a thin smile touched with sympathy for this foreign woman began forming on Naamah's face. Here she was, all dressed up for her meeting with the head of the Mossad, which she undoubtedly hadn't a clue about. Naamah's smile broadened, filling with compassion, knowing that Helena had nothing to look forward to; that up in the hotel coffee shop they had no good news for this fair and pretty woman standing in front of her, looking as though she had stepped out of a European fashion magazine.

Naamah and Helena had met on rare occasions when the squad members and their spouses got together with operatives who had left the squad. They stayed away from one another, barely speaking, since Naamah could not be bothered with the niceties of protocol, making small talk with the woman Gadi held so dear; and Helena had no idea how to approach the steely Naamah. Naamah did not want to think about what this woman was turning Gadi into, just as Helena preferred not to imagine the stormy sex that Naamah, who seemed wild and unbridled, had dragged Gadi into. Now, suddenly, these turned into advantages in Helena's eyes. Naamah had an interest in Gadi's success, and it didn't matter what the reasons were, just as she herself wanted Ronen to return safely for her own reasons.

"They summoned you here, too?" Naamah asked gently.

"Yes, but I'm running a bit late. The kids, traffic jams."

"I left Lital with Ronen's parents and raced here straight from school," she said, indicating her jogging suit.

Helena hesitated. The Mossad chief was waiting for her, and was probably cross, and the psychologist, too, but it seemed to her that Naamah was the one who would have the correct solution to the Beirut ordeal. A halo of affinity encompassed the two women against the backdrop of the last colours left behind by the sun as it disappeared into the darkness encroaching from the north and south and east, and the wind from the sea, and the roaring waves; Helena did not wish to leave it behind with the darkness. She did not want to part from Naamah.

"Do you have time for a cup of coffee?" she heard herself asking.

Naamah smiled, surprised. "What about them?" she asked, gesturing toward the hotel.

"I'm planning to make it a brief meeting, really just a courtesy call. I don't see how I can possibly help them. Could you wait a few minutes for me?"

Naamah responded warmly that she could, thinking there's more to her than I thought.

Watching from a distance, Haramati scratched his brow. Had he stumbled onto a real conspiracy? He continued following Helena as she quickly crossed the street.

Ronen's rented BMW, driven by Gadi, approached the entrance to Bir-el-Abed, Abu-Khaled's neighbourhood. Before nightfall Gadi had removed a bulb from one of the headlights so that they shone unevenly, like many of the other cars on the road. That way perhaps the BMW would be less noticeable. They had debated for a while which car to use: the BMW stood out more, though they knew from experience that there were quite a few wealthy people with BMWs, even in the Shi'ite quarters; the Ford Mondeo was mostly used by car rental companies. And in case of a hostile escape, a BMW had certain advantages.

"I gave them the story about Dr Itzmat when I came in. How about you?"

"Me too," Ronen laughed.

"It works. Let's stick with it."

"Can it be backed up?"

"Now? Of course not. After we were exposed they got rid of the infrastructure. I'm relying on the guards not to call, and if they do, well, you're pretty good at karate."

Ronen was disappointed to discover that Gadi's compliment meant so much to him.

"Just don't do anything without my orders," Gadi took care to add, and the pleasant feeling was replaced in an instant by the old bitterness. So he still doesn't trust me, Ronen thought. And why should he?

Why, indeed, was he going along with this madness? When had he agreed to it? Gadi had taken command and he had got dragged in after him, just like the old days. After all, he hadn't been convinced that Abu-Khaled shouldn't be killed. It would bother him, but not that much, if Abu-Khaled's wife and children were killed: Abu-Khaled's suicide bombers had certainly killed enough women and children. A mishap like the car exploding when empty or the mess that that might or might not cause on Israel's northern border were too theoretical compared to the tangible risk he and Gadi were taking. So why was he going along with it?

The moment Gadi announced he was going to dismantle the charge, come what may, things had changed. That much was clear to Ronen even through all the fog that had engulfed him. Without the remote he had no control over the charge, and no way to prevent Gadi from defusing the bomb. What could he do, try to stun him? Call the police? Out of the question. His operation was dead; if anyone were still to be killed as a result, it would probably be Gadi.

Because Gadi was going all the way with it, at all costs. It was crazy enough thinking that only two people could pull off such an operation; there was no way he could let him do it himself. It wasn't guilt that Ronen was feeling, or even responsibility for the situation: he was only responsible for his own madness. Gadi's madness, which was dictating their actions now, was Gadi's alone. Ronen simply could not leave him now, that was that. He preferred not to put a name to his motives.

Gadi slowed down, but only a little, when they spotted the roadblock, a small lighted booth at the side of the road. A lone guard with a Kalashnikov rifle signalled them to stop. He approached Gadi's window while two others, who had emerged from the booth, cocked their guns when they discerned that the car was rented.

"Passport, please," the guard said, aware from the first moment that they were foreigners.

Gadi removed his passport from his jacket and handed it over, then took Ronen's and passed it on. Because of the two guards standing on either side of the car, their weapons poised, Gadi and Ronen would have no time to react – should it be necessary – but after glancing briefly at their passports, the guard returned them to Gadi.

"'Passport, please!' Ever heard that before? That's the first time I've been asked for my passport here. Hezbollah's really created a state within a state," Gadi said, a couple of minutes after driving off.

"What do you think's going on? Has the bomb already gone off and they've received new instructions?"

"I doubt it. They wouldn't have let us pass so easily if that's what had happened. I think that was a local initiative."

"Or, they wanted to know if those foreigners who keep

visiting Dr Itzmat really are just innocent foreigners," Ronen said.

"If they were at all suspicious they could already have discovered there's no one by that name, and at the very least they would have questioned us. We're now inside Bir-el-Abed so, let's concentrate on our mission."

Gadi's practicality did not quite ease Ronen's mind. What if it were a trap? But Gadi then repeated the exact words he so disliked hearing from the division head: "There are always reasons *not* to carry out an operation". It would take more than ungrounded fears to keep Gadi from his goal now. Once again Ronen felt as though he had acquiesced to someone stronger than he. After a pause, Ronen spoke.

"About defusing the bomb, Gadi, we aren't sure what happens when you disassemble the timer from within, or if there's some sort of trap. Peter's probably home by now so if we call him he'll have to answer us without contacting Doron."

Gadi pondered this. What Ronen was saying was true: they would benefit greatly from such a phone call. If disconnecting the timer activated the charge it could prevent the bomb exploding in his face. But there was still the possibility that all the department heads knew it was the intention of headquarters to bring them back: the moment Peter took the call he would pass on the order that they return to Israel.

"I have an idea. Let's drive past Abu-Khaled's home and see how the land lies," Gadi said. "If we can do it, we will, and if there's too much going on and we need to kill time, we'll call Peter. If he tries to stop us, I'll know what to do; after all, I don't have to take orders from him. And Ronen…" he added after a short pause, waiting for Ronen to turn his head to him, "thank you."

"For what?"

"For deciding to stay. I know how hard it must be to change sides, especially when our chances for success are borderline. You can still take off, if you want to."

Ronen turned his head away. "Step on it," he said.

He had no time for sentimentality. Their situation was dire; they were at great risk of being discovered and getting caught up in a chase, or waiting for the neighbourhood to go to bed and then blowing up along with the charge. Gadi was the one who had decided to do this, but it was he, Ronen, who was responsible for getting them stuck in Beirut. So Gadi's "thank you" was superfluous, as was the option he had given him to take off. He would have preferred Gadi to curse him, which is what he should have felt like doing, or else to shut up.

They drove past Abu-Khaled's home. The Mercedes was not there. Shit, they said simultaneously. Now they would have to kill time and there was no way of knowing when he would return.

"In the meantime," Ronen said, swallowing a smile, "at least maybe he'll explode." Gadi slapped him lightly on the neck, laughing and swearing. Then, suddenly serious, he said, "That's not funny."

Ronen was persistent. "Now, let's place that call to Peter."

"Problems? No way!" Helena said, imitating herself as she replayed her conversation with Beaufort and Benny for Naamah. "What? The Mossad chief didn't offer him help as soon as he requested it? Never! Doron appointed his replacement behind his back, even before he finishes his term? No way! The head of Personnel has been manipulating him and finding ways to trip him up in order to show him that the organization wants him to leave? How absolutely implausible!"

Naamah laughed. They were in a small, deserted café; empty coffee cups sat on the table in front of them. Helena had surprised herself, both by the gaiety she was displaying now and by what she considered to be the slightly exaggerated assertiveness she had used in the meeting. She was unaccustomed to being tough or calculating, she did not tell jokes, yet here she was, in the space of a few minutes, surprising herself twice. It was as though something of Naamah's spirit had accompanied her to the meeting, had spoken from her mouth.

"Anyway, that's all nonsense," she said, growing serious. "I could see immediately that I couldn't be of any help. What really worried me was that I didn't get the impression they're really going to do anything. That made me pretty mad. Did they really need this conversation just to cover their asses?"

Naamah could not suppress her smile at hearing that expression used by fair Helena, whose high-cheekboned face had blushed when she'd used it. Perhaps under that soft exterior there really was a hidden piquancy that Naamah had trouble believing Gadi could live without. Did that make it better or worse for her?

"I told them that it was just like before: they didn't back him up after the operation and they weren't backing him up now. They've left him to clean things up himself," Helena continued. Naamah tried to ignore the fact that the "dirt" Gadi had to clean up was Ronen.

"So now I'm going to leave you to clean things up by yourselves," she concluded, quoting herself verbatim. After reflecting for a moment, she added, "I hope that wasn't counterproductive."

"So do I," Naamah said, wondering to herself whether they hadn't missed an opportunity to get the Mossad to take action. The fact that Gadi had gone there alone had only become fully clear to her in her conversation with Beaufort, and only now – sitting with Helena – did she understand that he had done so without the backing of the Mossad. So it was Gadi the knight in shining armour versus Ronen the caged tiger; anyone else involved would fight them, not save them. "It's pretty frightening to think what could happen to them over there, in Beirut."

Alarmed at having mentioned the name of the city, Naamah looked around to see if anyone had overheard her. The café was empty except for a man who had just appeared in the darkened entrance. The waiter caught her glance and approached the table. Helena ordered fruit juice, Naamah another cup of coffee. In the silence that fell when the waiter left the table Naamah felt that she wanted to – and could – make the move that begged to be made towards this woman. Her unfinished business with Gadi, the feelings she still had for him, should not have come out in suppressed resentment towards Helena. If anyone should feel resentment it should be Helena. But Helena was the one who had told her that Gadi had made contact with Ronen in Beirut, thus establishing the basis for the sympathy Naamah was feeling at that moment.

"I want to thank you for phoning," she said. "Your call saved me."

Naamah could imagine the call had not been easy for Helena. It can't be pleasant to call your husband's former lover. The charged relationship she had with Gadi certainly had not escaped Helena's watchful eye, even if it had no external manifestations and was limited to the hidden meanings in their infrequent conversations. Perhaps this was the right time to heal old wounds.

"All these years I've known I love Ronen," Naamah said carefully, weighing each word, "but since he left I just feel crazy without him."

She was satisfied with these words, they were an accurate description of her feelings. Perhaps not the entire range of her feelings, but certainly the core. It was the truth, just not the whole truth.

"I was crazy with worry until Gadi called, too. I just didn't know who to be angry with. Him. The Mossad. You," Helena said, allowing herself to speak freely.

"Me? Why me?" Helena's willingness to voice her feelings was more disturbing to Naamah than the guilt.

"Because I don't think he would have gone there if he didn't feel something for you."

Naamah lowered her gaze and rolled a few responses around in her mouth. She could not deny that Gadi thought about her; Helena would never believe her and it would be a breach of the closeness that was just beginning to form like the fragile web of a spider. She would appeal to logic.

"If he really did feel something for me, do you think he would have taken such a risk in order to save my husband?"

"I thought of that, but with Gadi it's certainly possible."

Logic was no answer to suspicion or the seed of jealousy that has no cure once it is sown. She would have to turn the conversation in a different direction. Perhaps Helena was asking for answers, perhaps seeking peace of mind. But it was too soon for that; they weren't yet close enough to permit Helena to believe Naamah's denials.

"It would make a lot more sense to be angry with the real guilty party."

"Our husbands? The Mossad?" Helena wondered.

Naamah glanced around her again; this time Helena had indiscreetly made mention of the Mossad. The man who had entered the café after them had quietly seated himself at the table behind theirs, his back to her. What cheek, Naamah thought: the place is empty. But mostly she was filled with gratitude to Helena for saying "our husbands"; she did not blame Ronen alone.

"Each one of us has good reason to be angry with the other's husband, since each is responsible for landing the other where they are now. So let's agree to be mad at the… office," she said, carefully selecting the last word.

Helena quickly found justification for agreeing. "I don't know how it is in your house, but in ours, the office comes first, before everything else: before our love, even before the children. It's an absolute addiction."

"The same," Naamah admitted.

"You wanted orange juice, too?" the waiter asked. He had just come to the table with their order and thought she was speaking to him. The women burst out laughing. The waiter placed their cups on the table and handed a menu to the man at the table behind them.

"I know what that's like firsthand. Somehow I stayed connected to that world through Ronen. But with him there was no process of separation, it was an immediate and absolute detachment. Like a guillotine, as if he'd died. The people he left behind also treated him as if he were dead," she said, unable to keep from making a generalization that included Gadi. "Working there, you think there's nothing more important or fascinating. So when you leave, the separation is really difficult, especially when it's absolute, as in Ronen's case." She thought for another moment and added, "Maybe nothing really *is* as important or fascinating."

"I'll have a large café au lait," said the man behind Naamah.

It was the voice of the water filter rep who had called that morning.

The sound of Naamah's chair scraping the floor as she whipped round caused Haramati to turn his head.

"Why are you sitting right here, of all places?" she asked him, her face taut.

"Is there a problem?" he asked, feigning innocence.

"The problem is that I don't believe in coincidences," she said sternly.

"Do you know him?" Helena asked, realization dawning. "I think I saw him near my house when I left for the meeting, and just now in the hotel lobby, too."

Naamah turned her chair all the way around, placing herself at Haramati's side. He took a sudden interest in the menu. As far as Naamah was concerned he could be a tail sent by the Mossad, a journalist, or a foreign agent; each was equally possible. "Who sent you?" she asked, attempting to exploit his embarrassment.

Haramati continued to study the menu, but he understood this could end badly, not just because of his uncompromising exposure or his failed mission. He figured he could even find himself being investigated by the police, whom the women might call in at any minute. He thought if he were quiet maybe they would leave, but Naamah had no intention of permitting him the right to remain silent.

"Do you plan on answering me?"

The athletic woman in the jogging suit looked like she was about to boil over. The next stage was threatening to be even worse than he had imagined. He thrust his hand into the pocket of his jacket and produced a tiny leather case containing his business cards, which bore the inscription Dan Haramati, Journalist, along with the logo of the Israel Broadcasting Authority and a major afternoon newspaper.

"Well, if it isn't Mr Harry Potter under his Invisibility Cloak," Naamah blurted out. "You're a real pain in the ass, you know?"

"Comes with the job," Haramati joked dispiritedly.

It was clear to Naamah that there had been a leak and that someone was trying to gain a scoop. If she overreacted now, it would only confirm his suspicions. If she made a scene bigger than the one she was already making it would only give him the pretext to write something oblique along the lines of "Why Mossad Wives are Uptight".

She decided, finally, on a different course. "It doesn't bother you that you're preventing two friends from having an intimate chat?"

"On the contrary, it most certainly bothers me," Haramati said, recovering himself. "I'm quite interested in you two continuing your conversation."

"Let's go," Helena said, keeping her Nordic cool.

Naamah was finding it difficult to switch from the aggressiveness she was feeling to backing off, as the situation warranted. She couldn't shake off the desire to slap his self-righteous face or grab him by the neck and throw him out.

"Wait a minute. Why us and not him?"

The waiter, who had just re-emerged from the kitchen with Haramati's coffee, was surprised at the scene in front of him and stopped in his tracks.

"Never mind. Do you want to read about this in the paper tomorrow?" Helena asked.

Naamah realized that that really was the last thing they could afford to have happen, so she controlled herself. Just one word in the paper and their husbands could be in grave danger, and any rescue attempt by the Mossad would be called off post-haste. She knew the journalist's name and where he worked; she would have to alert the Mossad immediately in order to prevent the story from getting out. Helena had already pulled out a fifty-shekel note and placed it on the table. The two women departed.

Haramati smiled in relief, shrugged his shoulders, pulled a small tape recorder from his pocket and turned it off. He took a laptop from his briefcase and placed it on the table, then sipped his coffee while waiting for the program to come up. He then opened a new file with the title, "The Good Life of Mossad Wives". Directly below that, where the program asked for a subtitle, he added, "Husbands Living It Up Spending Israel's Money – Wives Do It at Taxpayer's Expense".

Haramati swallowed another mouthful of coffee and his long fingers began typing quickly. *The wives of two Mossad operatives were spotted in a café on the Tel Aviv promenade shortly after each in turn had enjoyed a cup of coffee – at a luxury hotel at the taxpayer's expense, of course – in the company of none other than the head of the Mossad. The women met to swap stories. Incidentally, their husbands are currently overseas, involved in what one source has called "one of the strangest missions the Mossad has taken on in recent memory".*

Haramati reread what he had written and sighed. He had seen not only the anger in Naamah's eyes, but the fear, too. He had exposed nobody and done no damage, but there were certainly enough hints to cause someone hateful or unscrupulous to use his scoop as a springboard. He highlighted the paragraph, took another sip of coffee, and read it again. He'd better have a word with Milken, he thought as he pressed the delete button.

"We've got to let the Mossad know about this," Helena whispered, the moment they were outside. "They've got to stop him publishing what he heard."

Naamah feared their chances of stopping publication were nil, just as there had apparently been no way of thwarting the leak that had reached Haramati. The word "conscience" was not in the lexicon of a journalist who had hit on a scoop; nevertheless they would have to do everything in their power to kill this scoop right away, before it killed their husbands. Every reporter knew how to circumvent the censor. Perhaps a phone call from the Mossad chief to the director-general of the Israel Broadcasting Authority or the editor-in-chief of the newspaper would put a stop to it. She pulled out her cell phone and called Benny, and then Tamar, so that the message would reach Beaufort from at least two different sources.

Like Naamah, Helena was none too hopeful. She remembered well Gadi's description of the publicity following their failed mission in Beirut, even before the operatives had managed to get out safely. Only a few hours had passed since Gadi had rescued Ronen and John from the angry mob. He had dressed their wounds at the end of a narrow alley, the getaway car placed strategically between the three of them and curious passersby. Amazingly, no major blood vessels had been punctured and no bones had been broken. Ronen and John had gritted their teeth and announced they were able to fly. Gadi ordered his people to get to their rendez-vous.

An operations assistant was already at the airport and had purchased tickets for Ronen and John, and for squad members to escort them to the first Western destinations scheduled for departure: London and Copenhagen. They needed to depart from Lebanon before the blood they were losing seeped through their clothes, before someone gave the order to close the airport. In consultation with headquarters, several options for an airlift or sea rescue were weighed, but since no report about the assassination attempt had appeared in any of the media, it was decided to bring them out on scheduled flights.

Gadi picked up the operatives from their rendez-vous, removed transmitters, microphones and any other incriminating evidence, encouraged them, explained what was happening, calmed them down. He left them at the entrance to the airport only minutes prior to each one's check-in, and the operations assistant escorted them to their gates. Over the next few hours, three planes ferried operatives to Western destinations and the operations assistant informed Gadi, with a naughty smile, that the next flight out was bound for Hong Kong. That didn't sound too bad. After that, there was only a night flight to Paris.

"You go to Hong Kong, I'll fly to Paris," Gadi said. A flight to the Far East would delay Gadi's return to Israel by two or three days and Gadi, who was terribly frustrated by the failure of the operation, wanted to get back to his people and the debriefings as quickly as possible.

He returned to his hotel. It was already late afternoon. He showered, then searched for bloodstains on his shirt, finding a few, instead, on his trousers. He washed them, packed his belongings and ordered a meal from room service. He knew that the hours ahead would be among the longest of his life.

Four hours before he was scheduled to depart for Paris, Gadi tuned his television to the Israeli evening news. On the snowy screen he could make out the newscaster; on her left sat Milken, the station's notorious scandal-monger. Gadi had a premonition of bad news. "According to reports on Radio Hezbollah which have not been confirmed by any other source," Milken began, "an assassination attempt was made early this afternoon on the head of Hezbollah's overseas terror operations. An unnamed assassin pulled a gun on him at the entrance to his office in Beirut, but due to some mishap did not open fire. The unnamed assassin escaped in a getaway car but policemen in the vicinity shot and wounded the passengers. These passengers managed to escape thanks to their fellow squad members and a search to find them is now under way. Bloodstains were discovered in the getaway car. According to various signs and according to Radio Hezbollah, the operatives in question are Mossad agents. As stated, this news has not been confirmed by any other source."

Gadi had felt a chill rising up his back. Helena, he thought. And Naamah. And everyone's parents, and their children. He glanced at his watch: Ronen would have landed in London by now, and John would be landing any minute in Copenhagen. Even if Ronen and John were still on their feet – with the help of their escorts – and even if they managed to slip through passport control before anything could be whispered into the ears of the border police, they still had to board another plane to Israel, and that could not happen for another few hours at best. And the others were still en route. There was no way of being certain they would not be detained.

News agencies rarely quote Radio Hezbollah. Numerous reports of battles with the Zionist enemy were proved, after the fact, to be fictitious, so the major networks stopped regarding their reports as a trustworthy news source. But if the Israel Broadcasting Authority had decided to report it, then it must be reliable. The news bulletin would spread in a flash, in no time it would be picked up by CNN and the BBC.

On the face of it, Gadi thought, this should not present a direct threat to his safety in Beirut, since the real challenge was with Hezbollah and the local security forces, not the European security agencies. But paradoxically the Lebanese security forces were more likely to believe an IBA broadcast than the hysterical reports they received from Hezbollah.

Who exactly had been so irresponsible as to authorize this news item while some of the Mossad team were in transit and others were still in Beirut? What kind of sick scoop-chaser would broadcast such a bulletin without proper authorization and without knowing where the people involved were or what might happen to them, or how their family members would react for that matter?

Gadi had continued listening. Someone had apparently intervened and nothing more was forthcoming on the evening news; Milken was forced to swallow his own poison and leave the studio quietly. After briefly weighing his options, Gadi decided to go to the airport at midnight as if nothing had changed.

There was indeed increased security at the airport, but from Lebanese policemen, not Hezbollah or Syrian forces. The authorities were not quite buying the story of the assassination attempt. Gadi was asked a series of questions – about his activities, his meetings, where he had spent his time – but after four hours preparing he'd had answers ready to every question. His smile and his relaxed and courteous manner did the rest, covering up his racing heart. He told Helena a short while after his return that among all the curses he wished to let fly, the biggest was at the Israel Broadcasting Authority.

Even after Benny promised Naamah and Helena that "everyone possible" had intervened, Haramati's report appeared in the paper the next morning. It had been toned down from the one written in the café but was still capable of causing damage.

"There was no reason to prevent publication," Avigur, the bureau chief, apologized, when he phoned them – at Beaufort's request – to explain. "I'm sure you understand that the power of the Mossad vis-à-vis the media and the censor's office is pretty limited these days. If you read the article, you'll see it doesn't do any real damage."

Long-standing members of the Mistaravim squad recalled briefings with Mossad chiefs that had lasted into the early hours of the morning and covered almost every detail of the operational plan. With the situation as it was, a detailed operational briefing was run by Doron and lasted until the moment the chief arrived. While Doron stopped to have a private word with Beaufort, the operatives took the opportunity for a short break that became an official coffee break when the kitchen surprisingly supplied trays of cakes, bourekas and sandwiches prepared specially for them. Beaufort brought Doron up to date with regard to his conversations with the wives, especially Naamah's offer to go to Beirut. "But I don't think it's necessary any longer," he continued, "in light of Gadi's last phone conversation with Helena. I'm under the impression that things are under control. In fact, maybe we shouldn't be too hasty with our operation."

"Not being too hasty means postponing by twenty-four hours at least, until tomorrow night, because there's no way of bringing in our team during the day," Doron said. "It could be too late. But on the other hand," he said, at last finding an opportunity to bring up the scheduling issue with the chief, "it would give us another day for preparations, which we could really use."

"The ramifications of postponing the operation are serious," Beaufort agreed. "I'll consult the Prime Minister about it after I've seen the results of the preparations," he said, nodding in the direction of the rows of benches and the table in front of them, and the partitions arranged behind them. Two more partitions had been added to the rest, and on all of them appeared enlargements of the aerial and ground photographs with beautifully rendered captions that the intelligence officers and draughtswomen of the Intelligence Department had managed to prepare over the course of the day.

Doron clapped his hands twice for attention and indicated that everyone should return to the benches. The Mossad chief would see what they had accomplished, would have the chance to make up his mind about the operation, and Doron, too, would have the opportunity to refresh his view of the whole plan, since for the past twenty-four hours he had been too involved in the details. Once they were seated, with cups of coffee and cake in hand, the assembled group fell silent when the Mossad chief stood to address them.

"To put it simply, you've been called on to rescue the nation from an entanglement, the results of which could well be worse than past failures." He passed his tongue over his lips, scanning those present with a penetrating glance and frowning. Did they understand the importance of this mission? Did they realize that their actions could either mire the country in quicksand, or rescue it? Did each one of the young combatants facing him – or their slightly older commanders – have enough wisdom, daring and flexibility to know just how far to push his luck? Did they know which risk was necessary and which should be avoided? When to push forward and when to make a fast getaway? How was it possible to pass on this sense to them?

"Most likely at this very moment in Beirut there is a former Mossad operative who is trying to settle his own personal score with the Mossad and/or with Abu-Khaled, who was the head of Hezbollah's overseas terror operations, and another Mossad operative trying to stop him, more or less on his own initiative. This afternoon we learned that they have joined forces and are working together. We do not know what this means. The assumption is that Gadi has stopped Ronen, and it is possible that they will be returning to Israel as early as tomorrow. On the other hand, it's anyone's guess, since Gadi has been acting on his own and all communication has been conducted through an unauthorized third party. We understand that there is some sort of complication with the charge that Ronen took with him. We do not know if that means the charge has been placed on the car or elsewhere. For all these reasons, we have come to the conclusion that there is no justification for cancelling the operation."

The Mossad chief felt himself on more solid ground when describing the official considerations and the various possibilities and ramifications on the strategic and political level than he did when required, as he was now, to get to the operational details. He made do with several general questions, which enabled Yoav to describe the operation from the time they would land in Lebanon to their arrival in Bir-el-Abed, then the meeting or abduction, and then the retreat. Yossi made use of the maps and aerial photographs to describe the options for escape, while Daoud and Moussa answered several specific questions about the abduction and getting past roadblocks. The Mossad chief had run out of questions.

"Does anyone wish to say anything? Does anyone have a comment, does anyone feel there are unresolved issues?" he asked. From the bench there came some murmuring, which faded. "Is that a yes or a no?" Beaufort grumbled.

"Just what we all already know," Doron intervened: "That an operation like this requires much longer preparation in order to minimize potential mishaps."

Doron felt these words were both the least he was obliged to reiterate and the most he could get away with in such a forum.

The moment between the end of the briefings and the actual departure is the time for tying up loose ends, the time when suddenly the picture comes into focus. This picture was beginning to take shape in Doron's mind as an operation with potential for success, even though it had seemed doomed to failure only a short while earlier. His staff had made use of the entire intelligence mechanism at their disposal and the results were beginning to flow in. Precise analysis and interpretation of the aerial photographs taken of Abu-Khaled's home and office and their surroundings identified all roadblocks in the area as well as the guard booth at the entrance to his home; even now, a team of photo analysts from Eli's department was checking the area of the landing field and access roads according to updated aerial photographs. The main roads from North Beirut to Dahiyeh had been checked and at any minute they expected to receive an updated report on checkpoints and the level of alert. The operatives were well-trained and it was important to remember that Gadi was assumed to be on their side – and Gadi alone doubled the strength of their team. Perhaps he had even settled matters with Ronen and had, in the meantime, overcome whatever problem he had had with what "Ronen took with him". Doron naturally was not blind to Gadi's capabilities. Looking at the situation with absolute optimism, the Mistaravim might simply be going to give Gadi and Ronen a lift home, or they might find the two had already departed. But even being slightly less optimistic, and taking into consideration all reservations and exceptions, this operation now had the potential to succeed. Ultimately, Doron thought, there are the doers and the talkers; as one of the wholehearted doers, when it was decided to go ahead with the operation, all departments worked to arm the operatives with everything they needed to succeed, instead of looking for reasons not to act. Just before letting himself get washed away in a sea of adrenaline he wondered whether he wasn't repressing those reasons.

Doron heard the Mossad chief wishing all those present the best of luck.

A team of technicians finished anchoring the Mercedes to the floor of the helicopter. Next to the Yasur the pilots sat alone drinking coffee and chatting amongst themselves while the soldiers, armed with long-barrel and sharpshooter rifles, night-vision goggles and personal missiles, formed their own group. The hangar doors opened and the Mistaravim made their way to the chopper accompanied by some of the officials from headquarters.

Doron and the Mossad chief stayed behind while Beaufort had a brief phone consultation with the Prime Minister and Doron listened in. Even before the conversation ended Doron sent his bureau chief to instruct the men to take their places in the helicopter. "The answer is going to be 'yes' so why waste precious time?" he said when he heard how the matter was being presented. On the phone to the Prime Minister Beaufort listed the most salient points: that Gadi was with Ronen but the status of the relationship between them was unclear; that there seemed to be some problem with the charge, the nature of which was uncertain; that the team was ready, even though twenty-four hours for preparation were not enough; and that further postponements would apparently mean losing any chance of intervening on time.

The Mossad chief hung up a minute later. "The final decision has been postponed for another ninety minutes, to just prior to landing. In the meantime, have them take off. Good luck, Doron."

The last of Doron's internal conflicts disappeared the moment the Mossad chief and the Prime Minister decided to go ahead with the operation. A lot was dependent upon the operational abilities of Yoav and his men. But if it were necessary to make decisions from the command room, the burden would fall to him and there was no one who would perform this task better than him.

The adrenaline that had started to pump through his veins attested to this.

"Do you want to see the men before take-off?" Doron asked.

"Yes, of course," the chief said, trying to conceal his fatigue and anxiety.

Doron and Beaufort drove the few hundred feet to the helicopter in the chief's car. They approached Yoav and his team, who were next to the ramp with a number of people from headquarters, and shook their hands. Doron called Yoav to one side.

"So far we've only got an okay for the flight. Make sure before landing that you have communication with us."

Yoav shook his head, dissatisfied. "What's going to change between now and then? I want my men to get into operational mode on the trip there, I don't want them floating around, unsure whether or not there's going to be an operation until the last minute."

"I'll leave it to you to decide what to tell them and what not to," Doron said, clapping him on the shoulder. "And good luck."

Yoav disappeared into the dim red light inside the helicopter behind his team. He in turn was followed by Peter, the chief weapons officer, who would verify that there were no technical problems at the last minute; Avi, the communications officer, who would activate the transmitters on landing, and Eli who would pass on any last-minute intelligence briefings and update any incoming reports. The three would be returning to Israel with the chopper after dropping off the Mistaravim. The back ramp rose slowly and closed shut. The light from inside the craft disappeared. The engines, which had been working on low volume, suddenly increased in power and the blades began rotating.

The Mossad chief climbed into his car without another word and drove away. Doron and the officers from headquarters continued to stand in a group, blinking from the dust and wind kicked up by the large rotor.

The helicopter rose straight up to a height of about twenty feet, tilted to one side then the other, lowered its nose and shot towards the sea. The group stayed rooted for some time, speechless. Suddenly Doron turned to them and shook their hands again; it was the gesture of someone who knew only too well that from now on too much was in the hands of Lady Luck, who chose not to shine her countenance on those who did not ensure their fortunes by taking care of every last detail.

"See you in the command room," Doron said with a dispirited laugh, hoping to crack through the wall of anxiety and tension – and perhaps even sadness – that had descended on them. He walked to his car. Headquarters staff were always anxious about sending operatives to hostile nations, and tension was a constant. Sadness was perhaps unique to this mission.

8.

THE PHONE CALL to Peter's house was an exercise in futility. He was not at home and his son knew only that "Daddy's at work and he won't be home tonight." What did that mean, damn it? There was no operation planned for the division that evening. Perhaps urgent preparations were keeping Peter occupied all night long, something connected to them? Gadi had hoped his soothing messages passed through Helena would keep the activists at bay, the ones who were undoubtedly pressing to take action. But there was no way of knowing whether his messages had had the desired effect. According to his behaviour at their last meeting, Beaufort would be the last one to push for undertaking a hasty operation in Lebanon. Harder to discern was Doron's position, especially if they had discovered that Ronen had stolen the explosive charge, making Abu-Khaled's assassination imminent. It was not impossible to imagine in a case like this, with two operatives on the loose, that the Prime Minister would permit Doron to send in a few people at short notice in order to persuade them to come home, or even to apprehend them. Perhaps Doron himself would show up, that would be typical of him; maybe he was already on his way and the command room was being manned, and that's where Peter was...

The feeling of urgency this scenario raised convinced Gadi and Ronen to try to make their move earlier. They were surrounded by enough enemies and they didn't need a team from the division prowling around the neighbourhood, too. The second house diagonally opposite Abu-Khaled's building offered the best compromise between the ability to observe, linger, hide, and provide explanations, if necessary. That's where they'd spent the previous hour, Ronen leaning, crouched against one of the pillars supporting the building, while Gadi, standing, peered over the hedge, observing the passersby and the guard's activities.

The interval between each passing car grew and the number of pedestrians shrank. Gadi counted five minutes from the time the last car had passed and seven minutes since the last pedestrian. Another car passed, then two girls who had been chatting by the building next door parted; one entered the building while the other walked off in the opposite direction. The street had not yet gone to sleep – nor had Abu-Khaled, who had arrived home only fifteen minutes earlier. The fact that his car hadn't blown up at midday indicated that the timer's default was not twelve hours, but most likely twenty-four. Someone could still take them by surprise by entering the parking area in which they were hiding, but midnight was fast approaching as was the end of the twenty-four hour setting on the timer – if indeed their estimation was correct.

Their main problem now was the guard, who came out from his booth on occasion to make his presence known when a car or people passed by. He was still too alert but if they were to neutralize him, an unconscious or absentee guard would cause any passerby to call in reinforcements. Gadi was forced to wait a little longer, to allow the street to settle down even more.

All the partitions with the maps and photos were now standing in the command room, which had been set up next to the bureau of the division head. Albert, assistant to the communications officer, laid various transmitters on the table with labels next to them: Communications with Team, Army Hotline, Mossad Hotline, Telephone to Guest Room, where representatives from the Air Force and the Navy were stationed, Intercom to Mossad Chief.

Arye, director of the Planning Department, who had arranged the command room while Doron was at the briefing with the Mistaravim, had stuck labels to the chairs to identify who would be occupying them: the division head in the centre, directors of the planning and intelligence departments to his right and left, and, further down, the officers from Weapons, Communications, and one of his deputies, who would take notes in the operations log book.

"I want Rami next to me, and Albert facing the

transmitters," Doron said immediately on entering the room. "Yitzhaki will sit across from me and man the maps and photos. I want a chart showing the code names for communications. And leave a seat for the Mossad chief." Yitzhaki, the intelligence officer serving in Eli's absence, hurried to position himself on the opposite side of the table, spreading out aerial photos of the landing field, a map of the route to Beirut, and, tucked underneath for later, a map of Beirut. Albert stuck the chart of code names, which he'd prepared earlier, to the tabletop, next to the transmitters. "I want one of your deputies to take notes in the operations log book and that's it, everyone else out," Doron said to Arye. The breaking developments of this operation could be so irregular that he didn't want any unnecessary pairs of ears in the vicinity. Final authorization for the operation would only come – or not – in another hour, close to landing, but as far as Doron was concerned, the operation was already under way.

Arye swallowed hard and took up the post next to the operations log, at the end of the table. Even without this minor insult he thought the operation was harmful and unnecessary, occupying everyone for several days. As a former squad commander, Arye made no secret of the fact that he thought Gadi was not behaving as a commander should. It was a breach of regulations, and Gadi should be judged and dealt with accordingly.

In the Mossad, where strict discipline prevailed even without ranks or a military court system, many thought like Arye. Any breach of the written – and unwritten – codes of behaviour or regulations was viewed harshly, especially in a case like this where operational discipline was compromised.

Benny the psychologist was one of the few who found anything commendable in Gadi's actions, or at least dared to say so. "It's important to have procedures and values, but when someone violates them it's necessary to ask whether that helps or harms the organization," he said. "We're not the kind of organization that checks its ethos on a regular basis."

Eli knew that while he was on the helicopter en route to Lebanon and back, Beaufort and Doron would be sitting in the command room waiting for developments and would undoubtedly discuss how they would deal with Gadi and Ronen. There was nothing to keep the Mossad chief from obtaining an order for their arrest, at least on the grounds of unauthorized entry into an enemy country. He thought that for a person who violates the rules in a patriotic organization like the Mossad, where power combines with self-righteousness, the results could be disastrous.

Just before climbing aboard the helicopter, Eli had managed to toss one thought on the matter to Doron: "Not every transgression of the rules should be punished in full. Remember that Gadi is trying to save the organization from itself."

Yoav had left a bit of unfinished business for the flight: he wanted to go over, with Yossi and Eli, a few of the navigation routes he hadn't had a chance to study properly; with the entire team he wanted to review the major contingency plans, which had been handed to him in a neat chart but which his subordinates had scarcely had a chance to look at; and mostly, he wanted to discuss what would happen at the very moment they found Ronen or Gadi. After all, even if they were forced into their worst-case scenario – a hostile abduction – it was important to keep in mind that these men were colleagues. He had about ninety minutes to accomplish it all.

Yoav was sitting next to Yossi in the front seat of the Mercedes, while Moussa and Daoud sat behind. On either side of the car, the soldiers and the three members of headquarters staff who had come along sat on the low benches that lined the inside of the helicopter. The chopper's internal lighting was extinguished, leaving only four green emergency lights blinking in the corners. The thunder of the engines, though dulled inside, shook the craft, and the darkness that could be glimpsed outside the windows created a unique atmosphere, peaceful and tense at the same time. No one spoke.

Yoav looked around. Yossi seemed pensive, and Yoav felt his own energy seeping away. He had spared his men the uncertainty, and having made their peace with the fact that the operation was indeed about to take place, Daoud and Moussa managed to sleep, the head of one on the other's shoulder. But it was the apparent certainty of the mission that was causing Yossi to withdraw into himself with thoughts of his newborn son, who had just come out of a long period of jaundice after the birth; and about his wife, who still had trouble walking but would nonetheless have to take care of the baby all on her own, but if everything went according to plan, he would be reunited with her in less than twenty-four hours. And if it didn't? Yoav's own children appeared in his mind's eye, along with his wife who, unlike the others, was happy with the pleasure he took in his special job and with belonging to the Mossad family. He knew these were thoughts he shouldn't be having at that moment.

"Feel like reviewing the routes, Yusuf?" Yoav asked, and he was met with a look of utter resentment: unlike a number of his colleagues, who had become enamoured of Arabic culture through study and work and had immersed themselves in it, Yossi didn't like being called by the Arabic version of his name. He maintained a complete separation between work and life. On second thoughts, however, he understood that Yoav was merely trying to get him into the mood of the operation, since in little over an hour they would become Yusuf the driver and Munir the head of the work crew and Moussa and Daoud the labourers, making their way from their villages to a building site in Bureij Hamoud. And when they passed Bureij Hamoud and crossed the Beirut River their story would alter. They would be on their way from their homes in Bureij Hamoud to the new development being built along the shore at El-Ouzai. And at the roadblocks into Dahiyeh their cover story would change direction completely, and they would hail from the south, from the Sidon region, on their way to meet with their contractor who was coming in from A-Sheikh, slightly to the north, and would take them with him.

But he wasn't quite ready to turn into Yusuf. In fact, neither as Yossi nor as Yusuf did he feel just then like reviewing the routes that Yitzhaki had crammed into his head for hours that day.

"All right, so just listen while I go over them with Eli," said Yoav. He asked Yossi to move to the back seat and called Eli into the driver's seat. Eli spread his neatly-folded, laminated maps across the steering wheel and the dashboard. The helicopter continued northwards, low over the sea.

After an hour or so the pilot's voice came over the loudspeaker. "Crossing the shoreline."

The sudden alertness caused the men's muscles to tighten. The soldiers instinctively felt for their weapons and the Mistaravim decided to check their own cache one last time. Avi, the communications officer, stood up as if it were already time for him to check the transmitters. They were over Lebanese territory now; at any time someone could open fire and they would find themselves in battle.

The helicopter was now some twenty miles north of Beirut, following a deep riverbed east and then southwards, a course it would maintain, undetected by radar, until reaching the landing point.

"Men, we still have some time," Yoav said, futilely trying to calm them. Their ability to concentrate, which had been low anyway, had by then completely evaporated. Yossi returned to the driver's seat and while his men were busy with last-minute preparations, Yoav pulled out the chart of contingency plans, shone the beam of the car light on it and began reading – though he, too, had trouble concentrating. Deep down in his belly a familiar chill took hold; in another few minutes he would know if the operation was necessary or not, would know whether he and his men were about to stick their heads in the lion's mouth or whether they'd be spared that.

"Five minutes to landing," came the pilot's voice. The helicopter came alive.

The soldiers put on their bullet-proof vests and their helmets and gathered up their various weapons. The Mistaravim moved to their correct positions after reconfirming that their equipment was with them and that nothing inappropriate had been left visible in the Mercedes.

The three men from headquarters gathered around the car and shook hands with the team. Yoav activated the hidden transmitters in the car. There was a light buzzing, and then static that faded out. The system wasn't reacting. The communications officer opened Yoav's door, leaned in and played with the knobs. A moment later they could hear static again.

"Three, three," Yoav said. "Awaiting authorization."

"We read you. Three. Hold." It was Albert's voice in the command room.

Yoav waited, tense and alert. His team didn't know what "three" was, did not know that only now was the final decision about this operation being made. If they were to turn back now, his men wouldn't bear a grudge against him; if they were about to continue then it was just as well

302

they had already entered into the spirit of a mission. The time this flight took was almost as important as the length of a pregnancy: in a short, compressed period you have to internalize the fact that you're on a mission and there's no turning back. At the end of the flight you'll be involved in a new reality that places new responsibilities and burdens on your shoulders. With their last checks and preparations, each team member – wordlessly, to himself – had taken leave of his loved ones. But Yoav still couldn't do so.

A minute passed, as long as eternity. What were they waiting for? Yoav thought. The chopper was about to land.

"Continue." It was Doron's voice over the radio. "Continue, and good luck."

Yoav took a deep breath. The pendulum of his feelings, which had been swinging between the desire to act and the hope that the operation would be deemed unnecessary and would be cancelled, ceased. In its place, all the details he needed to deal with crowded into his consciousness, knocking out every other thought. The operation had begun.

"One minute to landing." The emergency lights were turned off. They sat tight in a silence so complete that it was almost possible, above the dull roar of the engines, to hear their breathing, their heartbeats. From the windows they could see the dark side of the mountain, and above it the sky, slightly lighter.

The helicopter landed with the help of its instruments in complete darkness. The rotor continued spinning and the landing was so soft that the passengers did not feel it. The soldiers, laden with weapons and wearing night vision goggles, filed out of the two small doors on either side while the technicians began unfastening the metal chains that had anchored the Mercedes in place. Yossi started the engine. The ramp was unlocked and made ready for lowering.

The soldiers positioned themselves on their bellies, around the sides and front of the helicopter, their weapons pointed outwards. They reported that the area was clean. The ramp came down slowly and Yossi inched forwards, freeing the car from the track into which the wheels had been locked. Peter guided him out of the helicopter, the Mercedes gliding slowly and almost noiselessly to just beyond the ramp. Eli left the helicopter and standing by the car, he looked around, a pair of night vision goggles over his eyes, a map and a compass in his hand. They were in the middle of a harvested field on a very narrow mountain plateau. The GPS plotted their location quite accurately and he was able to find the direct line to the point from which the car would leave the field on a compacted dirt road that curved for a few miles before meeting up with a paved southbound road. He pointed to a spot to the right of the car. "Just over there, about three hundred feet from here, Yoav, Yossi, that's your dirt road."

The car began driving away, its lights off. Yoav was looking at the road, Yossi was occupied with night driving and only Daoud, in the back seat with Moussa, gave a faint wave of farewell.

In silence Eli, Peter and Avi watched the darkened

Mercedes until its occupants had found the path after two false starts and picked up speed – still without lights. The three returned to the helicopter, and a moment later the soldiers re-entered the craft as well. The engines thundered, the helicopter lifted off, kicking up a pillar of dust, veered to the right and flew off in the direction from which it had come.

"Seven, seven." It was Avi's voice they could hear in the command room, the noise of the helicopter in the background.

"Seven," Doron read from the chart in front of him. "Lift off from Lebanon."

"In just a minute we'll get an 'eight', from the car, when the headlights come on," Albert said, glancing at the chart. Doron shushed him with a wave of his hand. Yitzhaki shone his laser pointer back and forth on the enlarged aerial photographs that had been taken down from the partition, highlighting the dirt road across a field down which the Mercedes was now making its way in darkness.

But the transmitter was silent.

"Perhaps he's waiting for the helicopter to get further away," the assistant communications officer opined.

"It's a pretty navigable dirt road. Maybe he's got good visibility and prefers to get to the paved road without headlights," Yitzhaki said.

"If you keep talking we won't hear the report," the division head said.

A few more minutes passed in silence. The helicopter was flying further and further away; if the Mercedes had progressed as planned then they should have reached the paved road. The possibilities were numerous, and many of them passed through the minds of those gathered in the command room. Was there a problem with the transmitters? Highly possible. Mechanical difficulties with the car? An encounter with a farmer? An encounter with a security force, preventing them from reporting? Perhaps the car had overturned? It had all happened in previous operations.

"Okay Rami, give us your assessment," Doron said, striving to be relaxed.

"I'm with Yitzhaki. My guess is that visibility is good and Yoav wants to reach the main road without being spotted. Afterwards it'll be a lot easier with the cover story."

"Is that part of the contingency plans?" Doron asked.

"No," Rami smiled. "It's part of the tradition."

"Well from now on let's add it to the contingency plans. This operation isn't even under way yet, we've got a lot of hours ahead of us and we don't need all kinds of improvisations to make us tense," Doron said quietly. Only those who were particularly familiar with his composure and self-restraint could sense his anger.

Doron's secretary came in with a small tea trolley filled with drinks. Just inside the door she noticed the utter silence, left the trolley to one side and departed without a word.

Doron used the intercom to inform Beaufort, who was in his office reviewing intelligence material, of the delay. Beaufort was supposed to join the others in the command room when the squad reached Beirut since there was no need for his presence during the flight and landing; however, in the event of unexpected developments he could be in the command room within a minute.

The helicopter reported having crossed the shoreline. From here on in they would need to involve the commander of the Air Force if it were necessary to send the chopper back to Lebanon.

Several minutes passed before they heard Yoav on the transmitter. "Eight," he reported.

Yitzhaki glanced at his watch and shone the pointer on the spot – some ten miles from the landing field – they should have reached if they'd travelled at the planned speed.

"Or maybe they just finished fixing a flat tyre and they're still on their way down the mountain," Doron said, smiling for the first time. He leaned back to take a can of lemonade. "We're not expecting any regular reports before Beirut, are we?" he asked, glancing at the chart. Albert shook his head. "Good, then I'm going to report to the boss from my office. Rami, you're in charge."

With Doron's departure a number of staff members who had been waiting for news in the adjacent rooms poked their heads into the command room, and a whisper of relief floated through the air.

Immediately after turning onto the dirt road at the edge of the field, Yoav instructed Daoud to open the compartment at his feet and give him the package that was stowed there. Yossi smiled grandly as Yoav removed the

307

rags that surrounded the pair of night vision goggles he'd taken on his own initiative and told Yossi to put them on. Let Rami and Doron try and explain what four Palestinian labourers were doing in the mountains at that hour of the night. There had been no time to discuss the issue prior to departure, and Yoav wasn't going to let his men pay the price for the "minimum equipment" policy. He preferred to reach the first populated areas without lights – and without being discovered.

After an hour of driving through the hushed winding mountain roads that led from the landing field down to the shore, they reached the first permanent roadblock known to Intelligence, east of Jedeida near the Jounieh-Beirut road. The compartments holding the light weapons were made ready for fast access.

Two parallel rows of spikes were spread across the road, leaving a narrow diagonal path between them and the Mistaravim could see a bonfire burning nearby. Yossi slowed down, stopping alongside two policemen stationed next to the rows of spikes. The first requested their papers while the second peered at them, bored, from the other side of the car. Two other police officers were next to the bonfire, upon which was perched a finjan filled with Turkish coffee: one was crooning and the other leaping about and dancing. Yoav smiled at them, and Moussa and Daoud gave them friendly looks. The officer returned their documents and Yossi drove off. Yoav closed his window and Moussa started to croon like the policeman. "A cold wind is blowing," he sang, the start of a popular bonfire song. "Add a matchstick, keep the bonfire glowing," all four sang together.

✧✧✧

Gadi tapped Ronen's head. "Okay, the street's quiet. Let's go."

Ronen flinched. "I fell asleep," he said, discomfited.

"The guard's still coming out of his booth every few minutes. There's no choice, we're going to have to neutralize him as we discussed. At the moment he is inside the booth so cross the street now and approach him from the rear. I'll start moving in another minute."

Ronen emerged stealthily from his hiding place, looked both ways and then crossed the street to the garden surrounding the building next to Abu-Khaled's home. Gadi then stepped onto the street: there was no one to be seen in either direction. He crossed to the pavement opposite and continued in the direction of the guard booth. When he entered the guard's line of vision, he saw him stand up, firming his grip on the Kalashnikov rifle slung over his shoulder. From the corner of his eye Gadi could see Ronen climbing over the fence separating Abu-Khaled's garden from his neighbours' and approaching the booth in a crouch. The guard heard Ronen's footsteps and turned his head instinctively to the little opening at the back of the booth.

Gadi moved quickly to close the remaining distance between himself and the guard and punched him in the chest before he even had a chance to look at his attacker. Gadi felt his fist pass through cracked ribs; the guard groaned and fell forwards at the waist. Gadi grabbed him by the windpipe and lifted him up. The only sound coming from the guard's throat was a light grunt as Ronen quickly slipped a rope around his neck from outside the window of the booth, and pulled. The guard's body was pinned to the wall and, unconscious, his head lolled forwards. Ronen released the rope and quickly moved inside the booth while Gadi eased the guard onto the chair. He removed the magazine from the guard's rifle and threw it into the bushes nearby. Placing the weapon across the guard's lap and looping the strap around his neck, Gadi noticed a pistol in the man's belt. "We screwed up," he whispered to Ronen, "not noticing it." When discussing various plans for attacking the guard they counted on the time it took to lift, aim and cock a Kalashnikov. But to draw a pistol took no time at all, one second and you were ready to shoot. Gadi took the pistol, looked it over and stuffed it into his own belt, winking at Ronen.

"Are you sure we shouldn't tie him up?" Ronen asked. They had gone over every stage of their plan several times, but he still wasn't at ease about leaving the guard free right in the middle of their operation.

"If someone comes by and sees him tied up they'll alert the whole neighbourhood. This way they'll think he's sleeping, and he himself won't remember what happened to him," Gadi answered in a whisper.

He indicated to Ronen to stand a few feet away, near the pavement at the entrance to the car park where the streetlights did not reach.

"*You* stand there," Ronen retorted. "I'll dismantle it. I know how I attached it."

"It's no longer the way you attached it. Anyway, it was

my decision to dismantle it so I'll do it. Get over there!"

There was a certain logic to Ronen's offer, and Gadi appreciated his willingness at the moment of truth to assume responsibility and take the risk. But this wasn't the time for displays of chivalry.

Ronen did as he was told while Gadi, crouching, made his way to Abu-Khaled's car.

Yoav and his team bypassed Beirut to the east, winding down along Bureij Hamoud and Tel-a-Za'atar in a matter of minutes without encountering a single roadblock until they crossed the Beirut River, in the south of the city. The guards there were bored and lenient: a car ferrying Palestinian workers back to their homes late at night was not an unusual sight. From there they reached the El-Obeiri road. Yoav searched for Abu-Khaled's office by checking the numbers on the buildings, and when they drew close he told Yossi to slow down. As expected, the office was dark at that hour and the adjacent car park was empty. Yoav reported these findings to the command room and had Yossi turn the car in the direction of Abu-Khaled's home.

The roads were deserted, and Yoav decided to skirt the roadblock at the entrance to Bir-el-Abed. He pointed Yossi towards a narrow side street with a "no entry" sign, and from there to another lane. One block before Abu-Khaled's street he told Yossi to stop the car.

"Here's where we split up," Yoav said. "Moussa, are you ready? This is your street," he said, pointing to the right.

"We'll meet at the next intersection. If you see anyone or anything, let us know. Check your transmitter."

Moussa inserted the tiny earphone in his ear, got out of the car and counted in Arabic. Yossi adjusted the volume of the car radio.

The car moved on, stopped again, and let Daoud off to investigate the street that curved off to the left. Yoav and Yossi continued driving slowly towards Abu-Khaled's street.

Ronen saw the car approaching and took several steps backwards into the darkness. The headlights failed to pick him up, just as Ronen missed Yoav's smile when he noticed the sleeping guard. Yoav gave Daoud the go-ahead to patrol the street on foot while they continued to check the surrounding streets by car.

Gadi, under the Mercedes, found the charge dangling dangerously. One metal band kept it attached to part of the chassis while another held the receiver in place; the cable attaching the two had been severed. This time he was equipped with a small torch and cutters. Taking the wires apart gave him no trouble, but the cutters were ineffectual on the wide strips of duct tape. He had no choice but to find the ends of the tape and begin unravelling them.

He heard a stifled cough, which was the sign from Ronen that there was some sort of interruption. He minimized his movement but did not stop his slow removal of the thick tape.

A man emerged from the building, perhaps from the first floor, since the stairwell light did not come on. He crossed the car park and stepped out onto the street just a few feet from where Ronen stood, frozen in his dark corner. The man glanced towards the booth, from where he thought the cough had come, waved, and when no response came he assumed the guard had fallen asleep and continued on his way.

Ronen checked the guard, saw he was moving slightly, and, unwilling to risk his revival, applied a shoto chop to his neck. The man's head dropped forwards and his body lost its balance. Ronen caught him by the shoulders and propped him up against the back wall again. Only then did he clear his throat to signal to Gadi that everything was okay. But Gadi had continued with his work anyway.

Daoud made his way up the street towards Ronen. Ronen coughed again and Daoud caught a glimpse of him without turning his head or slowing his step, only just making out his shape in the darkness. He passed by without the slightest reaction, taking in the guard slouched in his chair. Daoud concluded that that was not the position of a man in slumber. He heard Ronen clear his throat and smiled at his use of the conventional signals. He continued another ten steps before whispering into the tiny microphone on his shirt collar.

"He found him!" Yoav told Yossi. "Pick up Moussa." Yossi made a quick turn to the street where Moussa was patrolling.

Daoud told them that there was no sign Ronen had suspected him, that he'd coughed when Daoud approached and cleared his throat when he'd walked away.

Moussa was in the car seconds later. Yoav activated the transmitter to Israel.

"Daoud has identified Ronen at the entrance to the object's building," he reported.

Yoav's words electrified the command room, which was more crowded now with Doron and Beaufort and the three members of headquarters staff who had returned from the flight. No one moved; the only sound was static from the receivers.

"Describe the situation," Doron said quietly.

The communications officer tinkered with the volume and Yoav's voice filled the room.

"The street is quiet, there's no traffic of any kind at the moment. I understand from Daoud that Ronen is a few feet from the pavement and that the guard has apparently been neutralized. Looks to me like the right conditions for taking action."

"Hang on, we're missing some information. Have you identified the object's car?"

"Yes, the Mercedes is in the car park."

"What about Gadi?"

"Unclear," Yoav said after a pause. "But he's apparently in the vicinity because Ronen was using some of the conventional signals."

"What's the situation with the roadblocks?" Doron asked.

"Only the permanent ones. We can make detours. All in all the situation is quiet."

"Get ready and wait," Doron said, ending communication. He turned to Beaufort, who was sitting at his side.

"I think this is it, they should make their move."

"I don't think there's enough information about Gadi to enable me to make a decision," Beaufort responded.

In the meantime Eli spread enlargements of the aerial photographs of Abu-Khaled's neighbourhood on the table.

Doron said, "I recommend authorizing Yoav to take action against Ronen. If Gadi shows up, the contingency plans make clear what should be done."

Beaufort was insistent. "I don't want any surprises. If Gadi *is* there, what are the Mistaravim supposed to do?"

"Our working assumption is that Gadi is on our side, and he'll help them."

"And if he isn't?"

"They can't overpower two of them, they haven't prepared for that scenario. I don't think we need to start creating unexpected contingencies at this point."

"What do you mean, 'unexpected'?" Beaufort said angrily. "We were aware they had joined forces, which meant one of two things: either they're both on our side or both against us. How can you say unexpected?"

Next, Yossi picked up Daoud, who had continued walking and was now out of Ronen's line of vision. Once they were in the car Yoav said, "Our assumption is that Gadi is on our side and Ronen is not. Until we know otherwise, we'll stick with that assumption. But we still don't know what's going on between them. If they're both near the Mercedes then maybe something has changed. That close to the guard there's no chance of persuading anyone to do anything: if Ronen is alone we'll abduct him. If Gadi is there too then I'll approach him while you three take Ronen. As far as we're concerned the guard poses a threat. I'll neutralize him as I see fit."

"In my opinion he's already been neutralized," Daoud repeated.

"Is he dead? Unconscious? For how long?"

"No clue."

"So he's still a threat," Yoav concluded.

He instructed Moussa to leave the car, tapping him on the shoulder. Moussa was short and broad with a moustache and curly hair. Due to a combination of his non-threatening appearance, his cool self-control and his incredible punch – which had provided dozens of knock-outs during his IDF service in another undercover Mistaravim unit in the West Bank – he had been selected to kick off the operation.

He began walking in Ronen's direction.

"I sent Number One," Yoav told the command room. "The street is deserted, I have good conditions for operating."

"The street is deserted and Yoav has already sent the first man. The conditions could change at any minute and we could miss the opportunity to act," Doron emphasized.

The Mossad chief thought for a moment. "Clarify the matter of Gadi with Yoav."

To Doron it was all clear, both the vicinity and the conditions. He knew that at the outset of an operation he couldn't start asking all sorts of managerial questions. Still, it couldn't hurt to remind Yoav's men, in the midst of their adrenaline rush, that Gadi was likely to assist them, and that at any rate he was considered an ally.

"I'll remind him," Doron said, "but I think we should respond to the situation as it's been described to us, that they've seen Ronen but they haven't seen Gadi. I recommend we take action."

"If you're convinced that the conditions are optimal," Beaufort said in a low voice, "and a delay of two minutes for clarifying matters will be detrimental, then I authorize you to take action."

"Okay men, move out," Doron said into the receiver. "Remember that you've got an ally there, and good luck."

Yoav tapped on Yossi's shoulder and the car inched forwards following Moussa.

Gadi finished dismantling the charge, placed it gingerly on the ground next to him and crawled out from under the car. He rolled over onto his stomach and stretched out his arms, sliding the charge close to himself with caution. For the third time, Ronen coughed and Gadi froze. Shit. Now he, along with the charge was exposed to anyone who might enter the car park. Slowly he began pushing the charge back under the car.

Moussa moved along the pavement in measured steps. Ronen, who had noted Gadi's position, decided to intercept whoever was approaching, and stepped out from the shadows onto the pavement. He couldn't let the stout little man turn into the car park. But the man seemed to be walking in a straight path so Ronen avoided making eye contact with him, instead turning his back on him as if he were waiting for someone to emerge from the building. At the very moment Moussa drew level with Ronen, the Mercedes with the rest of the team pulled up alongside them.

While still several feet from Ronen, Moussa had formed a fist with his right hand, weighing carefully just how far to jab it into his stomach. But when Ronen turned away from him Moussa changed plans. He grabbed Ronen around the throat, pressed his hip into Ronen's back and bent him backwards, increasing the effect of the strangulation.

Yoav and Daoud jumped out of the car, leaving the doors open. Yoav lifted Ronen's feet while Daoud grabbed him around the waist. Moussa, his arms clamped around Ronen's neck, slid into the car first with Daoud after him, but Ronen's flailing legs prevented Yoav from closing the door.

First, let's get out of here, Yoav thought. He let go of Ronen's legs, ran around to the front passenger's seat and the car lurched forwards. Yoav turned in his seat to get control of Ronen's legs. He tried to tell Ronen who they were, but a sharp blow to his chin from Ronen's knee cut him short. Daoud attempted to handcuff him but received several blows to his face from Ronen's right fist; Moussa maintained his hold around Ronen's neck while Ronen jabbed him in the eyes with his fingers of his other hand. Yossi slammed into the kerb and had trouble getting the car under control when one of Ronen's kicks landed on his neck.

"We're from the Mossad! We're on the same side!" Yoav said as he got yet another kick to the face. There's no choice, he said to himself as he delivered a powerful punch to Ronen's ribs and another to his stomach. Ronen was winded for a moment, giving the three an opportunity to handcuff him. But they couldn't keep the car moving with the door ajar so Yossi pulled over and they tried again to subdue him, telling him again who they were. But Ronen, barely able to breathe, and continuing to thrash about could hear nothing.

"Knock him out," Yoav told Moussa, who increased the pressure around Ronen's neck.

For a few brief seconds, Gadi could hear faint noises and then the sound of a car pulling away. He lifted himself up onto his knees and peered through the windows of the Mercedes: no one seemed to be about. Perhaps the guard had regained consciousness, or someone had come to relieve him, or a local patrol had passed by – a number of possibilities flashed through his mind. But where was Ronen? He could be hiding, but why would he stay hidden when everything was quiet? His concern overcame his caution and he hurried to the pavement.

Down the street, parked by the kerb, he could see an old Mercedes from which a pair of legs were protruding, kicking and flailing. Suddenly they were pulled inside and a long arm reached out from inside the car to pull the door shut. Ronen had been abducted.

"Uzubillah!" came a woman's cry. "Heaven help us! Mufik, come quickly!" The familiar voice resounded in Gadi's ears; once again it was that neighbour and once again Ronen was getting beaten up.

Gadi's whole being focused on the need to save Ronen. His first thought was that the kidnappers were local Hezbollah men. Perhaps someone had noticed the two foreigners prowling about the neighbourhood, someone – maybe even the man who had left the building earlier – had seen Ronen or the unconscious guard and had roused them, and they had done what the Hezbollah does best: abduct foreigners. Other possibilities – that this was a Lebanese security force or a Mossad squad – flitted through his consciousness and disappeared; either was highly unlikely, since the Lebanese security forces rarely ventured into Dahiyeh and the Mossad had little reason to stage an operation, as a result of his soothing messages. Whoever they were, these kidnappers, he knew that if he let them out of his sight his chances of finding them and rescuing Ronen were nil. Ronen's car was nearby and he was poised to dash over to it when he remembered the explosive charge.

He considered leaving it in the hedge but he wouldn't be able to return to dispose of it in the little time left of the twenty-four-hour period, but if it blew up, they would have caused the damage they had tried to prevent.

He picked up the charge and raced out to the street. The tail of the Mercedes was just turning right at the end of the street. He didn't have a minute to lose, since there was no way of knowing which way they would turn next. He would dispose of the charge at the first appropriate space he found on the way. But first he had to rescue Ronen.

At the very moment he sat in the BMW and lay the charge on the passenger's seat he knew that what he was doing was complete madness. Why did he have to push to the very limits, why did he always have to stand at the precipice, overlooking the void?

He raced off in crazed pursuit of the Mercedes, skidding through the right turn at the end of the street, accelerating then braking at every corner to search for the Mercedes. If the kidnappers were indeed Hezbollah they could turn down any little side street: any building could be their hideaway. Still, Gadi figured they would take him to Haret-Hreik, the very heart of their territory. When he failed to find the Mercedes he pointed his car in the direction of Haret-Hreik, speeding down a one-way street that would take him out of Bir-el-Abed without having to pass through any roadblocks, and slowing momentarily next to the stop sign at the entrance to the El-Obeiri road, the main artery separating the two neighbourhoods. Far off to his left he could make out the Mercedes as it continued eastwards down the main road.

Gadi thought they must be taking him instead to the

Beqaa Valley, which gave him a little time to get organized, to think, and to get rid of the time bomb on the seat next to him just as soon as they left this heavily populated area. He recalled that just before merging with the Beirut-Damascus road there was some derelict land; an explosion there would not lead anyone to blame Israel.

"Ronen is with me, he put up a bit of a fight. I'm on my way, don't have a clue about Gadi yet," Yoav broadcast into the transmitter.

Ronen was half-conscious, mumbling, his legs bound, too. Yoav's lip was bleeding as was Daoud's nose. Yoav was holding a mini-Uzi and another weapon lay across Yossi's lap. They made a detour around the roadblock and leaving the neighbourhood they raced towards the road that bypassed Beirut to the east. They needed to calm Ronen down before doing him serious harm. Yoav waited until they reached a less populated area, which they found at the southern edge of A-Sheikh. Yossi slowed the car down and Yoav raised himself onto his knees and turned around to face the back seat. He signalled to Moussa to ease up a bit on Ronen's throat. "Ronen," he said, "we're from the division. Listen to me, we're from the Mossad. Rami's squad. We were together in Damascus a couple of years ago. Look at me, you'll remember."

A spark of memory and comprehension flashed in Ronen's eyes, and he became aware of bits and pieces of the voices and conversation he'd been hearing but had been unable to process while he was fighting so wildly. Suddenly he understood that with the best of intentions, they had all – because of him – had a hand in leading Gadi straight to hell. Yoav motioned to Moussa to relax his hold on Ronen completely. When he spoke, his voice could barely be heard: "Gadi is with the charge next to Abu-Khaled's car."

Gadi was gaining on the Mercedes and considered whether this were the time and place to overtake the abductors' car. He pulled the guard's pistol – a heavy old Webley revolver – from his belt to check its contents and found the gun loaded with six nine-millimetre bullets. Since there appeared to be four people in the Mercedes he figured he would have to pull up alongside the car and shoot each one of them in the head before they understood what was happening and shot Ronen. Then he would have two more bullets to make up for whatever he hadn't managed in the first round. He was well-trained to shoot from a moving car, but had almost no experience shooting while driving. He would have to pull close to the rear of the Mercedes and take out the two in the back seat, who were holding Ronen, and then the driver and the one in the passenger's seat. If he missed, Ronen's chances of survival were slim, and even if he were successful he would have to drag Ronen to his car and escape: the road was hardly deserted, there would be witnesses. And then there was the bomb, still ticking away next to him. The plan was lousy: he would have to get rid of the charge first, follow the abductors until they were completely outside the city on the Beirut-Damascus road, and only then take action.

He eased up on the accelerator but to his surprise the

abductors' car slowed down, too. There was strange movement inside the car; it seemed as though the man sitting next to the driver had turned his whole body around towards the back seat. What were they doing to Ronen? Gadi glanced at the charge and cursed. Should he take a risk on the timer? Should he dump the charge and take a chance with Ronen's life? He couldn't postpone taking action.

The Mercedes suddenly veered off onto the shoulder of the road. Had they killed Ronen? Were they killing him at that moment? They came to a stop. He would pull up alongside them; stationary, they would be much easier to hit.

Gadi opened his right window, grabbed the gun sitting on the seat next to him and held it firmly in his right hand, his finger on the trigger. He slowed down, pulling up alongside the Mercedes, fixed his stare at the car and raised the gun.

He couldn't see Ronen but the the man leaning over the front seat was familiar. At that moment other faces turned towards him, the tense faces of the driver and the two men in the back seat. As the driver lifted a mini-Uzi Gadi took aim: In that split second Yossi saw Gadi's face behind the gun and Gadi realized that these men were the Mistaravim. He dropped the gun into his lap just as Yossi's arm came down, too. So the Mossad *had* taken action, and with what speed! Now he could see Ronen, whom Moussa had helped to sit up, and felt choked with emotion. They could just as easily have shot one another, a double hit in the outskirts of Beirut. The Mistaravim always quoted the Arabic expression about haste being a tool of the devil, but sometimes Lady Luck actually favoured the hasty.

"The charge is here in the car," Gadi said, as soon as he'd recovered. "I haven't defused it yet. Do you guys know how long the timer is set for?"

Yoav, too, had needed a few seconds to pull himself together before answering. "No, nobody thought of the possibility of having to defuse the charger. What are you planning to do with it?" he asked.

"Toss it over there," Gadi said, indicating a derelict plot of ground between two buildings to their right, "and then get the hell out of here. But inform the command room in case they have some other suggestion. Get them to ask Peter how long the timer's set for. If he's certain there's time then I'll defuse it."

Gadi had pulled up in the right-hand lane, and several passing cars honked at him. He moved the BMW a few feet ahead of the other car and on to the shoulder, too. While he was waiting for the others to contact Peter he began removing the charge's plastic cover in case he was told there was time to defuse it.

Ronen, no longer bound, came limping over to Gadi's car, holding his aching side. A smile formed at the corners of Gadi's mouth at the sight of him. How many ups and downs their relationship had endured during these two days! But this wasn't the time for a class reunion…

"Gadi, what are you doing!?" Ronen was astounded to find Gadi working on the charge. "What does it matter what they say in the command room? Enough with your crazy tenacity, just get rid of it!"

"I'm giving them another couple of seconds. Do they have an answer for me yet?" He looked back down to the charge and resumed his efforts with the cover, saying quietly, "Get out of here, Ronen. It would be a shame if you got blown up, too."

"There's no talking to you," Ronen mumbled. He limped back to the Mercedes and pleaded with Yoav: "Tell him he's got to get rid of that charge, that he should quit this insanity before he blows us all sky high."

Gadi was fully aware that he had placed himself once again in one of those knife-edge situations he didn't seem to be able to prevent. It wasn't some kind of flirtation with death, as a few of his friends had called it. Death was the yardstick by which he judged his life. The knowledge that death was inescapable caused him to define what he wanted from life, as well as which goals were meaningless. He wanted to love Helena, and Ami and Ruth, he wanted to devote part of his life to that extended family, or tribe, or people, to which he belonged, just as his genes dictated; he did *not* want to devote energies to making a name for himself that would be remembered after his death, when it would no longer hold any meaning for him.

Death was a certainty, the only real question was when: that outlook enabled Gadi to handle dangerous assignments almost calmly. There was also the adrenaline that coursed through his veins at times of danger, just as now, and as it had done countless times before. Another factor, however, was madness, pure and simple. Otherwise he would have disposed of the charge immediately. After all, there's no point in *forcing* death to hurry up. Still, he should be allowed that madness: this line of work really wasn't for normal people.

9.

BETWEEN THE TIME that Doron gave Yoav the go-ahead and Yoav's report that Ronen was in their custody, only a few minutes had passed – minutes of deathly silence in the command room, during which each man was alone with his own thoughts and fears. It was not clear from his report whether they had left Dahiyeh, the area of immediate danger. Beaufort, like Doron, suppressed his desire to ask. "Our curiosity is not a factor," he remembered Doron saying during a previous mission. "They'll report when it suits them and according to regulations," he had said.

A moment later Yoav's voice broke the silence again when he reported that Gadi was now with them along with the explosive charge, and was awaiting instructions.

"The situation is unclear," Doron said into the transmitter. "Explain."

"I'm east of Hadet. Gadi is here with a car, and the charge. He wants to leave it here in a derelict spot between two buildings. He requests an answer from Peter about the timer setting, how long it's set for." They could hear

Ronen's voice in the background. Yoav added, "After the antenna cable has been disconnected. If there's time he wants to defuse it."

A sense of unease rippled through the command room. The situation was still unclear, including the status of the cable. Peter was trying to remember.

"I'm almost certain the default setting is for twenty-four hours, but I wouldn't swear on it," he said at last. The import of his words was clear to everyone: if he were wrong, it could either cost Gadi his life, or cause the charge to be abandoned in the outskirts of Beirut. An explosion at the time when the operatives were making their way out of the city was fraught with its own complications, especially with regard to vigilance at roadblocks.

"There's no such thing as 'almost certain' in these cases," Doron said with a piercing gaze at Peter.

"I've got the information in my office. I can run back and look for it. It's been a few years…"

"So run," Doron said, interrupting him. Peter, embarrassed, took off at a sprint.

Doron decided to clarify matters further before receiving Peter's answer.

"When and how was the timer activated?" he said into the microphone on the transmitter.

"What does that matter?" the Mossad chief said, coming to his senses. "It's clear he needs to get rid of it."

However, before Doron could respond, a partial answer came from Lebanon: "Last night around twelve-thirty." All eyes turned to the large wall clock – it was almost twelve-thirty.

"Have you all gone mad?" the Mossad chief asked. "Gadi wants to sit in Beirut defusing a bomb? Tell him to get rid of it immediately."

Beaufort had not a clue about Gadi's ability to defuse charges, nor was he interested. It was the fear that the charge would blow within the next few minutes and complicate matters terribly that was unbearable, and completely disproportionate to an unidentified bomb exploding in some derelict area in Beirut.

Doron reddened and swallowed the insult. "Let's hear from Peter first, perhaps there's still time and we won't have to leave a bomb in a populated area. It could explode when there are children around…"

"Or in Gadi's face, at this very moment. Tell him to get rid of it immediately. Even the minute you've just wasted was critical," the chief retorted, furious.

Doron slowly lifted the microphone.

No one ever knew who raised the alarm, whether it was the hysterical neighbour or a suspicious passerby who witnessed the car chase. Or perhaps it was simply a passing Hezbollah security patrol, in a Land-Rover with a flashing orange light, that had noticed two cars by the side of the road and had pulled over to see what was happening. Ronen, who was still standing alongside the Mercedes talking to Yoav, had seen them coming. He warned the four men in the car and Yoav transmitted the information to the command room: "A patrol car just arrived, I'm shutting down." He switched off the transmitter, concealed his mini-Uzi with the silencer under his coat and opened his door. "No one shoots except on my orders," he said before approaching the Land-Rover.

"Good evening, sir," he said in Arabic to the policeman in the passenger's seat.

At the same moment the driver climbed out of the patrol car. As he drew level with the Mercedes Moussa and Daoud, in the back seat, spoke to each other in Arabic while Ronen remained standing where he was. The policeman ignored them, his eyes fixed on the shiny new BMW.

Gadi had carefully removed the cover of the charge. The complex mechanism of electronic circuits and wires lay exposed before him. So immersed was he in his task, he did not notice the flashing orange light.

They've had enough time to let me know, he said to himself, their time is up. He looked around to make sure the area where he planned to leave the charge was clear and it was only then that he noticed the security patrol. A second later he saw the policeman approaching. He picked up the pistol; with the charge exposed on the seat next to him he had no choice. He would have to shoot him in the head the moment he reached the car and then run to the security vehicle in case Yoav was in trouble there.

Ronen, too, realized he had no choice. He could not speak Arabic, could not engage the policeman in conversation to prevent him from reaching the BMW and he had no intention of letting him see Gadi with the charge. He took a quick stride forwards, grabbed the policeman around the throat and bent him over using maximum force, until he was lying on the ground between the Mercedes and the BMW. He let go of his grip just long enough to enable him to give a powerful blow to his neck. The man groaned slightly and passed out.

Yoav, who had just given his papers to the other policeman, reacted in a split second. He opened the door of the Land-Rover: with his right hand he bent the man forwards and with his left delivered a sharp blow to his neck. But the roof of the car prevented Yoav from gaining enough momentum and his opponent, a large man, tried to sit upright, striking Yoav and reaching for his pistol. Yoav pulled out his own gun, and two muffled shots split the Hezbollah man's head open.

Nice work, Gadi thought. He climbed out of the car, took the charge in his hands and walked towards the open tract of land. He just needed to find something to cover the charge so that children or passersby would not be drawn to it.

Yossi and Ronen held the unconscious policeman under the arms and dragged him to the Land-Rover. It was their good fortune that no traffic was passing by. Together they lifted him into the driver's seat, his head falling onto the steering wheel.

"We should get rid of him, too," Daoud said. Yoav saw that all eyes were watching him for an answer. As far as their own safety was concerned, they were right. The driver would regain consciousness and the search would be on for the Mercedes and the BMW. He considered matters for a moment: the situation was ambiguous, there was no clear and present danger. He needed to decide right away before another car had a chance to stop. There was no time to return to the Mercedes to ask for advice from headquarters. They needed to make a hasty departure. Yoav turned his mini-Uzi around and rammed the driver's head with it.

"It'll take him a while to remember what happened here," he said.

Daoud and Moussa looked doubtfully at him.

"I have an idea," Ronen said suddenly. "May as well go all the way with this," he said. He ran to where Gadi was about to cover up the charge with a few pieces of old junk.

Less than a minute later the charge was in the Land-Rover and the Mercedes and the BMW were on their way.

When Yoav stopped broadcasting a second before Doron was able to give him the chief's instructions, the atmosphere in the command room turned tense and angry.

Beaufort groaned, thinking they never should have been tempted to carry out this operation. He had recommended leaving Ronen to his own devices: just as the Egyptians had their "crazy" soldier at Ras Bourka who had killed Israeli tourists and the Jordanians had their "crazy" soldier at Naharaim who killed Israeli schoolgirls, so, too, did the Israelis now have their very own crazy soldier. But the Prime Minister had not wanted to hear of the possibility of doing nothing, so Beaufort had suggested letting Gadi handle him alone. His instinct had been to maintain as low an operational profile as possible, and he had been right. Bringing in these four fully-armed Mistaravim to carry out an abduction had been dangerous and unnecessary. What if even now the bomb was exploding leaving dead bodies, and wounded, and captives in Beirut?

"Get me the Prime Minister," Beaufort said. "Now."

Yoav's voice came through the transmitter. "The incident is over, the policemen are sleeping in their Land-Rover and we've got rid of the charge."

The sound of relief that wafted through the command room was so loud that Doron was forced to pound his fist on the table for quiet.

"What state are the policemen in?" Doron insisted on knowing.

"They're in their Land-Rover, one resting in peace and the other on his way."

Doron was flooded with affection for his men.

"What about the charge?" he asked, trying to squelch the emotion in his voice.

"We put it in the Land-Rover."

An interesting decision, though odd. It was not at all clear that that was the right thing to do. Doron wanted to exchange a word on that with Beaufort. If they were still in the vicinity perhaps something other should be done.

"What is your present location?"

"We're approaching the Jedeida roadblock," Yoav said.

That meant that the charge was history; better not to mention it again. "Where are Gadi and Ronen?"

"Behind us. Tell me, before I close, do you want us to bring a new BMW home instead of our old *Junker*?"

"We'll talk again before you reach the landing field," Doron answered, "and have a safe trip. Nice work, men."

Yoav had clearly given a convincing cover story to the guards at the roadblock, since they simply waved the BMW through. They should have coordinated that in advance, Gadi thought as he and Ronen followed the old Mercedes. The Mistaravim should not have associated themselves with the passengers of the BMW. But before Gadi could complete this train of thought they heard the dull roar of an explosion in the distance.

He glanced instinctively at his watch. Would he have managed to defuse the bomb in time? His eyes moved to the rearview mirror, to the guards at the roadblock they had just left behind, but they were busy checking another car.

While the outcome of this whole rescue mission – his and that of the Mistaravim – would render it a success, it could never meet the standards of any investigative committee. So what did that mean? Should the Mossad, too, change its motto of "zero mishaps" to "he who dares, wins"? Was that even possible when society and the media and the Mossad itself were so intolerant of mishaps?

Cooling night air blew in through the open window as Gadi and Ronen followed the Mercedes off the coastal road past the entrance to Antalis and climbed the pot-holed road up into the hills through dark and sleepy villages. No other vehicle was following them. Even if there was some sort of commotion in the city just then, or if warnings were being issued to the roadblocks, not a soul knew where they were.

Ronen was back behind the wheel. Gadi slapped him on the shoulder.

"So," he said with a smile, recalling the conversation they had had in a Beirut café just before Ronen had snatched his car keys. "I guess we did away with the 'rights of lawmen in a foreign state.'"

"There wasn't much choice. He was set on getting to you and checking out what was happening in the BMW. Anyway, we'd already done away with those rights when we took care of Abu-Khaled's guard, but it's nice for once that you've accepted my opinion."

"You'll be surprised, but that's not the only matter about which I've accepted your opinion."

Ronen waited to hear more.

"I've had a lot of time these past two days to think about this organization that we're a part of."

"That *you're* a part of," Ronen corrected him.

"The fact that you're not is exactly the heart of the matter. If everyone within the organization were to back each other up, if they were able to give credit where it's due or at least if they were able to be a little forgiving, it would be possible to handle the external hostility. I'm not talking about what you and I just did, which merits neither forgiveness nor support. I'm talking about regular operations, where only one out of hundreds is a failure."

✧✧✧

Rami and Arye were driven to the landing pad, where they would board the Yasur helicopter on its way to pick up the operatives. "We haven't solved the riddle of Gadi and Ronen yet," Beaufort told them, "and I need you there to make sure that everything runs smoothly and that they make it back here safely."

"I know you were opposed to this operation," Doron said to Arye, "but that's no reason for you to get into an argument with Gadi or Ronen. You're the onsite commander from the moment you land, but I need you simply to babysit, unless problems arise. And if that happens, you have Rami and his men." He turned to the commander of the Mistaravim squad. "Rami, please give our thanks to Yoav and his team. A lot of people here thought they were on a mission that was doomed to failure from the outset, but they pulled it off in style."

"You realize this will have to end with legal proceedings," Beaufort said when he and Doron were sitting in Doron's office waiting to be called back to the command room when the helicopter approached the pick-up point.

"We have two people on our hands who entered Lebanon without authorization. The situation with Ronen is naturally far more serious due to the explosive charge and everything that entailed."

"If Gadi claims there was a misunderstanding between you and him it will be difficult to prove that he entered Lebanon without authorization," Doron said after a moment's reflection. "And as far as the charge is concerned, that's problematic too. We know that Ronen entered the warehouse but we don't have any proof that he took the missing charge or that he made use of it. We'll only be able to charge him on that if he confesses or if Gadi testifies against him."

"So divide and conquer," the chief said. "Anyway, I have less of a problem with Gadi, his intentions were good from the beginning and without him I don't know where we'd be right now. He deserves a lot of the credit the Prime Minister is going to give you and me."

"I don't think it's right to dump everything on Ronen and clear Gadi of any responsibility. We've been here before with these two, that's actually what the commission of inquiry concluded. I can't let Gadi come back to the division a hero, he should take some of the fallout, too."

"Well then, here's your opportunity to do what you've been trying to do for months – dump him," Beaufort said. "Although I've never understood why it was so important for you to get rid of him. It's true he's unconventional, but he gets the job done."

Doron remained silent, dispirited.

"At least," the chief summed up, "we agree on Ronen. There's no room for compromise, he's no longer a Mossad operative and I have no intention of standing up for him. I imagine he'll claim that our treatment of him is what drove him to these actions, but I have no interest in giving him the opportunity to air his complaints. Get our legal counsel on this now and make sure Ronen is picked up as soon as the helicopter touches down."

"What about Gadi?" Doron persisted.

"Inform him he's prohibited from entering the division…"

"…and the squad," Doron added. "It's important to pass along a clear message. Opinions about Gadi are divided, but a clear message from management will cause everyone to fall in line. Everyone, that is, but the inevitable two or three righteous types."

"As you wish. I'll put out a notice to all employees to the effect that these two will be punished to the full extent of the law, et cetera. But let's not get carried away. This ordeal is ending well, we should be grateful. I'm not planning to start some devil's dance that won't make either of us look too good."

Ronen was following a steep and winding road past the village of Bekfaya. At the approach to each village there was the occasional single streetlight, but thereafter the road was completely dark. The headlights occasionally lost sight of the road due to the curves and inclines, causing Ronen to brake suddenly in order to keep from plunging into the abyss.

"I've been doing a bit of soul-searching these past few days, and I've actually come to the opposite conclusion from you," Ronen said quietly. Gadi watched him with interest, abandoning his watch over the dark roads.

"The Mossad doesn't owe us anything and the friends we have there – had there – don't owe us anything either. We're not exactly miserable wretches. Very few people have had the opportunity to experience what we have. True, we were there because we're Zionists, but also because we enjoyed what we were doing."

Gadi said nothing.

"And about what happened with me," Ronen added when no response was forthcoming, "the person who screwed up was me, and I'm the one who needs to pay the price. Until yesterday I hadn't accepted that fact. I read the commission's report, I listened to what our friends said and I kept a long list of grudges against people I held responsible. I'm sure you realize you were right at the top of it," he said with a smile on his face, stealing a glance at Gadi before returning his eyes to the road ahead.

"It was an operational failure for which I bear sole responsibility. All the rest is bullshit. I didn't notice early enough that his little girl had got out of the car and was running to him, and I decided that in such a situation I couldn't shoot. After that I chose not to shoot the two policemen that blocked our way. These were *my* mistakes, every one. If the Prime Minister tried to exploit us for his own political reasons and if the Mossad chief should have stopped him but didn't and if you made me Number One when I wasn't ready for it, well, each of you needs to do your own soul-searching. No one pointed a gun at my head and made me take part in this operation or agree to be Number One. So from the moment I accepted and set out on this mission, the mistakes were mine. End of discussion. And if I have a problem because of Lital," he said, his voice cracking, causing him to cough and clear his throat, "it's untenable that she could keep me from carrying out my mission, for which the People of Israel wind up paying the price."

Ronen's remarks raised a chain reaction of thoughts in Gadi's consciousness. The words and sentences that had tumbled about inside him for nearly a year were suddenly falling into place.

It was *he* who should have ignored the pride and status of the Mossad chief and the division head when together they sat facing the Prime Minister; he should have told him it was impossible to engage in such a mission on so truncated a timetable. The Prime Minister could not have known this on his own, nor could the Mossad chief; he hadn't come up through the ranks of the Operations Division. And even if the division head knew and should have brought it up, that in no way minimized his own responsibility and his own guilt for not having said what should have been said.

What had prevented him? Was it the loathsome tradition that kept them from expressing an opinion contrary to their own commander's in front of a senior commander? Did he lack the necessary courage – civilian courage – to say what needed to be said, preferring instead to hide behind the limitations of his rank and Mossad hierarchy?

In his own realm, he was the only guilty party, and as Ronen had said, all the rest was bullshit.

The road – only partially covered with asphalt, the rest a mix of stones, gravel and holes – ended east of Biscanta. The Mercedes had stopped and Ronen pulled up behind it. They waited as Yoav got out of the car and approached them.

"I have to contact the command room now. The chopper is over the sea waiting to cut in over land as soon as he hears from me. There are another ten miles or so of dirt roads until we reach the rendezvous."

"And what was it until now?" Ronen asked, and Yoav laughed.

"Hang on, you have no idea what you're in for. I'm planning to drive without lights. Do you prefer to follow right on our tail without lights – it's a pretty clear night and you'll probably see me fairly clearly – or would you rather follow at a distance with your lights on?"

"You've already made this trip," Gadi said. "No nasty surprises along the way?"

"It's not the same road. The Yasur is landing at a different spot, about three miles from where we landed, just in case the first spot got contaminated and someone's waiting there for us."

"I'll give it a try without lights," Ronen said. "After falling into the first pot-hole I'll turn them on."

"Take good care of that car. The command room is supposed to let me know whether to bring back the BMW or the Mercedes, so try not to drive into any pot-holes."

"Whichever car we leave behind we'll push off a cliff," Gadi said. He was trying to let Yoav finish up his operation in his own way, but there were some matters, like this one, that required his superior rank and experience.

Yoav returned to the Mercedes and Gadi rolled up his window against the cold. It was after one in the morning and they were at an altitude of more than six thousand feet; freezing air permeated the car.

"If they leave the BMW here then my documents will be worthless. Nobody else will be able to use them," Ronen said.

"True, and leaving the BMW here will also indicate that this is a landing field. Anyway, don't let your documents worry you too much. Mine neither. Our passports are pretty much worthless without exit stamps from Lebanon. Eventually the Lebanese authorities will discover that Messieurs Smith and Ford remained in their country. They entered and never left."

"So we'll still wind up on the list of abducted persons after all," Ronen said. "But really, isn't it a shame about your passport?"

"I don't think I'll be needing it any longer," Gadi said sadly.

Yoav returned to their car. "Okay, we're taking the BMW and we'll toss the Mercedes into one of the valleys near the meeting point. Take a transmitter," he said as he passed them one small unit and an earphone. "It's good up to a thousand feet. If we disappear into the darkness, call us."

Ronen started the engine and began slowly following the Mercedes. At bends in the road the car's silhouette stood out clearly against the cloudless sky, but when it was directly in front of them the car dissolved into the mountain range.

"From what you were saying before about the

passport, I understand that you've made a decision to quit?"

"In effect, I quit the moment I boarded that plane to Beirut," Gadi answered.

"I wouldn't recommend it," Ronen said, leaning forwards, concentrating on his driving. "It isn't easy to find yourself on the outside, especially when you see the tremendous capability of the organization. Like now, for example, how they pulled this business with the Mistaravim together in a single day! You'll be sitting at home watching reports of terrorist attacks on television and you'll know who is preparing to take action and you're not even a player any more. It'll eat your heart out. Also, you should realise that you'll be completely cut off from them, just like I was. Leaving on bad terms is really tough. You won't believe how suddenly all the friends you had there will disappear. Don't even expect Izzy to invite you to parties for those who retire. He won't. The more you helped someone get ahead, the faster he'll drop you."

"I know I'll miss the people and the operations, and that this was the most significant part of my life," Gadi said, "but I feel there is no longer any compatibility between me and the organization. Every mistake we made in Beirut last year they repeated with the Mistaravim in this mission. And why is that? Because you can count on those colleagues and the culture of over-achievement kept them from speaking out."

"Good little boys," Ronen said with a smile. "Yes-men."

"I'm not cut out any more for keeping quiet or saying

the right things," Gadi continued. "I myself didn't speak out when I should have, and I have continued to display 'criminal tenacity'. I did things I didn't believe in because I had completely absorbed the rules of the organization. But that's no longer good for me or for the organization. Once upon a time we were in love, we had a great marriage, but that's all over now," he said with a melancholic smile.

"I'm sorry you feel that way," Ronen said. The speeches Gadi gave on behalf of the Mossad – and in fact on behalf of society at large, in the face of his own verbal attacks – had paradoxically injected Ronen with some hope. He needed to clarify the issue further. "So tell me, does this mean you've woken up to the matter of the question, and society as well?"

"I don't feel I'm in the position right now to judge anyone but myself. Let them all – society, the media, the Mossad – let them judge themselves. There's a Russian proverb that sums it all up pretty well: 'A nation that no longer honours its heroes will no longer have heroes to honour'."

The car took a sharp turn and they were both suddenly breathless: at an altitude of nearly eight thousand feet the view to the southwest from the southern edge of Jabel a-Ruissa opened up before them, first to Beirut and then southwards: Sidon, Tyre, the glow from Nahariya in northern Israel beyond the cliffs at Rosh Hanikrah, Acre, the towns around Haifa Bay – itself crouching in darkness in the shadow of the arc of lights – and above it, high and shimmering, sparkled Haifa.

Ronen braked and for a long moment they gazed at the enchanted sight at their feet, until Gadi came to his senses and radioed the Mistaravim to stop and wait for them.

For Ronen, Haifa, the port and the bay were an inseparable part of his military experiences. Not only did they dive and sail and practise manoeuvres there, it was where they had walked about in their Navy uniforms and later showed off their commando insignias and picked up girls. There were always the girls who waited for the seals, year after year, group after group, at the same clubs and pubs. It was also where they fought with their rivals, always from Tirat Hacarmel, and where Ronen had lived while serving with the naval commando for two additional years after his mandatory service.

Gadi knew this would be the last time he would see Israel from the other side of the border. Gazing at Israel, especially from the east, but from the south and north as well always filled him with emotion. He could recall precisely what the Golan Heights looked like from the Syrian side of the border during the day, but especially at night, the lights of its settlements glowing yellow. He remembered how exciting it was for him to view the squares of green and brown and yellow and blue of the Jordan and Beit She'an valleys from his vantage point in Aqraba, high above the Yarmukh River, or from Umm-el-Kis. Whenever he could see Israel while standing in an enemy state his feeling of loneliness was more acute than ever.

And this was the last time, his parting from Mr Ford

and all his doubles, the end of viewing Israel from angles that very few Israelis got the opportunity to experience. He was leaving behind such a very important part of his life.

"We're on our way to you," Gadi said into the transmitter. "Watch through your night vision goggles and let us know the minute *before* we plunge over the edge."

Ronen changed gear and continued slowly forwards.

This time the landing field was a small flat spot in a sort of hidden plateau on one of the mountain ranges. Yoav asked Ronen and Gadi to wait on the road while he and his men scanned the small valley and everything around it.

"All's quiet here," he said when he came back, "and the chopper will land in another fifteen minutes. We'll remove our equipment from the Mercedes at the landing field then I'll pitch the car into the valley." He disappeared into the darkness again.

The stillness, the sombre mountains, the freezing wind that penetrated the car even with the windows closed combined to give Gadi and Ronen that familiar shiver deep inside. In another few minutes, when the weapons and the transmitters had been gathered at the side of the landing field and the Mercedes had made its final journey to the bottom of the valley, they would be at the stage where they no longer had a cover story, and only firepower could rescue them if they were taken by surprise by an unexpected military patrol. Their trip without headlights had reduced the chances of this happening, but they could have passed a shepherd who hurried off to a neighbouring village to report what he had seen. Or a village guard, bewildered by the sight of two strange cars travelling on a road that leads to nowhere, who had passed his suspicions on. They also had no idea what kind of searches and patrols the security forces were employing as a result of the explosion in Beirut. At times like these the wait was harder than ever.

Ronen broke the silence. "Would you finally tell me what your briefing for Number One is? The one you didn't have time to give me before our last operation in Beirut?" He had asked Gadi to do this several times since their failed mission. The private, whispered meeting between Gadi and the person designated to pull the trigger was a known ritual, but Ronen had missed it because of their reduced timetable. After their mishap, Gadi did not see the point in reconstructing the briefing he had not given, but now it seemed right to grant Ronen's wish.

"I'll give you the condensed version, the major points," he said after a short pause. "I'll skip the Zionist part and go straight to the second section."

He paused as the Mercedes was driven away from the landing field and towards the edge of a cliff with Yossi and Yoav inside, before continuing. "You're going to kill a terrorist who has murdered and plans to murder again, and you have all the justification and backing from your country. But he is a human being, with his own reasons, and you are going to do this because you have chosen to. You are not a cog in a machine. So now you have two options: you can say this wasn't your choice and you can stay at home. Or you can set out after having made your peace with what you are about to do.

"If you have chosen to continue, you need to take into consideration that something could go wrong. Not only operationally but what I would call morally as well."

The dull roar of the Mercedes tumbling down the mountain and crashing on the rocks below reached their ears, and he paused again.

"So think about our country, about the terrorist attacks that will take place if you don't shoot. And afterwards remember that the decision about what to do in the new situation that could arise was yours, and yours alone, and that it derived from everything that you are and that you represent: an operative, an Israeli, a caring person, let's say even a logical person," he said, stealing a glance at Ronen, a smile spreading across his lips, "but primarily a human being. That's what I told Number Ones in the past and that's what I would have told you if we'd had the chance."

The back door opened and Yossi and Yoav climbed in. The inside light blinked on for a few seconds and Gadi thought he saw a trail of tears spilling down Ronen's cheek. Facing Abu-Khaled and his daughter, Ronen had behaved exactly as the briefing he had never been given would have permitted him to: like a human being. It had taken until now, a year later, for him to receive legitimacy for that.

Ronen would never know of the quick adjustments Gadi had made to his short speech, especially for him.

"Let's go," Yoav said. "The chopper will be here in five minutes."

348

He passed the night vision goggles to Ronen and they drove the few hundred feet to the landing point, weaving between stones and pot-holes: Moussa and Daoud were standing next to a pile of equipment.

"I know what they mean by five minutes," Gadi said as he reclined his seat backwards – to Yoav's dismay, since he had planned to sprawl out on the back seat. "Wake me up when that flying jalopy gets here."

10.

GADI HAD NOT yet managed to fall asleep when the earth beneath him began to rumble and the giant CH-53 helicopter, a huge black spot on the sky, rose up from one of the ravines and paused briefly in the air to enable its men to scan the area with their equipment. By using the transmitter, Yoav directed the helicopter to where they were standing and, as it made its descent, a cloud of dust rose skywards, engulfing the entire landing field.

Relying on Yoav's men, who were on the lookout in all directions, the soldiers in the helicopter were instructed to forego the regular security procedure. When the ramp descended, Arye and Rami exited to greet the squad. They assisted in loading the equipment, saving handshakes for inside the craft, after takeoff.

Ronen steered the BMW into the chopper and the ramp lifted back into place. After one last look around they took off, barely two minutes after the helicopter had landed. Ronen climbed out of the car and helped to anchor it, then joined the Mistaravim and the soldiers sitting on the benches lining the inside of the craft. He was not interested in talking to a soul. After briefly exchanging compliments and slaps on the back – with a bare minimum of enthusiasm due to Ronen's presence – Gadi, Arye, Rami and Yoav sat inside the car. At first there was no conversation between them; although the situation was similar to previous airlifts from enemy states, this one had no feeling of joy. It had ended quietly, but it had all been unnecessary, completely pointless, and there were those who would suffer the consequences.

Ronen sat lost in his own thoughts, imagining what was awaiting him. This time it wouldn't end with a commission of inquiry, but with a criminal trial, probably even jail. If the country's security apparatus were to consider him an enemy, every judge would accept their warnings and incarcerate him according to their instructions. Who would be willing to listen to him explain that he had only wished to make right what he had failed at in his previous state mission, to put an end to the activities of a terrorist who, because of Ronen's own bungle, had continued to murder Israelis?

In the dim glow cast by the emergency lighting of the westward-bound craft, Ronen traced the line of his long hands and the pointy knees drawn up to his chest and felt completely strange in his own body. It was as if these hands, which only one night earlier had planted the bomb, were not really his. In the sobriety that had flooded his consciousness he failed to explain to himself what had come over him, as though part of him had been left behind in some terrible nightmare he realised could not be real and from which he was waiting to awaken. But the men sitting to his left and right, some of whom he knew but who did not exchange a word with him, made it clear that this was no dream.

Suddenly he wished Naamah were there. Then, too, he would not speak, but at least he could lean his head on her shoulder, entwine his fingers with hers and inhale some of her warmth to counter the chill that had enshrouded his entire body.

After nearly twenty minutes of silence the pilot announced that they had crossed the shoreline. They were out of Lebanese territory. There was still a long trip ahead of them, they were over the sea north of Beirut, but no shoulder-launched missile or anti-aircraft artillery could threaten them now. A feeling of relief passed through the men. But Ronen remained cut off from the others, still lost in his own thoughts and reveries.

Only now did Rami and Arye permit themselves to ask Gadi and Yoav how it had gone. Yoav provided a short summary of events after which Gadi said, "Drop it. There's certainly going to be a commission of inquiry; why should I get entangled in conflicting versions?" If he remained silent they would have very little on Ronen. They would press charges on both of them for entering an enemy state but beyond that, what did they know for sure?

"That's true," Arye said. "An investigating officer has already been appointed, but in the meantime we only want to check how the explosive charge was stolen."

"Is there anybody left who is not either an investigator or under investigation?" Gadi asked.

"Not many, but soon there'll be none," Rami answered from the back seat.

Addressing Gadi, Yoav added, "Do you think they won't investigate you? After all, you went without authorization."

"What about *you*?" Gadi said with a smile. "Do you think you'll get off so easily? After what you did to that policeman, and the fact that we blew them up." Yoav's sudden outburst of laughter came to an abrupt halt. He had had every reason to assume he was returning a hero, but suddenly he understood that under the present circumstances there was a reasonable chance he would have to explain to a commission of inquiry why he had fired on the Hezbollah man, and why he had authorized placing the explosive charge in the security vehicle.

The pilot announced that Beirut was on their left, and several heads moved to the windows for a glimpse. Gadi, sitting in the driver's seat of the BMW, did not look. It was all over for him, better to retain in his memory the clear view stretching several hundred miles from Mount Lebanon past Beirut all the way to Haifa. He thought about how far he had come since the first time he had seen that marvellous sight as a young officer in the paratroops on a mission at the summit of Mount Hermon. They had begun their ascent at dawn and every few hundred feet exposed another stretch of brown squares with patches of snow that had not yet melted, all the way to the top. There they found Damascus spread before them in the middle of the valley to the east, Beirut and the sea to the west, when they turned around, the Golan Heights and its mounds of snow like heaps of cotton wool, and from there down to the Galilee, and all the way to verdant Mount Carmel and the Haifa Bay. His breathing had been laboured, but not enough to prevent him from quoting a letter written to him by his girlfriend – at that time on a post-army trip to South America – who wrote from one of the mountains that that was how God Himself must see the world.

His long road had always seemed fascinating to him – indeed, few had merited so many trips, adventures and achievements – but suddenly the world was shrinking, and the Mount Hermon of then and the Mount Lebanon of today seemed very similar, as did all the capital cities and metropolises and provincial towns in which he had pursued terrorists, arms merchants and scientists who had sold their souls to the devil. And all the hotel rooms on five continents in which he had spent his few free hours in taut sleep seemed like one hotel room, with one double bed, one side of which always remained unrumpled.

Gadi felt that this trip had brought him full circle, that it had atoned for the sins of his previous trip to Beirut. But accepting this did not appease him. He felt sad at opportunities missed. Something was wrong here, and he did not know if it was him or the Mossad or the incompatibility created by both.

But this was not all that was bothering him. He lacked

the ability to continue living in that dark, deceptive, treacherous world in which you can never really know what is good and what is evil, in which the permissible is forbidden and the forbidden permitted. A world in which even if you don't murder an old lady with an axe, but rather are authorized to shoot a terrorist, it is still a sin of sorts and punishment will be forthcoming. He admired all those who were capable of carrying on with that Sisyphean work, but he was no longer among them.

For the first time Gadi thought that maybe he was not simply unsuited to this work, but unworthy as well. He might just be lacking the modesty necessary to toe the line even when the line was pulling, in general, in the right direction.

The engines of the helicopter fell silent. The passengers did not feel the touchdown, only knew of it from the sudden quiet. The lights came on and the men, awakened from their sleep, stood up. The Mistaravim collected their equipment and departed through a side door. The soldiers were assisted in gathering their weapons together by a team that had been awaiting their arrival. The chopper team conducted their own checks. An officer from the Weaponry Department released the BMW while another of the division's drivers steered it out. Gadi waited for Ronen, who had remained seated, still shut off from the world. Bags in hand, they came down the ramp together alongside the BMW, which was gliding slowly out.

"I hope they thank you for this little gift," Gadi said as he patted the metallic roof of the car.

A sad smile spread across Ronen's face. He was exhausted and did not know what he was supposed to feel. Mixed up inside him was a blunted joy at having returned safely, a fear of what lay ahead, and a deep sorrow, which pinched his heart, at having brought all this to pass.

The pre-dawn air that greeted them was more than thirty degrees warmer than the chill of Mount Lebanon, which they had left behind a mere ninety minutes earlier. Although the air was mixed with fumes from the helicopter's engine, Gadi breathed it deeply into his lungs. The scent and the wind were so pleasant to him; the blast of warm Tel Aviv air at the doorway of an aircraft was one of the things he loved about this strange line of work.

The few landings he had made in a helicopter at a military base or on board a ship at the navy base in Haifa had been accompanied by a festive feeling; on a chopper or a ship he and his people were given their own private corner and it was not hard to discern the looks of admiration on the faces of the soldiers who had just removed the Mossad operatives from the heart of an enemy country. At air bases or jetties they were always met by a joyous reception committee sent by the division.

This occasion, however, was a strange mix: there was a helicopter and a rescue mission from an Arab country, but the atmosphere was foreign and alienating.

Gadi and Ronen stepped away from the area of bustling activity near the helicopter. They could see Rami, Yoav and their men assembling at the edge of the landing field next to a van with a few well-wishers from the division, and could hear laughter coming from that direction. Behind the chopper, the soldiers were arranging their equipment next to a military vehicle that had joined them. The ground crew was checking a number of pipes and openings in the helicopter.

The chopper was parked in the middle of a paved expanse lit solely by yellow projector lights around the perimeter. On one side Gadi and Ronen could make out a row of low buildings, on the other a long string of landing lights. Far off in the distance they could see the lights of Tel Aviv, from behind they could hear the sea and from out of the darkness in front of them, two white Mazda Lantises were making their way straight towards them.

Gadi identified his own car, with Helena sitting next to the driver. Naamah stepped out of the back seat of the other Lantis – one of the general division vehicles.

"Two cars, they've gone all out for us!" Ronen said with a dispirited smile as he walked towards Naamah. Only after a lengthy embrace during which he almost missed her "I love you so much" did he suddenly notice, over her shoulder, Lital sitting in the car seat.

All the air in his lungs was sucked up into his throat, and whatever did not stop there and choke him moved up to his eyes, releasing in an instant, as if by air pressure, his tear ducts. Ronen detached himself from Naamah, threw open the car door and pressed his lips against Lital's tiny head. He covered her with kisses, then buried his head in her lap and sobbed. Daddy, the little girl said, hitting him lightly and pulling his hair. His bobbing shoulders tickled her stomach and caused her bursts of uncontrollable laughter. Naamah stood over them, tears falling from her eyes.

Gadi held Helena's face in his hands.

"De very last time?" she half asked, half stated. Her accent brought Gadi back home, to her, to Ami and Ruth, to everything he knew, with the absolute certainty that this would be his one and only world from then on.

"De very, very last time, no going back," he said, laughing. He grabbed her around the waist, lifted her off the ground and swung her about in the air. Helena, surprised and embarrassed, hugged him tightly around the neck, her face glowing.

A moment after returning her to the ground, Gadi looked over at the Dolev family. Ronen was sitting next to his daughter. Naamah was standing by the car, and their eyes met.

Thank you, Naamah said, though the sound of her voice did not reach his ears, and he figured it had not even left her mouth. But the shape of her lips was easy to read.

A third Lantis stood to the side in darkness. Inside sat Doron and an officer of the Central Unit of the Israel Police, a longtime secret partner of the Operations Division.

"Are you certain we won't be needing reinforcements?" the officer asked.

"Don't get carried away. This just needs to be handled with tact. I don't know if he's expecting it or not, and I don't know what kind of shape he's in. Let's start to move in. I'll do the talking, you'll just be my legal back-up. We'll let him see you so that he can start to get used to the idea."

"The other guy won't interfere?"

"I hope not. We're letting him go home. We'll meet with him later on and then decide how to proceed."

The Lantis moved slowly forwards, stopping next to Naamah. Doron got out and shook her hand. Ronen climbed out of the back seat and Doron proffered him his hand, too. They stared at one another until Ronen glanced to one side and, noticing the police officer, understood. A cold lump filled his chest. He had expected this, but only when he saw the officer did he realize how much he had hoped matters would be settled internally, that even if he had to stand trial he would not have to go to jail.

The police officer's fears had been unwarranted, Ronen had no intention of resisting. His whole being was filled with sadness, and from this sadness arose acceptance and a new clarity. Here he was, Ronen, about to pay the price for something he *should* pay for. And after he had paid up, this chapter of his life – the chapter of his time with the Mossad, which had been troublesome – would be behind him, and his detachment from it in the future would be absolute. He knew now who he was: not Abu-Khaled's assassin, just Lital's father and Naamah's husband. The death of that old chapter fanned his expectations for the start of this new chapter.

*

Gadi watched as Doron slung his arm over Ronen's shoulder and led him off to one side. After a moment or two Ronen returned to Naamah and talked quietly with her, while Doron walked over to Gadi. He nodded at Helena and he and Gadi shook hands.

"We have a lot to talk about," he said dryly. "Beaufort and I want to meet you tomorrow morning at eight at the operational apartment on Ben Yehuda Street. Until then, don't contact anyone from the squad or headquarters."

Out of the corner of his eye Gadi could see Ronen and Naamah hugging and kissing. When Ronen made for Doron's car, the picture was clear to Gadi: they were distancing him, Gadi, from the Mossad and from his squad and putting Ronen behind bars.

"You couldn't even give him one day with Naamah and Lital?" Gadi said angrily.

Doron did not answer. He looked away, and it was clear that he wished to end this meeting as quickly as possible.

Gadi saw how completely Ronen had accepted his fate and he felt full of compassion for him. He could understand the reasons for arresting Ronen but he refused to let this pattern, so familiar from the commission of inquiry, repeat itself. He could not return home with Helena while Ronen was going to a holding cell and Naamah would be left alone.

There were a lot of unknowns in this new situation. They might offer him a deal he was very likely to refuse, in which case he might find himself in the cell next to

Ronen's. All that would become clear in the morning. The least he could do now was to stay with Ronen up to the very last moment he was allowed to. Gadi turned to Helena.

"Iloush, I need to be there, with Ronen," he said, kissing her forehead. Helena stared at him in astonishment, and Gadi explained to her in a few words what was happening.

"But you won't…"

"No, I won't be put in jail. I just want to be there with him. Do you understand?"

She did not understand.

"Just to accompany him, stick by him. I'll be home later," he said, and Helena watched, dumbfounded, as Gadi moved away from her.

Gadi climbed into the back seat of Doron's car and sat next to Ronen.

"Can I come along?" he asked a startled Doron.

"We do not allow voluntary incarceration," the police officer said.

"What is this, the beginning of a beautiful friendship?" Doron asked, overcoming his discomfort.

"No, the end of a beautiful career," Gadi said.

But the picture from the window of the car did in fact attest to a beautiful friendship as Naamah came to Helena and hugged her.

"Looks like Gadi won't be using his car. Shall we leave together?" Helena asked. Naamah kissed her cheek. They sat on either side of Lital. The driver, surprised, shrugged his shoulders and began following Doron's car towards the exit of the military airport.

The two women were momentarily blinded by a flashbulb at the exit gates. They had seen the flash a moment earlier, when Doron's car had passed through ahead of them, but they had not yet realized the light had come from a camera.

"Wait a minute," Helena said. "Wasn't that what's-his-name?"

"Stop, stop!" Naamah shouted, and the driver came to a halt. It was Haramati.

"I know exactly what I'm going to do now," Naamah said.

"Are you going to hand that over nicely, or not?" she would ask, extending her hand towards the camera.

"How about not at all?" Haramati would answer in his smart-alec manner.

Naamah would take hold of the camera with one hand and with the other give him a slap across the face. Not the kind of blow she had learned in years of training, but rather something between a slap and a punch that would be the outcome of the anger and contempt she would feel. He would stagger backwards, the camera would remain in her hands as Haramati hit the ground. In an instant she would open the camera and expose the film under the light at the gate. After that she would drop it, gently, onto Haramati's body.

"I hope you're not going to react," Helena said. "Gadi and Ronen and Doron didn't. If we give him ammunition to write an article we won't be able to settle anything quietly."

"But we already know the censor will do nothing." Naamah stared at Haramati for a moment and thought. "All right, go on," she said to the driver. "Let the dogs have their day."

Haramati breathed a sigh of relief watching the car pull away, and turned to answer his cell phone.

"No," he said, "Nothing."

Milken's angry voice shouted through the phone. "You don't give up on a scoop like this. Do you know how hard it was to obtain such specific information?"

Haramati could only imagine; he was in awe of Milken's excellent connections. Not only knowing that something was happening but also exactly where and when it would end. He had seen the police officer, seen Gadi and Ronen in the back seat of the car, and surmised that they were being arrested or taken in for interrogation. He had seen, too, the wives, had discerned the expression on Naamah's face. He could guess the nature of the debate they had had concerning him. Haramati knew only too well the hugeness of the scoop, and what it would do to these people.

"Sorry," Haramati apologized. "I have nothing to report."

Acknowledgements

Duet in Beirut was first published in Hebrew in 2002, three years after I had left the Mossad. In 2008, the head of Hezbollah's security and overseas terror operations, Imad Mughniya, was killed by a bomb planted in his car. Hezbollah blamed the Mossad, but no one has ever claimed responsibility for this killing.

To my dear colleagues in the Mossad I send my heartfelt thanks for twelve fascinating years.

After leaving the Mossad I studied screenwriting and my final project was the script upon which this book was based. For their encouragement, I wish to thank Idit Shehori, head of the School for Screenwriting, my teachers and fellow students.

Uri Adelman was present at the ceremony at which the script won a prize and suggested that I turn it into a book – an idea that had not occurred to me, since I had ascribed fictional "action" to film. If it had not been for Uri this book would never have been written. I owe him my deepest appreciation, too, for his useful comments.

The book was subjected to a long process of censorship; military censorship, the Mossad and the Ministerial Commission for Publications by Public Employees. I wish to offer my thanks to the representatives of those organizations for their openness, co-operation and professionalism.

The authorization process of this book demanded great patience from the publishers, Keter Publishing House, Ltd. Thanks to chief editor Zvika Meir and the rest of the people at Keter for believing in this book.

A major role in this book – as in life – is played by the wives of Mossad employees who, along with their children, pay a very high price. I wish to thank my family – my wife Shina, and my children Shiri, Regev and Omer – from the bottom of my heart for accepting the price with understanding and love.